They're brothers in arms, Navy SEALS risking their lives for their country... and the women they love.

This is Luke Harding's story.

Six months in a desert hellhole taught Navy SEAL Luke Harding things he never wanted to learn about life and death. Only tender memories of the beautiful brunette he met a few weeks before his deployment helped get him through the torturous days and nights. Back in the States after a perilous rescue, physically and emotionally damaged, Luke's about to plunge into a new kind of war. In a seemingly bucolic Idaho town, Sally Duncan faces real—and unpredictable—danger.

All Sally ever wanted was a safe place to raise her nine-year-old daughter. Her identity hidden behind a façade of secrets and lies, can she trust Luke—a man she barely knows—with the truth? Even as they give in to long-denied passion, a killer with a personal vendetta is setting an ambush that will leave them praying for a miracle and fighting for the future they may not live to see.

Heart of a SEAL

Dixie Lee Brown

LYRICAL PRESS
Kensington Publishing Corp.
www.kensingtonbooks.com

LYRICAL LIAISON BOOKS are published by

Kensington Publishing Corp.
119 West 40th Street
New York, NY 10018

All Kensington titles, imprints, and distributed lines are available at special quantity discounts for bulk purchases for sales promotion, premiums, fund-raising, educational, or institutional use.

Special book excerpts or customized printings can also be created to fit specific needs. For details, write or phone the office of the Kensington Sales Manager: Kensington Publishing Corp., 119 West 40th Street, New York, NY 10018. Attn. Sales Department. Phone: 1-800-221-2647.

Lyrical Liaison and Lyrical Liaison logo Reg. U.S. Pat. & TM Off.

First Electronic Edition: April 2018
eISBN-13: 978-1-5161-0648-6
eISBN-10: 1-5161-0648-2

First Print Edition: April 2018
ISBN-13: 978-1-5161-0651-6
ISBN-10: 1-5161-0651-2

Printed in the United States of America

To Jodie, my friend, my cheering squad and my awesome critique partner.

It's much more fun with you!

To the Floozies, who share your talent, advice and encouragement without hesitation.

To the Diamonds, you never fail to show up when I need you.

I love you guys!

Thank you from the bottom of my heart!

Chapter One

Heart pounding, Luke bolted upright, wide awake, as though a dose of adrenaline had shot directly into his bloodstream. The sound—no, more a feeling than a sound—came again, pulling him back from the edge of his nightmare—the same damn one he'd had last night and the night before that. The pain in his shoulders and arms was bad, intensified by his sudden movement. Yesterday's interrogation had been more brutal than usual. *Don't think about it. It's only going to get worse. Focus.* Something had jolted him from what passed for sleep these days. After nearly six months in this filthy, godforsaken POW camp, not much surprised him. Yet the strange vibrations that still pulsed in his nerve endings were somehow different.

Hell. What did he know? It wasn't exactly unusual to wake battling a gut-wrenching, hard-to-get-enough-air sensation that sapped his strength and made him want to scream to the God he was slowly beginning to doubt existed. With the dream fresh in his mind, how the hell was he supposed to distinguish reality from the warped images taking up residence in his fucked-up brain?

He lowered himself to his sleeping pallet and strained to catch the sound one more time. His gaze raked the shadows beyond the wire fence that segregated his two hundred square feet of Afghan sand and scrub brush from the rest of the compound. Within its confines, he was allowed to move around as much as he wanted. That was his one freedom, but his harsh captors provided little else. A frayed and rat-eaten tarp to keep out the rain and provide shade from the desert sun. Still, he could be grateful for the times he *was* allowed to stay inside his prison...away from this ruthless and unpredictable terrorist group. Militant jihadists who'd spun off al-Qaeda after Osama bin Laden was killed, they now claimed ties to ISIS and made his life a living hell on a daily basis.

It was unnaturally quiet in the compound, yet something lingered on the stillness of the night air. A sound so familiar it was as though, without it, he hadn't been complete. Shit. He was finally going crazy. Luckily, crazy was preferable to his other options.

A lone spotlight perched atop the locked gate at the north end of his stockade, interrupting the darkness. The moon, a mere sliver, was barely visible behind a thin veil of mist that would leave the ground wet with its touch before morning. The nights were getting colder. Late September or better. Fall already, with winter on the way. The seasons were the same as they were back home, except more extreme. Would his captors give him a blanket to fend off the freezing temperatures of winter? Would he survive long enough to worry about the weather?

Every nerve told him something waited in the dark just outside the fence. The skin on the back of his neck did that creepy-crawling thing he hated, assuring him he was being watched. Instinct screamed for him to stand and fight his unseen enemy, or at least defend himself. But fools perished quickly in this hellhole, and he wasn't fool enough to start a war he couldn't win. Attracting attention was never a good idea. For now, he would lie still on his worn sleeping mat, tucked beneath a shabby canvas lean-to in the darkest corner. His time would come soon enough.

Luke waited on high alert while minutes ticked slowly by. Nothing. No unusual sounds. No indication the fighters were any more vigilant than normal. Damn. It was probably the dream that had him imagining things. He'd have laughed at his paranoia, but his sense of humor had been the latest casualty of his months in captivity.

With an effort, he resisted looking toward the empty mat in the opposite corner of the lean-to. Before his buddy, Ian, had died, Luke at least had had hope. Since the chopper crash that killed three members of their team and stranded them deep within land held by the terrorists, they'd kept their spirits up by planning how they were going to escape. Admitting they'd probably die in the attempt, they'd agreed it would be worth it…as long as they took a shitload of terrorists to hell with them. Yeah, revenge was sweet.

Now, every time he closed his damn eyes, he saw the sword fall again, heard Ian's scream turn to a gurgle as his body jerked and twitched in agony. Each time the death scene played out in his mind, Luke struggled against unseen bonds, to free himself and help his friend and fellow SEAL…to no avail. It'd been nearly two weeks since Ian's death. And Luke was on deck. He knew that…but he wasn't going out without a fight.

Slowly, moving only his arm, he reached beneath the edge of his sleeping mat and pulled a picture free. The meager light was barely enough to make out the image. Sally Duncan and her eight-year-old daughter, Jen. With his thumb, Luke gently stroked Sally's cheek in the worn photograph.

The smoking-hot brunette had captivated him, and the kid, Jen, had flat-out won his heart. They'd met three weeks before he deployed, and he'd instinctively known some bad shit had gone down in Sally's life at some point. Whatever had happened had made her skittish, especially with men, and he didn't have to be told he wouldn't last ten minutes if he moved too fast. He'd played it cool. Didn't rush her. Many a night he'd ended the evening alone in a cold shower because of the petite, sexy woman whose Mona Lisa smile always made him think she had a secret. And damned if he didn't want to know what it was. The night before he flew out, he'd kissed her—really kissed her for the first time—and asked for a picture.

Jesus! The guys in his unit would have laughed him out of the platoon if they'd ever found out what a wuss he'd been.

But that kiss and this picture had kept him sane through countless days of pain, depravation and intense hatred. She wouldn't let him give up. He had one purpose: to stay alive to see her again. To hold her and feel the warmth of her body against his, see the sparkle in her deep blue eyes as she laughed at one of his dumb jokes. Marvel at her appreciative smile when he did something nice for her. What he wouldn't give to sit with them again in their living room, Sally on one side, Jen on the other, while he held a huge bowl of popcorn on his lap and pretended to groan through some chick flick they'd picked to watch.

The faintest swish of something moving in his peripheral vision jerked his attention to the guard's platform towering over the desert floor a hundred yards to the east. And then he heard it again—the sound that had woken him. The *whop, whop, whop* of a Blackhawk, coming in low and fast. He sprang to a crouch, his heart thumping fast and loud.

The guards on the platform rushed to the far side, pointing and yelling. Then one of them hit the alarm, and its screech drowned out everything else. An instant later, a missile launched from the helo and streaked toward the camp barracks across the compound. The detonation knocked Luke on his ass and lit up the night sky. When the .50 caliber machine guns mounted in the bay of the Blackhawk opened fire on the guard tower and the few unfortunates who escaped the barracks, he decided it was best to stay down.

What the hell were they doing? They had to be Americans, but this was no high-value target. They didn't know he was here. They were just as likely to take him out, along with the dirty bastards who ran the place. It wasn't like he could take cover inside his open-air accommodations. What was he waiting for? There'd never be a better time to make his escape.

He scrambled to his feet, tucked Sally's picture in his pocket and ran for the gate. The barracks were all on fire. A few enemy fighters still fled the burning buildings, screaming and slapping at the flames that hungrily devoured their clothing, while trying to outrun the merciless onslaught of bullets from the chopper. The smell of smoke, gunpowder and burning flesh turned Luke's stomach and propelled him on. He had no sympathy for them, any more than they'd had a gnat's compassion for Ian as he died. *Let them all burn in hell.*

One of the hostiles ran by the outside of Luke's enclosure with a rocket launcher on his shoulder, dropped to one knee twenty feet away and aimed the weapon at the Blackhawk that was still picking off ground forces.

"*Hell no!*" Luke veered toward the corner of his yard, the closest point to the chopper, and waved his arms wildly over his head. "Get the hell out of here! Go!" A direct hit at such close range would drop the aircraft like a rock. It didn't matter why they were here. He had to warn them.

Not a chance they heard him—he could barely hear himself. It was even less likely that they saw him…but somehow, they knew. The chopper lifted up and away at a steep angle, just as the rocket fired. Even then it only missed the underbelly of the craft by a matter of inches. The Blackhawk continued to move away, circled the blaze they'd created and disappeared behind some hills to the west.

Fucking A! They're safe. Now it was his turn. He swung toward the gate…and halted abruptly. Abdul Omari, commander of this little resort, had apparently managed to hide his sorry ass and survive. He stood a few feet inside the wire, brandishing a pistol, flanked by two of his most depraved underlings with semiautomatic rifles. The only good news was the gate stood open behind them…but Luke would need a miracle to reach it alive.

"Where do you think you are going?" Omari's sneer made his heavy accent even more pronounced.

Luke studied the three. He had no personal knowledge of the man on Omari's right, but he knew the other man too damn well. Ahmed Kazi returned Luke's stare. Blond-haired, blue-eyed, American born and raised, the turncoat was now an interrogator and assassin for the terrorist network. He obviously held a deep-seated hatred for his former countrymen and had brought that to bear with a vengeance on Ian and Luke.

He'd been one cold son of a bitch when the sword he'd raised over his head had ended Ian's life with a hollow thud. Luke would never forget

Ian's murderer. How could he? The man's fucking face appeared in his dreams every night. Rage, as black as the pits of hell, burned just beneath the artificial composure he presented to them. His fingers itched to be around the bastard's throat, squeezing the life from him.

Omari spoke a few words in one of the regional dialects. As one, his men raised the barrels of their weapons and pointed them at Luke.

Well, hell. Apparently, there wouldn't be time to come up with Plan B. Out in the open with no cover, his only option was to fight. Seriously outgunned, his odds weren't good. All he had in his arsenal was the training provided by the Navy SEALs—which was considerable—but he'd have to get much closer if it was going to help him against three armed men. Then, if the planets aligned just right, maybe he'd have a chance. Still, going down fighting was better than dying where he stood.

Luke straightened to his full height and raised his arms, threading his fingers together on top of his head. He dropped his gaze in mock submission as he walked slowly toward his enemies. "Commander, you have many injured men outside. I've trained as a medic. Let me help them."

"You would have me believe you care about my men?"

"Hell no, but I wouldn't allow even an animal to suffer if I could help it." Luke lifted his gaze to take in the commander's skeptical expression. *That's right. Don't believe me, you bastard. Just let me get close enough.*

A handful of men rushed by the gate with weapons drawn, heading toward the west, the direction the helo had disappeared. Ahmed and the other guard returned to the gate, stepping outside to question the leader of the small group.

Omari turned his head for only a few seconds, but that was all Luke needed. He launched himself across the few feet that separated them, grabbed him from behind and applied just enough pressure to snap the bones in his neck before the commander could make a sound. When Luke let him go, his lifeless body slid to the ground. Seizing the Russian Makarov pistol the dead man had dropped, Luke opened fire on the two guards, while the group of men scurried for cover.

The heavily guarded gate was his only way out. Luke was as good as dead if he stayed where he was, so he might as well get in the game. Bending low, he raced a zigzag path toward the opening, ignoring the pain in his extremities from the cruel tortures he'd endured. He was counting on the notoriously poor marksmanship of the local recruits with the Russian-made AK-47. Three men outside the gate went down under his offensive, including Ahmed, before the pistol Luke continuously fired ran out of ammunition.

He shrugged off a twinge of regret that Ian's murderer had gone down so easily. A slow, painful death would have been Luke's first choice.

The men crowding around the outside of the gate fired wildly in his direction, but Luke kept moving forward. An instant later, something slammed into his chest, stealing his breath and stopping him in midstride. Unable to move or even breathe, he hung there for a split second, while time stood still. His gaze locked on his goal, a mere half-dozen feet ahead, and he staggered backward, his efforts to stay on his feet ineffectual, until he sprawled in the dirt of his prison yard.

Damn! Get up! Pull it together! He tried to position his legs to stand, but his body wouldn't cooperate. Then the first wave of pain seared his nerve endings. He couldn't catch his breath. He'd been hit. *Those lousy desert rats got in a lucky shot!* The taste of blood filled his mouth. Panic seized him, but he refused to give it more than a few seconds. *New objective—stay alive. Failure is not an option.* The SEAL mantra had been drilled into him again and again during his training until it automatically followed *fuck this* in his vocabulary. One corner of his mouth curved upward in a half-assed grin, and he managed to draw a partial breath.

His gaze focused on the light at the top of the gate, he moved his hand upward toward the source of the pain, stopping when he felt the warm, sticky liquid that coated his shirt. He squeezed his eyes shut and struggled until another breath temporarily took away the ache in his lungs. *Failure is not an option.*

It sounded like a full-fledged war was being waged just outside his containment area. Every bit of his training demanded he get up and fight, but he needed a little more time to rest.

"Stay down!" someone yelled from not too far away in a pretty good imitation of English.

Who are they talking to? Does somebody need help? In a minute, I'll be strong enough to get back in the fight. Failure is not an option.

A sound close by forced Luke's eyes open, and he looked in to the gloating face of the remaining guard. Blood seeped from at least two wounds in his torso, but still he aimed his rifle at Luke. When the sound of the shot reverberated across the open desert, Luke's body jumped in anticipation of the slug tearing through his flesh. Instead, blood ran down the officer's chin, and he did a face-plant in the sand beside Luke.

Then there were people all around him, everyone talking at the same time—in *English*!

"Damn fine shot, Davis! Now, let's get our friends and get the hell out of here before reinforcements roll in." An American soldier, dressed in full battle gear, stood over Luke and talked into a small radio.

More unfamiliar faces appeared behind the first man, each yapping about something that seemed insignificant from Luke's position. He wanted to shout at them to shut up, but apparently there was no longer a connection between his brain and his mouth. *Not that there ever was much of one. Oh, great—now I get my sense of humor back.*

"Are you Petty Officer Second Class Luke Harding?" The man in battle gear knelt beside him.

As hard as he tried, Luke couldn't make a sound—or even nod his head. All he could do was stare until his eyes misted, and he squeezed his eyelids shut so he wouldn't fucking humiliate himself.

They know my name. Somebody knows who I am. Gratitude washed over him even as sorrow intruded into his momentary peace. Except for two short weeks, he could have celebrated with Ian.

The warrior reached for Luke's hand, gripping it firmly. "It's okay, son. You stay with me. You hear me, sailor? That's an order." He leaned over Luke, and there was understanding in his eyes. "We're here to get you home alive, and failure is not an option. You copy that?"

Luke would have smiled if he could have. Did the guy know the phrase he uttered so effortlessly was the only thing holding Luke together?

"Medic!" the man yelled over his shoulder, and two seconds later, another warrior stuck his head into Luke's space.

It was getting harder to breathe. His rasping and gurgling grew louder and filled his ears.

"Chest wound." The second man applied pressure, none too gently, to the hole in Luke's torso.

Jesus, you stupid SOB! Luke would have given anything for the strength to shove him away, while using every four-letter word he knew, but the most he could manage was a pained groan.

"Hang in there." The first man pulled Luke's attention from the medic. "I know you're in pain. The chopper will land any second, and we'll get you onboard. Next stop—a nice, clean hospital and then…Stateside. We're going to give you the good shit so you can sleep through this next part. You're going to make it, sailor, so start planning your homecoming."

Sally. The image of the sweet brunette flashed in Luke's mind. He barely felt the prick of the needle before his eyes fluttered closed on his last memory.

* * * *

This was definitely going down in history as one of the worst ideas she'd ever had. Sally pulled the door handle of Emmett's Chevy Tahoe and jumped out before he'd even come to a full stop in front of her house.

Dating her new boss—had she gone completely mad? Now that he'd proved to be a total dickhead, telling her exactly what he expected of his new office manager...outside of the office...she'd had no choice but to suggest he drop dead, using the f-word, which hadn't crossed her lips since Jen was born. Of course, that meant she'd be pounding the pavement tomorrow, looking for a new job. *Really?* How could she have been so foolish? She needed that job too, especially after her old Explorer had finally died and she'd had to go into debt to get the needed repairs. If only she could have a do-over for...oh, say, the last year of her life.

"We're not done yet, Sally." The SUV's door slammed shut and hurried footsteps followed her up the path toward the lights that glowed from the windows of her rented home.

Sally kept on walking. Her head throbbed as though someone had taken an electric drill to her temples. *Please, God, don't make me listen to anymore.* She shivered and drew the lightweight pashmina tighter around her shoulders. *What the hell was I thinking...wearing a short dress with no sleeves and strappy heels—at night in the middle of April—in the mountains—in Idaho?* Strong fingers circled her arm and bit down as he tightened his grip, jerking her around, making her forget the chill in the air, and bringing her face-to-face with one irate man.

She tried to shrug off his grasp, but he only pinched tighter. Sally swallowed an outraged cry, not willing to let him know he was hurting her. With composure she wasn't exactly feeling, she met his angry gaze. "Look, you made me an offer—I refused. I have a daughter and she comes first. Even if I wanted to become your...slut...I'd never set that kind of example for Jen. Surely you can understand that." Wary of the temper he'd exhibited on the way home, Sally refrained from telling him what a jackass she thought he was for pretending to be nice and normal until she agreed to go out with him. Then he'd hit her with a proposition that would have made a hooker blush.

Emmett yanked her closer, sliding his arms around her waist. "Well, *slut*'s a little harsh, darlin', but whatever you think. This has nothing to do with your kid. I'll find someone to watch her twenty-four/seven because that's how much of your time I'll need."

Anger sparked at his callous disrespect for Jen. Who the hell did he think he was? Of course, she already knew the answer. He was Emmett Purnell, owner of the biggest logging operation in Idaho. He was loaded and charismatic when he wanted to be and didn't like taking no for an answer. He'd smiled, turned on the charm and played the part of a gentleman until he'd managed to break through her barriers and she'd finally agreed to go out with him. *Idiot, idiot, idiot!*

Sally shook her head firmly. "Not interested."

Emmett's hands slid down to cup her bottom and pull her against him roughly. His intentions quickly became apparent as the hard ridge of his erection pressed into her stomach. Shock gave way to fury. She drew her arm back and swung, and her fist met his jaw with a resounding wallop.

Clearly taken by surprise, his head snapped back, but he recovered quickly. His lips thinned to the point of nearly disappearing, and his eyes darkened to glittering black orbs. "I like it rough, baby." He backhanded her so fast and hard, Sally hit the ground before she'd even registered the blow. The ringing in her ears made it impossible to hear...or think. A thousand needles pricked her cheek as the pain and taste of blood sent her to her knees, tying her stomach in knots.

She scrambled to stand, but dizziness and the pain in her still-fisted hand hindered her efforts. She refused to scream—that was sure to bring Jen and her babysitter, Tiffany, out of the house. Sally couldn't take the chance they might get hurt. Besides, screaming wasn't really her style. The best she could do at the moment was crawl out of the reach of the enraged lunatic and hope he came to his senses.

"Go ahead. Touch her again and see what happens, you fucking coward." The suggestion, coming from the darkness behind Emmett's vehicle and delivered with steel-edged composure, took her completely by surprise.

Sally swung toward the new player, forgetting Emmett for the moment. The voice was all too familiar, stirring unwelcome memories. Eyes watering from the blow, she squinted to see the man standing in the darkness just beyond her yard.

"Luke?" Sally staggered to her feet, clenching her teeth against the sick feeling that swirled in her stomach.

It couldn't be *him*. Not the man she'd fallen hard for before he deployed with his SEAL unit over a year ago. Not the man who'd refused to see her when she hurried to the hospital in Bethesda after hearing he'd been rescued from a terrorist prison. Rushing to his side because she'd thought they meant something to each other, she'd quickly learned the truth of the matter. His disregard had let her know, in no uncertain terms, that the feelings had been one-sided. *That* man had no reason—or right—to show up at her door.

Sally searched the shadows near the street, where the voice had originated. When she finally made out his silhouette, her breath caught in her throat.

Luke didn't spare her a glance.

"Who the hell are you?" Emmett turned to face him.

"Does it matter?" Luke's words contained a dangerous warning that Sally had never heard before.

As he stepped from the shadow of the SUV, his military fatigues and the duffel he carried reminded her of the homeless people who'd camped on Elk Creek last fall. A knife in a leather sheath hung at his side. His face was etched with lines of exhaustion, and he might have carried himself stiffly, but otherwise he was the same man she remembered. Light brown hair, longer and a bit more disheveled than the last time she'd seen him, always tempted her to run her fingers through it...even now.

"I'll need your name to give to the undertaker," Emmett sneered.

A humorless smile bared Luke's teeth as he let the duffel drop to the ground. He shrugged out of his jacket and tossed it over the bag. A black Navy T-shirt stretched across his obscenely well-muscled torso, just the way Sally remembered. Dog tags rested against the contour of his chest. His thick arms hung relaxed at his sides, his nonchalance chilling by itself.

"Okay, hotshot, you've got about a second to get the hell out of here if you want to avoid the beating I've got for you." Emmett started toward him at a brisk walk.

Despite the pain that had long since festered into bitterness, she couldn't stand by and let Luke get hurt. He'd been wounded, seriously. He looked strong enough, but what if he wasn't fully recovered? She glanced around for something to use as a weapon, but Jen had cleaned the yard last weekend and put all the garden tools away. Sally backed toward the house, unable to take her eyes off the disaster unfolding in her yard.

Luke's expression didn't change. He remained motionless as Emmett approached.

Her boss took a swing as soon as he was within arm's length. Luke ducked, evading the blow effortlessly, then shoved Emmett against the front of his Tahoe. He held him there in some kind of a headlock until Emmett's legs folded and he slid to the ground, apparently out cold. Luke opened the SUV's door, yanked Emmett off the ground, as though the man who'd towered over her weighed nothing, and stuffed him into the front seat before slamming the door shut.

Luke didn't look at her until he'd retrieved his jacket. As he threaded his arms into the sleeves, he turned to run his gaze over her, his expression dark and brooding.

"What are you doing here, Luke?" Sally's leftover concern gave her voice a trace of impatience.

"It's good to see you too, sunshine." He bent to retrieve his duffel before walking toward her. "Let's go in the house. He'll be out for a few minutes. I'm staying until he wakes up and takes off without causing any more trouble." A gentle hand stroked her cheek, where Emmet's blow had landed, and Luke's piercing gaze dared her to argue. He turned her toward the house and fell in beside her, pressing his hand to the small of her back. "What the hell are you doing, hanging out with a guy like that anyway?"

It wasn't like she didn't already know she'd screwed up. She didn't need a lecture from this man, who'd picked today to show up on her doorstep after he'd cast her away like so much trash. Sally's annoyance grew to irrational irritation. The nerve of him, even if he did rescue her from an uncomfortable, possibly dangerous situation. He had no right to judge her, despite his scent of freshly mown hay with a touch of cinnamon that teased her senses. She didn't have to defend her actions to him...and yet she couldn't keep from doing just that.

"Not that it's any of your business, but he seemed like a decent-enough guy until he'd had a couple of drinks. This is Huntington—not LA or New York. The dating pool here includes anyone single, employed and under fifty." Besides, who would have thought she couldn't trust her boss—a respected local businessman? *Well, he's not my boss anymore. Did one have to give notice in situations like this?*

Luke stopped and turned to face her, his brow shooting upward toward the hair that cascaded over his forehead. Rich brown eyes held her gaze, and she was powerless to turn away. Finally, a smile broke free that reminded her of the man she'd known before he'd gone through hell. "Well...it's good I'm here, then." He winked before opening the door and pushing inside, leaving her standing on the steps with her mouth open.

An instant later, the sound of Jen squealing and shouting Luke's name was followed by small feet running across the room. The wonderfully deep and warm male laughter that spilled through the doorway brought Sally images of Luke catching her daughter in his arms and twirling her around, exactly as he'd done a year ago. Jen had gotten attached to Luke too, and it'd taken her a long time to accept the fact he wasn't coming back. Now, her childish giggles, mixing with his masculine voice, meant trouble and heartache.

Damned if I'll let him hurt my daughter again.

Hands shaking slightly, she covered her face and tried to get her head back in the game. Part of her struggled to understand the toll Luke's ordeal as a POW had taken on him, and she wanted to weep for the man he'd been. Another part wanted nothing more than to hold him and let him know it didn't matter—not to her. But the sting and humiliation of his rejection when he'd refused her entry to his hospital room hadn't yet faded. Maybe she could have forgiven him if it had only affected her. Fortunately, Jen had remained in Huntington with friends, thereby spared the debacle at the hospital, but Luke's actions had hurt her too. Neither of them were up for a repeat performance.

Straightening her spine and squaring her shoulders, she took a moment to compose her expression. The coming confrontation would likely make her extremely unpopular with all parties concerned...but it couldn't be helped.

The sooner Luke left, the better for all of them.

Chapter Two

Holding that little girl while she squeezed his neck, giggled and repeated his name over and over, was just about the best feeling Luke had experienced in damn near forever. Close on the heels of that came the familiar guilt for sending Sally away when he'd returned to the States, wounded and broken, and for not making contact even after his health had stabilized… until now. He'd had his reasons, and they were good ones at the time, but the longer he stayed away, the harder it became to face her. He probably wouldn't have mustered the courage to walk up to the door tonight either, if shitface out there hadn't assaulted her in the front yard. Luke's vision had blurred to red, his rage taking over when that lousy piece of garbage backhanded her. The dirtbag was lucky to be alive.

No doubt Sally would run Luke off as soon as this crisis was over. He had no right to be here. As though he wouldn't have been able to figure that out on his own, his brother had pressed the point home in their last phone conversation. Sally hadn't been the only one pissed off by the way Luke had treated her. In addition, he was almost positive Sally wouldn't appreciate him turning into a damn stalker in the last week since he'd been here, driving past her house, parking down the street, wanting to go back in time and somehow become good enough for her again.

He hadn't begun his journey with that intention. Leaving Dad's house in Los Angeles ten days ago, his destination had been the home of Ian Mathias's brother, Daniel, a few miles north of Sandpoint, Idaho. Daniel had come to the hospital in Bethesda four days in a row, just to sit and talk about his brother with the last man to see him alive. Luke felt a kinship with Daniel, identified with the honest grief he expressed for Ian. He reminded Luke of his own brother. Before he left, Daniel extracted a promise from

Luke to visit him and his family—also a promise way overdue. Somehow, the route he'd chosen to travel took him close to Huntington and Sally's home, and he'd lost sight of his goal, replaced by the need to make sure she was okay...and, if possible, make things right with her.

Luke spun Jen around fast, the way she liked, then set her on her feet. Kneeling in front of her, he lifted one hand, inviting a high five. She obliged with a decisive smack.

Sally entered the house quietly, closing the door and leaning against it, rather than moving farther into the room. A second later, she dropped her purse, keys and cell phone onto the top of a cabinet that rested along the wall to the right of the door.

Tiffany, the teenage girl from next door, who he'd met a year ago, when she babysat for Sally, unfolded her legs from the couch and stood. She strode toward him, obviously with a purpose, and stuck out her hand. "Thank you for everything you did over there, Mr. Harding."

Aw hell! He never knew what to do or say when good-intentioned civilians verbally expressed their gratitude. In most cases, they had no idea what he'd done—what he'd seen over there—or that he'd never again be the same person he'd been. Months with a shrink had brought him to the place he was now, knowing he might as well live with his memories because he sure as hell couldn't change them.

He grasped Tiffany's hand, because that was what was expected of him, met her somber gray gaze and nodded. Thankfully, she turned away quickly, as they almost always did. Apparently, some sixth sense warned them they really didn't want to know what went on in his head after the lights went out at night. Not that he didn't appreciate Tiffany's gesture, but the military had been his *job,* and he didn't want or need accolades. After his captivity, everything had changed. His job had become staying alive—failure was not an option. Their image of a hero returning from war was all a lie, and it stuck in his craw.

He forced his attention back to Jen, and the welcome in her eyes soothed his turmoil. "Hey, midget. How old are you now? You're getting too big for me to twirl around like that." Luke teased her with the nickname he'd tagged her with a year ago.

As expected, she pointed her spindly finger at him and gave an exaggerated sigh. "I'm nine...too old for that name. Besides, it's not PC."

Luke threw back his head and laughed. "PC, huh? I guess you *have* grown up since I've been gone. When I was your age, I didn't know what *politically correct* meant."

The grin faded slowly, replaced with a tilt of her chin. "You were gone a long time, Luke. Were you mad at us?"

His guilt mushroomed at the uncertainty in her small voice. He leaned toward her, moving his face close to hers. "No. Never. I was just detained longer than I'd planned. I came to see my two favorite girls as soon as I could." Luke wasn't sure how much to tell her. Apparently, Sally hadn't discussed with her his time in captivity. And probably not about being turned away at the door to his hospital room either.

The silence stretched for a moment, while Jen looked at her mother with an I-told-you-so grin. It did Luke's heart good to witness the exchange, and Jen's unconditional acceptance might make it easier finding favor with Sally.

"Well, I don't usually worry too much about being PC, but if I was to change, what should I call you? Princess? Rambo? What's your pleasure?" Luke swept his gaze over her.

She must have grown a good four inches since he'd seen her last, but she was still as slender as a reed. Her chin-length brown hair, a shade lighter than her mother's, bounced every time she moved, which was a lot. She had Sally's light blue eyes, and Jen's now sparkled with mischief.

"No!" She laughed, as if he was the funniest person in the world. "My name is Jen. Maybe you could call me that until we think of a nickname that fits."

"You know what? Jen is a beautiful name, just right for a beautiful girl, but what's this business about you being nine? I thought you were eight."

"Silly. I had a birthday in February." Once again, her smile faded. "I wanted to invite you, but Mom said you couldn't come."

The sadness in her baby blues bit him in the ass...hard. He felt like a total jerk. Luke reached for her and drew her into a hug. "I'm sorry, Jen. I wish I'd been here. Tell you what. Let's pick a day and go shopping for a birthday present. Anything you want—well...except a car...or a pony." He crossed his eyes and made a funny face.

Jen laughed, her momentary sadness apparently forgotten. "*Anything* I want?"

"As long as it's okay with your mom." They both turned to look at Sally, and Luke didn't miss the wariness and anxiety in her expression.

She was so much more beautiful in person than in the faded photograph in his pocket. Long, dark brown hair hung in wavy tendrils to the middle of her back, its silky texture begging to be touched. Petite in stature, she was almost a full foot shorter than him, but she worked out regularly, or at least she had when he'd first met her, and her body was lithe, agile and strong. He loved her sexy blue eyes and the way they lit up with amusement, mischief and, once in a while, lust. He'd give anything to see happiness in her eyes now, but instead, she avoided meeting his gaze.

Why kid himself? If he was a betting man, he'd wager her unease had nothing to do with what he might buy Jen for her birthday and everything to do with the fact that he was kneeling in the middle of Sally's living-room floor. Truth be told—he wouldn't fault her for being cautious. It was a good trait to practice. If only she'd been a bit more circumspect before choosing to go out with the sleazeball in the driveway.

"Is it okay, Mom?" Jen's excitement erupted with another bounce.

He wouldn't have blamed Sally for not wanting him to spend time with her daughter, but Jen's smile of joy was apparently too brilliant to squash. "We'll talk about it tomorrow, okay, honey? It's way past your bedtime now. You get ready for bed while I walk Tiffany home." She grabbed her purse from the cabinet near the door. "I'll only be a minute."

"Bye, Tiffany," Jen said.

"See ya, girlfriend." The babysitter gathered her sweater and purse and started toward the door.

"Hold up a minute. I'll walk Tiffany to her house. You stay inside." Luke pushed to his feet, hoping Sally wouldn't argue simply because she was annoyed with him. He didn't want to remind her in front of her nine-year-old daughter that the man who'd caused the bruise forming on her jaw and cheekbone was still parked in the driveway. In a short time, those bruises would be noticeable enough for Jen to spot, and Sally could answer her daughter's questions however she saw fit. For now, he was relieved when Sally nodded, pulled some bills from her purse and handed them to Tiffany.

Jen touched Luke's arm as he moved to follow the teenager outside. "You're not leaving, are you?"

He wasn't going anywhere until the loser in the Chevy Tahoe out front left. After that, he needed fifteen minutes alone with Sally to say what he'd come to say. Then, if she wanted him to leave, he'd move on with a clear conscience…and a heavy heart. He gave Jen a quick hug. "I'm not leaving yet. In fact, I'll be staying at a friend's place north of here for a while. It's not that far away, so I can come anytime you want to see me. Don't forget, I promised you a birthday present and I meant it, even if I have to go shopping alone." He glanced at Sally, but he couldn't read her expression.

"I mean…you should stay here tonight…with us. Then we can talk more in the morning." Jen's small fingers squeezed his arm.

"Jen, that's enough, honey. I'm sure Luke has somewhere he needs to be." Sally stepped behind Jen, placing her hands on the girl's shoulders, and gave Luke an apologetic smile.

God, she was pretty…and so damn transparent. It was clear she wanted him out of there in the worst way—something she wasn't going to get until they'd had a chance to talk. He grinned as he met her gaze. "Actually, I don't have anywhere to be. I was planning to sleep in my vehicle again. Your couch looks pretty comfortable compared to my old truck." He hated himself for the cornered-prey look that invaded Sally's eyes. "If you've got eggs in the house, I'll even cook breakfast."

"Please, Mom. Please say yes." Jen hugged them both as she bounced up and down.

Sally's expression hardened and her cold eyes regarded him as though he was something the cat had caught and left on the doorstep. She cleared her throat, sounding suspiciously like she'd growled at him. "I suppose it would be all right for one night. Jen, find a pillow and a blanket for the couch."

The girl hugged her mother around the waist and Sally bent to kiss Jen's head. Lucky for Luke, Sally would do anything to make her daughter happy. Apparently, that included allowing the proverbial leper to sleep over. Now, if only he could get Sally to talk to him before she gave him his walking papers in the morning, Jen's efforts on his behalf wouldn't be wasted.

Luke continued to the door and gave Jen a thumbs-up before he followed Tiffany outside. It took him a couple of minutes to deliver the girl to her door and he was halfway back to Sally's steps when the Chevy Tahoe parked at the curb roared to life and the headlights split the darkness. He continued to walk until he reached the path leading to the front door, then turned to face the lights, legs spread slightly, hands fisted at his sides. If the guy wanted to take out his frustration on someone, Luke was happy to oblige.

The man revved the engine loudly three times before he rammed it in gear, and the big SUV lurched forward onto the grass. Luke advanced quickly, sidestepping the front of the vehicle. The driver threw the transmission in Park and climbed to the ground.

Luke stepped close, invading the man's personal space, struggling to control the white-hot fury he and his shrink had labored for months to lock away. His lightning-fast temper had been a surprise even to him after his physical body began to heal. Harder to fix, his mental state had become his nemesis—one that could keep him from the two people he cared about the most.

Sally opened the front door and stepped partway out. He couldn't see her eyes at this distance, but he felt her gaze on him as though a soft breeze, carrying the scent of carnations, swirled around him. She had always smelled of carnations. Now, her very presence was a physical restraint, tipping him back to the side of sanity.

"No one's been hurt seriously so far. Wanna keep it that way?" Luke stepped back, giving the driver some breathing room.

The man studied him with a steady glare. "You seem like a smart guy. Do me a favor, would ya? Tell the ice queen she's fired." He jerked his head toward the house. "You, on the other hand—I could use a man like you on the payroll." He pulled a business card from his front pocket and flicked it to the ground near Luke's feet. "If you ever need work, give me a call."

Yeah right. When hell freezes over, buddy. "No, thanks. I'll pass."

"Suit yourself." The man started to turn toward his vehicle but stopped and swung back slowly. "I wonder how well you know that little gal in there. I never hire anyone unless I do a thorough background check. People hide things, and when you're running a business, it's smart to find out what those things are." He crossed his arms and cocked his head toward Luke, as though trying to decide if it was worth his time to share his findings.

Luke stopped short of asking what line of work the guy was referring to. He probably didn't want to know. Besides, it didn't matter. Anger resurfaced as he prepared to defend Sally from what had to be nothing but a pack of lies. "If you've got something to say, spit it out."

"Sally Duncan has secrets and they're buried deep. Not even *my* people could dig up all the answers. My advice is, watch your back if you plan on spending time with her." He turned abruptly and climbed behind the wheel.

"That's all you've got? Sounds like bullshit to me, man. This—whatever this was—it's over. The lady won. Time for you to head back to whatever rock you crawled out from under. And you can do me a favor too. Don't come back." Luke's last words fell quiet and even, the outward manifestation of his simmering anger.

The man's gaze swept over Luke, obviously taking his measure, before he laughed and swung his door closed. He slammed the SUV into reverse and spun his big tires, leaving wide ruts in the grass until he squealed onto the street. Shifting into Drive, he apparently floored the gas pedal and wound the engine up tight, blowing through the stop sign at the end of the block.

Luke kept vigil until he could no longer hear the Tahoe's engine. When he turned toward the house, Sally stood quietly in the open doorway, the light shining around her with a halo effect. Her shuttered expression gave him no clue what she was thinking.

Luke held her gaze as he approached the house. She stared back at him with wide eyes, triggering his protective instinct. He had to fold his hands behind his back to keep himself from reaching for her, tucking her against him and laying her head in that spot beneath his chin. She'd felt so good there all those months ago. The effort it took to let her turn and retreat into the house awakened the panic in him. He had to tell her what he'd come to say before he lost his nerve.

As much as he tried to block out her former boss's accusations, the insidious whispers in his head started almost immediately. Was she hiding something? Was that why she stayed here in this backwater town with no family but Jen and a few friends? Her life seemed to revolve around that little girl and her friend, Rachel, who, coincidentally, was his brother's fiancée. At one time, Luke had hoped to be a part of the picture too, but now he wasn't so sure he'd make the cut.

He stepped across the threshold behind her, closing the door and turning the dead bolt.

In the center of the small living room, she whirled to face him. "What did he say?" Wariness crept into her expression, giving credence to his unwanted suspicions.

Luke shrugged. "Said to tell you you're fired. Everything else was just male chest-thumping." He caught the barest wisp of her smile as she turned away to straighten up the couch, where he'd be sleeping. A lump formed in his throat as he watched her. He loved the fact he'd always been able to make her laugh. The three weeks they'd spent together before he shipped out had been the most fun he'd ever had with a woman.

Without a word, he walked past her, through the kitchen, to check the lock on the back door. He'd spent enough time in this little house with her and Jen—cooking meals together, watching movies—he was familiar with her routines. Despite the fact this was a small town and everybody knew everyone else, Sally was strict—almost obsessive—about locking her doors. At first, he'd found it a little strange, but now he could be assured the house would be locked up tight until this mess had blown over.

The living room was empty when he retraced his steps. A pillow and neatly folded blanket were stacked on one end of the couch. He turned the switch on a nearby lamp, then returned to the door to flip off the overhead light. A good part of the room retreated into shadows. Luke dropped down on the couch, leaned over to unlace his boots and toed them off. Then he sat back and stretched, crossing his legs at the ankles. Out of habit, he pulled the picture from his shirt pocket. Creased down the middle, dog-eared and faded, the images of Sally and Jen smiled at him, never failing to make his heart beat a little faster, as though to prove he still had a reason to live.

A door opened and closed down the hallway to his right. A second later, Sally appeared, a green terry-cloth robe tied closed around her slim waist, leaving much of her legs bare. She glanced at him, then quickly away. Silently, she circled the room, picking up newspapers that had been left scattered on the furniture, empty dishes and cups and a game Jen and Tiffany had probably been playing. Finished with her chore, she folded her arms across her chest and turned toward him. The man-made chill in the room was enough to have him going for the blanket, but he stared right back at her.

"You never answered my question. What are you doing here, Luke?"

Right to the point. He'd expected that from her, and she'd get the same from him. "I came to see you. I meant to call first, of course, but I couldn't walk away while your friend was being such a jerkwad."

She straightened, dropping her arms. "Were you just sitting out there in the dark watching me?" Her voice conveyed the same disgust he saw in her eyes.

"Well, yes...and no. There were also a few drive-bys." He stopped at her disbelieving *humph* and raised his hands as though, by his sheer will, he could keep her from stomping out of the room. "I'm not a stalker, Sally. I know this sounds ugly and perverted, but I only kept my distance because I was having a hard time working up the courage to face you. And I couldn't leave without apologizing."

Sadness filled her eyes and her shoulders slumped as she turned away. "Do you know what you've done? If you're not here in the morning, Jen will be devastated. If you *are* here, she'll be shattered when she sees you walk out of her life. Either way, that little girl gets hurt, and that's the one thing I swore you'd never get the chance to do again."

Luke reached her in three strides, a hand on each arm, turning her to look at him. "You have to believe me—I never intended to hurt either of you, but especially not Jen. You know how I feel about her. This isn't easy for me either, but I owe you an explanation. I know I've fucked this up. I should have come a long time ago. Will you sit with me? Hear me out? Please?" He'd hurt her without even the courtesy of telling her why. Now he was asking for *her* time, and she had every right to turn her back on him. His chest constricted with the fear she might do just that.

Her gorgeous blue gaze drilled into him for a moment before she barely nodded. "You don't owe us anything, but I'll listen because I'd like to know where our signals got crossed." She slipped by him and strode to an armchair that sat to the left of the couch.

Luke followed, grateful to be able to breathe again. Scooping up the picture that had slipped to the floor when he'd risen to go after her, he returned to his seat, leaning forward with his elbows resting on his knees. Momentarily at a loss to start the conversation, he held the worn photograph out for her to see.

She searched his eyes before she reached for it and ran one slender finger down the crease, lingering on Jen's face. "You still have this."

It was a statement rather than a question, but it provided the opening he needed. "That picture was all I had of you and Jen over there. It meant everything to me. The prison guards let me keep it, then found every opportunity to tell me I'd never see you again. But I didn't believe them because you and Jen wouldn't let me give up. I know that sounds nuts, but trust me, I've been checked and rechecked by the best military psychiatrists available, and I'm completely sane. You and that picture are the reasons I didn't throw in the towel after the first month."

Sally sat up even straighter, if that was possible, and leaned to hand him the photograph. "As you can probably tell, Jen is still quite attached to you. When your brother called to say you'd been captured…by terrorists I couldn't tell her that. She was too young, not equipped to handle something like that. Lord knows I wasn't either. So, I'm very happy you came home, but I'm confused. I rushed to Bethesda when I heard you'd been rescued, only to be told I was on the short list of people you didn't want to see. No explanation. I had to wait for your brother to visit you to find out how you were doing. I was scared to death for you, and hurt and embarrassed for me. Oh, don't worry. I'm over it. I didn't have any claim on you. But why show up now? You must know how hard this will be for Jen when you leave again."

Luke folded his hands, resisting the urge to succumb to his guilt and look away. He was also very aware Sally hadn't said his leaving would be hard on her. "What did Garrett and Rachel tell you?"

She smoothed her robe over her thighs, her forehead furrowing. The dim lighting made her bruises appear larger and darker. "They said you'd been seriously wounded during the rescue…that the doctors wanted to stabilize you before surgery…and that they were only allowing family to visit." A harsh laugh punctuated her words. "I went to the hospital for three days anyway…just in case. The last day, I arrived in time to see three sailors leaving your room, all smiles. I was ecstatic, thinking you were better. When I asked at the nurses' station, they didn't know anything about a family-only order. One of the nurses asked my name as she was reading your chart, and she got this look on her face like she had a mouth full of something she couldn't possibly swallow. That poor woman was the only one brave enough to tell me it was only me you didn't want to see." Her eyes, full of hurt, drifted away from his, studying something on the wall behind him.

"Guilty as charged." He recalled the day she was referring to as though it was yesterday. His SEAL unit had returned Stateside, and three of his best buds...and Ian's...had surprised him at the hospital. Not that he was thrilled to have them as visitors either, but he'd learned three things about true friends that day. They wouldn't let you piss your life away feeling sorry for yourself. They were willing—even eager—to tell you when you'd screwed up. And they *always* had your back. They were quick to tell him he owed the truth to the mystery woman in the picture he was always scrutinizing. Where she went with it after that was up to her. Unfortunately, he'd come around to their way of thinking a day too late.

She jerked her gaze back to him, her jaw set in stony resolve. "When Rachel and Garrett learned it was you and not your doctors behind the order to keep me out, they were mad as hell. I made excuses for your behavior, blaming your injuries and frame of mind after the ordeal you'd been through. Garrett was set on confronting you, but I begged him not to. I couldn't handle being the cause of an argument between you and your brother. You needed him...and you'd made it clear you *didn't* need me. Garrett was sure you'd come to your senses after you'd had some time to deal with the trauma. I wasn't so sure, but I went home trying to fool myself into believing it was true."

Luke hung his head with the weight of his regret. "I was a damn fool. You and Jen were with me every step of the way in that desert. When the rescue unit found me, the captain in charge said to start planning my homecoming, and you were the first person I thought about. I couldn't wait to see you again." Luke paused as his memories pressed in on him.

"Then what was it?" Disbelief closed over her features.

He could have reached for her hand and threaded his fingers through hers, but her guarded expression told him how foolhardy that idea was. Misery rose up like a living thing and tried to deter him, but he raised his gaze to hers. Memories closed around him.

"Everything changed when I woke up on a hospital ship...paralyzed from the waist down." It had taken everything he possessed to force the words out without also giving away the bone-deep terror he'd become acquainted with that day.

Sympathy lined Sally's face, and though he hated her feeling sorry for him, Luke couldn't stop now if he was going to get through this.

"Doctors said the round missed my heart by a fraction of an inch and lodged right up against my spine. Swelling had caused the paralysis, but they couldn't operate until the inflammation was gone. In either case, they weren't giving me very good odds I'd ever get out of a wheelchair."

It was obvious now he'd made a hasty and ill-advised decision, but it hadn't been so easy to call when nurses had performed every humiliating service he needed while he looked ahead to nothing but more of the same. Somehow, he had to make her understand. "Whether you knew it or not, you saved my life in that prison. I couldn't saddle you and Jen with a cripple—or worse yet, leave you to make a choice you'd probably never forgive yourself for."

Something like anger flashed in her eyes and she started to speak, but Luke raised a hand.

"There's more. Please let me get this out. If you can't bring yourself to forgive me, I'll live with that."

Sally pressed her lips together.

"I was more like an animal than a man when those soldiers rescued me from that prison. I'd been living like one for months. Wallowing in filth. Eating slop—God only knows what they fed us—and we were glad to get it. Taking whatever they decided my punishment was for being alive each day. Living in a blind rage every minute, but knowing that to give them even one provocation would mean my death. I was on the fucking edge *all* the time. I wasn't safe to be around."

Even delving into his memories far enough to give her a summary of the hell he'd lived filled his nostrils with the putrid stench of death, and his stomach churned into a knot the size of an Idaho mountain. He dropped his head and fought the smells and sounds of the illusion that wanted to claim him again. *It's not real. It's in the past. I'm home...with Sally.*

He raised his head and met her gaze. "I didn't want you to see me like that...or feel sorry for me and possibly get trapped in a relationship you never really wanted. I tried to get my brother to stop you from coming to the hospital, but Garrett threatened me if I even suggested that he or Rachel lie to you. So, *I* lied to them about visitation, and then I told myself what I was doing was best for everyone." He tried a half-hearted smile, but she looked a little pale, biting her lower lip nervously. At least she didn't seem quite as angry as she had before.

"I'd just gotten my courage up to tell you everything...ask you to go home and forget about me...when Garrett said you'd left. I'm sorry I hurt you and Jen—actually, sorry doesn't begin to describe the regret that weighs me down every hour of the day." This time he couldn't help himself. He reached toward her, covering one hand as it rested on her thigh. She made no move to welcome his touch so, after a few seconds, he pulled his hand away. "Please don't blame Garrett or Rachel. I begged them not to tell you how serious my injuries were, both physical and mental. I told them I'd tell you when I was better. I'm pretty sure Rachel may never speak to me again, but here I am, as promised." Although his explanation was way too late if the distrust in her eyes was any indication.

"My father stepped up—you remember the senator, don't you?" Right before Luke had deployed, his father had caused no small commotion, showing up at his Aunt Peg's lodge in a helo, complete with bodyguards, to tell his sons that their formerly estranged and currently deceased mother had tried to kill them when Luke was five. Talk about a cluster.

Sally barely nodded.

"The senator whipped out his checkbook and hired a panel of shrinks to make me right in the head. Man, I hated him for that, for noticing how fucked up I was and calling attention to it. Mind you, I'm still not a hundred percent, but now I can at least admit the old man probably saved my life.

"It was three weeks before the doctors would chance the surgery to remove the bullet lodged near my spine. A full month after that before I got any feeling or movement in my toes. And months of physical therapy. Every time I had a good day, I promised myself I'd call you. Then I'd have a setback and…I couldn't. Pretty soon, it just got to be too long—too much time had gone by. You'd no doubt gotten on with your life, and who was I to get in the middle of that? Now it's easy to look back and see what a coward I was."

A rueful laugh drew his gaze to hers again. She still held herself stiffly. "What made you change your mind? I mean…here you are in the middle of my life." She emphasized the last few words as her brows rose questioningly.

Luke swiped a hand through his hair and slouched against the cushions on the couch. She might not be as angry anymore, but there was no trust anywhere in her expression "Maybe I should have left well enough alone, but the way I treated you was killing me slowly. Besides, I never said I was a smart man."

Sally's brows knit in a frown. "That's good, because you were wrong at nearly every juncture. If you're looking for a woman in your life that'll be happy with you making all her decisions, let me know how that works for you. That's a deal breaker for me, so I guess this *did* turn out for the best." She glanced toward the hallway and Jen's room. "I'm sorry for what happened to you, Luke. I can't imagine what it must have been like over there. I understand it was tough recovering mentally, emotionally and physically...but you didn't have to go through that alone."

She whipped a hand in the air. "You know what I mean. I know you've got family, and I'm sure they were all there for you, so you were right—you didn't need me anyway. The three weeks we spent together before you left, the phone calls and the e-mails afterward made me think we had something. That's why I dropped everything and rushed to Bethesda. Not because I wanted to see how badly you were damaged so I could decide if I should cut you loose. If I believed that, you must have thought I was pretty shallow, but then, we didn't really know each other, did we?"

"There's not a shallow bone in your body. You're as beautiful inside as you are on the outside, and a kinder soul has never drawn breath. I couldn't get past the idea you deserved better than half of a man, and I guess I felt responsible for making sure you got that. I was a jerk—I admit it, but at the time, how my injury and my mental state affected your life was the only thing I had any control over. I'd change it all if I could, Sally, but the damage has been done."

Sally's back remained ramrod straight while he bared his soul. Her eyes had misted like she was close to tears, but the firm set of her jaw clearly said she wouldn't cry in front of him. He didn't blame her. There'd probably been more than a few tears shed because of him.

This wasn't going well, but no worse than he deserved. He should have called first, but that little item of etiquette had been yanked out of his hands. His sudden appearance had upset her, hard on the heels of the date from hell. Red and blue bruises had become clearly evident on the side of her face in the last thirty minutes. A rush of anger made him drop his gaze. She'd probably have a black eye too. Hell. All in all, she'd had a memorable night. Still, she'd allowed him to say his peace. He respected her for that. It'd been foolish for him to expect forgiveness. Probably best to slink off into the night before the evening got any worse.

"Look...no one knows better than me I screwed up, and I hope someday you'll be able to forgive me." Luke leaned forward and reached for his boots. "Thanks for hearing me out. I'll lock the door behind me. My truck is just down the block. Everybody will be more comfortable if I sleep there, but I'd be grateful if you'd let me come back in the morning to fix breakfast for Jen. Then I'll go."

Sally regarded him with disbelief. "I suppose I'm the 'everybody' you're referring to? You're really quick with that, aren't you? You did it at the hospital and you're doing it now—deciding what I want—what I'm comfortable with." She stood and paced a couple of steps, her frustration obvious. "You suffered more than I can ever imagine—I get that. But you basically turned your back on me…and Jen. Why? Because you didn't want me to see you like… what? Hurt? Beaten and bruised? Angry? Unconscious with tubes sticking out all over? Or was it just that you didn't want me to see you weak and not in control for the first time in your life? Well, I expect a little more from any man I'd bring into Jen's life."

"Please believe me—I thought I was doing the right thing for you and Jen. Turned out to be a bad decision…one I'll regret for the rest of my life." The need to move on had him on his feet. He'd said what he'd come to say. He loosened the laces on one of his boots and positioned it to slide his foot inside.

Tears welled in her eyes as she tossed her hair with a shake of her head. Luke had only seen her cry once before and knowing his unannounced appearance was the cause this time didn't sit well. He shoved his hands in his pockets to keep from reaching for her. It did nothing to stop him from feeling like an ass, however.

"I'm going to bed." Sally halted after she'd skirted around him. Silence stretched for a moment before she sighed and looked over her shoulder. "You're sleeping on the couch and you're fixing breakfast for all of us in the morning, and don't forget you promised Jen a shopping trip. We'll set something up before you leave tomorrow. And…don't make decisions for me." Her short robe bounced against her thighs as she strode quickly toward the hall.

Luke watched her disappear, slightly breathless from the sudden turn of events. He folded his hands behind his head and leaned back. A small smile tugged at his lips. She hadn't taken the opportunity to kick him out when he'd handed it to her. That had to be good. He'd be allowed to go birthday shopping with Jen. That was even more telling. No way would Sally let him near her daughter if she thought he was beyond forgiveness.

He pulled his T-shirt over his head and turned off the light. Situating the pillow, he spread out the blanket before he pulled his Glock from the waistband of his fatigues and slid it carefully beneath the cushion where his head would rest. Sally's former boss was a dangerous man. Every instinct Luke possessed told him so. Hopefully, the loser would go home and forget about his humiliating night, but it wouldn't hurt to be ready…just in case.

Sleep eluded him, but that wasn't unusual. He hadn't had a full night's sleep, or one undisturbed by dreams, in over six months. A weight had lifted from him tonight, though, and for the first time in a damn long time, regret hadn't formed a ball of apprehension in his stomach when he lay down.

Now that he'd seen them again and confessed his deception to Sally, it wasn't even half enough. As much as he hated to admit it, he was in love with the sweetly innocent, slightly sassy brunette he'd pledged to return to when his mission was over. She'd tried hard to make it sound as though she was done with him, but the fact he was still here, stretched out on her couch, meant he still had one more chance. In the morning, over breakfast, perhaps he could break through the walls she'd erected. Maybe it wasn't too late to win her heart.

* * * *

Luke tossed and turned on the edge of sleep, coughing against the tickle in his throat. A large inhale preceded a coughing fit that brought him fully awake. His eyes burning and his breath wheezing in and out, he rolled off the couch to his hands and knees, the effort causing another round of hacking.

Fire! He couldn't see any flames. It was still too dark to tell where the smoke was coming from. Reaching for the lamp beside the couch, he turned the switch only to have the room remain in total darkness. He might as well have been blind. Feeling for the Glock, he slid it in his waistband, then quickly rose to a crouch and shoved his feet into his unlaced boots. He found his T-shirt and jerked it over his head on the fly.

Entering the hallway, he went automatically to Jen's room—the room where she'd begged him to read to her on more than one occasion. He threw her door open and his heart nearly stopped at the flames licking along the ceiling in the center of the room. The smoke was noticeably thicker.

"*Sally!*" He banged on the wall between her room and Jen's. If she was awake and smelled the smoke, she'd go to Jen's room first. He'd bet on that. Ignoring the ever-present stiffness in his back and shoulders, Luke dropped to his hands and knees and crawled the rest of the way to the bed positioned against the opposite wall.

Jen was a lump in the middle of the full-size mattress. Was she just a sound sleeper or had she already inhaled too much smoke? Dread tightening like a band across his chest, Luke scooped her up with her blanket and turned to rush from the room.

Chapter Three

As though from a great distance, banging intruded into Sally's exhausted sleep. She groaned and tasted the acrid dryness that, for some reason, rested in the back of her throat. *Water.* She uncurled from the tight ball she slept in and rolled onto her back, sliding her legs over the edge of the mattress. Hot air swirled around her bare thighs. *It must be a hundred degrees in here.* Barely a second passed before she made the connection. Her eyes flew open only to burn and tear with smoke from the flames that licked along the ceiling above her. Sally jumped to her feet as terror engulfed her. A coughing fit doubled her over and left her struggling for air.

Fire! I have to get Jen and Luke! Hastily, Sally shoved her feet into a pair of slip-on canvas shoes she'd left at the foot of her bed and sprinted toward the door. Fear for her daughter galvanized her movements and gave her purpose. Still, her heart hammered so hard and fast, the sound of its beating was all she could hear.

Reaching the door, Sally stretched for the knob, but the door flew open, barely missing her as she stumbled backward. A tall, broad-shouldered form stood just outside, the glow from behind her highlighting the relief on his chiseled features.

Luke held a squirming bundle close to his chest with one arm. *Jen!* He reached for Sally with the other, urgently tugging her into the hallway. His presence, and Jen's, momentarily eased her panic.

"Luke? Is Jen okay?"

"She's fine." Luke tugged on her arm again. "We need to go." He had to raise his voice to be heard over the roar she hadn't noticed until now.

Fear squeezed Sally's stomach as she stumbled after Luke. A glance over her shoulder caught flames clawing across the ceiling and down the wall by the window, engulfing the drapes in a barrier of fire. Drapes that had cost her a small fortune—gone in the space of a heartbeat.

Oh my God! That could have been me. Her involuntary gasp forced more smoke into her lungs, and her protesting airway took over again. The more she coughed, the more smoke she inhaled. Her eyes burned and watered until she could barely see.

The farther they got from the bedrooms, the less smoke choked the air. Exiting the hallway into the living room, she jerked her arm from Luke's grasp. "Are you sure Jen's all right?" She tried to untangle the blankets that held her daughter.

As though in response, the bundle in his arms stretched until two arms poked from the blanket and curled around his neck. Luke's brief smile held relief. "I've got her. She's okay." He hooked his arm around Sally's waist and guided her toward the front door, speaking calmly in her ear, loudly enough to be heard over the fire and the blood pulsing in her temples. His voice, sure and confident, called her back from the edge of terror.

Luke turned the dead bolt and opened the door, then dashed toward the couch and grabbed his duffel bag. At the last second, Sally spotted her purse atop the cabinet where she'd forgotten it after his unexpected appearance earlier. Her credit cards were in there, as well as what little money she had. Somehow, she'd have to put a roof over their heads—they'd need clothes and other essentials. She snatched the bag and her cell phone, threw the strap over her head, then noticed a pair of Jen's tennis shoes beneath the cabinet and snagged them before rushing through the open doorway with Luke on her heels. They jogged down the front steps, both dragging fresh air into their lungs, causing them to work overtime to force the smoke out. When Luke finally stopped, she dropped to her knees in the grass at the edge of the street and gave in to the uncontrollable need to cough.

Finally, she was able to take a breath and then another, without her lungs starting to spasm. She wiped her eyes and eagerly turned to Luke as he dropped to the ground across from her and set the precious contents of his bundle on the ground. Jen shrugged out of the blanket, her eyes wide, but otherwise she was perfectly safe. Tears welling, she reached for Sally and sank into her arms.

Sally sought Luke's gaze as she hugged her daughter, needing him to know how grateful she was for saving her little girl. He was staring over her head, and the flames, leaping from the blackened shell of her home, reflected in his eyes. A chill feathered up her spine and she trembled.

Luke lowered his head and met her gaze. "Are you okay?"

Sally held Jen tighter. "Yeah...now I am. Do you know how the fire started?"

He lifted one shoulder in a half-shrug. "No, but old houses usually have old wiring. An electrical surge or a spark from a bare wire could have ignited whatever you had stored in the attic."

"Why the attic?"

"The fire started above us, burned across the ceiling and down the curtains before the main floor became engulfed. The local fire marshal should be able to determine the cause after it's out." Luke stretched full length on the grass, leaning on one elbow, and searched her face.

He looked away, a sad expression dulling his eyes, reminding her how they'd left things between them. Their earlier conversation seemed as though it had taken place a lifetime ago. The world had changed in an instant. As hard as Sally had been sleeping, absent Luke banging on the wall, it was doubtful she'd have waked before inhaling enough smoke to kill her. And Jen—she couldn't even think about what might have happened to her daughter.

She owed Luke a debt she'd never be able to repay...for saving both of them. The slight she'd suffered in Bethesda no longer seemed the unforgiveable sin it had before. He'd come here to explain and apologize... and ended up saving their lives. That was worth something, wasn't it?

Jen pulled free of Sally's arms, sliding down onto the grass beside her. It was all Sally could do to let her go. "Are you hurt anywhere, honey? Are you warm enough?"

"I'm fine, Mom. May I go talk to Tiffany?" She pointed toward her babysitter and some other girls she knew from the neighborhood a few feet away.

Let Jen out of her sight? "Oh, honey. I'd rather you stayed right here so—"

"Sally?" Luke drew her attention, his voice brimming with quiet strength. "She'll be all right. I'll go with her. Okay with you, Jen?" He stood and offered her a hand up.

"Sure." Jen reached for his hand and scrambled to her feet. "Is it okay, Mom?"

Sally managed to nod even though the last thing she wanted at the moment was to be separated from her daughter. She did a halfway decent job of returning Luke's smile before he and Jen walked away.

Gradually, Sally became aware of other people standing nearby, of voices and sirens in the distance. She recognized Tiffany's mother, Gretchen, when the woman who'd lived next door for the past ten years bent down and squeezed her shoulder.

"I called nine-one-one as soon as I saw the flames coming from the roof. The fire trucks will be here any second. Are you and Jen all right?" Gretchen eyed Luke curiously.

That explained the sirens getting closer by the minute. Sally patted Gretchen's hand. "We're fine now. Thanks for calling the fire department." Gretchen nodded and moved away to await the firemen before Sally could tell her they might not have made it out if it hadn't been for Luke. She looked around for him and found him standing nearby, one arm around Jen's shoulders.

The fire engine, sirens screaming and red lights twirling on the roof of the truck, raced down the block and stopped in front of her house. Firemen jumped from every opening and began unrolling hoses. They pushed the small crowd of neighbors that had gathered farther into the street as they prepared to douse the flames with water.

Luke knelt in front of her with Jen's blanket in his hand, and placed it around Sally's shoulders. It wasn't until then she realized she was sitting in her front yard with nothing on but a stretchy knit tank top and panties. She experienced a brief moment of wishing she could drop through the earth's crust until she put it in perspective: being alive was the only thing that mattered. Still, she had no doubt her face was crimson when she met Luke's gaze.

"Thank you," she whispered.

He smiled, regarding her with those expressive brown eyes that had hypnotized her more than once. Though very glad Luke was here, this wasn't the time to explore residual feelings. He must have come to the same conclusion. Rising to his feet, his gaze swept the milling crowd. She searched for Jen again and found her, her small hand held in Tiffany's larger one as they both sat on the curb beside Gretchen. Reassured, Sally turned to watch the firemen efficiently quenching the flames on the roof. From the corner of her eye, she saw Luke pull his cell phone from his pocket and move away from the noise of the group clustered in front of her house.

"Sally, what happened?"

She dragged her attention from Luke to the man who knelt beside her. "Sheriff Anderson. I wish I knew. I really have no idea." Sally covered her forehead with one hand and tried to squeeze her burgeoning headache away. It didn't work.

"Are you and Jen all right?"

"We're fine, considering. I mean, it looks like they're getting the fire out, so it won't be a total loss, right?"

The lean, dark-haired lawman studied the progress of the fire for a moment. "There'll be smoke and water damage, Sally. I wouldn't count on saving much. Looks like the roof and attic have sustained the worst of it. You'll need someplace to stay until the landlord gets the needed repairs done."

"Great. This is the last thing I needed right now." Sally clamped her lips closed on the rest of her complaint. Her lack of employment wasn't any of the sheriff's concern, and he probably didn't need to know she'd started and lost a new job in the same month.

"Do you have someone you can stay with for a couple of months?"

A couple of months? "I'll figure something out."

"I spoke with Gretchen a minute ago. She mentioned you have someone staying with you." Ben removed his ball cap and gave her an apologetic smile. "Gretchen is quite a busybody."

Tell me something I don't know. "An old friend stopped by unexpectedly. Luke Harding—he got us out of the house, Sheriff. Otherwise, I don't know what would have happened."

The sheriff drilled her with his gaze. "Harding? As in Garrett Harding's brother?"

"Yeah. That's me, Sheriff." Luke stood a few feet behind them.

The sheriff rose slowly and swiveled toward him. "Ben Anderson." He offered his hand. "It's a pleasure to meet you, Luke. Your brother is a friend of mine."

Luke hesitated slightly before accepting the sheriff's hand. "My brother is a good man to have as a friend."

"He's sure proud of you." Maybe Ben noticed the barely perceptible narrowing of Luke's eyes and the tick just above his jaw too, because he pivoted quickly back to Sally. "Do you have a place to stay tonight?"

"Yes, she does," Luke said.

That was news to Sally.

If the sheriff noticed her surprise, he didn't let on. "I'll check in with you tomorrow. Meanwhile, if there's anything I can do, just let me know."

Before Sally had a chance to thank him, the night sky erupted in a deafening explosion. What was left of her house shot into the atmosphere as though in slow motion, and the shock waves rocked the ground beneath her. Instinctively, she scrambled toward Jen as pieces of what was once her home began to rain down around her.

Luke whisked Jen from Tiffany's care, pointing her and Gretchen to the opposite side of the street. Both men shielded Sally and Jen from the worst of the debris as they ran for safety. Firemen yelled commands. People screamed. And above that, the roar of the out-of-control fire fueled a terror in Sally the likes of which she hadn't known for a number of years.

No matter how hard she tried to ignore it, the truth wouldn't go away. This was no accident. Someone had started her house on fire and then blown it up...to make sure no one survived. It was after midnight. She and Jen would still be sleeping if not for Luke. But that didn't change the facts—someone had tried to kill them.

By the time they'd reached a safe distance in the neighbor's yard across the street, the firemen had already switched gears. They'd gone to work saving the nearby houses, counting hers a complete loss.

"Sally, you got any enemies?" The sheriff's straight-faced question at her elbow almost made her laugh.

As a matter of fact she did, and as soon as she could get a private moment, she'd have to make the call she'd dreaded for almost nine years, but right now she'd put on her game face and lie like hell. "No, Ben. Everybody loves me. You know that."

"Well, that's what I always thought, but do you mind telling me how you got those bruises on your face?"

In light of everything that had happened, Sally had practically forgotten about the altercation with Emmett and the bruises that had obviously appeared since then. Emmett was a creep, but blowing up her house and trying to kill her wasn't *his* handiwork. She started to shake her head.

Luke pushed one side of her hair behind her shoulder, gaining her attention, then pointed to Jen, standing graveyard still at his side. "I know what you're thinking, but what would it hurt to let the sheriff check him out? He deserves to at least answer a couple of questions to prove his innocence. If he's guilty, you and Jen won't have to worry about a repeat of this."

He was right, of course. Sally believed she knew who the responsible party was, but what if she was wrong? She glanced at Jen again. Thank goodness her daughter had fallen asleep earlier with sweats underneath her nightshirt. The air could get a little nippy in the mountains in the middle of the night. Sally owed it to her little girl to check out every viable suspect until she knew, beyond a doubt, who'd destroyed their home and their lives. Her very real fear of retribution from Emmett once he learned she'd named him as a suspect would have to be set aside.

She was going to need some strong mojo for her headache before this night was over. Sally chewed her bottom lip as she faced the sheriff. "Emmett Purnell."

"Oh shit." Ben massaged the back of his neck absently. "What happened?"

"Can we just say a date didn't end the way he expected and he made threats against me and Luke?" Sally looked at Ben hopefully.

"Who is this guy? I thought he was just your boss." Luke's gaze swept from Sally to the sheriff.

"Emmett runs the largest logging outfit in the state. He's got some big money and questionable associates behind him." The sheriff frowned at her. "I thought you were smarter than that."

What? Sally struggled to subdue the rush of anger his words triggered. "Ben, you and I have known each other since the day I moved to Small Town USA, but that doesn't give you the right—"

Luke stepped between her and Ben. "This isn't the time for making judgment calls. Is Emmett Purnell capable of this kind of violence because a woman refused to jump in bed with him?"

"Maybe, maybe not, but I think it's important to at least rule him out. Problem is, with the fire and the water, there won't be much forensic evidence left. I'm going to visit with the fire chief—see if he's found anything. You're welcome to tag along if you want." Ben set his cap back on his head and started toward the man standing beside one of the fire trucks, shouting orders into a handheld radio.

Luke pivoted to face Sally and pulled her blanket around her more securely. Concern emanated from him as his eyes searched hers. "The sheriff didn't mean anything by that. He's worried...and apparently doesn't have a friggin' clue how to talk to women." His trademark grin slipped into place. "Will you be okay for a few minutes? Stay right here and wait for me?"

Sally smiled half-heartedly and gave him a casual salute, which almost caused the blanket to slide off her shoulders.

One corner of his mouth hitched up and he leaned toward her as though he was about to kiss her, but he merely adjusted the blanket before he strode off after the sheriff.

She missed his confidence as soon as he was gone. Normally, she possessed all the self-reliance needed, but it had deserted her tonight... about the time Luke showed up and turned her world upside down. If she and Jen were going to make it through the days to come, she'd need a good offense. Fishing through her purse, she found her cell phone and scrolled through the list of contacts until she found the right one. Greg Lambert. She stared at the name for a moment, then hit the button to dial the number.

"Lambert." The phone was answered immediately.

She started to hyperventilate and could barely speak. "Marshal Lambert? This is Sally Duncan. I think...I have a problem."

"Are you somewhere safe?" Greg's voice was familiar, though she'd only spoken with him twice before.

"Yes, for now." Sally glanced around at the neighbors she'd known for years. There'd been some turnover during that time, but it had been a safe place to raise Jen...until now.

"Tell me what's happened." Greg was moving around now, making noise as though he was getting dressed.

Sally shook her head, a silent refusal to the worthless tears that threatened. "Someone set my home on fire and then blew it up. I had a house guest who woke up in time to get us out. Otherwise Jen and I would both be dead."

"Any sign of Clive or any of his men?" The jangle of keys came over the phone, along with Greg's ridiculous question.

A shiver raced through her at the mention of the name. She'd known Clive Brennan better than anyone. He was her father, after all, but it had been years since she'd thought of him as Dad or Papa or anything other than Clive Brennan, cold-blooded murderer. Even now, if she closed her eyes, the horror of his crimes flooded her, bringing more tears that stung the backs of her eyelids. The Biloxi family he and his henchmen had butchered were people she'd known all her life. The killers hadn't seen her come calling that day...they didn't hear her quietly step through the half-open front door...her gasp of shock had been swallowed up by the screams of the innocent people in the sunken living room. The shame of backing away—leaving her friends in their moment of need—to call the police still tormented her, even though reason said there was nothing she could have done to save them. Surely sometimes the right thing must be the *unreasonable* one.

Apparently, Clive's alibi hadn't held up, and the prosecutor had already established a motive, so all they needed was Sally's testimony to place her father at the scene of the crime. Still traumatized, she'd agreed, not realizing to what extent it would change her life forever.

And then it had changed again three months ago, when Clive was released from prison. "Of course not. If I'd seen anyone even remotely familiar, don't you think I'd have called you before now?" As soon as the heated words were out, Sally regretted sniping at him.

Greg chuckled. "Good girl. Get mad and stay that way. You'll have to get yourself and your kid out of sight and keep your head down until I get there. I'll call when I'm close."

"Then what?"

"Then we start over from scratch. A new identity. A new life. Except this time you have a daughter." Greg's statement was punctuated by the slam of a door and then a car engine started. He was already on the move.

Sally's gaze flew to Jen, who'd moved to join a circle with Tiffany and a few of the neighbor children, who were up way past their bedtime. She fought the urge to snatch her away from the group and hug her tightly. It would only scare her. "I can't do that to Jen. She has friends here. A life. I can't just rip her from everything she knows and expect her not to be devastated." Her voice was starting to rise, but she couldn't seem to stop the flow of words.

"Your daughter nearly died tonight. Is that what you want?" Greg's voice was still calm and patient, despite the seriousness of his words.

"You know it isn't! I just...I need some time to think."

"Sally, you know as well as I do that if Clive Brennan was responsible for the explosion at your house, he knows where you are right this minute and he's already working on plan B. Now listen carefully. Don't trust anyone." His voice hardened. "Take your daughter and find a safe place to stay. I'll be there by noon tomorrow and we'll figure this out. Okay? Now hang up and get moving."

"No. I'm not ready. There must be some other way. Wait!" Sally was talking to dead air.

Greg had disconnected. The hand that held the phone dropped to her side. Was he right? Was it possible Clive knew where she was and was already planning his next move? Could he be here in this crowd? She raised her eyes and ran right smack into Luke's gaze, staring curiously back at her. He strode toward her, across her neighbor's grass, concern and determination in his expression.

Clearly, he'd overheard her on the phone. As she dropped the device into her purse, she went over her conversation with the marshal in her head, but other than ranting about not taking Jen away from her home, Sally didn't think she'd given up any secrets. But she could trust Luke, couldn't she? He'd be the perfect person to help her figure out what to do. Was it asking too much of their strained friendship? All she needed was a little advice. There *was* no one else.

The marshal's words came back as though he stood directly behind her. *Don't trust anyone.*

Chapter Four

By the time Luke reached Sally, she'd stashed her phone in her bag and regained her composure somewhat. She'd blinked away the desperation he'd caught for a moment, leaving only exhaustion and dark circles beneath her eyes. "Everything okay?" Damn, her teeth were practically chattering. Probably more from shock than the cold, but Luke couldn't help stepping into her and drawing her against him to share his warmth.

Sally reacted as though his touch had burned her, backing away from him.

Luke dropped his hands to his sides. *Okay. It was too soon.* Should he ask her about the phone call? He'd overheard only bits and pieces of her conversation—enough to surmise she hadn't liked what she'd heard. Who called her in the middle of the night? Or…had she placed the call? Each question brought up two more, and Luke wanted answers, but his gut told him she was in no mood for sharing. Obviously, he needed to try a different tact.

"Sheriff Anderson said we can leave. I gave him my phone number so he can contact us if he learns anything new." Luke raised his arms slightly, and she followed their movement. "It's freezing out here. Let's get Jen into my pickup and blast the heater. Then we can talk about where to go from here."

Her reluctance was written in every worry line on her forehead. A few feet away, Jen was talking quietly with her friends, and Sally swiveled to watch her. Soon, her stance softened and some of the tension left her face. A smile smoothed the frown she'd been wearing. Jen didn't appear cold, but the suggestion had been planted, and the mama bear in Sally took over.

Luke didn't give her a chance to change her mind. While Sally took Jen's hand and visited briefly with her friends, he'd explained to Gretchen where they'd be staying—even though he hadn't broached the subject with Sally yet. Then he guided both mother and daughter down the street toward his old truck.

"This is it. She's old and rusty, but she runs like a champ. Heater works too." Luke motioned toward his 1989 Ford pickup, while directing his comments to Jen, hoping to engage her in conversation and give Sally some downtime, even if it was only a couple of minutes. "We'll find a warm, quiet place to get some rest. It'll be easier to figure out what comes next when we're not so tired. Sound good?"

Jen remained silent, and when Luke glanced her way, she was staring straight ahead, her eyes more closed than open. It was apparent she'd stayed on her feet as long as she could and was slowly shutting down. Luke pressed his palm to the small of Sally's back to move her toward the passenger side of his truck, tightening his grip around Jen's small hand at the same time.

Bristling with protectiveness, he kept a close eye on the people who stood on their lawns or in the street watching the firemen contain the blaze in Sally's house. Even more carefully, he perused the shadows and the windows of darkened houses along the street.

Someone had almost killed everyone in the house while they slept. Why would Sally have a target on her back? She couldn't possibly have any enemies…except maybe Emmett Purnell. Luke didn't like the guy, but Emmett simply didn't fit the profile of a killer. The sheriff would question him, but Luke already had a hunch they were on the wrong trail. One thing was for sure—whoever had set the charge would be extremely unhappy when he learned he'd failed.

He opened the passenger door and boosted an ominously quiet Jen onto the bench seat, then offered his hand to Sally to help her up. When she spun and strode toward the back of his truck, Luke turned again to the girl. "Hang tight, Jen. Okay? We'll just be a minute."

The keys still hung in the ignition—he'd forgotten everything when he'd seen Sally being knocked around by that sorry bastard. He stretched across the seat and Jen's lap to start the engine. "Give it a couple of minutes to warm up, then turn on the heater. This controls the fan and the temperature." Luke tapped the correct knob.

Jen gave him a ghost of her normal smile. His chest constricted with the need to replace at least some of what she'd lost tonight, starting with a safe place to lay her head. He patted her leg and closed the door.

Sally leaned against the box of the truck, her arms crossed and her gaze on the ground at her feet. Luke lined himself up next to her, shielding her from the cold breeze that evidently blew straight off the snowcapped mountains. She was practically irresistible with her slender legs bared below the blanket wrapped around her torso…and he'd better damn well forget that line of thought before he did or said something totally out of line.

Luke cleared his throat and met her gaze, heavy with defeat. "This sucks, Sally, and it won't all be smooth sailing from here, but we'll get through it."

"*We*?" Sally's warm exhale condensed into a visible mist between them. Her gaze jerked to his and, for a moment, she stared at him as though he'd sprouted horns and carried a pitchfork. "What does *that* mean exactly?" Her lips thinned and her baby blues held more than enough disdain to make it clear there was no *we* in her mind.

He stepped in front of her and placed his hands on her shoulders. "It means you, me and Jen. I know you can take care of yourself and don't need me, but you're not going to get rid of me until you land on your feet someplace where you feel safe." He wasn't about to leave her and Jen, especially after what he'd overheard her saying on the phone. He didn't understand what it all meant yet, but he'd get it out of her. He could be patient…and charming, if that was what it took.

Instead of jumping in the middle of his shit the way he expected, she rubbed her forehead as though trying to keep a headache at bay.

He dropped his hands and went back to leaning on the bed of the truck. "You can try to shut me out, but it won't work. Not now. So, you might as well decide you can trust me."

"I do," she said quietly.

"Yeah? Then when you're ready, maybe you'll tell me who you were talking with on the phone. What can't you do to Jen? It's obvious you're worried. Someone or something scared you, and I can't help if you don't fill me in." Luke shrugged. "I know—you think if you start to count on me, I might let you down again. Maybe I deserve that, but I'm going to prove you're wrong." He turned her chin with his thumb and forefinger so she'd look at him again. "Our best chance is to work together…but you have to make that decision."

Sally raked a hand across the top of her head, pulling her hair back from her face. "I know how much you care about Jen, and I've always appreciated that."

Finally. Some common ground. "Damn straight." Luke stopped short of adding how much he cared about her too. *Don't push her.* Personal feelings were on hold for now. He had a number of more pressing concerns. The first order of business was getting Sally and Jen off the street for the remainder of the night. Besides, Aunt Peg would have a thing or two to say if he didn't deliver them safely to the lodge after he'd called and told her to expect them.

"Let's just go with that for now. We both would do anything for Jen." He flashed a crooked grin. "We'll build on that foundation when it feels right. Okay?" He stepped aside and motioned for her to precede him to the passenger door. They'd have time to talk tomorrow, away from the smoke and rubble that had been her home. She'd had one hell of a night. Luke expected that she'd have more than a few issues to deal with in the days to come, several more critical than his sudden appearance in her life. Meanwhile, he intended to make sure no one else hurt them on his watch.

Sally hadn't moved, still studying his face. "There's something else I need to say. I haven't been fair to you. I should have accepted your apology earlier. I don't know why I didn't—stupid pride, I guess. I don't harbor any ill will toward you, and I want to thank you for your help tonight—for saving Jen and me. I won't ever be able to repay you for that." Her voice cracked.

Almost afraid to move and somehow shatter this fragile moment, Luke searched her face. Vulnerability mixed with her sweet, girl-next-door persona. Sally reached out hesitantly, and Luke craved her touch so much, he couldn't help leaning closer. He hadn't realized he'd actually been holding his breath, but when her hand brushed his arm and settled on his chest, he suddenly needed oxygen in the worst way. Her eyes were clear and bright for the first time since he'd disrupted her date.

His hand covered hers over his heart, a compromise to what he really wanted to do—draw her close and never let her go. Her emotions were all over the place. He could only guess at how that felt from the inside out, but he wasn't going to do anything that might push her away again.

"You don't owe me anything, Sally." Accepting his apology and extending the forgiveness he craved was payment enough. And yet he suddenly needed more. Her love. "I was such a fool. I'd like to think I could make it up to you someday. Obviously not today—we're a little busy. And probably not tomorrow. But maybe…next month sometime." He grinned at the slight twitch of her lips. "If you don't believe anything else…believe this—I'm here until you send me away. I'm not turning my back on you this time, and I'm going to try my best to make you forget I'm an idiot."

What sounded like a muffled laugh escaped her lips, and he struggled to suppress a chuckle.

She cocked her head slightly and her gaze swept his face. Whether she was looking for confirmation of his promise or simply checking to see what had changed between them, Sally studied him intently for several seconds. Just when he began to fear she would peel back too many layers and discover his remaining insecurities, a smile curved her lips, and her relief was evident.

The dull ache in his chest receded a little farther. It was a start. Threading his fingers with hers, Luke took a step back and nodded his head toward the cab of the pickup. "That little girl in there is practically sleepwalking. I called Aunt Peg and she's expecting us. She said you're welcome there for as long as it takes. Sorry I didn't ask you first, but I really think Cougar Ridge is our best bet...unless you've got a better idea."

A little over twenty miles away, the Cougar Ridge Hunting Lodge and Resort had been owned and operated by his mother and his Aunt Peg until his mother's death two years before. Luke and his brother had inherited their mother's share, and Garrett had lived nearby ever since. Although, if his brother was truthful, he stayed primarily because of Rachel, the sassy little redhead he'd met on his first visit and subsequently asked to marry him. The lodge was secluded and secure. Sally and Jen would be surrounded by people they both knew and trusted.

She looked away for a moment before she nodded. "It's nice of Peg to put us up. A day or two at the most. I'll have to make other arrangements for Jen. She can't miss too much school." She sighed. "It'll be good to see Rachel. It's been a while."

Luke stepped toward the passenger door and gripped the handle. "Is that my fault too?"

Sally shrugged. "I suppose so, if you want the truth. Our friendship was never the same after Bethesda."

Rachel and Sally had been best friends since Jen was born. Luke scowled, irritated all over again that his actions had driven a wedge between them. He opened her door and closed it carefully after she'd climbed into the cab. Then he circled the bed of the truck and clambered behind the wheel. Once they were in the clear, he'd see what he could do to repair the rift.

"Where are we going?" Jen sat straight in the middle of the bench seat, her face even paler in the moonlight that shone meagerly through the windshield. Though the interior of the cab was several degrees warmer than it had been, her lips still trembled as the words escaped. Immediately, Sally whisked the blanket from her own shoulders and wrapped it around Jen.

Unable to resist, Luke dragged his gaze from the creamy skin of Sally's bare thighs, all the way up to where the small patch of fabric covered her crotch. His arousal was instantaneous, rock hard and reaching the uncomfortable stage before he had the presence of mind to look away. He cranked the heater up a notch and reached into the backseat of the extended cab, grabbed his duffel and hauled it onto his lap. He chose one of his Navy T-shirts, wadded it up and tossed it over Jen's head to the sexy brunette, who blushed appealingly as she caught the garment with one hand.

An instant later, she yanked it over her head and squirmed in the seat until she'd pulled it down almost to her knees. Then she glanced at him with an is-that-better look, and Luke wanted to kick himself for being instrumental in covering any part of her beautiful body.

He smiled at Jen instead but suspected it looked more like a feral baring of teeth. "We were talking about going to Cougar Ridge. How do you feel about that?"

She considered his words solemnly for a moment, then nodded. "It feels safe there. I'd like to see Rachel."

Luke was concerned about the detached quality in her voice. His gaze flickered toward Sally and caught her chewing worriedly on her bottom lip. Even bruised, homeless and scared, her apprehension centered on her daughter's state of mind. The phone call he'd overheard earlier had made it clear someone wanted to take Jen away from Huntington, and Sally apparently hadn't been in full agreement. No way in hell anyone was taking a nine-year-old girl away from her mother. All Luke had to do to stop it was find out who, when and why. *Shouldn't be that hard.*

He patted Jen's knee. "We'll be there before you know it. Why don't you stretch out between your mom and me and catch a few z's?"

At once, Jen moved to do as he suggested, laying her head in her mother's lap and curling her legs so her bare feet were braced against his outer thigh. With one final look at the smoldering glow and the firefighters still bunched around the ruins of Sally's home, Luke pulled away from the curb.

Before they'd even left the lights of Huntington behind them, Jen's soft breathing made it clear she was sleeping. From the corner of his eye, Luke watched Sally rub Jen's back and shoulders gently through the blanket. "She'll be fine, you know. I've heard kids are amazingly resilient creatures."

Sally met his gaze and nodded. "I know." Her voice caught, and she cleared her throat. "I can't even speculate on what would have happened if you hadn't been there tonight."

"I'm glad I could help. I mean—I'm not really a big believer in fate, but sometimes things happen for a reason. Maybe your boss decided to use you as a punching bag so I wouldn't be able to put off facing you any longer and you'd have a light sleeper in the house tonight. And maybe, because we're working hand in hand with fate, you won't hold it against me for dropping by without calling first." He offered what he hoped was his most charming grin. "It's really a minor offense among my other screwups."

She ducked her head, but he saw the beginnings of a smile, and when she glanced his way again, her eyes held amusement. "I didn't think you'd be able to do that."

He turned his gaze to the rearview mirror. "Do what?"

"Make me forget long enough to find something funny in anything tonight—but then, you always could make me laugh."

"Well, that's because I was a clown in my previous life." He cocked his head as he hummed a few notes of a circus tune that popped into his mind.

Sally smiled and seemed to relax. "Are you sure it's okay—just showing up at the lodge?"

"Are you kidding? I get the feeling Aunt Peg will hunt me down and have me drawn and quartered if you and Jen don't show up there soon. She always did like you best."

Sally went still, and when he glanced over, she was stroking Jen's hair with such tenderness he wished, for just a heartbeat, he could be the recipient of her attention.

The dark outline of a bruise on her jaw caught his eye, and he reached out to stroke her cheek. "Your friend Emmett packs quite a punch when it comes to beating up women."

She toyed with a lock of her hair. "Emmett wasn't half as mad tonight as he'll be when the sheriff comes calling to ask if he had anything to do with destroying my home—especially when Ben tells him it was my suggestion."

"Technically, it was mine. You let me handle him from now on. He won't hurt you again. That's a promise." Luke dragged his hand across her shoulder and down her arm, until he folded her small hand in his where it rested on Jen's back. The fingers of Sally's other hand combed through Jen's curly hair while she stared at the darkness beyond the side window.

Luke squeezed her hand until she turned. "Want to talk about it? I'm a good listener." He smiled, hoping to coax a reciprocating grin from her. What he got was more of a grimace.

"It's all so overwhelming…I don't know where to start. Finding a place to live…and a new job. Who's going to rent to me if I don't have a job? Jen and I don't even have a change of clothes…or a car. The Explorer was in the garage. I just got it out of the shop." Sally pulled her hand from his and combed both of hers through her hair, her frustration clear in the clenching of her jaw.

"Take it easy. All that stuff can be replaced, Sally. Do you have insurance?"

She moaned and covered her face. "Renter's insurance is a luxury I can't afford. If I could have hung on to my job for a couple of months, I might have gotten caught up. Maybe then—"

"Okay, we'll worry about the money later. You and Jen weren't injured and you're together. That's the important thing. I'm not saying it's going to be simple, but you're not alone. My family already considers you one of the clan. You don't have to do this by yourself."

She dropped her head into her hands and her muffled words were barely audible. "You don't understand." Those three words were laced with resignation, sadness and a bone-deep weariness.

What the hell was she not telling him? Luke let the silence stretch for a few seconds while dread formed a black hole in his gut. "I'd like to." He tried to keep his sudden suspicions from influencing his voice.

She jerked her head up and, for a moment, it appeared she might confide in him. Then she shook her head and turned her face away, resuming her perusal of the darkness beyond the glass.

Luke allowed a few minutes to pass before he couldn't stand it any longer. "Something's bothering you that goes much deeper than your house burning down. I didn't mean to eavesdrop on your phone conversation earlier, but I know there's more you're not telling me. I want to help you, Sally, but, if you don't level with me, you're tying my hands. What are you afraid of? Let me in, sunshine."

Her hands stilled in Jen's hair while she regarded him for several seconds, but she turned back to the side window without a word. For a long time, she remained quiet while they sped along the deserted country road. When she finally looked over her shoulder at him, it was with a forced smile before her gaze darted quickly away. "You're wrong. There's nothing bothering me but the fire, and the explosion and almost dying tonight. I think that's enough. Don't you?"

Luke recognized her question as the distraction she no doubt intended it to be. She wasn't ready to confide in him yet. Every sense he possessed told him whatever she was withholding from him was of paramount importance. Her behavior was uncharacteristically veiled, and she was a lousy liar. He'd drop the subject for now, but he wasn't going to engage in the argument she obviously wanted. Sighing, he raised his eyes to the rearview mirror just as dual sets of headlights came into view.

The two vehicles appeared to gain on his truck in the time it took Luke to check the road in front and glance in the mirror again. It was nearly three in the morning. To encounter one vehicle on this deserted stretch of road would be unusual. Two was clearly improbable. Especially when they were hauling ass up behind them.

Chapter Five

Damn it! Why had she called Marshal Lambert? Sally's skin prickled with a case of nerves, making it nearly impossible to sit still. She was scared and confused…and irritated with herself for being that way. Luke knew she was lying. What must he think? Lying was so unlike her, and she hated the person she'd become to protect herself and Jen. Luke was trying to help. What if he decided to dump her at the lodge and get as far away as he could? She wouldn't blame him. Sally caught herself biting on one of her fingernails and quickly brought her hand down, slipping it beneath her leg. She had to get a grip. Anxiety had made a mess of her calm-cool-collected veneer…and that only made her angrier.

Hell, she deserved to be angry. Her house and everything she'd owned was gone. Her security was shattered, and if Marshal Greg Lambert had anything to say about it, what was left of Jen's peaceful existence would soon be a thing of the past as well. Even thinking about what that would do to her baby sent shards of pain through her chest. But she couldn't lose it now. She had to hold it together for Jen. Drawing on the inner strength she'd developed out of necessity over the past ten years, Sally went back to chewing her fingernail and forced her thoughts elsewhere.

Luke. That subject was no better. Why had he picked now to reappear? Was it too much of a coincidence that he'd walked back into her life and saved her twice in one night? She glanced from beneath lowered lashes at the daunting figure behind the steering wheel. He'd cooled his questions—the ones she couldn't answer—and wasn't paying any attention to her, so she took the opportunity to study his profile.

He was a couple of inches taller than his brother, which made him somewhere around six foot three. Still a strong man, despite his months of captivity, his chest was broad and muscular, his arms and thighs thick and powerful. His size dwarfed her decidedly *un*muscular five-foot-four-inch frame. Light brown hair, considerably longer than it had been a year ago, scraped his collar. His square jaw gave him the appearance of stubbornness, but if Sally were able to see his face, she had no doubt there'd be kindness in his rich brown eyes…and mischief. He'd always been smiling or laughing, saying something silly to get her to laugh too. Apparently, his sense of humor had failed him this time.

As Sally watched, Luke reached to adjust the rearview mirror, then glanced toward her side of the truck. Her eyes flew wide as she took in the rock-hard line of his jaw, his furrowed brow and the intensity in his gaze that clearly said he wasn't happy about something.

She tensed, instantly on guard. Twisting around as far as she could without disturbing Jen, she barely caught the lights of a vehicle behind them. "What is it? Who is that?"

Luke gazed at her expectantly. "There are two of them. I was hoping you'd tell me who they were. In fact, now would be an excellent time."

Jen stirred and tried to sit up, but Luke pressed her down gently. They turned a corner and the road straightened in front of them.

He stepped on the gas, and the pickup accelerated smoothly. "Hold on." Luke placed one hand on Jen, and Sally wrapped her arms around her tightly—just in time.

She heard the roar of a vehicle behind and to the left of them a heartbeat before something slammed into the side panel of Luke's truck bed. Jen whimpered as the pickup swerved one way and then the other, and they were tossed side-to-side in the cab. Regaining control, he floored the gas pedal, and the vehicle on their tail hit them again.

Luke must have been ready for it this time and brought the pickup out of its swerve effortlessly, accelerated and momentarily left the pursuing vehicles behind. His familiarity with this stretch of road, a result of the many trips he'd made from his family's lodge to see her, no doubt gave him the edge. In her side mirror, Sally could now see the two sets of headlights, and it was apparent, whoever the drivers were, they weren't giving up.

Was it Clive? Who else *could* it be? She turned toward Luke, ready to tell him her sordid life's story if it would save Jen's life, but the regret in his eyes as he met her gaze stopped her cold.

"We can't outrun them. This old truck wasn't built for mountain races." His eyes darted to the mirror.

Reeling from his words and what they meant, Sally pushed her daughter toward Luke. "This is my fault. Stop the truck—let me out." *Luke will keep*

Jen safe. She reached for the door handle as Luke maneuvered through the next set of turns. Her whole body shook with the adrenaline that pumped through her veins.

Luke grabbed her arm. "No one's getting out yet. I'm not giving up either one of you. Just tell me one thing: Are these the scumbags that blew up your house?"

Sally nodded unevenly. "I…I think so."

Jen threw her arms around Sally's neck, and the girl's heart drummed against her. "It's okay, sweetheart," Sally whispered in her ear, knowing it wasn't.

"Okay. You can tell me the rest later. Right now, we'll assume they're probably not in a negotiating mood. We already know we can't outrun them, so our only option is to hide until they give up." Luke accelerated again on a straight stretch, and the lights of the other vehicles dropped back as the drivers slowed in the treacherous curves.

That didn't leave them any options. "If we can't outrun them, how are we going to hide?" Sally's breath was coming too fast, and her fear was threatening to swamp her.

Jen squirmed into a sitting position between them, and Sally quickly buckled her in the seat belt. "Like they did in that movie, *Run for the Border.*" Jen's small voice garnered their attention. She looked excitedly between Luke and her mother, then rolled her eyes, apparently disgusted by the blank stares she received. "On the way to the lodge, there's a big drop-off. Remember, Luke? You have to be real careful because the road's so narrow."

"I remember. It's a dangerous spot." Luke gave Jen a curious glance, and his gaze swept over her head to meet Sally's.

"In the movie, some men were being chased. They got far enough ahead that the bad guys didn't see them jump out of their car, and then they let it go over the edge. The bad men shot at the wrecked car until it exploded. It was okay, though, because the good guys were hiding in the trees." Jen's words tumbled out in a rush and she threw her hands in the air at the climax of her story.

Sally would have chuckled if their situation hadn't been so dire. "Honey, we can't expect Luke to run his pickup over a cliff."

"Wait a minute. She might have something. We're not far from the spot she's talking about. If we can get ahead of these characters before we get there, I could let you two out, head for the cliff and jump out at the last minute. We could meet on Elk Mountain. They'd never find us up there." Luke actually sounded as though the plan he and Jen presented was a viable solution.

Has the world gone mad? Sally forced her mouth closed rather than say something that might hurt her daughter's feelings. *But holy hell...* "Luke, there has to be another way."

He eyed her over her daughter's head. "I wish we didn't have to do this in front of Jen, but we don't have a choice. If these are the same people who planted a bomb in your house, can we assume they're following us now to finish the job?"

Jen squeezed Sally's fingers in a gentle grip, and Sally was blown away by the fact that her nine-year-old daughter seemed to be dealing with all this better than she was. "Yes." Her voice was just above a whisper.

"They're not going to leave any witnesses, Sally."

A cold chill wound around her heart as she jerked her gaze to meet Luke's. *He means Jen! Her baby would die too. Oh my God!*

"Do you have a better idea?" His question was softly spoken and filled with understanding.

The seriousness of their position stole her voice momentarily. *Her position...yet* Luke and Jen would suffer equally in her fate if Clive's men managed to run them off the road. She grimaced and shook her head. "No, I don't. I guess I'd better get behind Jen's idea." She forced a lightness into her voice she didn't feel for her daughter's benefit.

"It'll work, Mom. Right, Luke?"

Sally met Luke's eyes again and read the deep regret in his piercing gaze. And she knew—Jen's plan was all they had. Luke wouldn't say the words so Jen wouldn't lose hope, but Sally saw it there in his bleak expression. If the vehicles got close enough to ram them again, now that the drivers knew what to expect from the curvy mountain road, Luke, Jen and she would be toast.

"We're going to give it the old college try." He glanced in the mirror. "That last hairpin turn must have gotten their attention. They slowed a bit. We've got some distance on them." Luke ruffled Jen's hair. "You ready?"

She nodded, and the force of Luke's gaze drilled into Sally. "When we get through the next set of curves, if we're in the clear, I'll stop. Everything depends on you getting out as fast as possible and finding a place to hide before they come around the corner." He glanced back to the road, stepping on the gas until the pickup surged forward. "After their vehicles go by and disappear, you and Jen cross the road. Head uphill toward the lodge. Ready?"

Sally felt his gaze on her again as the headlights revealed the curves ahead. For a moment, she thought she would choke on the fear in her throat. *No, I'm not ready! I'll never be ready.* Mechanically, she released Jen's seat belt. "What about you?"

He had the nerve to laugh. "Don't worry about me. I've got the easy part." He nodded toward the front, the tension in his voice belying his humor. "Almost there." He focused on the mirror as they entered the tight curves. A few seconds later, they caught a straight stretch again. "Let's do it."

The trees created a curtain, shielding them from the lights behind. Sally threw open the door as Luke slid to a stop. She practically fell onto the shoulder of the road, regaining her balance just in time to steady Jen as she leaped from the seat.

Luke leaned over and caught the door, ready to swing it shut behind them. "Get going. Remember, head uphill. I'll find you." His voice wasn't nearly as confident as it had been a moment ago.

Jen tugged at her hand, and Sally tore her gaze from Luke's. Without looking back, they sprinted for the tree line. She heard the pickup's door close and the truck's engine revved. Tires spun. Then he was racing away in one direction and she and Jen in another. The trees reared up in front of them, looking like skinny, twisted giants in the moonlight. Sally spotted a downed log and pulled Jen toward it, dropping down on the other side just as the first vehicle's lights rounded the corner.

Sally hugged her daughter's small body close, holding her breath as the two cars sped after Luke's pickup. She waited a minute, and then another, before she peeked over the log. The road was empty and dark as far as she could see. Even the sound of Luke's loud mufflers had been drowned out by the quiet of the forest.

"They're gone. Luke said to cross the road. Ready, sweetie?" Sally brushed the hair from Jen's face, spreading some moisture in the process. Tears. Her baby must be so scared and confused. Sally's heart ached for her.

"Mom, who were those people? Why are they trying to hurt us?" Jen's expression was sadder than Sally had ever seen.

"It's a long story, honey. It started way before you were born. It's time I told you, but not now. We have to do what Luke said and get someplace safe. Let's go."

"Okay." She got to her feet. "Luke will be all right, you know."

Sally smiled. She didn't want to admit, even to herself, how concerned she was about Luke.

She held Jen's hand as they stepped over the log and approached the roadway. After listening for a moment for any indication the vehicles might be returning, they jogged across the pavement, up the bank and into the cover of the trees.

After they'd walked uphill silently for a few minutes, Jen suddenly stopped. "Mom, there's a GPS in your phone. We can find the lodge easy with that."

Sally pressed a hand to her throat, experiencing a moment of panic when she remembered where her phone was. "I left it in my purse...in the pickup." Damn it! What a monumentally dumb move. Her phone, her money, her driver's license—everything was in that purse, which was probably at the bottom of a canyon if things went as Luke had planned. *God, please let Luke be all right.*

Her emotions barely in check, Sally kept placing one foot in front of the other as they forged uphill. She grasped Jen's hand close to her side, even though it made walking cumbersome, unwilling to take the chance of being separated from her daughter too.

A few more minutes of walking and she pulled herself up short. They'd traveled a zigzag course up the north side of Elk Mountain for at least thirty minutes. She'd go right by the lodge if they stayed on that course. Time to level off and head northeast. She might not have a GPS, but she could see the moon. Rachel's friend, Jonathan, had taught both of them the basics of finding their way by the moon's position.

Suddenly, the thud of muffled gunfire jerked her attention to the east, as though she'd be able to see the ribbon of asphalt Luke had followed. Jen wrapped her arms around Sally's waist and buried her head in Luke's overlarge T-shirt.

Sally backed into a small thicket of young pine trees and lowered herself carefully to the ground along with her precious cargo. "Luke's going to be okay, remember?"

Her daughter cried softly.

"You'll see, sweetheart. He'll catch up to us any minute and he'll be like 'what took you so long.'" Sally mimicked Luke's teasing banter.

Jen giggled reluctantly, followed by a sniffle. "I'm really glad he's here, Mom. Aren't you?"

The question she'd dreaded...and Sally still didn't know how to answer. One thing was for sure: After tonight, her daughter had proven that she could handle the truth, so the truth was what she would get.

"I am," Sally said, not really surprised by how easy the admission came. "But I don't think he'll be staying, honey. I know you like him a lot and I hope you won't be too disappointed when he leaves."

"Why, Mom? I thought he liked us." Tears glowed in Jen's eyes again. "Is it because of me?"

"Of course it's not, baby. Don't ever think that. It's just that Luke is from California. That's where he lives—where his friends are. He comes here once in a while to visit his Aunt Peg and his brother, Garrett…and to see you. It's just like when we went to the Grand Canyon last year. We met some people there, but our lives were back here in Idaho. So, when our vacation was over, we went home…and so will Luke. But I bet he'd let you e-mail him if you asked. Then you could keep in touch all the time." Sally was grasping for a positive way to spin the ultimate good-bye, but it was hard to be upbeat for Jen when Sally couldn't get a grasp on her own feelings.

Jen sat up straight and wiped her eyes. "Maybe that would be all right… but it won't keep you from missing him."

Sally pushed Jen's curly locks behind her ears, then pulled her closer for a kiss on the head. "When did you get so grown up anyway, Ms. Duncan? Don't you know that you're all I need?"

Jen rolled her eyes in the typical preteen answer to everything and pushed to her feet. "Whatever."

Sally snorted and Jen snickered, and immediately the tears and gunshots were pushed to the back of their minds. This time Jen fell in behind her as Sally set a quick pace—as quick as they could manage across the rough terrain of Elk Mountain.

Twenty minutes later, they stumbled onto a little-used forest service road. It wasn't much, but enough that Sally wanted to sing a couple of choruses of "Hallelujah." One look at Jen changed her mind. "Let's rest for a bit, honey." Sally sat against a tree trunk and patted her lap.

Jen didn't waste any time snuggling against her, trembling from the chill night air and her exertion.

Sally brushed Jen's hair as she spoke soothingly. "We're almost there. I remember this road from hiking with Rachel. It meets the lodge road not too far from here and then it's just a short walk."

"What about Luke?" Jen's face was pale and etched with fatigue.

"He'll be okay, honey. He'll find us. Or maybe he's waiting at the lodge." Luke had to be all right. Sally couldn't give any thought to anything else— not after everything he'd done for them tonight.

Suddenly, Jen sat up straight. "Mom, I saw a light through the trees… there." She raised her arm and pointed across the overgrown road, her voice low and urgent.

Sally's heart hammered erratically as she searched the area Jen had indicated. After a few seconds, the flickering light appeared, bouncing up and down as though someone carried it and then disappeared again.

"Quick. Follow me." Sally pushed Jen to her feet and clutched her hand as they moved off the open roadway into the shadow of the trees.

"What if it's Luke?" Jen whispered.

"Even if it's Luke, we need to stay out of sight until we know for sure." As soon as they were within cover of the trees, Sally kept Jen moving, stopping only when she found a close grouping of young pines with needles scraping the ground. She pushed her way through the supple fronds and dropped to her knees, pulling her daughter down beside her. Silently, she placed one finger in front of Jen's lips, then positioned herself so she had a view of the road. It was so dark within the forest, the only way she'd see anything was if it moved or carried a flashlight, but she settled down to wait. The only sound in their enclosure was the wind rustling the pine needles and Jen's soft breaths, both of which calmed her frazzled nerves.

Several minutes passed before the bobbing light came into her line of sight. Sally studied the figure who held it. Hope plummeted at first glance. It wasn't Luke. This man was taller and broader across the chest and shoulders. Was it one of Clive's men? How had they found her? The federal witness protection program was supposed to be secure, if nothing else. Marshal Lambert would have to explain this before she'd agree to anything more… providing she survived the night.

The big man stopped when he reached the spot in the road where Sally and Jen had rested. Slowly, he turned in a circle until he faced back the way he'd come. "Do you smell that?"

Startled, Sally realized he was talking to someone who was following—someone she couldn't see. Her gaze darted back to the man with the flashlight. Something about his voice…or was it just wishful thinking?

"I don't smell anything. What is it?" The breeze carried the second man's words to her, distorted by the sudden stomping sounds of deer or some other four-legged creatures obviously made unhappy by the proximity of humans in their territory.

The first man turned slowly again, stopping when he faced directly toward her. Sally ducked down as though it might be possible for him to see them through the thin moonlight and the tree branches.

The man looked back toward his companion. "Perfume. I smell perfume. I think we're close." The echo hadn't died from his last words when frenzied barking broke out. "See. Cowboy smells it too." He turned back and cupped hands around his mouth. "Sally! Jen!"

"It's Jonathan and Cowboy!"

Sally still whispered, despite her relief, and hot tears welled in her eyes. Determined not to let them fall, she pushed Jen through the pine boughs, then took a moment to compose herself. Jonathan worked for Luke's Aunt Peg at the lodge. Besides Rachel, he was Sally's only close friend. What was he doing out here looking for them? Was he with Luke? Eager to know Luke was all right, Sally stepped out of the trees just as Cowboy, the former military K-9 Luke's brother had brought back from Afghanistan after they both were wounded, bounded to Jen and danced around her excitedly. Jonathan laughed warmly as he scooped her daughter into a bear hug.

He stopped when he saw her just standing there. "Sally? Are you okay?"

"Almost." She strode toward him, suddenly self-conscious of Luke's T-shirt and her disheveled hair. "I didn't expect to see *you* out here."

Jonathan grinned. "Well, I didn't really expect to be out here looking for *you* either."

"Is Luke with you?" From the corner of her eye, she caught a movement and turned, expecting to see him smiling at her. The smile was familiar, but it was worn by Luke's brother, Garrett, as he covered the last few feet to join them.

He placed his cell phone to his ear. "We got 'em...yeah...see you in a few...yep, here she is." Garrett extended the phone to Sally, and he didn't have to tell her who it was.

Knowing Luke was alive turned her knees to rubber, and it was all she could do to force herself to take the phone. Somehow, she rasped out Luke's name.

"Are you and Jen all right?" He sounded exhilarated and relieved at the same time.

"We're fine, Luke. Are you okay? Where are you? What happened? We heard gunshots."

"Slow down. We'll catch up later. I'm not far from you. I called Garrett as soon as I crashed my ride. He and Jonathan came to help me find you." He paused, and Sally got the feeling he was listening to her erratic breathing. When he spoke, he was dead serious. "I told you I'd find you, babe."

Sally nodded but didn't know what to say to that. "Is your truck history?"

Luke snorted. "That gutless piece of shit? It's time I bought a new one anyway."

They laughed together and, for the first moment in a very long time, Sally felt whole. Was it possible to go back? Recapture something that had died such a resounding death? Sally shook her head and squeezed her eyes closed. She'd never know unless she opened herself up to the possibility, but the thought of trying and failing again scared her to death.

Chapter Six

Luke reached the abandoned logging road, where Garrett had told him the vehicles would be parked, before anyone else arrived. His brother's Jeep and the lodge's old beater pickup that Jonathan drove glimmered in the starlight ahead. Approaching cautiously, Luke focused all his senses to discern whether any unwelcome visitors waited there. Satisfied the area was deserted, he dropped his duffel—saved from the doomed pickup at the last moment—and knelt in the shadows by one of the Jeep's wheels. Still on high alert, he was anxious to see with his own eyes that Sally and Jen were unharmed.

He didn't have long to wait. Quiet voices drifted to him, and he studied the darkness until he caught sight of the beam from the flashlight moving through the trees. Cowboy loped into the clearing first, followed by Jonathan, carrying Jen. Luke rose silently and moved a step away from the Jeep. Jonathan evidently spotted him, bent at the waist and set Jen on her feet.

The little girl jogged toward him. At the last second, Luke dropped to his knees and caught her in a hug.

"Luke!" Her voice was low, yet filled with excitement and joy.

He held her tightly, picking her up as he got to his feet, her heart beating rapidly against him. She wound her arms around his neck and her quiet sniffling gave away her tears. Strong emotions formed a lump in his throat.

Damn. He loved this little girl and he wouldn't handle it well if anything happened to her. "It's all right, Jen. You're safe."

Luke couldn't read Sally's expression when she finally stepped into the feeble light cast by the moon. Worry was obvious and understandable. The axis of her world had just tilted several degrees. He'd fix it if he could, but it wasn't within his power. All he could do was give his life if that was what it took to keep them both safe.

He settled Jen on one arm and held his other out to Sally. She hesitated a moment, searching his eyes, then shuffled toward him. Luke reached for her when she paused and pulled her in for a three-way hug. Once she was beside Jen, Sally relaxed against him and her stuttering sigh yanked at his heartstrings even as her warmth reminded him of comforts he'd not thought of for a long while.

Jonathan strode toward his pickup, and Garrett was futilely trying to control a pleased grin when Luke frowned at him over Sally's head.

Garrett cleared his throat, propped his hands on his hips and became the serious big brother. "Mission accomplished. Now let's get you back to the lodge. These two young ladies are asleep on their feet." He walked to the Jeep and opened the driver's door.

Luke released Sally, then set Jen on her feet next to her mother. "We won't be going to the lodge."

Sally's surprised gaze darted toward him.

Garrett's raised eyebrows clearly said he thought Luke had lost his mind. "What? It's the safest place. Where else would you go?"

"Those jerks trying to run us off the road changed everything. I don't know the whole story…yet." He met Sally's gaze before turning back to his brother. "What I know is if they find out Sally didn't die in the crash, you can bet they won't give up. If we go to the lodge, they'll come after us. Think of Aunt Peg and Rachel."

The muscle flexing in Garrett's jaw told Luke he'd made his point.

"What makes you think they won't come anyway?" Jonathan stood at the rear of his pickup, concern evident in his stance.

"They might, but you'll be ready for them, and when they don't find any sign of us, they won't have any reason to stick around." Luke glanced between Garrett and Jonathan, their silence signifying they didn't like his idea one bit, but they apparently agreed with his reasoning.

Sally turned, her hand on Jen's shoulder. "I can't ask you to do this, Luke. You've done enough. You should stay here with your family."

Luke tousled Jen's hair and weighed his words carefully. "I'm aware you haven't asked me to go any farther with you, but like it or not, I'm not letting you go by yourself."

Sally shook her head sadly. "You don't know everything."

"Then fill me in." Luke leaned back against the Jeep and crossed his ankles as though he had all the time in the world.

Sally's eyes took on that deer-in-the-headlights look, darting around the small clearing, finally landing on her daughter.

Jen smiled with maturity beyond her years. "It's okay, Mom. We'll keep your secret."

Sally allowed one sob to escape as she hugged the girl, and it was a moment before she found her voice. "I'm in the witness protection program. I have to assume whoever blew up my home and tried to run us off the road was sent by the man I testified against eleven years ago. The marshal in charge of my case is on his way to pick us up and find us a new place to live…and new identities."

Luke did the math in his head. They'd celebrated Sally's twenty-eighth birthday before his deployment. That made her twenty-nine now. She'd been only eighteen when she testified and gave up everything she knew to go into hiding. No wonder her scumball boss hadn't been able to dig up anything on her.

Her story also made those thugs who evidently wanted her dead a whole lot more serious than they'd been a few minutes ago. International espionage or organized crime could be behind the attempt—something he hadn't considered until now.

Sally's guarded expression made it clear she expected him to change his mind. No chance of that happening. "All the more reason we shouldn't hang around in familiar territory. We need to disappear tonight, before they regroup and come back to check their handiwork."

She started to interrupt, and Luke held his hand up to stop her. "Your problem became my business when my truck went over the cliff. Those men were trying to kill all three of us…not just you." He glanced toward Garrett. "Can I borrow your Jeep?"

The keys were already in Garrett's hand and he tossed them through the air. "Where will you go?"

Luke caught the keys easily. "A place the people looking for Sally won't know anything about. It's better if you don't know either."

Garrett's lips settled into a firm line. He obviously wasn't happy with that answer, but he knew it was the right move. "Check in when you get where you're going." It wasn't a request.

Cowboy whined, his tail moving slowly from side to side, clearly reacting to Garrett's change of mood.

"We will." Luke studied his brother's concerned expression for a silent moment before his gaze swept to Sally, trying to gauge how much argument was left there. He was pleasantly surprised when she slid an arm around Jen's shoulders, stepped away from him and guided her daughter to the Jeep.

His brother stepped toward him, and Luke shook his hand with a firm grasp meant to convey he had this under control, knowing full well his big brother would worry about him anyway. When they turned away from each other, Luke shook hands with Jonathan before tossing his duffel in the backseat and climbing behind the wheel.

"One more thing, Bro. If you could call a tow truck and get what's left of my ride out of the canyon before those creeps climb down there and find out there aren't any bodies or footprints, we might stop them right here."

Jonathan, returning from his truck, shoved a blanket through the window into Luke's hands. "Jen might need something comfortable to lay on." The big guy had such a soft spot where the girl was concerned. Luke could identify.

"Thanks, man." He accepted the offering and placed it between the seats, then started the Jeep and listened to its quiet purr as the two men stepped away from the side. With one last wave, he shifted into reverse, backed a tight horseshoe and crept slowly down the mountain. After turning right on the county road, where he'd ditched his truck, he drove without benefit of lights, watching the mirrors carefully for another mile or so before he flipped on the headlamps.

An audible sigh of relief came from Sally as the lights lit up the area in front of the vehicle. It was the first sound she'd made since she buckled her seat belt. Jen, bless her heart, knelt between the bucket seats with a hand on each of their shoulders. She should have been in her seat belt too, especially on this damn road, but Jen apparently needed their contact as much as Luke needed hers. *In a minute, I'll ask her to sit down and buckle up.* For right now...he reached around her head to pull her close for a kiss on the cheek.

She grinned in delight. "Did it work just like in the movie?"

A tiny sound that might have been a laugh came from Sally's half of the cab. Luke glanced her way, but she was still concentrating on the view out in front of them.

He swept his attention back to Jen. "Not quite. I revved the truck up and headed for the edge of the canyon." He made the sound effects and waved his arms in the air, letting loose the steering wheel for a second, chuckling as Jen got into the story. "Then I remembered my duffel... containing the only clean clothes we'd have until we could get to a store. I grabbed it, along with a couple other things I thought we might need, and jumped out at the last minute, like we planned. The duffel broke my fall, which was good, but the bad guys were too close. I didn't have time to cross the road and get into the trees."

Sally swung around to stare at him. "What did you do?"

"Well, there I was, hanging over that cliff, with that heavy canvas bag in one hand, while my truck ground and scraped all the way to the bottom and then started on fire. Those clowns—there were four of them—got out of their vehicles and looked over the edge as though they were afraid of heights or something. I could tell they weren't about to climb down and make sure we were all dead. But I didn't know how long I could hold on either." He paused for dramatic effect and smiled at Jen's impatient sigh.

Sally was halfway grinning now, and damned if it didn't seem like all the ugly stuff that had gone between his leaving her and his coming home no longer existed. Interesting that he thought of this place as home.

"A couple of them began shooting down in the canyon. I guess they thought they might get lucky and hit something. Then one of them started talking. It wasn't English, but I couldn't hear well enough to recognize the language. And, thankfully, they didn't stick around much longer."

Jen giggled, jumping up and down on the floorboards in her excitement, and Luke laughed...until the stricken expression on Sally's face pulled him up short. His first instinct was to comfort her, but when he touched her shoulder, she tensed.

"Where are we going?" Jen yawned through the question.

"To stay with a friend of mine for a few days, until the heat is off here. Then we'll get busy finding you and your mom a new place to live." Luke wrapped his arm around her slender shoulders. "How's that sound?" Providing the heat *did* die down in Huntington. There was a good possibility it would never be safe enough for Sally and Jen to return and resume their lives, but he'd break the bad news to Jen when it became necessary.

"Good." She leaned close enough to whisper in his ear. "Mom needs a job too."

Luke nodded his head. "Right. A job." Hopefully, one where she wouldn't be persuaded to date the boss. He now understood her reticence to have the sheriff question Emmett Purnell, because it was highly unlikely he was involved in the destruction of her house. If Luke had known her history, he'd have been okay skipping that step. It stood to reason Purnell wouldn't take his implication in the crime lightly.

Jen clutched her blanket, pushed herself onto the backseat and wiggled until she apparently found a comfortable position. The seat-belt buckle clicked into place, making Luke smile. She unfolded the blanket and draped it over her body. When Luke glanced in the rearview mirror next, all movement had stopped. Soon her breathing slowed and deepened into a peaceful sleep. Luke lit up the face of his watch. Zero five hundred hours. *Hell, it's morning.*

His gaze swept to Sally. Her long brunette hair hid most of her face, but he could tell by her crossed arms and stiff spine she wasn't asleep. Not even close. "We need to talk, Sally."

She straightened even more, then slowly turned her head to look at him. Her eyes were wide with dark circles beneath them. Worry drew her brows together, but the rest of her expression was flat, as though she'd turned off her reaction to everything.

Sally squared her shoulders. "Yes, we do. I'm so sorry, Luke. Sorry you got involved in this. Sorry about your truck. Why are you so calm? You should be mad as hell."

Luke chuckled. "If you knew how many anger management classes I've attended since I got back, you'd have a whole different opinion of me. Why would I be angry with you? None of this is your fault."

"You don't know that," she said.

"Yeah...I do." He reached for her hand and wrapped it in his larger one. "Are you ready to tell me everything yet?"

"There's not much to tell. I witnessed a murder, and when I went to the police, they arranged for a US Marshal to pick me up. I eventually learned I'd be placed in the witness protection program in exchange for my testimony. When it was all over, they found me a place to live in Huntington."

Luke squeezed her hand. "Who was it? Who did you testify against?"

Her reluctance was noticeable. "His name is Clive Brennan. A natural-born US citizen, but it turned out his allegiance was with Russia. It was probably a Russian dialect you heard while you were hanging off the cliff. My testimony put him away for fifteen to twenty years, a travesty in itself. Mississippi has a ten-year minimum, so, with time off for good behavior, he was released three months ago."

Luke frowned. "Why is he after you now? You can't hurt him after he's served his time."

"I don't know." Sally's gaze danced away from his for only a second, but it was enough to make him wonder why she was withholding information.

He wouldn't push her now. Her emotions were too raw. His presence too new and unexpected. "What about this marshal that's supposed to show up?"

"Marshal Greg Lambert. He's been my contact for nine years. I've spoken to him a few times on the phone, but I've never met him before. Now he's on his way to pick Jen and me up to hide us away again." Sally scooped her hair back from her forehead angrily.

"You're not in favor of that?"

"I wouldn't care if it was just me, but Jen doesn't deserve that. She won't understand. All she'll know is I'm tearing her away from her friends and the only life she…" Sally's voice broke on the last word and she quickly glanced away. "She hasn't done anything to deserve this."

Sally hadn't done anything to deserve it either. Luke felt a jagged hole open in his chest at the thought of never seeing her and Jen again. Was a new identity really the best thing for them? The only way to keep them safe? Was he being totally self-serving to want to find another way—to believe he could protect her as well as the feds? She at least deserved another option. "If you decide that's not what you want, you can count on me. I'll stay with you all the way, sunshine."

Sally smiled for the first time since she'd walked out of the forest, and Luke's heart melted. She squeezed his fingers. "Are you sure, Luke? I mean, I haven't exactly greeted you with open arms. In my own defense, showing up the way you did brought up all the bad memories. Do you have any idea how much I worried about you…all those months?"

"In *my* defense, I was half loco when they rescued me." He focused his attention toward the front, emotions swamping him.

"You really hurt us, Luke. You hurt Jen." Her voice cracked, but she pushed through. "Don't hurt her again."

Luke turned toward her, and the plea in her glossy eyes broke him into little pieces. No anger or bitterness lingered in her expression—only a fierce love for the daughter she'd brought into the world. That was one of the things he loved about her. Still, Luke had no trouble believing he'd kiss his chances with her good-bye if he crossed that line again.

He could live with that, because he would no more hurt Jen than willingly return to Afghanistan.

"You have my word. Hurting you or Jen in any way was the last thing I wanted to do. The two of you are important to me. If you don't believe anything else, please believe that. If there was a way to get back the time we've lost, I'd do it in a heartbeat. In fact, there's *nothing* I wouldn't do for you and that little girl right there." He looked in to her eyes for a second, warmed by the acceptance he found there, as though he'd finally said something right. Perhaps he should have copped an insanity plea right up front. Maybe his actions were more understandable under those circumstances. *Figures.* The bad news was: There was a distinct possibility the crazy still resided within him.

Luke brought her fingers to his lips for a kiss before he released her hand. "You're exhausted. Why don't you lean that seat back and get some sleep?"

She glanced at him again, a slight tilt to her head. "You have to be just as tired. I'll stay awake and we can talk or play a stupid game."

Luke grinned, reminded of the times the three of them had played Jen's word games until all hours of the night and the hilarity that had ensued. "Sounds fun, but it's not necessary. I don't really sleep much anymore." He felt her looking at him and braced himself for the questions he knew would follow...and the truth he was determined to share.

"Ever? Surely you must sleep sometime." Her voice was wary, as though she had to ask but wasn't sure she really wanted the answer.

"Unfortunately, that's true. I catch an hour or two now and then before I wake up in a cold sweat. My experiences with Uncle Sam changed me—and not for the better. I have nightmares and headaches. I get startled easily, and when I do, I come up swinging. But I'm better than I was, and I'm grateful for that. Mostly I try to stay awake."

"How long has that been going on?"

Luke shrugged. "Started while I was over there...in that filthy prison." A shudder worked its way slowly through him. "I thought I'd seen it all with my SEAL unit, but I didn't have a clue. After my team member, Ian Mathias, and I were captured, the interrogator at the camp where we were held started his psychological warfare. Ahmed Kazi was his name—the name he took when he converted to Islam. He was born in New York, but, man, that guy hated Americans, and military personnel were apparently the lowest in his opinion. He had it in for us from day one. A master at the art of torture, he wanted us to anticipate what was going to happen next.

"Ian drew the short straw—he didn't make it." Luke struggled to keep his voice steady. "I dream about him a lot. Relive that helpless feeling when I'm filled with so much hate my heart's pumping like a locomotive and there's not a fucking thing I can do to save him." Anger filled Luke, and he clenched his hands in a death grip around the steering wheel to keep his rage from escaping.

"My God." Sally's whisper was nearly inaudible, but her warm, caring touch on his leg snatched him back from the brink. "I knew it was bad, Luke, but I didn't realize you still lived with it night and day. Is there anything I can do to help?"

Focusing on her face, he fought to get his anger under control. He never wanted her to see that side of him. "You already have. That picture. I wasn't kidding about you and Jen saving my life. You kept me from giving up. Gave me a reason to keep fighting. Calmed me when I woke from a dream, breathing so damn hard my ribs ached. After Ian was killed, you were all I had." Luke paused to see if he was giving her too much information—convincing her he really was crazy. Her rapt attention as she turned toward him seemed to ask for more.

"The bond we had before I deployed took on new meaning after I was captured. I…took some liberties—embellished a bit. Hope you don't mind." He stole a glance in her direction, and she still hadn't looked away. Might as well get it all out in the open. "I've imagined making love to you in a hundred different ways. Just so you know, sunshine, we were incredible together." Was that a grin working at the corners of her lips or just wishful thinking? "That's what makes what I did to you so terrible. You never gave up on me once, yet I took it on myself to decide you wouldn't want half a man back from the war." He stopped then, strangely bereft of words.

"That *was* wrong of you." Sally nodded her head in agreement. "But I can't begin to comprehend what you went through. Nor am I qualified to decide how you should react to everything that happened." She looked in to his eyes. "I'm really glad you're here, Luke."

Luke's surprised gaze collided with her sure and steady one. A full-on gorgeous smile blossomed across her otherwise tired visage. He reluctantly jerked his eyes back to the road, unable to control a pleased grin. "Yeah? Does that mean you'll give *us* another chance?"

"It might…on one condition."

"Which is…?"

"Honesty is a big deal for me. I won't settle for less." She flinched as though something pinched her on the last word, regret worrying her gorgeous eyes for a split second before she blinked it away and smiled a little too brightly.

Luke frowned. Was she still haunted by his lie? He knew only too well what it was like to be unable to forget, and he didn't want that for her. It wasn't conducive to the plans he dared have for their life together.

Luke spotted a turnout ahead and stepped on the brakes, pulling over a little quicker than he should have. He leaned toward the woman whose opinion meant everything to him, took her hand again and placed it over his heart. "You won't ever have to settle, sunshine." Releasing his seat belt and then hers, he hooked one arm around her waist, pulling her to the edge of the seat until she was close enough her breath tickled his cheek. He leaned in slowly with a grin, almost touching, then nibbled and teased the corner of her mouth before he took possession of her lips. She responded to him as though she'd wanted this as badly as he had, opening for him when he ran his tongue across the seam of her lips. When he delved inside like a starving man, she met his searching tongue with parrying thrusts of her own. She tasted of honey and smoke, and he couldn't help a rumbling laugh against her soft lips.

"What's so funny, sailor?" Sally kissed him again and then drew back to look in his eyes.

"We've been smoked. Do I taste like a bonfire?" His hand settled on her neck and stroked gently.

"A little. Me too?" She obligingly bent her neck so he could take full advantage of her satiny skin.

Luke pulled her toward him again. "I love the way you taste."

She leaned into him as he nipped at her bottom lip before he pressed his mouth to hers and lost himself in the homecoming he'd dreamed of so many times. He pressed her back against the seat and deepened the kiss, needing to claim her as his own so there'd no longer be any question. By her soft moans and the way she fisted her hand in his hair, she was as caught up in the heat of the moment as he was. In only a few minutes, they were both breathing heavily.

Remembering where they were, why they had set out and the nine-year-old girl sleeping in the back, Luke reluctantly released Sally. He pulled back to his own side of the vehicle and leaned against the steering wheel while he caught his breath. Turning an apologetic smile her way, he shifted the Jeep into gear. "That was a hell of a lot hotter than anything I imagined."

One side of her mouth shot upward in a smug grin, and she placed her hand, palm down, on his thigh. The warmth of her touch set off a chain reaction that ended with his jeans becoming tight and uncomfortable.

She lowered her voice to a sexy murmur. "Speaking of that—you've got your work cut out for you, Luke Harding."

He eyed her curiously. Should he be worried by the obvious challenge in her smile? "Yeah? How's that?"

"I fully expect you to show me those hundred different ways you've imagined us making love."

Luke coughed, steering the Jeep onto the roadway again. "Damn it. You're killing me here."

Her sweet peals of laughter were music to his ears.

Chapter Seven

Four hours later and a few miles north of Coeur d'Alene, Luke had finally given in and let her drive. Sally could tell by his heavy eyelids and the slight slur to his words that he'd needed to rest, despite the dire description he'd given of his sleeping issues. She'd managed to doze some while he drove. Though not well rested by any means, she was alert enough to take the wheel. He'd fallen into a restless slumber almost immediately upon switching places. So far, he'd mumbled unrecognizable phrases, but otherwise he seemed like anyone else catnapping in a car.

Midmorning on a Saturday meant more traffic than she was used to. Huntington never saw many travelers other than locals. The sky was overcast, but the clouds were breaking up to the north. Seeing the sun would be a nice touch after the night they'd had. Jen squirmed on the seat behind her but settled in again without waking. Sally stretched taller so she could see her in the rearview mirror. *Peaceful. Beautiful. Poor baby must have been exhausted.*

Every few minutes, Sally's glance fell on Luke, asleep in the seat beside her, his rolled-up jacket forming a pillow where he leaned his head against the side window. Warmth invaded her belly, making her smile secretly. His muscled chest moved up and down gently with each breath. The urge to touch him was nearly overwhelming. The memory of his lips on hers sent electrical pulses all the way to her toes. She was as giddy as a teenager, falling in love for the first time. The difference was, she'd been in love with Luke for a long time…and now he'd come back, professing an interest in starting over. She wanted to believe he felt the same way she did, but her heart was still raw—a gentle reminder the world could change in a heartbeat.

She'd meant every word, but was it possible to spend time with him, let him touch her...make love to her...and not risk her heart? Even though intimately acquainted with the shattered pieces he'd reduced her soul to after his rescue, she still wasn't willing to give up this time with him—this possibility. Their relationship *could* work. She'd never know unless she let go of her fears long enough to give him a chance.

Masochistic much?

Never in her life had she acted like an irresponsible child. She'd grown up at fourteen—the day her mother died, leaving her in the care of her only living relative. Her father...Clive Brennan. Apparently, she was making up for lost time now, her insides turning to mush at the mere thought of Luke's touch. To have so quickly abandoned her determination not to trust the man who'd broken her heart had to be foolish to say the least. Didn't it? After all, hers and Jen's lives depended on the decisions she made in the next few days.

What if she was wrong about him?

This is Luke.

She scoffed soundlessly, chastising herself for even thinking he could be anything other than honorable. Sally glanced at the sleeping military hero beside her and slowly shook her head. *No. There's not an unprincipled bone in his body. He's come back a slightly different man—but the same in every way that matters.*

The heaviness of guilt bore down on her again, as it had earlier, when she'd told Luke she wouldn't settle for anything less than honesty. Wasn't *she* guilty of withholding the truth from him—information that could easily put her life in jeopardy? Sure...she'd told him about Clive Brennan's crime, her testimony and the resulting witness protection gig, but she'd left out the part that humiliated her to the bone—the fact that the monster was her father. She'd wanted to tell Luke—to have everything out in the open—but when she'd formed the words in her mind, her mouth had gone dry to the point her tongue refused to cooperate, the breath caught in her throat and her world began to spin. If Luke hadn't reached to steady her on that mountain road in front of Garrett and Jonathan, she'd have hit the dirt for sure.

Still, it was crucial not to lose sight of what was important. Jen's safety came first. Besides, Marshal Lambert was on his way to find her with plans to stash them back in hiding before the day was out. A sudden memory brought her up short. She'd left her cell phone behind when Jen and she jumped from Luke's truck. It was going to be hard for Lambert to find her if she didn't answer her phone. She couldn't even call him because his number was pre-set in her contacts and she had no idea what it was.

Equal amounts of fear and relief surged through her, along with a hefty dose of excitement at the feeling of freedom from the bonds that had held her for so many years. To no longer have the federal government responsible for her safety brought mixed emotions—and possibly it was premature to be celebrating. On the other hand, the feds certainly hadn't done such an outstanding job keeping Clive and his men away from her last night.

At that instant, Luke jerked forward, grabbing the dash with both hands, his eyes wild. Every muscle in his arms and legs strained in the throes of whatever nightmare had woken him. "Get back! Get the fuck back!"

Startled, she slammed on the brakes and the Jeep fishtailed to a stop on the side of the road. "Luke?"

For a fraction of a second, the blank look he gave her held no recognition. His features twisted into a mask of rage as he grabbed the steering wheel. Jen moaned and stirred on the backseat but apparently slipped back into her deep sleep. Sally cringed away from Luke's obvious anger and, suddenly, concern for Jen's safety and hers became Sally's overriding thought. Would she upset him further if she tried to reach her daughter?

It's still Luke! She forced herself to focus. He was still the man she cared about, and he was obviously hurting somewhere deep down inside. She wouldn't cut and run at the first sign of trouble.

Sally placed her hand firmly over his where he gripped the steering wheel. "Luke, wake up." She'd tried for calm and had managed a small amount of bravado.

Confusion surfaced in Luke's expression and, as suddenly as it had begun, his glazed eyes cleared and a scowl hardened his features. He let loose the dash and steering wheel, dragging his hands the length of his stubble-covered face as he leaned back in the seat. "Sorry. I'm okay."

Not wanting Luke to see how much he'd frightened her, Sally stepped on the gas again, guiding the Jeep into the northbound lane. Her heart still pounded as she stole a glance at his profile. Was that what it was like all the time for him? He'd warned her, but she'd had no idea his episodes would be so intense. Thankfully, Jen hadn't witnessed his outburst. She wouldn't have understood.

Silence resumed in the cab until, a few minutes later, he slid his hand onto her knee and turned his head toward her. "I'm sorry, babe. Are you okay? I didn't mean to startle you."

She smiled. It was still Luke. He was having a hard time right now and he needed her to be strong. Her heart swelled to overflowing for her Navy SEAL and all the wounds he'd suffered. "I'm fine. Go back to sleep."

He squeezed her knee before settling back in the seat. Heaven help her—she loved him. The need to touch him came again, stronger this time. *We deserve a little happiness—all of us. It's not like I'm going into this with blinders on.*

Forty miles later, on the outskirts of Sandpoint, Sally yawned as she pulled the Jeep off the highway and into the parking lot of a small, tired-looking motel. The sun had broken free from the clouds and now hung directly overhead.

Instantly, Luke sat straight and scanned from right to left, his gaze finally coming to rest on her. "What's up?"

"We're stopping. I need food, a shower and a clean bed to stretch out in, not necessarily in that order."

Luke looked toward the rustic motel, its faux log cabin sides missing chinks of plaster here and there. Huge, old air-conditioning units hung on the front of each room, lined up alongside a dozen doors, painted neon green, all in a row, ending with a glass door bearing a sign saying "Check-in." His nose wrinkled. "Is this the best we can do, babe?"

Sally shoved the gearshift into Park and rested her head on the steering wheel. For a moment, she considered kissing the doubtful grimace off his face but dismissed the idea when she heard Jen rustling behind her. "Yes. For now, it will have to do. I don't have any money, Luke, but I'll pay you back every cent."

"No need. Money should be the last of your worries right now." Luke raised up slightly and inserted one hand into his right front pocket. "Besides, Uncle Sam has been taking care of my expenses for a while now. So, I've got a bundle saved."

"I appreciate that I don't have to worry now, but *I will* pay you back, so get used to the idea."

Luke grinned as he pulled his hand from his pocket and handed her the wallet she'd left in the truck. "I almost forgot. Your purse spilled on the floor while I was taking a corner pretty fast. I grabbed a couple of things I thought you'd need." He reached into his left-hand pocket and came out with her cell phone. "I turned it off. Didn't want those thugs to hear it ring while I was clinging to the side of that mountain."

Sally stared at the phone and, suddenly, the weight of the world collapsed on her shoulders again. Now she would have to turn it on. Answer it when it rang. Tell Marshal Lambert where to find her. She took it from Luke tentatively and smiled a thank you she didn't mean.

He caught her arm as she swiveled to nudge Jen. "Hey. You okay?"

His sincerity and concern banished her pity party, and she nodded, raising her lips to his. Luke pulled her closer and she pressed into his warmth as their lips met in sensuous exploration. She wanted to stay right there, but she pulled away as soon as she heard Jen stir and come fully awake. Sally didn't want to give her daughter false hopes. Until she talked to the marshal and figured out the next move, their lives weren't their own. She pushed Luke back and frowned at his humorous smirk.

Jen yawned and rolled toward the bucket seats. "Mom, I'm hungry," she whispered.

"Me too," Luke said. "I didn't think you'd ever wake up." He tossed a wink at Sally, and she had to bite her lip to keep from smiling. "Tell you what: Why don't you ladies wait here while I get us a room? After we're settled, I'll run into town and grab us some breakfast. How's that sound?"

"Can we have pancakes?" Jen slid to the edge of the seat, shook her curls out of her face and grasped the front seats to pull herself up. Her clear eyes and excited manner alleviated some of Sally's worry. Her daughter appeared no worse for wear, despite the past several hours.

"You can have anything you want." Luke landed a kiss on the top of her head before he opened his door and stepped out. "Figure out what your mom wants while I'm gone, okay?"

As Luke disappeared inside the motel's office, Jen crawled into her lap and wound her arms around Sally's neck. "Mom, what happened to your face?" Her small hand gently touched the bruise on Sally's jaw.

How could she explain the black and blue marks without destroying her daughter's trust in men? She'd promised herself, when Jen was barely able to walk, that she'd always be honest with her—something Sally's own father apparently hadn't known the first thing about. It hadn't always been easy. Like when Luke was captured overseas and wounded and Sally had been sure she'd never see him again. Things like that were hard to explain to a child—so she'd omitted parts of the truth to protect her daughter. That wasn't the same as lying, was it?

"Remember I told you I had a date with my boss last night?"

"Yeah," Jen said.

"Well, not all men are nice. Some of them are bullies, just like in your school."

"He hurt you? Did you tell Luke?" Placing her fingers under Sally's chin, she turned her mother's head and studied the abrasion on her cheekbone.

"Luke knows." Sally went for the simplistic answer rather than also explaining Luke's sudden appearance.

"Good. I bet that bully won't bother you again. Mom, when can we go home?"

Apparently, her daughter was full of hard questions today. This was one Sally hadn't wanted to field so soon. She pulled her daughter's arms loose and took her small hands in hers. "I don't know, honey. It might be a long time. There wasn't much left of our house. The landlord might decide not to rebuild." Sally tucked a lock of Jen's hair behind her ear. How would her nine-year-old daughter handle such devastating news?

Jen stared at her thoughtfully for several seconds, then leaned into her again, and Sally hugged her small body close. "That's okay, Mom. It'll be like an adventure. As long as Luke is with us, I won't miss home that much. Will you?"

Sally should have known her daughter of nine…going on thirty…would take everything in stride. She smiled, a genuine smile of relief. "Why would I miss home when I have everything I care about right here?" She tickled Jen's ribs, mother and daughter giggling together.

The passenger door opened and Sally jumped. Jen laughed when she spotted Luke in the doorway. He held out both hands toward her, and she clambered across the seat and flung herself into his arms. Luke let out an *oof* and mumbled something about her being so big.

He situated Jen on his left side, reached for his duffel and nodded his head in the direction of the line of motel rooms. "Ours is the last one."

Sally hurried to keep up with Luke's long stride, but when he reached the last bright green door, he unlocked it, shoved it open and stood aside, waiting for her to go ahead. The musty, closed-up smell hit her first, and she kept walking to the far side of the room, where she wrestled with the window for a few minutes before she gave up. Frustrated, she turned and surveyed the rest of the room. Shag carpet, two full-sized beds with mattresses that dipped in the middle, covered by worn bedspreads of questionable cleanliness. It was all she could do to keep from shuddering as her gaze drifted to Luke.

He set Jen on her feet and straightened. A crooked smile slid across his countenance. "Next time I choose the accommodations."

His dark brown eyes, sparkling with amusement, were her downfall. She coughed to disguise the laughter that sputtered from her throat, but when Jen and Luke broke up, Sally lost it too. She hadn't really laughed in so long—since before Luke was deployed. It felt good to be reckless, impetuous and carefree.

Luke collected himself first and eyed Jen. "Did you find out what your mom wants for breakfast?"

"Oh shoot, I forgot." Jen sounded truly repentant, and Sally was relieved when Luke turned his best smile on the girl.

"No worries. I'll get it out of her." He grinned at Jen, and she dropped on the edge of the bed, watching to see what would happen next.

"Okay, pancakes for Jen. You want anything else with that? Sausage? Bacon?" Luke pretended to pull a waiter's order pad from his pocket and began writing with the tip of his finger.

Jen dissolved into giggles. "No. Just pancakes and milk."

Luke pretend-jotted another note. "You got it, miss. And for the beautiful lady?" His gaze locked on Sally's.

She could practically feel the heat emanating off him from where she stood a few feet away. Between that, him calling her beautiful and the lust in his eyes, she found herself stumbling for words. "Um…I'll have… whatever you're having will be fine."

He raised an eyebrow as though he doubted her decision but folded the pretend notebook and put it back in his pocket. He strode to the door and stopped. "I won't be long, but one of you might have time to get in the shower. Help yourself to anything I've got in the way of clean clothes. We'll do a little shopping before we hit the road again. Pick up a few essentials. The place we're heading to is out in the sticks, so if we don't get it here, we'll have to go without until we get back to town." He paused and frowned. "Lock the door and don't open it to anyone while I'm gone." His gaze fell on her again, and she gave him her abbreviated version of a salute. He smiled, but this time the humor didn't reach his eyes.

As soon as he left, Sally strode across the room and locked the door. His ominous warning, accompanied by obvious concern, had left a dark cloud over the occupants of the room. Even Jen seemed to feel it, so Sally hurried her into the bathroom and turned on the water, adjusting it to the right temperature. Then she left her daughter to the shower and returned to the other room to search through Luke's bag. She settled for a T-shirt that would pass as an oversized dress on Jen's small frame. It would have to suffice until they found something better.

She chose a button-up, light blue shirt for herself, mostly because it smelled like Luke, and carried the clothes into the bathroom. Jen was just stepping out of the shower, so Sally helped to pat her dry, then pulled the fresh shirt over her head. They had a good laugh over how it hung off one shoulder.

Luke still wasn't back, so after reiterating his instructions about keeping the door locked to Jen for good measure, Sally peeled off her soiled clothes and crawled under the inviting spray. She couldn't remember when a shower had felt so divine, although it would probably take more than one to get the smoke out of her pores. With the soap and shampoo provided by the motel, she did the best she could. Then she dried off, ran her fingers through her hair in a last-ditch attempt to restore order without the proper equipment and wrapped Luke's shirt around her shoulders, slipping her arms into the sleeves. She breathed in deeply of the slightly spicy, slightly fresh-mown-hay scent that clung to the fabric. Luke's smell…it brought back all kinds of memories she'd tried to forget.

When she left the steamy bathroom, Luke and Jen were sitting at the table eating breakfast from Styrofoam containers and discussing the end of the school year, which was only a couple of months away. God only knew when Jen would see the inside of a classroom again.

Luke did a double take when he saw Sally and, feeling self-conscious, she tugged on the bottom of the shirt to make certain everything was covered. Heat invaded her cheeks anyway, and she was sure she'd turned a bright shade of red. Suddenly, she was regretting her decision to rinse her tank top and panties and leave them draped over the shower curtain in the bathroom. When she pulled out her chair and sat to eat, Luke's gaze remained on his food. Was it just her imagination or did his pained expression and stiff spine mean he was uncomfortable for some reason?

Pancakes, eggs and sausage seemed to be the fare everyone was enjoying, and Sally dug in without hesitation. "Oooh…this tastes really good. Thank you." She smiled her gratitude at Luke.

When he glanced at her briefly and nodded, she was startled at the nearly black color of his eyes and the intensity burning in them. She started to ask if he was all right, but he averted his eyes and the words caught in her throat.

Jen sat back and dropped her plastic fork onto her empty plate. "Mom, can I be excused?"

Sally dragged her gaze from Luke's profile. "Sure, honey. There's probably a garbage container under the sink for your paper and plastic."

Jen jumped up, tossed her plate and utensils in the trash, then skipped around the table and landed a kiss on Luke's cheek. "Thank you for breakfast."

"It was totally my pleasure." He returned the peck before she scooted away to flounce on the end of one of the beds.

"Is it okay if I play a game on your phone, Mom?"

"Sure. You'll have to turn it on first. Just for a few minutes, though. I don't want to run the battery down." The only charger she'd owned had been incinerated with the rest of her belongings.

Jen found the phone, where Sally had dropped it alongside her wallet on the nightstand and propped herself on the pillows of the far bed.

Sally turned back to her breakfast and caught Luke studying the blue button-up shirt she'd pulled from his duffel and slipped on. The grim set of his mouth seemed a lot like disapproval and emphasized the emotional distance between them. Suddenly uncomfortable, she laid her fork down. "Should I change? You said to help ourselves, but—"

Luke's gaze slowly rose to her eyes, and the heat in his glance warmed her skin as surely as if he'd touched her. "Do you have any idea how damn sexy you look in my shirt? Hell no, I don't want you to change." A glimmer of his familiar grin banished his serious expression. "We just need a certain little girl to go to sleep." His words were a conspiratorial whisper.

Sally gave a dismissive wave of her hand. "I wouldn't count on that. She slept practically all the way here."

"I know." His lips contorted into a half grimace, half self-deprecating smile. "I need a shower anyway. I guess it'll be a cold one."

Luke finished the last of his food and pushed his chair back. He leaned toward her and swept her hair behind her shoulder, baring her neck to the gentle brush of his lips. "You don't mind if I imagine you in there with me, do you?" A tip of his head indicated the bathroom door, and his gaze did a slow burn over her breasts to her lap, and the spot on her thigh where his shirt ended.

A tremor surged through her torso, and her stomach felt as though it flipped clear over as his head slowly lifted until he focused on her face again. His lips met hers, a silent promise of more to come. Another few seconds and Jen rolled over, breaking the spell. Luke stood. With a smile of regret, he dumped his trash, grabbed his duffel and disappeared into the bathroom.

Sally let her breath out slowly. Clearly she was putty in his hands, unable to form a coherent thought if he was within arm's reach. What did Luke expect from her—besides the sexual intimacy that he obviously craved? Was he interested in an overnight family—forever? Because that was the only kind of relationship she'd bring into Jen's life. She and her daughter were a package deal.

Luke had made it obvious the sun rose and set with Jen, and Sally had no doubt he'd take on the role of father with all his heart. Her little girl thought the world of Luke too. Sally pushed her remaining eggs around with her fork, no longer hungry. That only left her—what did Sally want?

She loved their reawakened closeness—the sexual tension that zinged between them. Sally wasn't immune to Luke's charm and devastatingly good looks, and there'd been a time she'd dreamed of a hero riding in on a black steed, offering the house in the country with a white picket fence… and maybe more children someday. She'd be lying if she didn't admit the prospect of sex with Luke Harding excited her. A slow smile faded as quickly as it came. If only she could keep from dwelling on the rubble of her house and her current situation.

There were problems with her happily-ever-after scenario. The man who'd sired her apparently wanted to make her life significantly shorter in retribution for sending him to jail. Marshal Lambert wanted to protect her but, in the process, would completely destroy her current existence.

Neither was acceptable. Both were reasons why she shouldn't waste what little time she and Luke had.

Sally pushed to her feet, finished clearing off the table and glanced toward Jen. Her daughter was completely engrossed in the game she was playing, and experience had taught her Jen would continue happily until asked to stop.

The shower turned off, and Sally's imagination kicked into high gear—Luke stepping from the steamy cubicle, running the towel over his muscled body, soaking up the water droplets. She shook her head. She couldn't just walk in on him…could she? *What if Jen sees me?* Sally glanced toward the bed, where the girl lay propped on her elbows, thumbs pounding out a rhythm on the phone's face. Jen was obviously in her own world at the moment. She wouldn't notice a brass band parading through the room. Sally grabbed a napkin and absently wiped down the table where they'd eaten. If she was honest…it wasn't Jen's reaction she was worried about. What if Luke didn't want her there?

Huh? Get a grip, girl. How much more transparent could he be? If she'd doubted he was attracted to her before that sizzling kiss, she didn't any longer. He'd made himself quite clear on the subject. It was time she reciprocated. Too bad she was scared to death. *All the more reason…*

With one last glance toward Jen, she strode to the bathroom door and knocked quietly.

"Be right out." Luke's deep voice came from the other side.

Sally straightened her spine, pushed the door and slipped inside.

Chapter Eight

Luke stepped from the shower and made quick work of drying off before wrapping the towel around his waist. Sandy-colored clumps of wet hair stuck out every which way as his image stared back at him from the mirror. He raked his fingers through the strands, in serious need of a haircut, and called it good. Grabbing the shaving cream from his kit, he applied it evenly to his whiskered face and dragged the razor down his rough skin, systematically shaving from right to left. He paused for a heartbeat when he heard a knock.

"Be right out." Luke turned the water on as hot as he could get it and let it run. Jen probably had to use the bathroom. He'd throw on some clothes and finish up in here later. A smile formed beneath what was left of the shaving cream. There wasn't much he wouldn't do for that little girl.

An instant later the door opened behind him, and the razor went still in his hand.

He stared at Sally's reflection in the steamed-over mirror. Her in that damn shirt of his, leaning against the bathroom door, both hands behind her back. A good deal of shapely thigh led his gaze to well-toned calves. He followed them down to pretty pink toenails on bare feet. Did she know what coming in here like that would do to him? He took the last two swipes of shaving cream off with the razor, rinsed his face in the hot, running water and patted it dry. Barely able to swallow and momentarily unable to form an articulate sentence, he turned slowly.

Her blue eyes went wide as her gaze dropped below his waist, immediately answering his unspoken question. Evidently, she *could* see the hard-on he sported beneath the form-fitting towel that hugged his hips.

He took a step toward her. "Sally?" That was all he managed to force from his mouth. It sounded more like a command than the question with which he'd intended to rule out the possibility something was wrong.

A secretive smile played on her lips as she brought one hand up and raised it in front of her with a dismissive shake of her head. "I'm sorry. I don't know what I was thinking. This can wait till you're finished." Her gaze dipped once again to the towel draped around his hips, and she swiveled with a hand on the doorknob.

Oh no. Hell no. He wasn't letting her escape that easily. He was damn sure she'd stepped out of her comfort zone for a reason and her baby blues were daring him to find out why. He closed the gap and caught the door as she opened it a sliver. Peering through the opening, he saw Jen, still intent on her game. A glance toward the motel room door confirmed that the dead bolt was thrown and locked. They could have a few minutes of privacy.

Luke pulled Sally away from the door, ignoring her squeak of surprise and trying not to react to the violet hues that darkened her eyes at the same time her pupils dilated. Oh yeah. She knew what she was doing, all right. Sally wanted him as much as he wanted her. He stepped close, sandwiching her between the sink and himself, hands braced on the counter, one on each side of her. "So, you missed me, huh?"

Sally glanced up, her brow furrowed as though giving the question heavy thought. As soon as he touched her rib cage in a spot he knew she was ticklish, she folded into laughter. "I might have." She finally forced the breathless words out.

He snorted. "Not good enough. Why did you barge in here?" He lifted her to the edge of the counter and inserted himself between her legs, his hands on her bottom, pulling her against his growing arousal.

She wrapped her legs around him, and he felt some of her tension ease as she threaded her fingers in his hair and pulled his head toward her. "I don't want to waste any more time, Luke." Moisture shimmered in her eyes as he smoothed the hair back from her face.

"Then we won't. Not another second." His mouth claimed hers. The desire that raced through him like electricity had nothing to do with his arousal and everything to do with her admission. He'd almost convinced himself he'd screwed up too badly—that she'd never let him close again. But the beautiful blue-eyed brunette in the picture he'd carried for months was giving him another chance, and he wasn't going to fuck it up this time.

When he leaned away, she held on to him, and her sad smile tugged at his heart. What troubled her was no mystery, but he wanted her to understand she wasn't alone. He wrapped one arm around her, pulling her tight again, then tilted her chin up so he could see her eyes. "I'm not giving up on us... ever, and I don't want you to either. Do me one favor, babe. Trust me to keep you safe."

Her eyes scanned his. "I trust you with my daughter, Luke. There *is* no more trust than that." Her fingers stroked his cheek and he caught her hand, pressing a kiss to her palm. "She's in as much danger as I am now, and I can't stand the thought of her being hurt because of me. And now you're involved, and I'm terrified for both of you. I don't know what to do. Maybe we should run. Leave the country."

Luke dropped a string of kisses on her neck, right above her collarbone, and gave some thought to her suggestion. "If that's what you really want, I can make it happen."

"But...?"

Smart girl. She recognized his reluctance. "We'll be looking over our shoulders for the rest of our lives. I could be wrong, but I'm betting you've had enough of that. The only way to hang on to something you want to keep is to stand and fight for it."

"Even if we're going to lose?" He could hear how tired she was. It was clear the constant battle had already taken its toll on her. She didn't want to fight anymore.

Luke grinned as he lifted her off the counter, pivoted, took three strides and pressed her against the wall. "Who says we're going to lose? As long as we stick together, no one can stop us." He kissed her again, with all the passion he'd held in check during the past few minutes. His tongue swept the inside of her mouth, twisting around hers. Tilting his head, he deepened the kiss until she placed a hand on his chest and pushed back.

"I have to check on Jen." Was it disappointment that shadowed her eyes?

Holding her gaze, he ground his hips into the warmth at the apex of her legs. He nodded toward her undergarments drying over the rod that held the shower curtain. "Am I to understand there's nothing between us but a thin towel right now?" He punctuated the question with a nip to her neck.

A rosy hue enveloped her cheeks, but a persistent smile seemed to dare him. "You're very observant."

"SEAL training. Always important to know if the enemy is wearing panties."

Sally laughed and squirmed against him.

He was using up a good portion of his self-control on this exercise, but he wouldn't push her if she wasn't comfortable, whether because of Jen or for some other reason. Luke leaned toward her ear and teased her with his nose while he spoke. "If Jen wasn't awake in the next room, I'd be happy to show you one of those hundred ways right here. Then I'd carry you to the bed and show you a couple more." He groaned as he kissed her lips hard. "But I can wait…and when we come together, it'll be spectacular. I promise." That earned him a sexy smile as he lowered her feet to the floor. "Now go, before I change my mind."

He opened the door and guided her out, patting her round derriere as she went by, and was rewarded by an insincere glare. Damn. A groan bubbled up in his throat. Letting her go was harder than he'd thought. Hopefully, they'd find some private time…and soon, but hell, what did he know about living with a kid? Privacy could be a rare commodity.

Another quick and cold shower later, Luke slipped into an old pair of sweats and reentered the bedroom. One glance told him Jen had fallen asleep on top of the comforter in the middle of her game. Her mother had closed the curtains and covered her with the blankets from the opposite side of the bed, leaving Sally's side bare except for sheets. She was clearly exhausted, and he hoped to give her two or three hours of sleep before they headed out again. As he watched, she picked up the phone, turned it off and laid it on the nightstand. Then she spread out on the bare side of Jen's bed.

Luke poured a glass of water and drank it down. He'd never spent any time around kids until he'd met Sally. What was the proper etiquette here? Would it be so bad if Sally slept with him in the other bed? Of course they couldn't do any of the things he longed to do with her, but at least she'd be warm. The one thing he could be sure of was that whatever Sally thought was acceptable…she wouldn't compromise on the issue. It would have to be her idea.

He set down his glass and walked toward his bed. Removing his watch, he left it by her phone, then slipped between the sheets and moved to the far side, leaving the bedding folded down invitingly on the other. After a few minutes, he propped his head on his elbow and looked at her. Sally hadn't moved, her eyes open and staring at him over Jen's sleeping form. He held her gaze as he crooked his finger and patted the sheets beside him.

Sally shook her head, and Luke didn't argue. As soon as he lay down on the pillow, he saw her head pop up in his peripheral vision. He closed his eyes and pretended to ignore her, but he couldn't disguise his pleased grin. The ball was in her court. *Make it seem like it's her idea.*

"What's so funny, Harding?"

Luke heard the aged box springs creak, and when he opened his eyes, she was standing over him, hands on her hips. Her lips were pressed together, not in annoyance but apparently trying to forestall her own laughter. His arm snaked out and caught her by the shirt, pulling her in close and over his body to the other side of the bed, then rolled partway on top of her.

"Shh." He tapped her lips with his finger to remind her of the sleeping girl in the next bed.

He recognized the instant it dawned on her that she could wake Jen by the hand she threw over her mouth and the giggles it didn't quite contain.

When she'd composed herself, she looked in to his eyes, a you've-got-some-explaining-to-do tilt to her head. "What do you think you're doing?" Her husky whisper fell far short of the feigned indignation on her face.

Luke raised a hand and swept it toward his blankets. "Well, sunshine, I'm offering you a place in my bed for a little nap." She felt so damn good underneath him, her breasts plumped against his chest. He should really stop teasing her now before it came back to bite him.

A tentative smile hadn't wavered on her features. "Where will you sleep?"

A low laugh rumbled from his throat. "Funny girl. You're not really going to make me answer that, are you?"

Her smile gave way to worry and she shook her head. "We can't, Luke. Not with—"

He lowered his head and gently nibbled her lips, effectively swallowing the rest of her words. A few seconds later, he reluctantly drew back. "Yes, we can. We can sleep in this bed together and I can finally hold you in my arms. The only thing I can't do is have my way with you." One eyebrow arched upward as he dropped another kiss on her doubtful mouth. "I can live with that…for now. Can you?"

Sally visibly relaxed beneath him. "You're always thinking about her, aren't you? Do you realize how rare that is?" Her fingers traced a path from his shoulder to his rib cage.

Fire seemed to follow her caress, and he captured her hand in his to stop the torment before things could get out of hand. "I think pretty highly of that kid, and I'd never do anything to knowingly cause her harm. You know that. But right now, my thoughts are all about you." He met her gaze as she digested that information. Encouraged when her glance drifted to his lips, he covered her mouth again, kissing her long and hard.

She wrapped her arms around his neck and hung on, responding eagerly. Too willingly—a condition he'd wished for a dozen times but had never come to fruition while circumstances were in their favor. Now, with Jen a few feet away, Luke's control was becoming dangerously thin. If he was going to sleep with Sally wrapped in his arms as he'd said—as he'd imagined so many nights—he'd need to call a halt to this sooner rather than later. *There'll be time.* His raging libido wasn't convinced.

Luke backed away from the urgency, gently kissing her several times before he raised his head and shifted off her, just enough so she could move. "Roll over, babe. I want to spoon with my girl." Okay, so maybe he was rushing things a little, but the fact that she didn't get in his face and set him straight made him the happiest he'd been in a hell of a long time.

With a quizzical tilt to her brows, Sally turned her back to him, lay her head on his arm stretched beneath the pillow and scooted back until every inch of her touched him somewhere. His nostrils full of the fruity, coconut smell of her hair, he pulled the blankets over them and slung one arm over her hip, his hand splayed halfway between her rounded breasts and the oasis between her legs. His dick twitched in response.

Sally looked over her shoulder with a droll smile. "Um…are you sure this is a good idea?"

"Don't worry. I've got this." *Not exactly true, but I'll run with it.* "We should get out of here about noon. Do our shopping and hit the road. So sleep while you can, sunshine."

"That might be easier said than done." Amusement warmed her voice. She faced away from him again and snuggled next to him as though the two of them were one.

They lay still for a moment before Luke propped himself up so he could lean over and glimpse her face. "One more thing you need to know. If I fall asleep and start thrashing, acting out of my head, don't try to wake me." He'd been debating the warning since she'd allowed him to sleep on her couch last night. The dreams, and his inability to shake them, made him feel weak and out of control. He hated admitting his Achilles' heel to Sally. A woman should feel safe with her man, but he was telling her not to trust him when he was in the throes of one of his nightmares. Best-case scenario—he wouldn't be her man very long. Worst case—she might be afraid of him… in bed, for shit's sake.

She turned onto her back this time, disbelief staring from her expressive eyes. "Don't wake you? What would you have me do?"

"I want you to get out of the way. I've been known to swing on guys who've interrupted one of my dreams, trying to calm me down. It can get ugly pretty fast. You saw what I was like in the Jeep a little while ago. I don't want you or Jen hurt because of me. I'd never forgive myself. Promise, Sally."

She pursed her lips and studied him thoughtfully. "I'll make sure Jen isn't in harm's way, but that's the best I can do."

"Sally." He spoke the warning as sternly as he could manage, with a half-naked woman in his bed making him crazy.

She silenced him with an accusing glare. "Weren't you listening when we talked earlier? When we decided to give this thing between us another try?"

He held back a groan. She's going to pick now to argue? "Of course I was listening. What does that have to do with—?"

She flashed her palm at him. "So, are we just there for each other when everything's good? If that's the case, you should have gotten out of the way a long time ago, what with Emmett making a scene in front of my house… and someone trying to blow us up and run us off the road. *I don't want you hurt because of me.*" Sally lowered her voice to a pretty good imitation of his own as she repeated his words back to him. "So, you should probably be going."

The ornery woman tried to tug his covers away from him as she rolled onto her side again, and Luke had to talk himself down before he did something foolish such as laying a good smack on her sexy ass.

There was something inherently wrong with her argument. Hell, it was no argument at all. She'd just twisted his words around and fed them back to him. For some reason, he couldn't get the exultant smile off his mug. He was humbled by the meaning behind her words—dangerous or not, she intended to stand *with* him. No other woman he'd ever known had offered herself in that way. Luke still feared what might happen if she intruded into his nightmares, but damned if he could find the words to say that her loyalty, faithfulness and courage didn't mean the fucking world to him.

Combing her dark locks behind her shoulder with his fingers, he leaned close and brushed her lips with his, kissed her eyes and then her ear. "I'm not going anywhere…and neither are you." Locking his arms around her, he tugged her closer and lay his head down with a contented sigh. Damned if it didn't feel good to get the last word for a change.

A full minute passed before she spoke in a whisper. "I knew you'd see things my way." She shifted against him just enough to rub her luscious ass against his sweatpants-clad arousal.

Luke hardened even more, sucking in a breath and holding it as he refrained from grinding himself against her. She settled next to him, apparently ignoring the hard shaft that pressed unyieldingly against her backside. Unwilling to let her go after dreaming of being there beside her for so long, he opted to deal with his discomfort by concentrating on the balance of their journey.

The sun was shining brightly on the other side of the room's heavy curtains. It would be a good day for the drive north. Daniel Mathias's place was fifteen miles from the Canadian border. It was rough and wild country, according to Daniel. Would Luke be able to arrange some alone time with Sally once they reached their destination? Damn, he hoped so. He loved

Jen, but hell, he'd pay someone to watch her for an hour if he had to. Luke listened for the girl's quiet breathing. How long would she sleep? Was she a sound sleeper? Would Sally be quiet or would she scream out his name when he made her come?

Damnation! Quite possibly he was going to need yet another cold shower, and the sumptuous brunette in his arms would have the last word after all.

* * * *

Luke woke with a start, taking a moment to figure out where he was. The sweet-smelling angel in his arms was his first clue, the erect woody that pressed against her enticing behind his second. *What time is it?* He shifted to his back, groping for his watch on the nightstand. *Almost eleven hundred hours.* He'd slept nearly four hours straight with no interruptions. No dreams. God, when was the last time that happened?

Bedding rustled. He turned onto his left side to peer toward the other bed. Jen's cute-as-hell heart-shaped face, surrounded by a curly mop of light brown hair, appeared over her mother's phone. Jen tapped furiously on the device's screen with both thumbs, then threw her bony little fist in the air, obviously claiming victory for this round. When she glanced up and saw him watching, she smiled self-consciously.

"Hey. How long have you been awake?" Luke heard Sally stir behind him.

"A while." Amusement sparkled in Jen's mischievous eyes as she lay the phone on the nightstand. "You were snoring."

"Why, you little storyteller. I don't snore." Luke tried to feign annoyance, but when she began to giggle, he lost it too and chortled right along with her.

She was such a mellow, good-natured kid. She'd totally won him over by the second day they'd spent together. He'd never do anything to hurt her on purpose, but hell, he didn't know anything about kids. Would seeing her mother wake up in the same bed with him scar her young psyche? He should have thought this through before he fell asleep wrapped around Sally.

"Is all that noise necessary?" Sally rolled onto her elbow and stared sleepily at them.

Luke glanced over his shoulder and smiled at her tousled hair and the sparkle in her beautiful eyes. Her attempt at looking stern failed as soon as Jen launched herself from her bed, into Luke's arms.

Luke lifted Jen high and piled her on top of her mother, then tickled them both while laughing evilly and ignoring their demands for him to stop.

In the middle of the melee, Sally's phone vibrated against the top of the nightstand.

Chapter Nine

Sally's heart stuttered as the buzzing filled the room. Her gaze flew to Luke's composed expression, then swept to the phone vibrating closer to the edge of the stand every time it rang.

Luke stretched to snatch the phone just as it reached the edge of the table. He turned it over and studied it for a moment before his steady gaze clashed with hers, silently commanding her to calm down. That wasn't going to happen any time soon.

"Greg Lambert?" A frown creased his forehead.

Her whole body shook by the time the phone went silent, the call transferred to voice mail. Immediately, it started ringing again. Sally helped Jen move off her, then sat up and claimed the phone. *Any normal person would leave a message and hang up. Why did the marshal have to be so damned persistent?*

"What's wrong, Mom? Aren't you going to answer?"

Luke sprang into action, rising, grabbing a shirt and yanking it over his head. "Jen, want to go for a walk? Grab a sweatshirt and we'll go ask the manager where there's a good place to shop."

Jen looked questioningly between Luke and her mom but soon took the hand he offered to help her crawl off the bed.

The phone still vibrated in Sally's hand as Luke leaned toward her and spoke quietly. "Tell him you're not ready to make a decision. Tell him you'll call when you reach a safe place. Hell, tell him whatever you think is best, but don't give up where we are or which direction we're heading. You and I need to talk first. After that, if you choose to go with the marshal…I'll respect your decision." Luke's eyes held sadness as he closed in to brush her lips with his. A grim smile was his only good-bye as he took Jen's hand

and led her out the door. Luke's thoughtfulness in giving her some privacy warmed her heart, and yet she missed his calming presence. Between the ominous threat of hurling her breakfast and the inability to still the rapid beating of her heart, Sally regarded the phone as though it were a king cobra, poised to strike.

Her finger trembled as she pushed the button to connect the call. "Hello?"

"I was beginning to worry about you, Sally. Did you have trouble...or did you simply decide not to take my calls? If that's the case, I'm glad to know you've come to your senses." His was the same calm, undisturbed, nothing-wrong-in-my-world voice she remembered from the few times they'd spoken. She envied him.

Unfortunately, his detachment also ticked her off, and the crisp words that collected on her tongue wouldn't be held in. "I'm happy this is all so easy for you, Greg. Exactly how many lives have you altered, rearranged or phased out? Have you ever once imagined yourself on the other side of the equation? To be the one leaving everything familiar behind? Alone. Uncertain. Always looking in the rearview mirror. Or is the reason you're so good at your job *because* you don't give the people involved another thought after you go home?"

"I do exactly what needs to be done to do my job. When it's all said and done, that's what you want, isn't it? I don't have time to feel sorry for you. My pity won't save your life, Sally."

He was right—but so was she. They each had their jobs to do. Hers was to decide what was best for Jen...and she didn't know how to make that decision.

"Where are you, Sally?" His tone was colder; his words more clipped. Apparently, her accusation had hit a sore spot.

Not her problem. "There's someone else besides my daughter. I can't leave him. Not yet anyway."

"That's not part of the deal. An extra person changes everything. It takes time to create another identity...get authorization...approval for funding. Those details don't happen overnight, and we can't afford to wait. You and your daughter are targets. That makes you the priority for relocation."

"No. You misunderstood me. I'd never ask him to go into hiding with us. I just...I can't disappear from his life. Not now." Maybe not ever. She sighed, Luke's instructions running through her mind. "I'm not ready to make a decision yet. I'm sorry I inconvenienced you."

"Think about what you're doing, Sally. This delay could cost your daughter her life. Are you prepared to accept the responsibility for that?"

His words wrenched a sob from her throat, and she covered her mouth so he wouldn't realize the fear he'd struck in her soul. Luke's quiet words came back to her, and she was finally able to swallow around the lump in her throat. "Marshal Lambert, I need time. I'll contact you when we get to a safe place." Sally disconnected the call before he could say another word, but it seemed certain she'd just stomped all over the good marshal's willingness to help.

She stared at the dark screen of her phone for a moment before she turned it off and tossed it toward the end of the bed. It slid over the edge and hit the floor with a thud. She'd have given anything to curl into a ball, pull the covers over her head and stay there forever, but that wouldn't change a thing. *Don't stop.* She had to keep moving…for Jen. One step at a time. *Get up. Get dressed. Never give up.* Rather than giving in to the tears that ached to be shed, she was going to get mad—damn good and mad—because that was the only emotion strong enough to help her now.

When Luke and Jen returned a few minutes later, Sally was ready to go. She'd even found a belt in Luke's bag that she was able to wrap around her waist loosely and buckle, giving her long shirt the respectability of a dress… albeit a very short dress. As long as she didn't bend over, she'd be fine.

Luke's dark eyes and low whistle telegraphed what he thought of her apparel, but she resisted the almost overwhelming urge to seek comfort in his arms. She was still apprehensive over her conversation with the marshal. Worried that she'd acted impulsively without thinking it through, she couldn't stop the dread that settled like a slab of granite in her belly. She'd seen the curiosity in Luke's expression. He deserved to know the outcome of Lambert's phone call and what her decision had been. She'd expect to be informed if the situation was reversed.

Too bad. She wasn't ready to evaluate whether she'd just made the biggest mistake of her life yet. Already hanging on to her determination by a thread, she'd surely lose her grip on her courage at the first sign of compassion or sympathy or Luke's oh-shit-you-probably-shouldn't-have-done-that frown.

As they were walking out the door, Luke spotted her cell phone where it had landed on the floor at the foot of the bed and went back to scoop it up. "Are you trying to ditch this on purpose?" His steady gaze held hers with a tinge of amusement while she made no attempt to take it from him. "You might need it again. I'll hang on to it for you." He winked as he shoved the device into his pocket and reached behind him to close the door.

Jen waited for them to catch up by the passenger side of the Jeep. Luke raised his hand and pressed a button on the electronic key. The sound of the vehicle unlocking was loud in the quiet parking lot. Jen opened the door and scrambled into the front seat.

Sally paused before stepping off the curb. "I don't think he'll be calling any time soon."

Luke hadn't asked, which heaped guilt on Sally for being silent about her conversation with Lambert. It wasn't fair to keep it from Luke when he was as invested in their flight across the state as she was.

His expression immediately brightened. "Yeah? You're sticking with me, then?" The intensity of his rich brown eyes could be felt clear to her core.

"I told him I'd call when we got somewhere safe, but yeah, I'm sticking with you...if you'll have me."

Luke grinned as he took her arm and turned her toward him. "Damn, woman. I'd have you for breakfast, lunch and dinner if you'd let me." He glanced toward the Jeep's windshield, where Jen peered out. Laughing, he shook his head. "And if there weren't always little eyes watching. How do you ever get any privacy?"

Sally shrugged, his question doing a tap dance on her nerves, even though it was obvious he was teasing. She was supersensitive where her daughter was concerned—she knew it—and she didn't care. "It hasn't been a problem until now." She stepped off the curb, stopping when Luke's hand tightened on her arm.

"It's not a problem now, Sally. That's not what I meant."

She pressed her hand to her forehead, feeling the start of yet another headache, and raked it from front to back through her hair. "I'm sorry. I don't know why I'm so agitated." A small puff of breath punctuated her words. "You don't deserve that."

Luke caught her with his other arm around her waist and dragged her close. "I think I know why, sunshine. You've taken some serious hits in the last few hours." His lips tickled her ear as he whispered, "But it won't always be that way. We'll figure this out. I promise. Let me carry some of your burden. Hell, I'll carry all of it if you'll let me."

Sally bumped her forehead against his solid chest. "Are we being watched?"

"Yep. Her whole face is pressed against the windshield." Luke chuckled, his broad shoulders vibrating with mirth.

She raised her head, caressing his cheek with slow strokes of her fingers. "I guess she'll just have to get used to us kissing and holding hands, then."

Luke's eyes widened and a smile curled his lips. "I like the way you think." He wrapped both arms around her, pulling her so tightly against him, she could feel the rapid beat of his heart.

Their lips met and heat worked its way slowly from her head to the pit of her stomach. Desire hit her hard, and she had to lean against him to keep from collapsing. When he broke the kiss, she clung desperately to him, sure her legs would give out if they were forced to support her. Luke wore a contented look as he nibbled at the corners of her mouth and kissed her eyes and nose.

"You okay?"

She nodded, then laughed at herself as she tried to pull away and stand on her own.

He held her close for a moment longer. "Are we good, sunshine?"

Just then, another guest of the motel exited his room three doors down and strode toward them. As he approached, a scowl twisted his face. "Jeez, get a room why don't you!"

Sally met Luke's gaze, which mirrored the same humor she was struggling to contain. Finally, she couldn't hold it any longer, and they both burst out laughing. She barely heard the man continue his diatribe as he walked away. Glancing toward the windshield, she caught Jen smiling from ear to ear. When Sally cocked her head curiously, Jen raised her hand, thumb pointed up.

Sally turned back to Luke. "We are *so* good."

"You've just made me a happy man. Come on. Let's go shopping." Luke opened her door and helped her with the sizable step up into the vehicle, made more difficult by the hem of his shirt riding up her thighs. Jen used the bucket seat backs as leverage to swing into the back and plopped on the fabric-covered bench seat. With amusement crinkling the skin near his eyes, Luke tossed his duffel in the back across from Jen and slid behind the wheel.

Jen scooted forward again, hooking her arms around the corner of each front seat. "You guys were kissing." Her singsong voice made Sally's cheeks burn with embarrassment while Luke merely laughed.

He leaned sideways and hooked an arm over Jen's shoulder. "Are you okay with that? Would it be all right with you if I love both you and your mom?"

Did Luke Harding just say he *loved* her? Sally's gaze darted to his as her heart rate ratcheted up. He winked and turned his attention back to Jen.

"Will you stay with us in Huntington?" Jen's eyes were wide with excitement.

Sally waited, barely breathing, to hear his answer.

Luke's smile covered both of them. "If it's A-OK with your mother, I plan to be wherever the two of you are." He started the Jeep and drove from the parking lot.

"But Mom said you wanted to go home to your family."

"Well, I'll probably visit them once in a while, but I'd hope that you ladies would accompany me. Like a vacation. Would you like that?" He made a left turn before glancing toward Jen. His expression full of hope and happiness, he caught Sally's eye for a second.

She clenched her teeth to stop the tremor that fluttered through her body. A voice in her head argued logically that this was happening too fast, but Sally did her best to block it out. She'd loved Luke for a year. Giving up on her dream of a life with him had been the hardest thing she'd ever done. They'd all suffered, and now they had a chance of being a family. God, she wanted that.

"That sounds like fun, Luke. Doesn't it, Jen?" Sally could see that something was troubling her daughter and hoped getting involved in the conversation would convince her not all changes were bad.

"Sure. I guess." Jen appeared to have lost interest and started to turn toward her seat in the back.

"Hold it, Jen. What's bothering you? Let's get it out in the open so we can fix whatever it is." Luke pulled into the parking lot of a mall and quickly found a place to park.

Sally had seen Jen's expression many times—like when she knew she would have to stand in front of her class and give a book report, or when the teacher sent a note home saying Jen had been in a fight that day, even though it was to help another student who was being bullied. Sometimes Jen simply clammed up. Conversation over. Luke didn't know the routine, however. He took her hand and waited patiently, his quiet expectancy filling the vehicle.

"Will you…like…will you be my dad?" It was obvious she'd tried but failed to keep her chin from trembling.

Sally's heart broke with the weight of her daughter's question. "Oh, honey, that's not something—"

Luke's gaze shifted to her for a split second, accompanied by a nearly indiscernible shake of his head before his focus returned to Jen. "Would you like that?"

"Yeah." Her reply was half breath, half nervous giggle.

"Yeah? Me too…so, if your mom says it's okay, I'm going to see if we can't make that happen. I won't lie to you, though. It's going to take some time. There are a few things we have to do first. We need to find a place to live while we wait to see if your landlord will fix your old house up. Then—well, I think your mom and I have to be married before I can legally adopt you. What do you think about that?" Luke lowered his voice as though Jen were the only one to hear him, even though Sally sat less than a foot away.

Jen bounced up and down on her toes. "Really? You're going to get married?" Her excited gaze jumped back and forth between Luke and Sally.

"Hold on. Let's not get ahead of ourselves." He leaned close and lowered his voice again. "I haven't exactly asked her yet." As Jen glanced toward her mother, Luke grinned smugly.

Sally snorted but remained silent, her eyes narrowed in mock irritation. She couldn't be angry with him. Watching him confess his desire to be a dad to her daughter was the most endearing thing she'd ever observed, outside of a Hallmark Movie.

"Well, why not?" Jen was clearly perplexed.

A sparkle in his eyes gave away his enjoyment. "Can you keep a secret?" Jen nodded and Luke scrunched his face into a worried frown.

"I'm not at all sure she'll say yes." He shrugged and emitted a heavy sigh, earning a giggle from Jen. "So, will you help me win her over?"

"Sure. What are we going to do?"

Sally choked on a snicker at the secretive conversation going on within inches of her. Just one more indication of how messed up her life was. Was she living in some kind of alternate universe? Wasn't *she* supposed to find out first that the hero loved her and wanted to marry her? He was right about one thing: She was nowhere close to saying yes. It wasn't even twenty-four hours since Luke had decided to grace her life again. Forget for a moment she'd loved this man a year ago. Put aside the fact she went weak in the knees every time he got close enough to breathe the same air she did. Proposals were serious business—and marriage…was forever.

Luke and Jen laughed conspiratorially, and Sally wondered if she should have been paying attention. Oh well. Let them plan. She hadn't completely wrapped her head around his declaration of love yet, but knowing how much he cared about her daughter made her heart go all soft and gooey. Though she might be unsure of many things, without a doubt Luke would protect Jen with his life.

Signaling the end of the conversation, Luke swung his door open. "Ready? Oh, one more thing." He looked directly at Sally this time. "So we don't draw attention to ourselves inside by arguing, let's get this settled right now. Pick out everything you need for two or three days. There'll be a washer and dryer at my friend's place." He stopped abruptly.

"Why would we argue about that?" Sally waited for the rest of his speech.

"We wouldn't. After you've got what you want, give it to me." Luke tensed, apparently in anticipation of her argument, and suddenly she understood what he was trying to say.

She wagged her head from side to side. "You're not paying for our things, Luke. I have a credit card because you were kind enough to rescue my wallet. I've got it covered." His offer was generous, but being in debt to someone was no way to maintain a relationship. She pulled the handle and opened her door.

Luke's hand landed on her knee, and his frown was stern as his intent gaze pinned her to the seat. "This isn't about my possessive nature, although I admit I have one, and it's not about your pride. If this Brennan guy happens to have connections, he may be able to trace your credit card activity. And for damn sure Lambert can. If you think it's necessary, you can pay me back later any way you'd like, but for right now, I pay the bills." He paused and the hint of a smile appeared. "Now, come on. This'll be fun." He stepped out, leaving Sally no one to hear her rebuttal.

Okay. He's probably right. And he did say I can pay him back...any way I want. Sally felt only a little guilty for the erotic ideas that popped into her head. Pushing the door open, she slid down, carefully holding the hem of her shirt, and turned to catch Jen as she jumped off the seat.

Though Sally had been hoping for a Target or a Walmart, the mall held neither. It did, however, have everything they needed, as long as they were willing to pay the price. She and Jen had absolutely nothing except the clothes they'd been sleeping in when the fire broke out, so she was dismayed by the staggering amount of *stuff* they needed. Besides pants, shirts, underwear, a pair of shorts for Jen, and a bra for her, jackets, shampoo, a hairbrush, a new charger for her cell phone—everything right down to feminine hygiene products and toothbrushes. When they'd tried on their finds, at Luke's insistence, replacing his oversized garments with jeans and long-sleeved pullovers, and piled their selections on the counter in front of an excited salesclerk, he made her go back for lotion and cologne.

"Women like lotion," he'd said, his easy smile assuaging her guilt somewhat. After a few minutes, they'd both returned to the counter at the same time. Glancing toward Jen, where she was peering into the jewelry case, Luke tossed down a couple of shirts, a pair of jeans and an extra-large package of condoms. Sally was sure her face turned candy-apple red even while trying to contain her laughter at his snarky grin.

She was about to declare they were finished when he grabbed her hand and pulled her back to the apparel aisles, calling to her daughter over his shoulder. "Jen, come help us pick out something for your mom to wear out on a date."

Sally tried to extricate her hand, overly conscious of the cost of the articles already littering the counter. Luke was unrelenting, however, tugging her along until they reached a rack of skirts and dresses. He started sliding the hangers along the rack, looking at each new selection as it was revealed.

Sally shook her head and stepped between him and the row of apparel. "I'll take it from here, Harding."

He chuckled. "Whatever you say, sunshine." A wink made his agreement seem suggestive—or was that just her overactive imagination? "Why don't you try something on, and meanwhile, I'll take Jen to the arcade next door. I'll leave you my card and tell the clerk you're authorized to use it, although something tells me she's looking forward to a big commission and wouldn't do anything to kill this sale." Luke dug his credit card from his wallet and handed it to Sally. "Meet us at the arcade when you're done. We'll come back and get the bags later."

After Jen and Luke left, Sally found a skirt she liked and wandered the store searching for an appropriate top. He was spoiling her. What's more, he seemed to be enjoying himself. Far be it from her not to let him. It might take her forever to repay him, but maybe there was merit to that idea. Only time would tell.

Sally picked two silk blouses, draped them over her arm, and followed the short hallway toward the back until she came to the dressing rooms. She closed the door behind her and hung the articles carefully on pegs against the wall before she started to undo her belt.

A sudden staccato knock startled her. "Occupied," she said as she reached toward the button to lock the door. Not quickly enough, however. The door flew inward. Sally flung herself back to keep from being hit by the approaching plywood on hinges. She lost her balance and slammed into the wall behind her, headfirst with mind-numbing force. Dazed, her legs gave out, and she slid to the floor with a thump.

Sally shook her head and tried to focus on the looming figure who appeared in the opening where the door had been, but her vision blurred with the stabbing pain behind her eyes. It was obviously not Luke, so that left few possibilities in her mind. Only one man she knew of was looking for her. Only one trying to kill her. How in the hell had he found her?

She forced her gaze upward to where the huge apparition's face should have been. "Who are you and why are you here?" Damn. She couldn't keep her voice from shaking. A couple more blinks and her fuzzy vision began to clear.

"Sally, darlin', I'm here to thank you for the scintillating night you so graciously arranged for me."

She recognized that voice. Nothing about its scornful tone sounded grateful in the least. Squeezing her temples, she dragged her gaze back to his face, and this time she saw enough.

It was ex-boss and lousy date, Emmett Purnell.

Chapter Ten

Sally leaned her head gingerly against the wall and squeezed her eyes closed. With her thoughts scattered in a dozen directions and her head throbbing with every beat of her runaway heart, she couldn't come up with one good scenario for Emmett forcing his way into her dressing room. *Like there could be a good reason.*

The man had slapped her around last night because she refused to become his whore. She sported black and blue bruises on her right jaw and cheekbone as proof he wasn't a nice man. He'd obviously been hauled into the sheriff's office in Huntington and grilled about the explosion that destroyed her house. That had to be what he meant by thanking her for the evening she'd arranged. This time his sarcasm wasn't lost on her.

He intended to thank her, all right, no doubt with bodily harm. If he'd gone to all the trouble of tracking her down hundreds of miles away from home, he was obviously determined to have his pound of flesh. She struggled to swallow around the lump in her throat. Was he going to kill her?

Sally peeped through nearly closed eyelids when Emmett stepped farther into the tiny room and shoved the door closed.

"I don't appreciate being accused of arson, unlawful use of explosives and attempted murder by some Podunk sheriff," he growled, pacing in a tight circle, clearly agitated.

As unobtrusively as possible, she peered under the partial walls that separated her cubicle from the other dressing rooms. No other feet in sight. No sounds except muffled voices from the front of the store. It wouldn't do any good to scream. The young salesclerk would be more hindrance than help. Luke would be next door by now. Even if he was out front, attracting his attention would probably also bring Jen, and Sally would change her mind and gladly become Emmett Purnell's sex slave rather than endanger her little girl.

Though her head was spinning, she got the impression he was waiting for her to say something. What did he expect? An apology? An excuse? The pounding inside her skull precluded any formal speech. Her gaze drifted back to the gap between the floor and the cubicle wall. It had to be at least twelve inches. She could fit through—though probably not gracefully.

Emmett pulled a short stool from the corner, positioned it in front of the door and dropped onto it, raking one hand across the back of his neck and then over his face. Unexpectedly, he sighed and fixed his gaze on her again.

Blinking her blurry vision into focus, Sally got her first good look at his face and stared in astonishment. "What happened to you?" Yellowish purple bruises and cuts covered him from chin to forehead. His lips were torn in at least three places. Knotted bruises dotted his jaw. On closer inspection, she noticed he held his left arm tight to his side, and he bent slightly at the waist, the other arm cradling his ribs. The man had clearly been beaten unmercifully, and she had a terrible feeling in the pit of her stomach it had something to do with her.

"What happened?" she repeated, more forcefully this time.

Of all things…Emmett laughed, sounding almost embarrassed. "As pissed off as I was at you, that's nothing compared to the whoop-ass I'm gonna give the old geezer who ambushed me outside the sheriff's office this morning."

Wait a minute. *Was* pissed off? Did that mean he was over being upset with her?

Sally was grasping at straws. "You were mugged?" She couldn't help but wince at the ugly bruises and welts distorting his face.

"Not exactly. This was personal. The old man had a couple of thugs with him so he didn't have to get his hands dirty." Emmett's swollen lips gave him a lisp, but his anger and scorn came through loud and clear.

Sally shifted nervously, trying to gauge whether she could roll out of her cubicle into the next, jump to her feet and escape before Emmett moved his stool from in front of the door, caught up to her and choked her to death in a fit of rage. The odds weren't in her favor. Glancing in his direction, she saw that he was watching her intently…expectantly.

"Why are you here? You don't think I had anything to do with the attack, do you?" She recoiled at the idea.

"I came to find you, but damned if I know why I bothered." Emmett stared accusingly, then huffed a breath as though he couldn't believe he was sitting across from her in a tiny women's dressing room.

Join the club, buddy.

His gaze locked on hers. "The man that did this was looking for you, darlin'. I guess he thought I'd know where you were. Apparently, he doesn't know about your boyfriend with the dog tags…yet, but you might want to give—Harding, is it?—a heads-up."

Oh God. Clive Brennan wouldn't think twice about doing that kind of damage to another human being if he thought it would gain him the answers he wanted. Instinctively, she shuttered her expression and feigned ignorance. "Looking for me? Who was he?"

Emmett slammed his knuckles against the wall, and Sally jumped. "Don't test my patience, woman. I took this beating because the old man didn't believe me when I told him I knew nothing about a fire or where you'd disappeared to, but he made it crystal clear it was very important he find you. Call me suspicious, but I didn't get a good vibe for why he wanted you." He leaned forward, bracing his elbows on his knees. "I might have had too much to drink last night and I might have acted like a jerk. I'm not apologizing, mind you. It is what it is, but if he's looking for you… well, I decided I'd find you first."

Surprise cracked the walls she'd erected around herself. "You came to warn me?"

"Don't look so shocked. I have my moments. Are you going to tell me who the son of a bitch is?"

A ghost of a smile threatened, and Sally ducked her head until she wiped it away. Under the cubicle door, she spotted a pair of military boots two or three feet away. Motionless and silent, Luke waited, no doubt listening to every word. She should have known. Relief surged through her, and she turned her gaze back to Emmett so he wouldn't become curious about why she was staring.

"What did he look like?"

"Late sixties, gray hair, glasses, five-ten or so, thin, wore a dark trench coat. The two ballbusters he had with him were hard-core. Spoke with heavy accents. Russian, I think."

Sally nodded once. There didn't seem to be any reason to lie. This would be the second time in a matter of hours she'd spoken aloud the truth she'd kept buried for over ten years, and the words still came hard. "His name is Clive Brennan. It's possible he's a spy—I'm not sure. What I know is, he murdered a family in Mississippi years ago, and I testified against him. He went to prison and the feds put me in my own glass cage—witness protection. Clive was released three months ago. I'd hoped he would get on with his life and forget about me." She hadn't been totally honest with Luke when she told him, and she wasn't about to confide her most shameful secret to Emmett—that Clive was her father and not likely to ever forget her betrayal.

Emmett grunted. "Apparently, he still wants something from you—damn bad. Like I said…it seems personal. My advice is to leave the state. Get as far away as you can. Go somewhere he'd never think to look for you. Maybe he'll give up."

Sally's gaze flicked over his mutilated face. "I'm sorry you got caught up in this, Emmett. Sorry you had to come all this way. How did you find us anyway?"

"Once I found out your friend Luke was Garrett Harding's brother and that Garrett's Jeep wasn't anywhere around Cougar Ridge, I contacted a few friends of mine and put out the word. Didn't take them long to spot the vehicle, and I flew one of the company helos up. Then I just waited for Harding to leave you alone. I was beginning to think he'd never let loose of you."

"It won't happen again." Luke's sudden addition to the conversation from outside the dressing room startled Sally, even though she'd known he was close by.

The anger seemed to have left Emmett's face as they'd talked, but now that Luke stood outside the door, Sally studied Emmett carefully for any sign of the short fuse she'd come to know.

"Well, Harding, I was wondering how long you'd leave us unattended." Emmett seemed to enjoy trying to rile him.

Luke's boots moved closer to the door, and he tapped on the wall with something hard. "You want to step out here, or should I come in?"

"Put your gun away, Harding. I'm not armed." Emmett unfolded his tall frame, shoved the stool out of the way and offered his hand to Sally.

She hesitated before shrugging and allowing him to help her up. She still didn't trust him completely—probably never would—but she could believe he was single-minded enough to chase her down and warn her if he thought doing so would somehow exact revenge from the man responsible for beating the tar out of him. Mostly, though, if Emmett's intention had been to harm her, he'd had ample opportunity. He moved aside, and she pulled the door open and stepped out.

Luke caught her hand and tugged her to the side, bringing his firearm to bear on Emmett. "Are you all right, babe?" Luke's tortured eyes swept over her, worry, impatience and relief cascading across his face.

"I'm fine, mostly." She rubbed the tender spot on the back of her head. "Not his fault," she quickly added when Luke scowled. "Just my own clumsiness."

Luke squeezed her hand and then focused on Emmett. "Turn around and put your hands against the wall."

Emmett smiled coldly. "I told you I wasn't armed."

"Humor me."

Emmett stared at Luke as the seconds stretched, then suddenly laughed. "I knew I liked you, Harding. You remind me of me." He turned, leaned his hands against the wall and spread his legs.

"High praise indeed." Luke tucked his weapon in his belt and quickly searched the man.

"Luke, where's Jen?" Sally's voice was a strained whisper, unable to believe it'd taken her so long to miss her daughter's presence.

"Don't worry. She's out front with Maryanne, the salesclerk. I promised to double her commission if she kept Jen occupied for a few minutes."

Emmett swung around and glanced from Luke to Sally. "Satisfied?"

"More like surprised. You don't strike me as the type who travels without a bodyguard or a weapon." Luke pushed Sally toward the front of the store. "Go find Jen. I want a word with your friend here."

Emmett's grin was cocky. "This should be good."

Sally paused, looking between the two belligerent men. "Luke, you heard why he came, right? To warn us?"

Luke nodded, without taking his eyes off Emmett. "That's why he's still alive."

A gruff chuckle rumbled from Emmett's throat. "Darlin', go get your kid. We knights have some jousting to do."

Sally snorted scornfully. *Have at it, then.* She was too emotionally exhausted to care at the moment. Men with their wannabe balls of steel and their delicate egos—it would serve them right if their words dissolved into a free-for-all. As long as she...or Jen...didn't have to watch. Leaving the skirt and blouses hanging in the dressing room, she turned abruptly and marched toward the front of the store.

* * * *

That was the third time in the last twenty minutes Sally had glanced into the back of the Jeep, obviously checking on Jen. Luke couldn't decipher whether she was worried about Jen or just life in general. Every time he looked toward the little girl in the rearview mirror, she was intent on the new book Sally had bought for her after they'd left the department store.

He caught Sally's hand as she faced the front again. "Penny for your thoughts."

A genuine smile brightened her features for a couple of seconds before it faded. "Did you believe Emmett? You don't think he'll go back and tell Clive Brennan where we are, do you? Is that what you talked about?" Sally lowered her voice and leaned closer.

Luke brought her hand to his lips for a lingering kiss. He could almost feel her tension. "I think Emmett will do whatever it takes to get payback from Brennan. It was big of him to warn you, because he had no way of knowing you already suspected Brennan. Don't get me wrong—Emmett isn't a man I'd trust to watch my back. But in this case, I can't see him doing anything to help the man that beat the sh…crap out of him. And… let's not forget, he's a man with resources. Sometimes it makes sense to give the benefit of the doubt to a person like that…if you can stomach it." He covered her hand with his. "*That's* what we talked about."

Sally pulled away and unconsciously massaged the back of her head for a moment.

"How's your headache?"

She dropped her hands into her lap. "Better. Thanks. You haven't told me very much about this place we're going."

Luke slipped his phone from his pocket. "Hold that thought. I need to give Daniel a call." He found his friend's number in his contacts and pushed to dial, then hit the button to put the conversation on speaker. Ian's brother answered after three rings, but the connection was lousy. "Hey. It's Luke."

"Well…our long lost…a week ago." Daniel's side of the conversation was breaking up badly, but it didn't take a genius to figure out what he'd said. It was a totally legitimate gripe.

"I'm sorry, Daniel. I know I said I'd be there last week." Luke paused. "I got a little lost, I guess, but I found what I was looking for. In fact, I'm bringing a couple of friends with me, and we'll be there in about twenty minutes…if that's all right." How much of the conversation was Daniel getting on his end?

"No problem…ass up here. Couple things…tell you…cell phone…sucks. No surprise…don't go all apeshit…some…" The call abruptly went dead. Luke tried calling him back twice but got no answer. This wasn't the first time he'd phoned Daniel, so he was well aware the cell phone service was abysmal. But *don't go apeshit*? What the hell did that mean? He scowled as he dropped the device in the cup holder.

"Is he okay with Jen and me coming?" Concern wrinkled Sally's forehead.

"Oh yeah. No worries there." Luke smiled and locked away his apprehension. He wasn't concerned that Sally and Jen wouldn't be welcome, but Daniel had something going on he seemed to think would rile Luke. What that could be, he had no idea, and there was no sense worrying until he *did* know.

Sally, already agitated, would clearly be better off without him adding to her unease, so he shoved the issue to the back of his mind. "You asked about the place. I've never actually been there. Remember when I told you about Ian Mathias dying in Afghanistan, and his brother, Daniel, coming to see me in the hospital?" Luke flinched, first, because the memory of Ian's death still horrified him as though it'd happened only yesterday, and second, because he wasn't sure what effect the mention of visitors who'd been allowed in his room would have on Sally.

"Of course. He invited you to his home...and you were supposed to be there a week ago? He's probably been worried." If the subject of visitation upset Sally, she didn't let on.

"I know. I should have called way before now." Luke had avoided the entire topic of Sally when conversing with Daniel. Somehow, the matter of losing the woman he loved, though important to him, had seemed trite in comparison to a man who'd recently lost his little brother in the most gruesome way imaginable. "He's married with a daughter—five years old, I think. They own some rustic hunting cabins on the Kootenai River near Bonners Ferry. And by rustic, I mean...I hope you don't hate it there."

Sally arched an eyebrow. "You've seen my house, right? Before, that is. Now it's just a pile of charcoal. My point is, I'm not used to fancy. I think I can deal with rustic for a few days."

The sparkle in her eyes mesmerized Luke. He would have leaned over for a kiss if the sign heralding the turnoff for Kootenai River Cabins hadn't appeared up ahead with an arrow pointing left onto a narrow road.

He slowed to make the turn. "Ten more miles."

The first fifty feet of roadway was chip sealed and fairly smooth. After they passed the mailbox, adorned with the name "Mathias," all traces of *smooth* vanished. The track they followed was filled with rocks, potholes and mud. Luke crept along, conscious it was his brother's Jeep he drove, and still the occupants were bounced and jostled at every turn.

"I don't think your friend wants very much company." Sally held fast to the dash with one hand and the edge of her seat with the other.

Luke glanced in the rearview mirror to make sure Jen was buckled in securely. "I don't think that's it. He's one of the friendliest guys you'd ever want to meet. He and Ian bought this place together. Daniel ran the business while Ian went off to do his patriotic duty. Ian was the only family Daniel had, besides his wife and kid. He was a mess the first time I saw him—worse than me." Luke smiled at the memory of the man, who looked so much like his friend, Ian, walking into his hospital room. Luke had been on a rampage, alienating all the nurses because he didn't want anyone bathing him or helping him piss in a bottle. There were just some things a man couldn't abide.

"One day, Daniel walked in my room, pushed a chair close to the bed and sat down. He looked just like Ian, and I didn't have to ask why he was there. He had this haunted expression, and his eyes were red and swollen. Kind of gave him a crazy look. I figured I didn't look much better. He sat there for a while, just staring, and finally, he said, 'Is Ian really dead?'" Daniel's first words had hit Luke so hard he would have fled the room if he'd been able to move his legs.

"Oh, Luke. That must have been so hard." Sally's gaze burned into the side of his face, but he didn't turn.

He'd lose it if he saw the sympathy he heard in her voice. "I didn't want to tell him how his brother died at the hands of those animals, but he insisted. He wanted to know every detail. By the time I was done, we were both bawling our eyes out, but knowing what a hero Ian had been seemed to help him accept his death." For his part, the mere act of relating the details to another human being had probably saved Luke's sanity.

"Daniel came back the next day when three of my buddies were there. SEALs I'd served with."

"Yeah, I saw them." Sally's voice sounded strained, but there was still concern in her expression when he glanced over.

He reached for her hand anyway. "I'm so sorry, babe."

"You've already apologized. I'm just giving you a hard time. Too soon?" She clamped her teeth down on her bottom lip, obviously trying to keep the amusement sparkling in her eyes from traveling to her full, beautifully shaped mouth.

"No. You can give me as much crap as you want…as long as you don't change your mind about us." Luke released her hand so he could put both of his back on the steering wheel.

"That won't happen, Luke. Tell me about your three friends."

Luke couldn't help laughing. "They're a rowdy bunch. I thought they were joking when they told me they weren't signing on the line again. They were the best at what they did, and I couldn't imagine them wanting to punch a clock somewhere. What Ian and I went through in that prison was brutal, but apparently watching from the sidelines was no cakewalk either."

"No, it wasn't." Sally's eyes shimmered. "I imagine it was doubly hard for men used to taking matters into their own hands to stand idly by for months, knowing what you were going through, knowing the likely outcome and not being able to do a damn thing."

"Mom, language." Jen's admonishment came from behind them without her even looking up from her book.

Sally dropped her head. "Sorry, sweetheart," she said, her muffled laughter following.

Luke didn't laugh. He'd been selfishly blind all this time. Never dwelling on what his captivity meant to her, or his family or his friends and fellow SEALs. Even after his buddies had told him they'd had enough of the Navy…and why…he hadn't made the connection. She'd been waiting at home with no news, no hope and no end in sight. Then, as the fucking cherry on top of the sundae, he'd surprised everyone by coming home alive…and refused to see her. It took a special kind of jackass to be so self-absorbed. Yet she'd forgiven him.

He let the Jeep roll to a stop as he stared at her bowed head. She looked up and met his gaze questioningly as he put the vehicle in Park. Shame gripped his chest until he had to fight for his next breath, and he tore his gaze from hers. All those months—he'd had all the time in the world for introspection. Not once had he put himself in her place. Not one fucking thought about whether she cried herself to sleep at night, worrying about him—or maybe she'd been afraid to close her eyes in sleep…just like he'd been. *Shit!* Self-loathing rose and choked him.

Somehow, he got the door open and stepped out onto the muddy roadbed. With no destination in mind, he started walking, grateful for the air that filled his lungs. A few more deep breaths and he could almost think straight. He recognized the panic attack for what it was, courtesy of the thousand or so that had come before. What he didn't know was…why now?

Luke turned and marched back toward the Jeep. Sally watched him from the passenger seat, her expression apprehensive and wary. He stopped. That was it. He'd lost her once because he didn't consider her reactions… at all. Now, he was doing it again—shutting her out when he should be telling her what was going on in his head. He changed directions, skirting the front of the Jeep until he stood by her window. Damned if he would lose her again.

Sally opened her door, her eyes still holding a certain caution.

Luke closed the gap, lifting her off the seat and into his arms. Her heart was beating against his chest—in fear? Not acceptable.

"Jen, read your book for a minute, okay?" He barely waited to hear her grunt before he closed the door. Taking a step away from the Jeep, he set Sally on her feet and held her at arm's length.

"Was it something I said?" Her voice was low, sensuous and went straight to his heart.

"No, sunshine." He smiled and smoothed the hair behind her ears. "I just realized how lucky I am to have you in my life—how close I came to never being able to do this again." He leaned closer and found her mouth with his.

A buzz of electricity vibrated between them wherever his lips or tongue touched her, and he couldn't get enough. Sally fisted her hands in his T-shirt, her forearms braced against his chest, and gave back as good as she got. It was a couple of minutes before Luke remembered Jen. He broke the kiss, glanced over his shoulder, expecting to see her nose plastered against the glass, and breathed a sigh of relief when she was nowhere to be seen.

When he turned back to Sally, she was already laughing, and he chuckled with her. "You'll have to educate me on the nuances of living with a daughter."

Her mouth curved in the sexiest smile. "I'm pretty sure you already know as much as I do."

"Then we'll learn together."

Her smile faded. "Luke, let's not make promises—"

"This is the perfect time for promises, sunshine. I can't lose you again. I love you. *Marry me.* Let me spend the rest of my life cherishing you. That's my promise to you, Sally."

The regret in her eyes told him he'd screwed up big-time. He'd known better than to allow his emotions free rein, but he'd gotten caught up in his epiphany and the force of his feelings for her. He hadn't meant to push her. Now, his declaration was out there, and the I'd-rather-be-somewhere-else look on her face gave him her answer.

Time for damage control. He pulled her against him, sliding his arms around her waist. "Shh. Don't answer that."

Gently, he kissed first one corner of her mouth and then the other. Sadness stole over him, but he deliberately shook it off. Sally wasn't ready. She had a shitload of crap going on in her life and more important things to worry about than him. He could be patient.

He forced a grin as he ran his thumb over her lower lip. "Maybe I'll ask you again someday."

She held his gaze for a long moment before she blinked, and her sliver of a smile resembled a smirk. "Jen and I are homeless. An angry man is trying to kill me. I might be on the run for the rest of my life. This isn't the right time to make commitments. Hanging around me could get you killed. Even if Clive doesn't find me this time, what about the next time he gets close? What if you're sorry you got trapped in a relationship you never really wanted? I'm not going to let you do that." Satisfaction flashed in her eyes.

Luke frowned. *Shit!* He'd heard those words before. Hell, he'd spoken them...to her. Just as he'd made the decision that a disabled man wasn't good enough for her, she was throwing his logic back in his face. Deciding it was too dangerous for him to be around her—suggesting he'd be sorry someday and want out. It was the exact thing he'd done to her...and, damn it, she'd made her point.

She flashed him an impish grin.

Luke rubbed a hand across the back of his neck and laughed sheepishly. "Okay. I deserved that, but if you think you're getting rid of me, it's not happening. You're stuck with me, at least until this situation is resolved. I told you I wouldn't let anyone hurt you or Jen, and I'm a man of my word. Can we agree on that much?" Even if she couldn't, there was no way in hell he'd walk away.

Sally's playful laugh put him at ease again, loosening the knot in his belly. "I'm really glad you're here, Luke." She studied him, a flirtatious curve in her smile. Raising on her toes, she leaned into him until her breath warmed his ear. "After all, you've got all those condoms..." Her soft lips fluttered against his neck.

All the blood left his head for parts south, and a groan rumbled from deep in his chest. "Holy hell, woman, that's *so* not fair." He snagged her hand and tugged her toward the Jeep. "Let's go. Maybe Daniel has a two-bedroom cabin...with locks on the doors."

The look she flashed him was all innocence as he held the door for her.

The next few miles, silence reined in the Jeep's interior, interspersed with full-body perusals and sexy smiles from the brunette in the seat beside him. He'd always thought her fairly reserved sexually, but what she was doing to him now with only her eyes had to be intentional. The normal blue of her irises had darkened to sapphire, partially hooded by long lashes that softly brushed her skin with each flutter of her eyelids. Her sultry glances were driving him crazy. He shifted slightly, easing the denim fabric over his groin.

Luke welcomed the intrusion of Jen into his heated thoughts when she dropped her book, reached forward and tapped his elbow. "Are we almost there?"

"Just a couple more miles. Are you getting hungry?" Luke studied her in the mirror.

"No. Just tired of this bumpy road." She sighed.

"I hear that. When we get there, we'll have a look around, get settled in our cabin and meet our hosts. Then we can do whatever you'd like. How's that sound?" Luke felt Sally's curious gaze, but he only smiled.

"We'll be close to a river, sweetie. Maybe we can go fishing." Sally glanced over her shoulder.

Jen brightened. "From a boat?"

"Just so happens Daniel rents boats. We'll see what we can arrange," Luke said.

They crested a rise, and he braked. Below them, the road flattened out and became a well-groomed, two-lane gravel road. A green valley filled with wildflowers spread on both sides of a meandering river, and snow-capped mountains stood sentinel on three sides. A small cluster of brown cabins hugged the foot of the mountain about twelve hundred yards north of their current position. Considering they were the only cabins he could see and the gravel road ended in their midst, that had to be their destination.

Two minutes later, Luke parked beside an old white Suburban in front of the largest cabin and cut the engine. An equally old Ford pickup and a seventies' model Chevy Super Sport waited there as well. Daniel appeared, banging through the screen door, and jumped off the top step, followed more sedately by a blond-haired woman and a towheaded little girl. Luke turned to Sally and nodded his head toward his friend, including Jen in his gaze. "Come on, ladies. I want Daniel to meet you."

Luke exited the vehicle and strode toward Daniel. All six feet of his rugged build exuded the friendly welcome Luke had expected. When they reached each other, Luke grasped the extended hand, but Daniel pulled him in for a bear hug anyway.

"It's about time you showed up, Luke. Did you have some trouble?" Daniel's brow creased in concern.

"Some, but we can talk about that later. I want you to meet some very important people." Luke held his gaze for a moment.

Daniel nodded and a lazy grin appeared. "So that's how it is, huh?"

"Now, Daniel, don't you embarrass that girl." The woman who had followed Daniel from the cabin hooked elbows with him and reached to shake Luke's hand. "We're so glad you're here, Luke. I'm Ellen, Daniel's better half."

"True, that." Daniel nodded vigorously.

Luke enjoyed her teasing banter. "Nice to meet you, Ellen. I hope it's okay. I brought some friends."

Sally approached, her arm around Jen's shoulders.

"We love having company. The more the merrier, I always say. Right, Daniel?"

"That's the way of it around here." He patted his wife's arm.

Jen quietly slipped her hand into Luke's and her uncertainty came through loud and clear. "Daniel, Ellen, I'd like you to meet Sally Duncan and her daughter, Jen."

It always amazed Luke how quickly women made friends. Within sixty seconds, they were deep in conversation, headed toward the main cabin for a cup of tea. Of course, Sally had been reluctant to leave Jen, but he'd latched onto her hand and smiled his assurance, hoping Sally would get the message he could handle one nine-year-old girl. An instant later, the small blond-haired child, the spitting image of Daniel, stepped closer and fastened one spindly arm around her father's leg. He introduced Luke and Jen to five-year-old Bridgett, whose first words were, "Do you want to see my pony?" After a brief reminder from Daniel about safety, they ran off toward the corrals, visible behind the cabins.

Abruptly, a shrill whistle shattered the serenity of the valley, and everyone, including Sally and Ellen, stopped to stare in the direction of the river as a loud shout reached them. "Hey! Guys! He's here."

Luke recognized the voice at the exact moment he noticed the terror in Sally's eyes. Quickly, he jogged across the grass to her side, vaguely aware of Daniel following him.

"Where's Jen?" Panic strained her voice.

"She's okay. Listen to me." He placed both hands on her shoulders and turned her to face him. "It's *not* Brennan. Remember my friends—the ones you saw at the hospital? The one doing the yelling is Travis. I assume the *guys* he's referring to are MacGyver and Coop." He glanced sideways at Daniel, pacing nearby. "And this must be what you didn't want me to go apeshit over?"

Daniel nodded.

"Shit, man. You gotta do something about your cell service." Luke swallowed the groan building up within him. It wasn't that he minded his friends showing up at the same time he did, but fuck, given what Sally had been through, it would have been nice to have a little advance notice.

Daniel spoke up as though he'd read Luke's thoughts. "I tried to warn you."

Luke sighed. Yes, he had. Too bad it hadn't worked. Seeing his friends approaching from the corner of the cabin, he turned back to Sally. "Ready to meet them?"

She stood a little straighter, and a smile tugged at the corner of her mouth. Luke took that as a good sign. "They're a little rough around the edges, but they're good people. You'll like them—just don't believe everything you hear."

Chapter Eleven

Sally's gaze darted to the three tall, wide-shouldered men quickly approaching. Each had big biceps and broad chests, as though they spent their free time working out. Dressed similarly in faded, worn jeans and T-shirts stretched to fit, a seven- or eight-inch knife, matching the one Luke carried, hung off each man's hip. She could easily have mistaken them for a team of mercenaries on the set of some movie…except for their easy smiles, just like at the hospital. They wore their humor like pranksters. That must be why Luke warned her not to take them too seriously. Her face relaxed into a smile. Luke would no doubt be the brunt of their ragging and joking. Men being what they were, they'd probably say anything to get a rise from him. Her presence would most certainly be the fodder for their teasing.

Luke strode forward to greet them in typical male fashion. Lots of laughter, swearing, feigned shoulder punches and grunts preceded a round of handshakes and high fives. When the ritual was over, all three strangers turned as one and stared at her, a look in each set of eyes that seemed slightly suspicious.

The handsome black man who stood in the center of the group flicked his gaze over her. "You've been holding out on us, Harding. Who's this?"

Feeling much like a side of beef that these scoundrels hadn't found worthy of speaking to, even though she stood right in front of them, anger sparked to life, effectively trumping the embarrassment she'd been fighting. Sally stood straighter, lifted her head and returned their appraising stares.

"Hey, Travis." Luke's hand shot out, connecting with the man's abs. "Be nice or we're going to have a problem." His tone was friendly enough, but Sally detected an underlying thread of warning.

Obviously caught by surprise, Travis grunted and dropped back a step.

The last thing Sally wanted was to be the cause of an argument between Luke and the men he called friends. She forced a parade-waving smile and stepped forward, grateful for the arm Luke slipped around her shoulders. She was aware of Ellen beside her until Daniel grabbed her arm and wouldn't let her go any farther, even when she stepped on his foot.

That made it easier for Sally to keep her smile, and she turned it on Luke. "Are you going to introduce me to your friends?"

Luke studied her warily for a second with a cute little smirk on his face, then leaned toward her. "Only if you promise not to hurt them," he whispered.

She raised an eyebrow. "We'll see."

Luke coughed, no doubt to cover his amusement as he faced his friends again. "This is Sally Duncan. Sally, these are friends of mine—at least for now."

The guys laughed uncertainly, as though they weren't entirely sure he was joking.

"The blond on your left is James Cooper. Coop is an explosives expert. He saved our butts more than once."

"Nice to meet you, Coop." Sally extended her hand, and the muscles in his forearm flexed as he gripped it firmly.

"The loud mouth there is Travis Monroe, aka the Shadow. He earned his nickname by getting in and out of places no one else could, quick and silent, just like a friggin' ghost."

Travis doffed his ball cap as he shook her hand. "Just one of my many talents." His bedroom eyes narrowed and a suggestive smile played around his mouth, giving her a pretty good idea what he counted as a talent.

Luke groaned. "As you can tell, he's modest too."

Everyone chuckled, including Travis. If he could laugh at himself, surely he couldn't be as degenerate as his words and actions implied.

"The big guy is Matt Iverson. We call him MacGyver because he can fix things."

Matt appeared only slightly larger than Luke or the other men. His dark brown hair had been cropped close in a buzz cut. Her quick perusal brought a slight flush to his neck and face, yet he nodded politely, and his warm handshake restored some of her quickly diminishing confidence.

A natural smile fell into place as she swept her gaze across the line of curious faces. "Luke's told me a little—"

"It's her. The lady in the picture. Right?" Matt's gaze left her face and darted to Luke's. "She's the woman in that picture—the one you showed us—the one you had with you in that shithole." He focused on her again. "You're his angel. Aren't you?"

Luke's arm had tightened around her, and one look revealed the force of the emotions and memories he was dealing with. Sally instinctively pressed closer as he reached in his back pocket and drew out the folded, faded picture. He handed it to Matt, who studied it for a moment, handed it off to Travis, then dragged her from the safety of Luke's side and gave her a huge hug.

"Thank you," he whispered in her ear before he released her and stepped aside. The scene was repeated twice more, with Travis giving her an uncertain peck on the cheek and Coop squeezing her shoulders in a sideways hug while handing the picture back to Luke.

All three of them wore their affection for their friend as a badge of honor, and because of their loyalty to him, she'd been accepted and apparently thrust into the role of angel—one who'd helped to bring their wounded brother home. She was humbled and awed by the bond between these warriors, and another chink in her determination not to reach immediately for the love and security Luke offered fell away.

"Hey, where's the midget?" Matt turned to search the lawn near Daniel's cabin.

Luke flinched. "Uh-oh. Yeah, MacGyver, we don't call her that anymore. Apparently, it's not politically correct." He reclaimed his place beside Sally. "MacGyver has a soft spot for kids. I told him about Jen."

Sally weighed the nickname Luke and the others had tagged Matt with, rejecting it as she met his inquisitive gaze. "She and Bridgett went to see the pony." Sally glanced toward Ellen and caught her wiping her eyes. Obviously, Sally hadn't been the only one moved by the show of solidarity. Standing beside his wife, Daniel grinned and nodded toward the corral.

Sally warmed to the clearly softhearted Matt Iverson. "I'll introduce you, if you like."

He rubbed his hands together. "Let's go." He offered her his arm, then abruptly stopped and turned to face Luke. "Okay with you, man?"

In reply, Luke gripped his arm for a moment. "I have a favor to ask... all of you, but especially Daniel." His gaze swept around the gathering. "Keep your eyes open. If you see anything that doesn't belong, let me know ASAP. We may have a little trouble following us."

"I assume you'll tell us what we're supposed to be watching for, right, Bro?" Travis stood completely relaxed, as if Luke hadn't just dropped a bomb on their reunion.

"I was hoping to meet with Daniel tonight, after the kids go to sleep. If it's okay with him, you can all sit in." He glanced toward Sally, then focused on their host. "You may not want us to stay once you hear the details."

Daniel nodded, strands of his black hair falling over his forehead. "If there's trouble, we might as well all hear it at the same time and decide what's to be done. First things first. Your cabin is on the end." He pointed to his right, and Luke glanced quickly at the structure he indicated—closest to the river. Daniel stepped toward the parked Jeep. "I'll help you pack your things down there while Sally and MacGyver round up the girls. Dinner's in the main cabin." Daniel jerked his thumb behind him toward the building both he and his wife had come from at Luke and Sally's arrival. He shifted his gaze to Sally. "When you come for dinner, bring some nightclothes for the young one. If things go as well between her and Bridgett as I think they will, we can put them both to bed here and have our visit afterward. Agreed?" He quickly scanned the group but didn't leave much room for argument.

Sally's good mood dissolved at being the source of so much turmoil, and she couldn't help feeling it was only the beginning. Matt, the girls and the pony momentarily forgotten, she peered at Luke, whose supportive gaze couldn't rouse her from her self-imposed funk this time.

Sally's stomach was tied in knots, even though they'd left Daniel's place behind as they navigated the dark on the path to their cabin. Time had stood still in the Mathias family living area after the small group of men and women had gathered. Luke had related the events of the past twenty-four hours…and the reasons behind them, looking to her for confirmation when he got to the details that led to her entering the witness protection program. Having her past laid bare for all to see had been humiliating and not a little terrifying. After all the years of hiding, not letting anyone get too close and never uttering the name Clive Brennan, her mask had been ripped away, and she'd been left naked and exposed.

She'd wanted to run. The only thing that'd kept her there was Luke's warm and reassuring hand on hers. The angry expletives from Luke's friends and the acceptance she'd seen on Daniel and Ellen's faces had eased her anxiety further.

"Hey, you okay, sunshine?" Walking beside her as they picked their way over the uneven ground, Luke tugged on her hand until he pulled her off-balance and she bumped into him. Immediately, his arm went around her waist and brought her against his side.

"Yeah—just…" Her words faded and she shrugged.

"They're on our side."

He offered that as though possibly endangering the lives of six more people somehow made the situation better—or took away her shame.

"I get that you're uncomfortable with strangers knowing your life story, but Travis and the others are exactly the help we need. We couldn't ask for better. I don't know how Brennan could track us here, but if he does, we'll see him coming, and we'll have the experienced manpower to discourage him." He halted and stepped in front of her, his thumb stroking the smooth skin of her cheek. "Trust me, Sally. We're safer here than out there on our own."

Sally forced the corners of her mouth upward and swallowed the words that had been caught in her throat all evening. Everyone at the meeting had expressed surprise that Brennan had waited ten years to seek revenge. "He had the resources and manpower to reach out from prison and not have to get his hands dirty," Travis had said. "This feels personal."

That had been her opportunity to come clean. She'd wanted to tell them—tell Luke—that Clive Brennan was her father. That when she chose to testify against him, she not only put a murderer away…she betrayed the one man who no doubt expected her undying loyalty. His vendetta was almost certainly *personal*. She expected nothing less. Sally had tried to form the words…but the conversation had taken a turn and the moment passed.

Focusing her attention on Luke's tired eyes, she forced her guilt to a place where it was less noticeable. She'd deal with it later. "I trust you, Luke. You know that, right?"

"Talk to me, then. What's up?"

Sally looked away from his gaze as she searched for a safer topic. Her daughter. It'd been just her and Jen for a very long time, and tonight it'd proved extremely difficult for Sally to leave her asleep in Daniel's cabin. Ellen had assured her that Jen would be comfortable and safe in Bridgett's room for the night. "She's sound asleep, Sally. No sense waking her," Ellen had said.

Sally cocked her head and gave another quick shrug of her shoulder. "I know Jen will be fine with Daniel and Ellen. It's just…I'm not used to being away from her."

She shivered as Luke trailed his fingers down the side of her throat, then tipped up her chin. His expression held a mixture of sadness and contentment. "I know how hard it was for you to walk out of there without her, and I had a hunch you might change your mind. We'll go get her right now if that's what you want." The conviction in his eyes told her he meant every word.

Letting Jen stay at Daniel's cabin meant she and Luke would be alone for the first time since he'd reappeared in her life. Without reservation, he'd offered up that time for her state of mind and Jen's safety. Tears prickled her eyelids at the realization of how much she loved him. She'd be crazy not to snatch him up and never let him go.

Blinking the tears into submission, she shook her head. "No, but I might need a distraction." She traced one finger down his chest.

Luke flashed his signature grin. "I can guarantee that." He leaned in and nibbled her lips gently. An instant later, he groaned, stepped away and continued walking toward their cabin, grasping her hand in his.

She lengthened her stride to keep up.

They'd left a light on in the two-room dwelling on the banks of the river and brought in dry wood, kindling and newspaper for the fireplace before they joined the others for dinner. Daniel had said it could still drop below freezing at night this far north.

An arm around her shoulders, Luke hurried up the gravel path, jogged the four steps to the porch that lined the front of the cabin and shoved the door open. With a sweep of his hand, he stepped aside and let her go first.

An amused grin curled her lips as she stepped across the threshold. "What's the rush, Harding?"

He caught her hand and spun her around to face him, then backed her against the wall, kicking the door shut as he moved closer, a devilish grin parting his lips. His hands circled her waist and held her tightly against him while he leaned in slowly and kissed her, his tongue stealing between her lips to claim hers in a sensuous dance.

When Luke raised his head, a slow moan escaped her, much to her chagrin.

He smiled, lifting one eyebrow inquisitively. "There's no rush. Now that I have you to myself, we're going to take everything nice...and slow."

His voice was so low and sexy, Sally's breath stuttered, and again he smiled. Clearly, he knew exactly what he was doing.

He kissed her again, long and hard. This time when he released her, he stared searchingly into her eyes. Suddenly, he cleared his throat and took a step back. A trace of uncertainty crossed his face. "Daniel said he stocked the wine cupboard. Would you like some?"

"That would be nice." Sally studied him for the cause of his mood change. Although the temperature had chilled noticeably, she couldn't detect the reason for it.

Luke stepped toward the kitchen area, which consisted of a coffeemaker, a microwave, a small refrigerator and a sink. He searched the nearby cupboards until he found the one he was looking for, reached inside and came out with a dusty bottle of red. A drawer yielded a corkscrew, and then the hunt was on for what Sally could only suppose were wineglasses...or glasses of any kind.

The silence thundered around them. The distance she sensed settling between them confused and saddened her. Was it something she'd said? Had he suddenly realized how much trouble she was bringing to the relationship? She certainly wouldn't blame Luke for thinking twice, but she hadn't expected the sense of loss she experienced to be so great.

She took a couple of steps toward the small bedroom. "I think I'll freshen up, if that's all right?

"Ah, here we go." Luke pulled two wineglasses from a cupboard above the sink and turned to look at her. "Of course. Take as long as you need. I'll have this wine poured by the time you're finished." He smiled, but his eyes remained guarded.

Sally hesitated. She should ask him what was wrong. Easy enough to say, but her courage failed, and she walked purposefully toward the back of the cabin and the tiny room where she'd left her new belongings earlier. As soon as she was out of sight, she released the breath she'd been holding to maintain her forced smile. Perhaps it was Jen's presence that made them fit together so well. Sally had never been alone like this with Luke before. If Jen was there, they'd be worrying about where everyone would sleep in this cabin obviously intended to house only two people. Luke would no doubt insist that she and Jen take the bed and he'd make do on the couch. Maybe they needed her daughter as a buffer between them.

She flipped on a lamp by the bed and pawed through a department store sack for something to sleep in, then changed her mind, grabbing a new toothbrush instead. There was barely enough room to turn around in the bathroom, but she managed to wash her face, brush her teeth and comb her hair without claustrophobia setting in. Her mind was a whirl of questions and regret. Luke was attracted to her—Sally had no doubt about that. And she couldn't imagine anybody more right for her. So what was the problem? To find out, she'd have to put on her big-girl panties and have a grown-up conversation.

Sally groaned, picturing the very small swaths of fabric she'd purchased for panties earlier in the day. *I guess they'll work just as well.* She pulled her long-sleeved T-shirt off, unsnapped her bra and let it slide down her arms, then unbuttoned her jeans and kicked them off as she moved toward the bed. Luke's duffel sat at the foot, and she plucked the same light blue, button-up shirt from its place at the top of the bag and slipped her arms in, letting it settle comfortably around her shoulders. Securing the front and smoothing her hair, which fell in waves down her back, Sally returned to the door and pulled it open, stepping into the front room just as Luke turned from the sink, a glass of wine in each hand.

Her smile fell back in place and she held it, even when something unidentifiable flared in Luke's eyes and a muscle flexed in his jaw.

"Mind if I wear your shirt again?" She stepped toward him.

His gaze swept over her body before he frowned and seemed to finally remember the wine he held. He offered her one of the glasses. "I don't usually let women wear my shirts, but I'll make an exception for you."

Sally accepted the wine, expecting a smile, a wink or, at the very least, his trademark grin. He'd told her this morning, in no uncertain terms, he appreciated how she looked in his shirt. In the bathroom at the motel, she'd felt the evidence of his arousal firsthand. Yet, he seemed almost annoyed with her now, his gaze wandering away as he brought the wineglass to his lips. Their banter, returning to the cabin, had been light and easy... intimate...exciting. Then, in the space of a kiss, everything had changed.

For the first time in nearly twenty-four hours, Sally felt safe...because Luke was with her. Because he cared about her and Jen and had brought them to a place of refuge. At least for tonight, she could rest easier, and she'd wanted this night with Luke...for a very long time.

The evidence of the miles that separated them was subtle, but Sally felt it in every nerve and synapse. Emotions tingled across her skin like small bursts of electricity, which was probably why she ignored her better judgment and reached out to touch Luke's forearm. From the way he jumped, he must have felt it too.

Dark eyes settled on her. With no way to read what he was thinking, Sally stepped into him, raising her lips to touch his, absorbing the heady taste of the merlot still lingering there.

Luke responded, capturing her mouth with undisguised hunger...for a few seconds before his jaw tensed, and he quickly stepped away, walking toward the couch that sat in the middle of the room. Over his shoulder, his voice sounded dry and raspy. "Let's sit down. We should talk."

Sally turned and watched him retreat. *Great. What every girl wants to hear on her first real date. Let's talk?* At least she was starting to catch on—he did have something on his mind, and her heart told her she'd jumped in blind again, trusting him. With emotions racing to make a fool of her, she wasn't entirely sure she wanted to hear what he had to say. Gone was the Luke who'd proposed to her earlier in the day, replaced by a man who apparently wasn't comfortable even looking at her. Anger surfaced, and she shook her head. She set her glass on the counter and placed her hands on her hips. How was she going to get out of this one without having her heart shattered?

When Luke reached the couch and turned, it was obvious he'd expected her to follow, and surprise widened his eyes for an instant. His glance dropped to where her hands sat at her waist, before his gaze met hers.

"Sally…" Without taking his eyes from hers, he bent to place his wineglass on the coffee table in front of the couch. "Something wrong?" A tentative grin appeared but didn't dim the caution in his eyes.

Too little, too late. Sally drew a tired breath. "Seriously, Luke? Don't you think we should start a relationship…before you break up with me?" A short laugh, shamefully close to hysteria, escaped her, and she dropped her gaze to the floor.

"What are you—?" He took a step toward her.

Quickly, Sally raised her hands, hoping to convince him to stay where he was. "You know what? It's okay. For whatever reason, you've changed your mind about wanting to be with me. I don't even want to know why. Let's just be glad you realized it before we did something crazy." She dropped her hands and backed away, turning and breaking into a jog, desperate to reach the bedroom before her tears betrayed her.

One stride from the seclusion of the other room, Luke reached her, lifting her off her feet and pulling her against his muscled body. A heartbeat later, his arms cushioned her impact as they collided with the sturdy bedroom door.

Giving her no time to collect her breath, Luke covered her mouth, his tongue demanding entry between her lips, effectively stopping any arguments she'd thought to voice. Her hands, pushing for space between them, soon fisted in his T-shirt to pull him closer as he branded her with his scorching kiss. He positioned his hips against her abdomen, and the full length of his arousal pinned her to the door. She reveled in his hard thickness and arched against him, causing a chain reaction of grinding bodies and groping hands.

His mouth left hers to push the blue shirt far enough out of the way to bare one breast. He sucked the taut nipple between his teeth, scraping it teasingly. Sally hissed and reached for the waistband of his jeans, undid the button and threw open the zipper. Encased in the black cotton briefs he wore, his shaft pushed through the opening she'd made, and she gripped him through the fabric, her fingers barely able to meet as she squeezed.

Luke tore his lips from her breast and regret marred his features. "Aw hell, babe. Let's slow this down for a minute." He gripped her elbows, took a step back and held her at arm's length. "Where did you get the crazy idea I was breaking up with you?"

In the grip of a lust more powerful than she'd ever imagined, Sally stared at him blankly for a moment, willing her brain to catch up. She shook her head, trying to remember anything that had transpired before the last two minutes. A self-conscious laugh escaped and brought a relieved smile from Luke.

"Believe me, that's the last thing on my mind." He released one elbow and brushed the hair back from her eyes.

"But you…you got all distant on me. You walked away." She pointed at him accusingly. "You said we needed to *talk*. That's never a good sign. I figured you finally realized what a bad deal you'd made." Sally clung to his smile, savoring the love that shone from his eyes. "If you're not looking for a way out of this, what do we need to talk about?"

He cocked his head and looked into her eyes. "Babe, I told you how I feel about you. That wasn't just some line I made up to get you in the sack. I don't *want* out of this."

"What then?"

Luke stepped closer. "After we left Daniel's cabin tonight, I started thinking about the way I've been acting. Pressuring you. Wanting you to make a commitment you're obviously not ready to make. Asking you to marry me. Buying condoms. Shit! That was a douchebag thing to do. Hell, it was only this morning you forgave me for my last stunt. I need to know you want this night together as much as I do. If you're not ready, I'll wait as long as it takes. That's a promise."

Too good to be true—the words flashed on the screen of her mind in neon orange, a last-ditch warning that she fully intended to ignore. Sally caressed Luke's cheek as she dismissed any remaining doubts about the man who held her heart in his hands. "But I do—I am. I don't want to wait. I mean—part of me doesn't even believe you're here, much less that you want to stay. But I think I could get used to the idea."

Luke's smile brought a sparkle to his eyes. "It's about time you realized we're meant to be." He reached for her, lifting her against him until her shoulders were even with his and then wrapped himself around her until she couldn't tell where she ended and he began.

Despite the events of the past twenty-four hours and the hard truth that she might be on the run for the rest of her life, Sally couldn't hold back an exultant laugh as she flung her arms around his neck. Truly free of regret for the first time in years, she leaned close to his ear. "I hope I live up to your overactive imagination."

He pulled back and met her gaze, all seriousness. "You're so much more than I ever imagined." His voice rasped and sent a shiver of anticipation through her as his lips captured hers, igniting a fire deep within her belly.

Chapter Twelve

Luke let her body slide down his, then scooped her up, one arm under her knees. She turned the knob on the bedroom door, and he carried her to the foot of the bed. Carefully, as warranted for the most precious cargo he'd ever carried, he set her on bare feet. His gaze swept over her. Damn, she was beautiful—and he'd never look at his blue shirt the same way again.

His hands moved to the buttons and started undoing them one at a time. He could tell the instant she became nervous, uncertain. She took a step back.

"Don't move," he whispered. "You wore this for me, didn't you?"

A faint nod accompanied her slight smile.

Finishing the last of the buttons, Luke softly caressed the underside of one of her breasts, where the fabric had fallen open. "You do a number on me in that shirt—no doubt about it. But I've got a hunch this is nothing compared to what's underneath." He tugged on the shirttails teasingly. The lamp, near the head of the bed, provided just enough light to see desire darken her irises.

Luke stepped toward her and, with a flick of his fingers at her shoulders, the shirt slid down her arms, landing in a blue mound of fabric behind her. He started to reach for her, then dropped his hands to his sides. Mesmerized, his gaze moved slowly over her, and the rightness of the moment amazed him. *Perfection.* Her long strands of wavy brown hair hugged the flawless innocence of her face, of which the focal point at the moment was her larger-than-usual, luminescent blue eyes. Surely she could see clear to his soul. Her small, rounded breasts and firm, flat stomach gave way to a tiny triangle of fabric—light blue—that barely hid her womanhood and disappeared between strong, shapely legs that Luke could almost feel wrapped around him.

She was exquisite in a world that had stopped making sense.

Sally took the step that separated them and tugged upward on the bottom of his T-shirt, her lips curved in a playful smile. "Your turn. I'm not going to be the only one in the room who's naked."

She didn't have to tell him more than once. He reached over his shoulder, grabbed a handful of shirt and peeled the garment off over his head and arms. Then he wadded it into a ball and, not caring where it landed, tossed it behind him. That brought a laugh from her, and he was just about to grab her in his arms and satisfy his burning need to touch her everywhere when she stopped him short.

"Don't move," she said in a sexy whisper that froze him to the floor.

Luke recognized his words of only a few minutes ago. She was turning the tables on him again, and hell if he wasn't inclined to let her do any damn thing she wanted. Although, considering he'd been hard and ready for a while now, this would be an exercise in self-control. He took a slow, deep breath and fisted his hands as she placed hers on his chest.

Sally skipped her fingers lightly over his pecs until his nipples peaked in eager anticipation, sending sharp pangs of need straight to his groin. She smiled in smug satisfaction when a groan tore from his throat. Any sign of humor disappeared, however, when she spotted his scar.

Nearly dead center, just below his heart, the bullet wound still ached if he pushed himself too hard. And he'd done a lot of that while trying to regain his strength after the surgery that gave him back the use of his legs.

Sally pressed her palm lightly over the scar, and he sensed her starting to pull back. Ignoring her directive to stay still, he tilted her head and gazed into her troubled eyes. Tears threatened, and he had no choice. He had to put a stop to this before she saw the rest of his body. The scar beneath her hand was only one of many. There'd be a time for full disclosure... but not tonight.

He bent slowly and kissed her lips. Then he framed her face with his hands, capturing her complete attention. "Tonight, we're looking ahead to our future. You, me and Jen. The past is behind us. It can't hurt us anymore unless we let it." He gently drew her hand away from his scar.

Sally's gaze flicked briefly to the rutted and pulled skin on his chest, then she firmed her jaw as she blinked away her sadness, and her fingers traced circles down his arms to his wrists. Her eyes shone with warmth and caring that lit up dark places within him—places that had known only emptiness for a long time.

Small hands landed on his open waistband, and a mischievous grin took up residence on her full lips. "Aren't you forgetting something?" She tugged his jeans down a couple of inches before she stroked teasingly around his engorged shaft, never touching him but managing to set every nerve on fire.

"No, ma'am. I'd *never* forget something so...essential." Luke pushed his jeans down below his knees and sat on the edge of the bed to unlace his boots, kick them off and jam his socks inside. Sally watched him intently as he stepped out of his jeans and briefs. Color flowed freely into her smooth cheeks when she grasped the narrow bands of lace at the top of her panties and stripped them down her legs, dropping them on the floor.

The knowledge that she obviously wasn't an expert in midnight trysts with men turned up the heat on his possessive nature. He wanted her all to himself when it came to shedding clothes. Her uncertainty appeared in her body language and her slight hesitation, yet she was willing to place herself in his hands. That meant the fucking world to him.

He quickly reached for her and pulled her against him, pressing the full length of his erection into the softness of her belly. Covering her mouth with his, he kissed her hard until she was breathless and his restraint was stretched to the breaking point. "Sorry, babe. It's been a while since...do you happen to know where those condoms ended up?" Luke moved around the side of the bed and began searching through store sacks.

Sally kneed her way onto the bed and stretched on her side, bracing her head on one arm. "How long has it been?"

He stopped and looked at her. "Well, not that this is appropriate first-time sex small talk, but...it was about a month before I met you."

She chuffed a laugh. "That's not so long. Try ten years."

His first instinct was to laugh at the improbability of that statement, but the acute embarrassment that washed over Sally's face told him she hadn't just pulled that number out of the air for the sake of topping his. And she wasn't talking about someone else. This was an incredibly personal confession. It was also too much of a coincidence that ten years would place her last sexual partner at about the time Jen was conceived. Even if he couldn't feel her anguish from where he knelt, the SEALs had taught him to discount anything that resembled a coincidence.

Luke had heard pieces of whispered conversation between Rachel and Sally, and he'd been the cause of their dialogue abruptly ending when they'd become aware of his presence. He'd had his suspicions about what they'd been discussing, but he'd respected Sally's privacy...until now, but damned if he didn't want to know what had happened to her that turned her off men for ten years.

He renewed his efforts to find the elusive condoms, finally locating them at the bottom of one of the sacks, and tossing them on the nightstand by the bed as he rose to his feet. Carefully composing his expression so Sally, hopefully, wouldn't notice how much her admission had affected him, he climbed onto the bed beside her. He slipped his arm around her waist and laid her down amid the pillows with him, gently smoothing back the hair that had fallen into her eyes. "Let me get this straight. Ten years ago, you had sex so incredible you knew every other man in the world would suffer by comparison...so rather than damage their egos, you've just been waiting until I came along? Well...no pressure there." Luke rubbed the back of his neck and let out a harsh breath.

The sweet smile he'd hoped to evoke spread across her lips, and he kissed both corners of her mouth before moving to her ear. Oh, he'd given her a pass—a way out without having to explain herself and a situation that he suspected had been just the opposite of the scenario he described. The anger that still stirred in his belly correlated to whatever had happened to Sally, and he'd wager it hadn't been good. Eventually, he'd find out what it was.

Luke slid his hand up her side until he covered her breast, his palm rubbing over her pebbled nipple, the sensation hardening his shaft even more, and he pressed the throbbing member against her. A growl worked from his throat as he took her breast into his mouth, his tongue running back and forth across the swollen tip.

Sally shivered in his arms, crooking her leg over his hip and pulling herself tighter. Luke guided her leg forward until he draped it over his shoulder, using it to push off and move his body down hers. Slowly, he kissed his way to her belly button, pausing to thrust his tongue in and out of the small cavity, a precursor to the hot, tight receptacle waiting for him only a few inches away. With an impatient snarl, he continued his exploration to the small rise of her stomach and then to the patch of hair that led to her folds. Her soft moans encouraged him as he cupped her delicious ass, pulling her toward him while he positioned himself between her thighs.

Sally raised her upper body, bracing on her elbows, and stared into his eyes. He met her curious gaze as he deliberately swept his tongue from one end of her folds to the other. He grinned when she threw herself down on the pillows, uttered something beneath her breath that sounded suspiciously like the f-word and fisted the sheets with both hands. The fact she was already wet and slick made the full length of his hard-on throb with impatience. God, he ached to be inside her warmth, and he wouldn't be able to hold out much longer.

"Oh my God! What are you doing?" She moved her hands to his hair, grabbing two fistfuls and tugging.

Luke quickly loosened her grip and pulled her hands free, holding both of them down on her stomach. "It'll become obvious in a minute, sunshine." He slid one finger deep inside her, followed by a second, and worked them in and out in a rhythmic movement. Each push inward allowed him to thumb her sweet spot hidden in the triangle of hair, resulting in her thrashing and pulling to free her hands.

"Luke! It's too much. I need you now."

He almost couldn't resist her plea. How long had it been since anyone had wanted him that badly? But it was obvious no one had ever tended to her needs before, and he meant for her to have it all tonight—wanted her to know how good sex could be...would always be. He didn't have as much control over himself as he'd like for their first time. Another day, he'd make up for that, when his need wasn't so raw.

Luke continued his sensory exploration, bringing her to the edge twice and backing off before she reached her release. He was fairly certain she issued the ultimate insult to his mother beneath her breath as he started over again. This time, when he felt her body tense and arch against him, he sucked her swollen womanhood into his mouth and rolled it unrelentingly between his tongue and teeth until she came, crying out his name.

He pulled himself alongside her, holding her until her trembling subsided. A drop of moisture rolled down her cheek, and Luke brushed it away, landing kisses on both eyes. "You okay?"

She nodded. "You could have warned me."

"About what?"

"That you were going to make me lose control. That I'd feel so alive it's scary. That one experience and I'd be addicted to you...and what you do to me. Great! I'm a sex addict!"

Sally's words, though apparently meant to sound accusing, had no sting. When she couldn't maintain a straight face any longer, a bubble of laughter surfaced. Luke drew his arms tighter around her and covered her mouth with his in a kiss bearing all the tenderness he felt for her.

"Don't let that get around, babe. Every male between here and the Montana border will want to supply your fix, and I'll have to fight them all." One hand stroked the silky skin of her back. It was hard not to be elated by her words, especially the addicted-to-him part. He was more than fine with that. "In my own defense, I didn't know that part of it was a first for you until we got into it a ways. You said you trusted me, so I made an executive decision. Would you rather I'd stopped?" Luke dropped a kiss on her lips, then cocked an eyebrow as he awaited her response.

A smirk lifted one corner of her mouth. "No. Stopping definitely wasn't an option."

"Okay. Good to know." He captured her lips again and rolled until his body covered hers and his arousal pressed against the warmth of her core. "Actually, I was hoping you'd say that, because we're not exactly finished." Luke rubbed his hard-on along her naked thigh. "Just one more little item."

Sally laughed and wrinkled her cute little nose. "It doesn't feel that little."

"I'm glad you think so." Luke took her mouth roughly, claiming her with an urgency he couldn't keep in check any longer. He pushed to his knees and reached for the condoms on the nightstand. Grasping the box, he ripped open the package, sending foil packets flying in every direction. Managing to locate one that had landed between Sally's legs, he freed it from yet more packaging and rolled it on, while she tried to stifle her giggles, unsuccessfully. Damn good thing he didn't have a confidence problem.

Spreading her legs wider, he lowered himself again, covering her mouth and swallowing the remainder of her laughter. With his shaft positioned snugly at her opening, he rocked back and drove in to the hilt. Her surprised cry went unheard as he plundered her mouth, probing with his tongue and savoring her taste. Her sweet warmth wrapping around his swollen manhood was far better than he could have imagined. Mind games had kept him alive for months, make-believe scenes just like this one, but his preconceived ideas crumbled into dust in the face of reality. This woman was real. He loved her so much his heart ached. She loved him too. He was sure of that, even though she hadn't voiced it yet. She was his now, and he'd never let her down again.

Luke stared at her beautiful face as he drew out and then thrust forward, seating himself deep inside her again, grinding his pelvis against her sweet spot with each pass. After repeating the sequence several more times, he increased the tempo. The blatant need in her eyes seemed to match his, and he let go of some of his control, driving into her harder. Though Sally hooked her legs around his hips and met him thrust for thrust, she was still much smaller than he, more delicate. He'd never forgive himself if he hurt her, even accidentally.

A sensual smile forming, she wrapped her arms around his neck and pulled his lips to hers, inserting her sweet tongue in his mouth while he sank into her. As he felt his release within reach, a tremor rocked her again, and she breathed his name before shattering in his arms. Gathering her tightly, he buried himself in her hot sheath as his climax slammed into him and he continued to pulse and twitch in rhythm with her spasms.

Long moments passed before Luke could shift positions and roll off Sally. "Don't move—I'll be right back." He covered her lips with his, reluctant to leave her even for a minute.

In the bathroom, he disposed of the condom, splashed cold water on his face and hurried back to the woman in his bed. How he'd lived without her up to this point was pure mystery, but sure as hell, he wouldn't make it a day without her now. Sliding in beside her, he patted his side in invitation, and she lay her head on his shoulder, one hand stroking his chest with a feather-light touch.

Luke kissed her forehead. "Love you, sunshine."

Sally smiled and stretched to touch her lips to his jaw.

Disappointment bit him when she didn't respond in kind, despite his inner voice telling him it wasn't all about him. It was okay she didn't say the words back to him. Things were great between them. Considering the emptiness in his life twenty-four hours ago, his circumstances had definitely taken a turn for the better. She was still reeling from the fire and explosion, probably nervous about the marshal and obviously scared shitless of Clive Brennan. So how about giving her a break…and some time to get used to the idea he was going to stick, no matter what.

Luke brushed her soft lips with his and gazed into her sparkling eyes. "Do you like to dance?"

Her eyebrows shot up. "Yes, but I'm not very good."

He guided her head back to his shoulder. "I'm no Fred Astaire either, but I'd like to take you dancing. Would you go out with me on a real date?"

"I'd like that." She traced a line from his cheek to his mouth, and he caught her hand, pressing her palm to his lips.

Two days ago, all he'd had was a picture to keep him sane. Here he was, lying in bed with her after incredible sex. She wasn't the kind of woman who slept around. How much more evidence did he need that she loved him?

It didn't matter. All his logic wouldn't change a thing. He wanted the words from her sweet lips, and he wasn't going to rest until she was his in every way.

Chapter Thirteen

Total blackness met Sally's gaze when her eyes popped open. Luke must have turned the bedside lamp out after she dozed off. The bedroom door was open, giving her a straight shot to view the front entrance to the cabin as her vision slowly adapted to the dark. The lack of anything but starlight from outside, combined with silence so absolute she could hear her own heart beating, gave the impression she and Luke were the only humans for miles.

Yet something had woken her, unleashing instant dread that pinged from nerve ending to nerve ending like static electricity.

She pressed closer to Luke, craving the heat from his body to banish the sudden chill in hers. Apparently, she wasn't the outdoorsy girl she'd thought she was. All this wide-open space made her edgy.

Sally sank deeper into the covers and forced herself to relax. They were in a cabin in the middle of the wilderness. The sound that had brought her from a deep sleep could easily have been an animal…making whatever noises animals made. An owl had hooted from a nearby tree as she and Luke returned to the cabin after the gathering at Daniel's home. That was probably what had woken her—or a raccoon, a deer, a wolf. Every noise she heard didn't necessarily mean her father was at the door.

The deck creaked as though an unseen weight had been brought to bear upon it, echoing through the silence of the outer room and drawing her rapt gaze to the door, where a silvery thread of light marked the threshold. *Maybe something a little bigger. A bear?* Mesmerized, she stared, her lungs aching for air as she held perfectly still. So intent was she that she nearly cried out when a shadow obscured the sliver of light for a second before moving on, rattling the doorknob as whatever it was continued its nocturnal exploration.

She propped her chin on Luke's chest. Maybe it *was* a bear. *Yeah, that's what it is. Nothing to worry about...as long as it stays outside.* Relieved that Luke and his macho friends hadn't witnessed her spinelessness, she settled more firmly into Luke's arms, still wrapped around her protectively.

Suddenly, Luke leaned over her, his lips hovering near her ear. "Shh," he whispered. His body lying partially over hers, he reached toward the floor and snagged the blue shirt she'd worn earlier. "Get dressed," he hissed, pressing the shirt against her abdomen. In one lithe movement, he pushed himself over her and landed on silent feet beside the bed.

Sally sat on the edge and slipped on his shirt. Her fingers trembled slightly as she worked the buttons. From lowered lashes, she watched Luke pull on his jeans and retrieve his handgun from the nightstand. Fear threatened to erupt into full-fledged panic, knowing Luke was on high alert. Did he think someone—maybe Clive Brennan—was outside their cabin?

Defending people clearly came naturally to Navy SEAL Luke Harding. He appeared completely comfortable with a gun in his hand. As he took her arm and pulled her from the bed, confidence and control emanated from him. He had a job to do, and it was obvious he took his promise to protect her seriously.

"Go in the bathroom and close the door." He still whispered, and his warm breath sent a chill clear to her toes. "Stay there until I come for you."

The cold detachment in his voice scared her to death. Sally stared as he fumbled for his cell phone, its face lighting as he sent a quick text message. She searched for some sign he was only erring on the side of caution. That he also thought it was probably a bear or a wolf—that no further danger lurked outside their cabin. What she received for her effort terrified her even more. The man she was falling in love with all over again had turned into a warrior right in front of her. He was preparing to do battle...for her...while she hid.

Her stomach clenched and she shook her head. "No. I'm going with you." This protecting thing between them went both ways.

Luke gripped her arms. "Huh-uh. This isn't optional. For me to do my job, I need to know you're safe. That means you stay where I say, for as *long* as I say. Trust me on this, sunshine. I know what I'm doing." He dropped a kiss on her forehead. "And I promise I'll let *you* boss me around later."

She could hear the teasing in his voice even as his rigid stance told her it was useless to argue. Despite her tenseness, Sally smiled. He was right, of course. She would only get in the way if she went with him. For sure, she'd be no help. No doubt she'd endanger him *and* herself. Still, she hated the idea of staying behind—of not knowing what was going on or if he was safe. "I'll hold you to that." She tried to adopt his unemotional tone, but there was no hiding her fear.

He turned her toward the bathroom, his arm around her shoulders. Sally followed woodenly, her head spinning with thoughts of everything that could go wrong. "Don't let anything happen to you, Luke." The vehemence of her demand surprised even her.

Something flared in Luke's eyes, and his familiar grin flashed briefly. "Don't worry, sunshine. I've got everything to live for, so I won't be taking any crazy chances." He pushed her backward into the bathroom and closed the door silently.

If Sally had thought it was dark in the bedroom, the tiny bathroom, without even a window, was pure inky blackness. She could hear nothing, not even Luke's footsteps walking away. Rejecting the idea of turning on a light, in case that would give away her location and somehow endanger Luke further, she braced against the dread clawing to escape as she tried to talk herself down. Claustrophobia had never been a serious problem. Until today. The walls were closing in on her. Her lungs burned for want of a complete breath. The room, a dark, lifeless tomb, stole not only air and freedom but her very life.

Sally groped for the doorknob, turned it as quietly as she could and pulled the door open a sliver. Her face pressed to the opening, the slight chill seeping through the crack brought reason back to her frazzled thoughts. The dim grayness that filtered through the bedroom windows grounded her. Dawn—it would be light soon. Relief washed over her, and she leaned her forehead against the cool wood of the doorjamb.

How long she stayed there before the sound of footsteps and voices reached her ears was unclear. Her head jerked up, and her breathing stilled as she listened. Male voices spoke in low tones from the front room, but she couldn't make out whose they were or what they said. Quietly, she slipped through the opening and tiptoed toward the open bedroom door. Lamplight suddenly shattered the darkness beyond, and she jumped, pressing herself against the wall near the doorway.

"Who'd you say you're looking for again?" Luke's voice sounded friendly enough, but she heard the wary edge embedded within.

"Don't play dumb, Harding. I'm too tired and too fucking pissed off to enjoy the game. Like I told you outside after you assaulted me, I'm a US Marshal. My name's Greg Lambert, and I'm here to take Sally Duncan and her little girl into protective custody."

Sally recognized the voice even before he gave his name. How had he found her? Why was he still looking after she'd told him not to? Thank God Jen wasn't there. She carefully peeked around the doorframe.

Luke stood near the lamp in the center of the room, his back to her. His gun was shoved in the waistband of his jeans, snug against his bare back. Tension radiated from him like sunlight.

He laughed mockingly. "I don't think Ms. Duncan is expecting you, Marshal. In fact, I'm damn sure she said she'd call you when she wanted you to drop by. Yet here you are, slinking around outside my cabin like a common thief."

Greg stood just inside the cabin entrance. He was armed as well. Sally could see the bulge of his handgun beneath the edge of his jacket. Short blond hair, fortysomething, a rugged face beneath a black cowboy hat and long, slender, jean-encased legs ending in cowboy boots wasn't exactly the picture she'd had of him, but she'd recognize his slight drawl anywhere. He was nervous and wary, never taking his eyes off Luke.

Greg spread his arms in an I-don't-know-what-to-tell-you gesture and a smile that didn't reach his eyes appeared. "There's a killer after my witness. I'm well aware of what she thinks she wants, but it's been my experience that women in Ms. Duncan's situation don't always know what's best for them."

"Oh, and you do, I suppose?" Anger flared hotly in Sally's veins as she pushed herself away from the wall and surged into the room. "You don't get to decide what's best for me, Marshal Lambert." She stopped just inside, feeling suddenly exposed and out of control, Luke's instructions echoing in her mind even as the realization it was too late dropped like a rock from a tall building.

The satisfied grin on the marshal's face did nothing to alleviate her annoyance, but it was the disappointment and apprehension in Luke's visage as he whirled around that made her regret her hasty entrance.

Then, as though to reinforce how badly she'd screwed up, the marshal pulled his weapon, took three long strides and pressed his gun into Luke's back, disarming him all in the space of two seconds.

"Why don't you have a seat, Harding? Are you going to give me anymore trouble? I know you think you're protecting Sally, and I can appreciate that. I won't cuff you…unless you make it necessary."

It was all over before Sally started breathing again. Luke's gaze pierced her as he raised his hands and moved toward the couch, with Greg prodding him in the back with his gun.

Regret formed a lump in her throat. Why hadn't she listened?

Greg faced her. "Let's go, Sally. Where's the kid?" His gaze traveled the length of her. "You might want to put some clothes on."

"I'm not going anywhere with you, Greg."

He dipped his head, and an impatient sigh issued forth. "We've got a long trip ahead of us, Sally, and you can argue the whole time if that makes you happy, but you *are* coming with me…with or without the kid."

Sally gasped. "You can't do that!" Fear constricted her throat. What if he did it anyway? She couldn't let that happen.

"That part's entirely up to you, but don't test me. I don't think you really want to leave Clive's grandchild behind, do you?" With his free hand, he motioned toward the bedroom.

"Grandchild?" Luke stared at her.

"She didn't tell you?" Greg laughed. "Yeah, it's her old man she's been hiding from all these years."

Oh God. It'd taken Greg only five seconds to out her in front of Luke. Five seconds she'd never live down. Shame and humiliation swamped her. The shock and revulsion in Luke's expression as he turned his face away left her empty and aching. "I'm sorry, Luke." The words were barely a whisper, and he gave no indication he'd heard them.

"Do as he says, Sally. Get dressed and go get Jen." Luke's gaze locked on the marshal. The bitterness in his voice cut her to the bone. "Tell Daniel and Ellen you couldn't sleep without her—anything to get her out of there without bloodshed." His gaze dropped to the gun in Greg's hand.

Sally stared at Luke until he looked toward her. She wanted him to know she was sorry…for everything. His dark scowl and the muscle that worked in his jaw wasn't conducive to explanation. Would he ever forgive her for betraying him?

Her heart beat wildly and weakness spread quickly through her limbs. Light-headed, Sally labored for her next breath, each inhale becoming harder and shallower than the last. The all-out panic attack had come from nowhere. The more she tried to calm herself, the less oxygen reached her lungs. Feeling faint, she looked around blindly for a place to sit before she made a complete fool of herself by passing out. Regulating her breathing was key to retaining consciousness—and now wasn't the time to keel over. Managing only short gulps of air, she fumbled her way past a bookshelf to a straight-backed chair along the wall.

A quick glance at Greg's worried countenance told her he'd noticed her distress…and that was when the idea came full-blown. She sagged in the chair, emphasizing the wheeze that was already present with each inhale. From beneath lowered lashes, she saw Luke sit forward, uneasiness furrowing his brow. Greg paid no attention to Luke; concern for his witness displayed on his face.

"Stay put." He tossed the warning to Luke. Greg holstered his weapon and stepped toward her. "What do you need? Got any paper bags around here?" He gently rubbed her back as he leaned closer.

"I don't...know. Maybe...some water?"

His gaze swept the cabin's interior, zeroed in on the sink and started that way. Sally rose silently to her feet as soon as his back was turned. A foot-tall sculpture of a bear on the bookshelf beside her caught her attention. Without daring to glance at Luke, she clutched the metal statue in both hands. Greg was filling a cup with water when Sally swung. At the last instant, she flinched and swung short, hitting him a glancing blow from the back of his head to his left shoulder.

He grunted and sagged over the sink, spilling the water down his front, and his free hand flew to the back of his head. As she recoiled in horror, Luke was beside her almost instantly, taking the marshal's gun and retrieving his own. Then he jerked the man up by his jacket and forced him down on the couch.

Greg swore under his breath as he held his head in his hands. "This is going to go badly for both of you." A groan punctuated his statement.

"You're probably right...unless we can come to some kind of understanding." Luke stood on the other side of the coffee table.

Suddenly, the door burst open and three huge, camo-covered men stormed the room, weapons drawn.

Sally started, still trembling from the idea of caving in someone's head with a piece of art, but neither Luke nor Greg flinched.

"What the hell, man? Are we late? Looks like you've got it under control." Travis lowered his weapon, looking strangely disappointed.

A smirk appeared on Luke's otherwise stony face. "Sally took matters into her own hands."

The men chuckled, but Luke didn't join them.

"I knew there was more to the little woman than met the eye." Travis ran an appreciative gaze over her.

"Sally, you might want to get dressed now." Luke gave her a cursory glance, as though he was embarrassed by her.

Wasn't that just the whipped cream on top of their reunion sundae? Heat flooded her cheeks as she dropped her gaze, unwilling to meet the uncomfortable glances of Luke's friends. Had she just made the biggest mistake of her life by angering Greg? Too late. The marshal didn't look like he was in to second chances at the moment. First order of business: get dressed. Second: find Jen. Then decide on the third thing.

"Would you boys mind staying with Sally for a bit? Marshal Lambert and I need to have a conversation." Luke glanced at each of them in turn.

Sally didn't expect him to look at her for approval, so she wasn't disappointed.

"Marshal?" The usually quiet Coop was the first to voice the question.

"Shit, Luke. What the hell?" Apparently, Travis was just getting up to speed, worrying about his involvement in obstructing justice.

"Marshal Lambert is in charge of protecting Sally." Luke turned back to Greg. "But the witness protection program is voluntary. Isn't that right, Lambert? You can discourage her from quitting, explain the danger and try to persuade her to accept the new identify you've procured for her and disappear. Kidnapping—removing her forcefully by threatening to leave her daughter behind—that's low. I'd think that would be frowned upon by the US Marshals Service."

Greg glared at him from the couch.

Luke nodded his head toward the door. "We need to talk about how this is going to end." He turned his back on Greg and stepped toward the door. Travis, Coop and Matt parted to let him through and then watched distrustfully as Greg rose and followed him from the cabin.

Sally quickly disappeared into the bedroom, closing the door behind her. Her emotions were all over the place. Anger, humiliation, frustration and dread—all playing hopscotch on her chest. If she'd thought it was possible to hide away in this room forever, she'd have given it a shot. Anything not to have to face the three men in the front room. And she wasn't so hot on encountering Luke anytime soon either.

She shook her head and her chin came up. She'd hidden long enough. It was time to take a stand and face things head-on. Starting with getting dressed and making a pot of coffee for the men who'd been left to babysit her. Sally pulled on jeans and a sweater, removing Luke's shirt and tossing it on the bed.

When she stepped from the bedroom, Travis was positioned by a front window, obviously on sentry duty. Coop sat on the couch, reading a magazine he'd picked up from the coffee table. Matt, bless his heart, was already brewing coffee. Sally nodded to each of them in turn and stepped toward the big man arranging five coffee mugs on the counter.

"How do you take yours, Sally?" Matt poured steaming hot liquid in four of them.

"Black is fine." She forced a smile as she gratefully accepted the coffee he handed her.

Coop and Travis sauntered over and each grabbed a cup.

Travis grinned at her, lifting his coffee in salute. "That marshal should have known better than to threaten Baby Bear. Mama bears never stand for that shit. Way to go, Sally."

Coop and Matt mumbled their agreement.

She grimaced, uncomfortable with their praise when Luke was so obviously displeased with her involvement. "Thanks, guys, but I can't help thinking I shouldn't have come here. It wasn't my intention to bring trouble into Daniel and Ellen's home. And you guys shouldn't have to take care of me either."

"Oh, hell. Daniel would do anything for Luke. He can take care of what's his too. If he's even half as tough as his brother, Ian, he's one tough mother. Pardon my French. Any friend of Luke's is a friend of ours." Coop glanced at the other two, who nodded their agreement.

Sally smiled half-heartedly as heat seared her cheeks. Luke wouldn't even look at her before he left with Greg. What would his friends think of her once they found out she'd managed to upset him to the point of turning his back on her?

Travis returned to his station by the window and Coop kicked back in a tweed recliner nearby, nursing his coffee. Sally glanced up as Matt stepped closer.

"Want to talk about it?" His voice was low, as though he purposely spoke so no one else would overhear their conversation.

Of Luke's three friends, Sally had been instantly drawn to Matt "MacGyver" Iverson. His compassion, his honesty and his obvious respect for Luke instilled trust in her for the dark-haired man. Still, she couldn't bring herself to tell him of Luke's anger.

"About what?" Sally met his gaze.

Matt chuckled. "Luke and I are tight. He wouldn't let a little thing like that marshal showing up here bother him overmuch. But he definitely had a mad on, so I'm betting something didn't go the way he planned."

Sally opened her mouth to deny having any part in it when Matt's eyebrow shot up and he crossed his arms, watching her expectantly. She snorted derisively. Matt might talk slow, but he didn't miss much. Still, she couldn't tell him the whole truth. Not the part about Clive Brennan being her father. And especially not how she'd betrayed Luke—betrayed them all—by withholding that information. She turned her back to Travis and Coop just in case they glanced her way.

"I'm afraid it's my fault. Luke told me to stay in the bathroom, but I started to have a panic attack trapped in there, so I opened the door. I just needed some air, but then I heard voices, and I snuck closer so I could hear. I overheard Marshal Lambert say he didn't think I knew what was best for me and Jen." Sally paused and raked a hand angrily through her hair.

Matt leaned closer. "Made you mad, didn't it? I don't blame you. How long have you been making decisions for yourself and that little girl? Nobody else knows what's best for the two of you. My guess is, that marshal only said it to get you to show yourself."

"Well, it worked. I went barreling out into the front room, not realizing what I'd done until I saw the expression on Luke's face. He looked so angry. I wouldn't be surprised if he got in his car and..." Sally took a small sip of coffee, needing a little time to fight back the tears that suddenly threatened.

Matt scoffed. "Ah, angel, Luke ain't goin' nowhere. That man's got it bad for you. He carried that picture of you and little Jen everywhere. He needs you like he needs air. He'll be back. You can take my word on that. He gets all tweaked sometimes—we all do, but he'll get over it. He knows you're the best thing that's ever happened to him...even if you don't follow directions very well." He gave her an exaggerated wink.

Laughter bubbled from her throat. "I may be lousy at following directions, but why do men think their instructions are irrefutable?"

Matt grinned broadly and clinked his cup with hers. "Because, darlin', we're always right."

With a roll of her eyes heavenward, Sally lifted her mug in silent appreciation for his friendship, a smile sliding easily over her face. It slipped away just as quickly as Luke strode through the door.

Chapter Fourteen

A stab of possessiveness hit Luke hard in the abs as he watched her interacting with MacGyver so free and easy, like she hadn't just met him today. And that asshole was eating it up. As quickly as the suspicion clenched his jaw, Luke shook it off. They had more important things to worry about than petty jealousy.

Travis walked toward him, and Luke shook his hand. Coop and, eventually, MacGyver joined them and huddled around the doorway. "We all good?" Travis's gaze swept over him, probably to determine if he'd gotten his ass kicked tonight.

"Everything's cool. I'll fill you all in later—after I talk to Sally." Luke glanced toward her, where she leaned against the sink, a coffee mug clutched tightly in both hands. She blinked and looked away.

The men started to file out. Coop clapped him on the back as he came alongside. "You got us up at o-dark-thirty...for nothin', man. It was all over before we got here. You *owe* us a skirmish, Bro. Don't forget."

Luke grinned. "You're supposed to be on vacation, Coop, but I'll see what I can do."

MacGyver stopped directly in front of him, his height giving him two or three inches of lean-over on Luke. His expression was stone-cold serious, though the bond between them shone in his eyes. "She's hurtin', Luke. Take it easy on her, huh?"

Luke nodded minimally, and MacGyver followed the other men outside, pulling the door closed behind him. Luke hung his head for a moment. His friend had spent all of ten minutes with Sally and picked up on the pain that he'd been blind to. Should have known better than to suspect the big man of making a play for his woman. MacGyver was one of the most honorable men he'd ever met.

Suddenly, the cabin was bathed in silence thick enough to butter bread. Luke turned toward Sally and caught her watching him again. Abruptly, she pivoted toward the sink, and her coffee cup landed a little too hard on the countertop. Damn! He'd give anything to know what she was thinking, but the only way to determine that was to have the conversation he was justifiably dreading.

He covered the distance between them and leaned against the counter a few feet from her. The smell of freshly brewed coffee grabbed his attention, and he claimed the last remaining cup, reached for the carafe and poured it full. A large swallow of the hot liquid braced him somewhat.

"Is he gone?" Sally spoke without looking at Luke.

"Yep."

"Is Jen all right?"

"She'll never even know the marshal was here." He should have known she'd be worried about her daughter. Luke set down his cup, his gaze directed out the small window over the sink, same as hers. "Are *you* okay?"

"I'm fine," she said, her voice distant, her words clipped.

She was angry with him. What had he done besides try to protect her? He'd been surprised and furious from the instant she'd appeared in the room, in essence turning herself over to the marshal who wanted to whisk her away from him. Then finding out Brennan was her father had tipped him over the edge. After cooling off, Luke had realized it was only the fear of losing her that had jump-started his temper. But there were things they had to discuss. The conversation he needed to have with her was going to make her angrier. He knew that. It might even make her decide she didn't want him around. Sweat beaded on his forehead. Still, he had to know he could trust her completely.

Luke took a deep breath and plunged in. "You were supposed to stay in the bathroom. We talked about why that was important. Remember? What the hell happened, Sally?" He strove to keep his voice from sounding harsh but was only partially successful.

She tensed and remained silent.

Luke sighed. "I thought you trusted me. If you don't, tell me now and I'll find someone else to protect you."

Sally flinched and crossed her arms over her stomach. She opened her mouth and closed it twice before any words came out. "I know I screwed up, but don't treat me like a child, Luke. I've been living this life a lot longer than you have. I didn't come out of that room because I didn't trust you or because what you said wasn't important. It doesn't even matter why. I just...*had* to." Her voice cracked, and she paused, pulling herself up even straighter.

Luke's heart constricted and his simmering anger fizzled and dissipated. All he wanted to do was fold her in his arms, the revelation that Brennan was her father temporarily pushed aside. When he took a half step toward her, she stopped him with a raised hand and a terse shake of her head.

"When I heard Greg talking about me as though I was an empty-headed bimbo who needed a man to make her decisions, I lost it. It was foolish. Greg might have hurt you...or worse...and it would have been my fault. I don't blame you for being furious. And I'd totally understand if you wanted me to leave."

Luke closed his eyes for a minute, relief washing through him like floodwaters in a dry creek bed. If she was leaving that decision up to him, damn sure she was staying right here. He tried to hide the grin he couldn't seem to wipe away. "I'm proud of you."

Sally glanced at him, clearly surprised, then looked away again.

"You used what you had—the beginnings of a panic attack—to cause a diversion that put us back in control of the situation without anyone getting seriously hurt. I had to go through Navy SEAL training to learn to think on my feet like that."

Luke stepped toward her, close enough he could brush back the hair that had fallen into her eyes. She was trembling, and her arms crossed in front of her seemed to be the only thing holding her up, but she didn't scoot out of his reach.

"I get it. No small rooms for you. I had a feeling it was a bad idea from the start. I was a little disappointed—okay, maybe irritated—when my plan fell apart, but I'm nothing if not adaptable. I can adjust if need be. We'll work out a better plan next time."

She huffed as she turned away from him. "First, the word you're looking for is *sullen*. Next time? I don't think so."

"Wait." Luke stepped in front of her and forced her chin up with one finger. "What's that mean?"

"It means you and everyone else will be safer if Jen and I leave." Sally's eyes filled with tears, and still he wouldn't let her look away.

Luke's sense of relief and well-being melted away and trepidation coiled like a snake in his stomach. For a few seconds, words escaped him. The idea of her leaving him was unthinkable. Hell no...he wouldn't let her go without him—plain and simple. Perhaps they had brought danger too close to Daniel and his family. With Travis and the boys here, though, Luke would bet on them coming out on top in anything short of a full-scale enemy attack. Surely Sally could see they were safer here.

Was she looking for an excuse to bail? He tried to clear the lump from his throat, but it still lodged there. "I see. So...you're still mad at me." His voice hardened slightly.

"No. I'm not mad at you, Luke." She pulled away from his touch.

"Okay. Then tell me what I've done to deserve you running out on me. We're relatively safe here. Travis, Coop and MacGyver have our backs. For someone in your position, it doesn't get much better. So, let's hear your reasoning. I deserve to know, don't you think? Unless I'm right and you're just plain-ass angry at me. Go ahead. Tell me. Yell if you have to." Luke could see her distancing herself emotionally and physically. He was pushing her intentionally, hoping to break through the barriers she'd apparently erected around her heart.

Sally turned away; her stream of mumbled words went unheard.

"What did you say? Speak up, sunshine. Or didn't you want me to hear your answer?" He bombarded her with questions.

She whipped around, her hands again fisted at her sides. "*I. Don't. Yell.*" The words, issued at the decibel level of a rock and roll band in concert, echoed in the silence of the room. Sally covered her mouth as remorseful eyes locked on him. Tears rimmed her beautiful blues and overflowed down her cheeks.

Luke raised an eyebrow, then threw back his head and laughed. A watery smirk appeared on her lips fleetingly, chased away by a stuttering sob.

He caught her before she could turn away and wrapped her tightly against him. "I love you, sunshine. Did you forget? Regardless of what you might think, I would be a basket case if you and Jen walked away. You can get mad and yell at me as much as you need to—I still won't let you go. Whether you know it yet or not, *you don't want to leave me.*" His mouth came down on hers, not a soft, gentle kiss but one of deep need and hunger.

Finally, her body relaxed against his and her arms threaded around his neck. When he raised his head, she stayed put, a smile riding her lips that made his heart ache deep down inside. Without a word, Luke swept her into his arms and strode to the bed. His heart wasn't the only thing aching. His arousal had swollen, hard and impatient, and now throbbed in time with his pulse. He placed her on her feet on the bed and pulled her jeans down to her ankles.

She squealed when he bent and jerked her feet out from under her, then ripped her pants the rest of the way off. The sexy woman sprawled on the bed wore no panties, which turned him on even more. He hastily got rid of his boots and pants and joined her amid the rumpled covers.

Luke locked his mouth on hers, plundering with lips and tongue. The soft mewls he swallowed said he must be doing something right, but it wasn't enough. He straddled her stomach and pushed her shirt up to reveal firm, ripe breasts. The nipples were hard and pebbled, and his rough hands surrounding them, pulling and tweaking, made her writhe beneath him and cry his name.

He grinned when she reached for his manhood, standing sentinel between them. He caught her hand and stretched it over her head. "Not this time, sunshine. I'm just barely hanging on as it is." Capturing her other hand, he joined her wrists on the pillow above her. Raining kisses over her face, neck and breasts, he smiled as she tried to pull her hands away. "In a minute. Don't get impatient."

He brought his hand to her mound, and she arched into him. His fingers split her folds once, twice, and then sunk deep inside. His thumb circled her sensitive core, coming closer and closer to her swollen nub, while he worked his fingers inside her. Damn, she was so wet and hot—and she was his...just like he was hers. She would know they belonged together before he was through.

His fingers found the spot that ripped a tortured moan from her lips, and he rolled her engorged center between thumb and forefinger. Sally reared off the bed with a cry and then came apart with a whimper beneath him. Her eyes were glazed and unfocused. She moaned, and her breath caught as he released her hands and sat back on his knees. Fumbling for a condom, he ripped open the package and had it seated in seconds.

Luke lowered himself between her silky thighs, his hard-on nestled in the warmth between her legs. She smiled lazily and brought his face to hers for a kiss. Raising up on his elbows, he studied her. "Tell me you're staying with me. I need to hear you say it."

Worry, or something worse, creased her brow. "Why haven't you asked me about...my father? I should have told you."

"Hell, if it's one thing I can understand, it's having family members you'd rather not claim. My old man is a perfect example. That the senator is my father is information I seldom volunteer." Damn straight—she should have told him, and it stung, more than a little, that she hadn't.

Her warm hands caressed his face. "I guess you're stuck with us, then."

Not exactly the commitment he'd wanted to hear, but he wouldn't push her—not yet. He searched her face for any sign of doubt and found none. "I want you so bad, sunshine. I don't know if I can be gentle."

"I trust you, and I'm pretty sure I won't break." Her lips at the edge of his mouth encouraged him.

Luke rocked his hips back and penetrated her tight sheath. The sound of her sudden inhalation reached him, but he was lost in her heat and the way her muscles squeezed his throbbing member. With a groan, he wound his arms around her waist, binding her to him, and began a slow and steady rhythm. Suddenly, he rolled over, clutching her tightly and bringing her with him until she sat, straddling him, impaled on his rigid shaft.

Surprise lined her face, but a sultry smile slid into place on her lips. "You might warn a girl," she whispered.

"I like keeping you off-balance. Always knowing what to expect is boring. Life with me won't be boring, sunshine." He held his breath when her brow furrowed for a heartbeat.

She hadn't committed to life with him or anything close, but that didn't mean he wasn't going to plead his case every chance he got.

"Good to know." Her faint smile returned.

Luke fastened his hands around her waist. "Are you ready?" He bucked upward and grinned when her eyes grew round. He was ready—that was for damn sure.

Her tender gaze, locked on his, was enough to help him find the gentleness within himself he'd been afraid he couldn't harness. He moved with her until they found the rhythm he craved so badly, and as her release crashed over her again, Luke took satisfaction in how perfect they were together.

Holding her tightly, he rolled her beneath him and plunged deep until, a groan escaping him, he exploded into fiery bits of pleasure and lust that left him depleted. It was a long time before his lungs recovered and he could feel his legs. When he moved off her, she curled up next to him, her head resting against his heart. Contentment and hope curved his lips into a grin as he pulled a sheet over them and wrapped his arms around her.

Chapter Fifteen

Daniel and Ellen's front room was a beehive of activity by the time Luke and Sally arrived at midmorning. Travis was on his way to the small utility area just off the kitchen, looking surprisingly domestic, carrying a basket of what appeared to be wet laundry. Coop and Matt were helping Ellen fold sheets, and Daniel strode through the back door with a large toolbox and a carpenter's belt buckled around his waist.

Jen and Bridgett struggled under a bucket loaded with cleaning supplies, rags and sponges. Jen helped Bridgett set down their burden and ran to throw her arms around Luke and Sally.

Hugging her daughter, Sally looked curiously at Ellen. "What's going on?"

Daniel's wife stopped folding towels and brushed a loose strand of hair from her face. "We got a big reservation this morning. One of our regulars from Spokane referred a large group of business associates. They'll be here tomorrow morning and are staying the week."

"Tomorrow?" Sally suddenly understood the reason for all the laundry and cleaning supplies. "They didn't give you much notice."

"I know, but this is really good for our business. Martin O'Sullivan is a real estate broker—the one who helped us buy this place. He sends us new clients all the time. He's been so good to us, we couldn't say no." Ellen glanced toward Daniel and smiled. "Besides, the early season is the toughest to book, especially when you're the new kids on the block. Unfortunately, none of the cabins are ready for the season, except the ones you're staying in. I've already imposed on Coop, MacGyver and Travis." Ellen smiled apologetically. "I was hoping you and Luke might lend a hand too."

"You bet we'll help," Luke said.

Sally grasped Jen's hand. "Tell us what to do."

"Daniel has a list of items that need attention on the cabins. How about if the guys go with him and we girls finish the laundry and then start cleaning?" Her gaze included Jen and Bridgett.

"Let's get started." Luke winked at Sally and tousled Jen's hair before he followed Daniel and the rest of the men outside.

The women made short work of washing, drying and folding the rest of the sheets and towels Ellen said she'd need. It didn't seem like work to Sally. Between the adult female conversation and the abundant laughter, she felt normal for the first time in days. It'd been a good idea, coming here, meeting Luke's friends. She could almost believe it was possible to have a new life, free of the shadow of her past.

Filled with expectancy and optimism, Sally slid her arm around Jen's shoulders and gave her a hug. "I love you, sweetheart."

"Love you most, Mom." Jen issued her standard reply, and they both laughed.

Ellen kept them busy throughout the day, scrubbing floors, organizing cupboards and making beds. As soon as they finished cleaning and stocking each cabin, she sent the girls off to Daniel with the to-do list she'd made as they discovered items that needed attention. The two girls ran in circles, chased each other and giggled as though they'd just been released for recess. Seeing Jen so happy was pure joy to Sally.

The sun was going down when Ellen finally set her hands on her hips and looked around, a hint of pride in her eyes. "I think we're ready." A tired smile gave her a soft glow. "We couldn't have done this without you and the guys. I'll never be able to thank you."

Sally hugged her. "That's what friends are for."

Ellen linked arms with her. "Come on. Let's go clean up and start some dinner. The men are probably starving."

Sally's stomach growled, and both women laughed. Jen and Bridgett had crashed a couple of hours ago, and Ellen had sent them back to her house to rest and have a sandwich. That sounded pretty good to Sally, but when they started up the path to Ellen's back door, the most scrumptious aroma teased her senses, magnifying her hunger.

Ellen lifted her head. "Something smells delicious. Daniel must be at it again."

"He cooks?" Sally's eyebrows shot up.

"Oh, honey, there's not much my Daniel can't do." The Cheshire-cat grin on Ellen's face made Sally snicker.

As the women entered the back door, arm in arm, all five men stopped the domestic chores they were involved in and looked their way. Matt was at the sink, presiding over a soapy stack of dishes. Travis and Coop had been hauling plates and flatware to the table. Luke and Daniel worked behind the big, industrial-sized oven, each with an apron tied around his waist.

Speechless, Sally exchanged a bemused glance with Ellen.

Daniel rapped on the countertop with a spatula. "Back to work." The activity resumed as though it had never stopped.

"What's for dinner?" Ellen moved around the counter toward her husband.

Daniel held his hands up in a don't-blame-me-for-this gesture. "Pizza. Luke's recipe. The jury's still out on whether it's any good or not."

Sally met Luke's gaze. "It smells wonderful."

"Thanks, sunshine. It's nice to hear from someone who appreciates good food. I've had to put up with these knuckleheads for the past hour." Luke swung his arm in an arc, indicating his three SEAL buddies and Daniel.

"Oh, boo hoo, Harding. Give it a rest, will ya?" Travis groused from across the room as he scattered the plates around the table in no particular order.

Luke chuckled and his familiar grin appeared. "Your dinner is about ready. Why don't you ladies get washed up?"

"Where are the girls?" Ellen gave her husband a quick hug.

"They grabbed a bite to eat a couple of hours ago and headed upstairs to watch a movie. Haven't heard from them since. I'll go get them—that is if Luke can get the pizzas out of the oven without burning them." Daniel strode toward the stairs, accompanied by male laughter.

"Everyone's a critic." Luke threw open the oven door and pulled out four large pizzas in quick succession.

Sally looked at herself, dirt and grime caked on the legs of her pants—not to mention under her fingernails. Her skin practically crawled with the sweat and dirt that covered her. "I was hoping for a shower and a change of clothes." She lifted her hands, afraid to touch anything.

Luke dropped his pot holders and circled the kitchen counter. He slid his arm around her waist and pulled her against him, his lips grazing her forehead. "We're all in the same boat, sunshine. Just wash off the worst of it for now." He lowered his lips to her ear and continued in a whisper. "When we get back to the cabin, I'll wash you...from head to toe."

Sally's gaze darted to his. Mischief shone warmly from his eyes. "Now there's an offer a girl can't refuse." She pressed close and lifted her lips to meet his.

Stepping back, she headed quickly for the nearest sink. Luke's low groan followed her.

"Bridgett and Jen said they're not hungry. Let's eat." Daniel made the announcement as he descended the stairs.

Luke pulled a huge bowl of salad and two bottles of wine from the refrigerator and handed them to Daniel. When they were all seated, Daniel blessed the meal and then bedlam broke out as they passed the salad around the table while everyone grabbed for slices of pizza.

"This is delicious," Sally said, a slice still clutched in her hand.

The others murmured their agreement, and Luke gave her a kiss on the cheek.

A warm sensation grew in her belly until a flush of heat on her skin made her look away.

"Ellen, what time will the guests arrive tomorrow?"

"Around noon. We'll check them in and get them settled first. We stocked the cabins with lunch supplies, but they'll take their breakfast and supper meals with us." Ellen glanced at her husband.

As though on cue, Daniel raised his wineglass and cleared his throat. "Obviously, Ellen and I couldn't have gotten this place ready in time by ourselves. Thanks to all of you, we got 'er done. It's a fitting tribute to Ian's choice of good friends." His gaze traveled to Sally. "And Luke's—who didn't stop talking about *you* all day."

Sally refused to blush but couldn't corral the pleased smile that spread of its own accord.

Luke chuckled and rubbed his hand up and down her back, then lifted his glass. "To Ian and good friends."

"May he rest in peace," Matt said.

"Hear, hear." Travis held his glass skyward, as though saluting someone the rest of them couldn't see.

Sally watched him as he solemnly honored his fallen comrade.

Silence settled over the group for a moment until Daniel coughed self-consciously. "You know, those kids are probably sound asleep by now."

Sally had been thinking the same thing. Before she could reply, Luke threaded his fingers through hers. "No problem. I'll carry her back to our cabin."

"Or...you could let her stay the night again," Ellen said. "I'm being selfish, of course, but Bridgett's been so happy since Jen arrived." A blush tinging her cheeks pink, she stood and started clearing the table.

All hands helped carry the dirty dishes to the sink until the men, with Ellen's prodding, filed outside and quiet descended on the room. In short order, the kitchen was spotless and the dishwasher purred softly through its cycle.

Sally dried her hands on a kitchen towel. "You look tired." She smiled at her new friend. "Tell me what I can do to help tomorrow."

"People don't come here expecting to have everything done for them. Our guests carry their own luggage and clear their place settings from the table. But…even we have to keep records and pay lodging tax. I feel bad even asking, but if you could drop in about noon and help me get them registered, that would really speed things up."

"Say no more. I'll be here." Sally hung the towel to dry on the oven door. "Well, I'd better go get Jen."

"Need any help?"

"Thanks, but I'll grab Luke if she needs to be carried." Sally appreciated that Ellen didn't bring up Jen staying over again. After everything that had happened last night with the marshal, she wanted her daughter close.

Jen and Bridgett were sound asleep on the *Frozen* comforter that topped Bridgett's princess canopy-style bed. Sally should've known, but disappointment bit her anyway as she halted just inside the door. For a moment, she stood watching her daughter in peaceful sleep while she made up her mind. Then, carefully covering both girls, she left them there.

Luke and Ellen stood in the open doorway of the cabin when Sally descended the stairs.

Ellen turned toward her, and her gaze swept to the upper floor. "Asleep?"

"I didn't have the heart to wake her. I'll leave her, if you're sure you don't mind."

"She'll be fine here, and don't worry about coming early to get her. We're going to take it easy around here in the morning."

Leaning against the doorframe, Luke studied Sally. "Are you sure, sunshine? I don't mind packing her back to our place."

Luke's sincerity was obvious in his expression, and she loved him for it. Meeting his gaze and holding it, she shook her head. "I think Ellen's right."

Daniel entered the cabin at that moment, pushing through the small group standing around the door. "My wife is always right. What's she right about this time?"

"That Jen will sleep here tonight." Sally caught Ellen's gaze and the woman nodded.

"I can't believe you even tried to argue with her," Daniel said as he edged Luke and Sally toward the doorway. "You two go on now…and have fun."

When they stepped onto the front porch, Daniel closed the door in their faces.

Sally raised an eyebrow and glanced at Luke. He stared at her, intensity in his gaze. His slow, sexy smile woke the butterflies in her stomach as he reached for her hand. "You heard the man, sunshine."

* * * *

"Regrets?" Luke slung his arm around Sally's shoulders as they left Daniel's cabin, partly because of the chill in the night air and partly because of her sudden silence. If she'd made the wrong call, there was still time to fix things.

She glanced up with a smile. "No, not at all." A tiny shrug lifted one shoulder. "Maybe I feel a little guilty leaving her. Can we do something fun with Jen tomorrow after the guests are settled?"

"I was going to suggest that. How about fishing? We can take Bridgett too. Give Ellen some time off."

Sally's sigh appeared to lift a weight off her. "Jen would love that. You're so thoughtful, Luke." An impish grin blossomed on her luscious lips. "Mmm...I'm so turned on right now."

He laughed aloud. "That's what does it for you, huh? A thoughtful guy?" Luke dipped his head toward her. "Listen, do me a favor and keep your observation to yourself. If Travis and the guys get hold of that, I'll never hear the end of it."

He stopped abruptly and brought her in tightly against him, putting a silencing finger to his lips. What the hell? Was that a flash of light down by the river? Several seconds ticked by and the shiny reflection didn't reappear. Sally had tensed beside him, and he could have kicked himself for scaring her. "Thought I saw a light near the river, but there's nothing there now. Just to be on the safe side, though, I'll have Travis check it out."

Luke dug his cell phone from his pocket and thumbed to the text message screen. *Possible intruder near river below cabin 3. Have a look around?*

Almost instantaneously, the reply came. *Got your back, Bro.*

Luke held Travis's response out for Sally to read, knowing it would ease her disquiet, as it had his. He was rewarded by her sensuous smile and an arm slipped around his waist as they started walking again. Luke's suspicion still nagged at him, and he searched the shadows that surrounded the line of cabins, especially the one at the end of the row.

"How did Marshal Lambert find me?" Sally lay her head on his shoulder and looked at him.

He'd wondered when she would ask about the marshal. Luke glanced at her with what he hoped was a reassuring smile, then resumed his scrutiny of the area they yet had to pass through. "I asked him that. Figured it couldn't hurt to know what we were doing wrong. Lambert said he has a buddy in Huntington."

"That's a bit coincidental, isn't it?"

"Exactly what I said. Apparently, he was already familiar with the town, through his buddy, before he chose it for you. According to him, he called his friend as soon as he heard from you the night of the fire and asked him to keep an eye on you until he got there. Had the nerve to bitch about us taking a little walk through the woods by Aunt Peg's lodge, but switching vehicles didn't throw our tail for long. Former military, apparently. He led Lambert right to us."

Sally was silent for a few seconds, no doubt digesting that bit of information. Travis, Coop and MacGyver would probably be skirting the river by now, but Luke would never see them. They were too good at what they did.

"How did you leave it with him? He *is* still alive, isn't he? Will he come after us again?" Sally's brow furrowed and worry deepened the crease on her forehead.

Luke shrugged. "He's alive...although he'll probably have a hell of a headache for a few days."

Sally groaned and covered her face.

"He was pissed as hell, but I convinced him we had everything under control. That instead of trying to make you disappear, he should be enlisting some of his buddies to find out what the hell Brennan is up to. It wasn't an easy sell, but he eventually came around. He even said to call if we needed anything. I think my charm won him over."

"Charm, huh?"

"Careful." Luke's gaze came back to her. "I can be charming when I put my mind to it."

"I know. Why do you think I'm here?"

Approaching their cabin at last, dark forms suddenly materialized in front of them. Luke had half-expected them, but Sally drew in a sharp breath. He was pretty sure his arm around her stopped her from giving one of them a black eye before they stepped from the shadows into enough light to be recognized.

Sally dropped her hands to her hips. "Didn't you ever learn not to sneak up on a person?" Her accusing words brought low laughter.

"Not really, ma'am," MacGyver said. "Just the opposite."

"No sign of anyone." Travis was taking care of business. "We checked around the cabins. Yours too. Nothing. We'll take another run through in a couple of hours, just in case. Not like you to see things."

"Thanks, fellas." Luke clapped Travis's shoulder, wondering how to break the news about all the things he'd seen that weren't really there since he'd returned from Afghanistan. Maybe it was a conversation for another day.

"Anything for you, Luke." Coop tipped his ball cap to Sally as he strode by. "'Night, Sally."

"Good night, Coop."

MacGyver headed out too, nodding to Sally and slapping Luke's back. Travis was the last to go, and he seemed to disappear into the shadows the same way he'd come. Luke opened the door and ushered her inside.

"Too tired for a shower?" Luke strode toward the bedroom, hoping it wasn't too late to get her mind off the scare he'd given her needlessly.

"Yes, but it doesn't matter. I can't go to bed like this. Besides, didn't you promise to wash me?"

Luke stopped in his tracks and turned slowly to face her. A grin was trying to slip free, but he wouldn't let it…not yet. He took a lazy step back toward her. "I *did* say that." Another step. "Are you up for that?"

She shrugged. "I think so. Are you?"

He covered the distance between them until they were a foot apart. "Oh, I'm definitely on board. You know we'll both be naked, right?"

"I assumed. Anything else I should know?" A sexy little grin rode her lips.

He leaned toward her and kissed both eyes and her nose before his mouth came down on hers, and he put all his longing for her into the kiss. When he came up for air, her eyelids remained closed for a few seconds before she opened them and pinned him with the darkest blue eyes he'd ever seen.

Luke linked his hand with hers and led her toward the bedroom. "I'll get the water warmed up. Join me whenever you're ready." He dropped a kiss on the column of her throat before he kicked off his boots and strode toward the bathroom. A minute later, his clothes lay in a pile near the wall and the hot, steamy water cascaded over his shoulders. Soaping a washrag, he removed the sweat and grime from the day's work, then shampooed his hair. Sally still hadn't appeared.

Just when he gave in to the conclusion she'd bowed out of their little rendezvous, a shadow slid in front of the lights. Luke glanced over as she pulled the shower door open a few inches.

She froze there. Luke stood still while her gaze slid over his body, starting with the scar, front and center on his chest, from a bullet he'd stopped on the day he was rescued. She paled but eventually moved on to his scarred back and shoulders, where his captors had sliced open his flesh time and time again. There was hardly a spot on his torso that didn't bare some reminder of his imprisonment.

He didn't need to be reminded—he remembered only too well.

Would she be able to cope with the stark evidence of his torture? Apprehensive that she might not be able to handle it, he waited for her to say something, turn away or join him in the shower.

Pushing the door open farther, Luke held his hand out to her. "Come on in. The water's just right."

Her gaze darted to his and held for the longest few seconds of his life before the corners of her mouth curved upward ever so slightly. This time, her bold gaze traveled over him like a slow caress, and his body reacted instantly, his manhood hardening to an incessant ache.

A sultry smile settled on her lips and made his heart do a little flip as she placed her hand in his and stepped over the edge of the shower.

Sweet Jesus! If he thought she was sexy standing outside the shower naked, it was nothing compared to her naked and wet. When she reached for him, curling her hand around his rigid shaft, he nearly lost his footing.

Sally gazed at him, a sly smile taking up residence on her beautiful face. "Tell me if I'm doing it wrong." Without waiting for a reply, she dropped to her knees.

A groan worked free from Luke's throat as her tongue spiraled up one side of his member and down the other. His eyes rolled back in his head when the tip disappeared between her full lips. As she took him deep, Luke ground his teeth against the release that was building, while fighting the urge to place his hand on the back of her head and direct her movements. With seemingly expert technique, she brought him to the edge of reason, and it was with supreme effort he kept from tipping over the edge.

So aroused it hurt, he pushed her away. Then, releasing a feral growl, he quickly lifted her to her feet, thinking only of his need to be inside her. Unexpectedly, Sally jerked free of his hands and shrank from him. As he met her gaze, uncertainty, bordering on fear, hardened her expression for a heartbeat...and then it was gone. Shit. He'd been too damn rough and he'd frightened her. Instant self-recrimination sucker-punched him.

Holding her gaze, he reached for her, raking his fingers through her hair, and drew her slowly closer until his lips met hers. She tensed but didn't resist. After a few seconds, she relaxed into him and responded with desire matching his. A sigh of relief escaped, and Luke mentally cataloged the incident for another time. Even so, anger still simmered deep down.

Someone had used sex to hurt her. He'd bet on it, and his money was on Jen's father. They'd never spoken of him, yet Sally had managed to convey to Luke that the topic wasn't open for discussion. Sooner or later, he'd convince her to talk to him, and if he found that the man who'd fathered Jen had put the look of fear in Sally's eyes in a moment that should be comprised of complete trust—heaven help him.

Luke plucked another washrag from the rack and slowly covered it with soap. Sally watched him, biting her bottom lip.

"Turn around, sunshine." He breathed the words against her ear.

A shudder passed quickly through her, and she complied with a nervous squeak.

Luke grinned in response. Wrapping one arm around her to hold her in place, he started with her neck and shoulders, rubbing the soapy rag from left to right.

"Raise your arms." She complied without hesitation and, looking over her shoulder, he glimpsed the smile that turned up the corner of her mouth as he spread soap from the tip of one hand, across her breasts to the other.

She giggled and bent forward when he got to her ribs, stomach and the sensitive skin at the apex of her legs. He had to bite back an expletive when her sexy backside brushed the length of his hard-on.

"Spread your legs."

Sally straightened, pushing her hair back from her face, and slid one foot over about six inches.

"More." Luke nipped her earlobe and soothed the bite with his tongue.

"What? No."

"Do it." Luke kissed the pulsing vein in her neck, bending her sideways until her legs parted to keep her balance. "Good girl. Now, don't move."

"Um...you've gotten a little bossy, sailor."

He brought the soapy rag down her back and across the cheeks of her delectable ass, eliciting a shiver from her, but she stood her ground. Stepping around in front of her, he knelt. "Grab my shoulders."

"I'm okay."

"Suit yourself." Luke soaped the rag again, slowly, enjoying the view from his position. His eyes on her, he finished bathing her legs from thighs to toes, paying close attention to her hair-covered mound and the slickness of her folds. Her breath had picked up over the past few minutes, as had the pulse in her neck, and her dark eyes watched his every move. He tugged her farther under the spray of water and let his hands slide over her silken skin as the soap suds ran off her in foamy rivulets.

He leaned toward her, placing his mouth over the swollen kernel at her core and sucked. Sally arched into him even as his name tore from her throat. Her legs gave out, and he caught her in his arms as she collapsed. He slid down to sit on the bottom of the compact shower stall with her on his lap while she trembled under the force of her climax. The way she responded to his touch…his kiss…his voice in her ear…was so damn hot.

After a few minutes, Sally's hand came up to cover her face. "You have to stop doing that."

Luke nuzzled her ear. "Is that really what you want?"

"Yes. No. No, of course not. But you could warn me."

Luke barked out a laugh. Then he leaned over her. "We're running short on hot water. Besides, I forgot to grab a condom, and I'm not done yet. I want to be inside you. Are you ready?" He breathed the words against her mouth.

She pulled him closer. "I'm always ready for you."

Her words wrapped a layer of warmth around his heart. They sounded closer to permanent than anything she'd said so far. He'd already decided he wouldn't give her up without a fight…and he could fight dirty if he had to, but it'd be the answer to his dreams if she wanted him badly enough to make fighting unnecessary.

He helped her out of the shower, towel drying her tenderly, and then she did the same for him. When he couldn't wait another second, he scooped her up, strode to the bed and tossed her onto the soft mattress. Ripping open the waiting condom, he rolled it on and crawled to the center of the bed.

"Care to make a little wager?" Luke braced himself over her, enjoying the instant challenge in her eyes.

"What kind of wager?"

"I bet you'll have a second orgasm before I have one."

"Oh, please. That *would* be some kind of a feat, considering I'm still breathless from the last one."

His muscles flexed as he shifted to bury himself in her warmth, the action sending a tremor through his body and producing a comfortable feeling of being home. He gritted his teeth and pushed deep. "Have a little faith, sunshine. I bet I can make you come all night long."

Sally tipped her head back and considered him with what appeared to be doubt. "Big words, sailor."

"Consider yourself warned." Luke brushed her lips with infinite care, moving slowly down her throat to the fullness of her breast, pleased by the way her pulse leaped in the hollow of her throat as he stroked the pebbled tips with his tongue. He had all night…and either way it went was a win.

Chapter Sixteen

Sally sat cross-legged on the foot of the bed, leaned her elbows on her knees and stared at Luke's sleeping form. The poor guy deserved to sleep in. He'd been awake most of the night—they both had. While his vigorous activities had evidently tired him out, she'd been completely energized. She couldn't seem to divest herself of the grin that came every time her mind wandered to the intimacies they'd shared.

Up early and raring to go, she'd showered and changed into khaki shorts and a white tank top, reserving a dark blue fleece jacket for the coolness of the morning. She'd entertained and rejected the idea of leaving a note for Luke and walking to Daniel and Ellen's house by herself. That would no doubt be careless after Luke had called out Travis, Matt and Coop last night to check out a flash of light down by the river. She wouldn't diminish Luke's concern by acting foolishly.

She looked yearningly through the open bedroom door, where the sun was just making an appearance through the front windows. It was going to be a gloriously beautiful day. She started to slide her legs off the bed when a warm hand grabbed her wrist. Luke pulled her toward him until she was sprawled on top of him.

Smoldering eyes regarded her from beneath lowered lashes. "You're dressed already? What are you doing up so early?"

"I'm too happy to sleep." Sally pecked him on the lips. "You, on the other hand—you led me to believe you didn't ever sleep and look at you."

"You must have put a spell on me. I haven't slept so soundly in over a year." Luke lay a finger alongside her chin, turned her head and landed a kiss on the corner of her mouth. "It's all you, sunshine. We're good together. You know that, right?"

"I'm starting to see the up side."

He snickered good-naturedly. "Yeah? Does that mean you're ready to accept my proposal?" Luke raked one hand through her hair, grabbing a handful, and made her look at him.

Words failed her, but, apparently, her stunned silence told him everything he needed to know. The hurt in his eyes pierced her like a knife. "I'm sorry, Luke. I thought you understood. Clive Brennan is a black cloud hanging over my head. My life hasn't been my own since I was eighteen. I can't give you all of me and I don't see you settling for less. My father overshadows every waking moment of my existence. It wouldn't be fair to you any more than it's been fair to Jen all these years."

Luke released a sigh. "I could argue that a hundred different ways... but I'm going to let it go for now. We'll find a way to entice Brennan out in the open and make him go away once and for all. You *will* be free of him—that's a promise. I can be patient until then, but don't expect me to give up. Just promise me one thing—let me be a part of your life, and Jen's."

Sally nodded, uneasiness stealing over her. That was a promise she'd really like to keep...but could she? She forced a smile. "Now, are you going to get up?"

Luke dumped her off to the side as he stepped from the bed in all his naked beauty, stretched and strode toward the bathroom. Sally never got tired of seeing him, touching him—never ceased to be amazed that someone so strong, handsome and kind would pick her from all the women who'd have loved to stand by his side. Women who didn't have murderous family members out to kill them.

Sally shook off the thought as soon as it came. She didn't want anything spoiling this day. Straightening the sheets, she made the bed and then moved into the front room to start a pot of coffee. The bright sun drew her to the window beside the door, and she gazed out longingly. So quiet out there. No sign of any of the men. When did the day start around here? The coffeepot made its final gurgle, signifying the dark brew was done. She rummaged for two cups and poured the liquid in both.

Luke was dressed in jeans, unbuttoned, and nothing else, when she stuck her head through the crack in the door he'd left. He smiled at her in the mirror, then turned to take her in his arms. The kiss he gave her was long, lingering and filled with the love he professed for her. She could get used to that.

"Ummm...you've had coffee," he said, smacking his lips.

"Yep. I brought you some." Sally handed him the full cup, and he growled his pleasure before taking a big swallow.

"Give me two minutes, sunshine. I'm almost ready."

"No hurry." It was a lie. Sally wanted to go now—needed to see Jen to make sure she was okay. Two minutes might as well be forever.

Sally clamped her lips shut on the unbearable need to implore him to move faster. Watching him sit at one of the dining chairs to slip on a pair of sneakers, she bit her tongue to keep it still.

At her second deep sigh, Luke straightened and regarded her with raised brows. "What?"

"Nothing." She dismissed his question with an impatient wave of her hand.

"Okay…but it *seems* like there's something." He leaned back and gulped another swallow of coffee while he studied her.

Sally would have made it if he hadn't smirked. Throwing her hands in the air, she stomped her feet petulantly. "Are you ready yet? What's the holdup?"

Luke had the nerve to chuckle. "My, we're impatient this morning. Tired of being alone with me?"

A roll of her eyes made him laugh out loud. "Don't be absurd. Can't you see the sun's shining? It's a gorgeous day and we're missing the best part. Jen's probably already up having breakfast. Get a move on, sailor. We've got things to do."

Luke stood so fluidly, he was halfway to her before his purposeful strides registered. The sparkle of humor in his seductive eyes was all that kept her from retreating. Stopping before her, he pushed her hair behind her shoulders. Cupping her chin, he kissed her soundly. "There's the sunshine I remember. It's good to finally see you happy. Dare I hope I had a little something to do with this turn of events?"

Sally's smile came unbidden. There was no mistaking the intensity of his love in the warmth that shone from his eyes. She wasn't alone anymore. Happiness filled her heart.

He must have found her answer in the sappy smile she couldn't rid herself of. With another smirk, his expression turned playful. "Tell you what—I have to finish getting dressed and tie my shoes yet. Then I'll give you a thirty second head start…and I'll still beat you to Daniel's cabin." The challenge in his voice was obvious.

Sally's excitement grew as her naturally competitive spirit surfaced. A race to reach Jen. Against a man built of pure muscle and trained by Navy SEALs to overcome obstacles the average person didn't even know existed. Though Luke had been a POW, tortured and seriously wounded, it was obvious he'd worked many long hours to rebuild what he'd lost and regain his strength. She'd never beat him in a fair race. The fifteen hundred yards she estimated was more of a sprint than a race. She'd need that head start and then some.

As soon as he turned his back, Sally jerked the door open, hurdled the steps and hit the grassy trail at a full run. Only then did she give any thought to being alone outside, but she couldn't stop now.

"So this is how you want to play it, huh?" His words followed her out the door, and she nearly choked on the laughter that bubbled free.

As soon as she heard the door slam shut and Luke land with both feet at the bottom of the steps, she forgot about humor and lengthened her stride. If she didn't put all her concentration into running on the uneven path, her ill-gotten advantage would be in vain.

Sally was no slacker when it came to running, yet in spite of pushing herself to the limits of her ability, Luke's footsteps still closed in on her. With Daniel's front door only a few feet ahead, she gave it everything she had. She could almost imagine Luke's breath on her neck as she bounded up the porch steps two at a time. Victory so close she could taste it, she caught her toe on the top step, stumbled and did a face-plant a foot away from her goal.

Her hands and knees took the brunt of the fall. The skin on her hands burned as she pushed herself up, then she winced as her right knee objected to holding her weight and she rolled hastily to her back. Lifting her hands for inspection, she groaned at the dozens of wood slivers embedded in each. Her knees probably looked similar, although a few slivers surely couldn't account for the throbbing in her right knee. What had she done?

Sally struggled to her elbows, but suddenly Luke knelt beside her, pushing her down, gripping her wrists and giving her hands a cursory inspection. "You're okay, babe."

If she was really okay, why did his brows almost meet over his eyes?

He directed a faint smile toward her. "You kinda had this coming—cheater."

"You're just pouting because I beat you."

"For your information, this race has been called due to clumsiness." He still held her wrists.

Sally laughed. "Let me up. I'll finish the race with or without you."

Luke's teasing smile faded. "Before I let you up, how are you with blood?"

He had to be joking. Why wasn't that roguish grin of his making an appearance? She hadn't landed hard enough to do serious damage. Still, her right knee throbbed like hell, and Luke wasn't wearing the face of a prankster.

Sally cleared the lump from her throat. "I'm a parent—I've seen blood before."

A muscle flexed in Luke's jaw. "How are you with your *own* blood?"

"You're scaring me, Luke." She struggled to free her wrists from his grip.

"Easy. Calm down, sunshine." He glanced toward her legs. "You're going to be fine, but we have a little problem we'll need MacGyver's help with."

"MacGyver—Matt? Luke, tell me what's wrong."

He held her gaze for the space of a heartbeat before he nodded. "You have a rather large splinter of wood from Daniel's porch in your right interior quad just above your knee. I'm not sure how deep it's embedded. There's some blood, but right now the splinter itself is keeping it from bleeding a lot."

Sally did her best to hide the shudder that washed over her. Common sense told her it wasn't serious, but it was probably good he hadn't allowed her to see the wound—although she wasn't going to tell Luke that. "Is that all? What now?"

"I'm going to get the big man out here to take a look." He leaned over her and stretched to bang on the door. "MacGyver was the medic for our unit. You're in good hands. How long's it been since you had a tetanus shot?"

Luke's brow, furrowed in concern, made it difficult to accept his optimistic remarks. Probably blaming himself for suggesting a race when it had been her stupid competitiveness that had caused her to wreck. Once Matt got her patched up, Luke would see it was nothing and she'd convince him later that it wasn't his fault.

The door opened behind her, and Luke glanced up. Surprise, followed quickly by anger, rolled across his face. He tensed and started to rise. "Where's Daniel? Who the hell are you?"

Sally pushed up on her elbows and swiveled to glance behind her. She gasped as fear gripped her with icy fingers and dread fell like a sledgehammer in her chest.

Clive Brennan. Her father. The man who inhabited her nightmares had caught up with her at last.

Luke gained his feet and inserted himself between Sally and the man who'd contributed sperm toward her birth and now was probably going to kill her. Instantly, a dark-haired man stepped from the shadows inside the cabin, advancing on Luke with a granite-hard expression that screamed cold-blooded and lethal.

Sally still struggled to find her voice. She had to warn Luke. He didn't know how great a danger he faced. She choked on the words as a sudden realization made her blood run cold.

Jen is inside the cabin.

"Luke, wait."

He and the dark-haired man faced off, Luke apparently determined to protect her even when the fight was stacked against him. If her father had one hired man out here, he undoubtedly had several more inside—with Jen.

"Luke!" Panic crept into her voice, and Luke's gaze swept her way and then back.

"Yakim." Clive Brennan spoke to the dark-haired man quietly, but there was no mistaking the absolute authority in his voice.

Yakim backed off immediately. "Sorry, Mr. Brennan."

Clive's charcoal-gray eyes locked on Luke's face. "It appears my daughter has been hurt. Bring her inside. My granddaughter will want to know she's all right."

Luke's gaze darted from her father's stony visage to the open doorway. "You son of a bitch. Touch that little girl and I'll kill you."

Surprise flickered in her father's eyes at Luke's threat, but no other emotions made it to his passive features. "We can debate the merits of that once my daughter has been made comfortable. A priority—don't you agree?" He was the picture of patience as he waited for Luke to arrive at the same conclusion.

When Luke finally dropped down beside her, his jaw was set in a hard line, and barely restrained anger reddened his face. Sally, unable to reconcile her father caring if she was comfortable with the man who was soon going to kill her, took hope from his strange assertions. The faintest of smiles, meant to reassure Luke, fell sadly short.

"How ya doin', babe?" Luke's answering grin was a poor imitation of the real thing.

"I think the bleeding stopped."

Luke stood and leaned over her. "Put your arm around my neck." As soon as she complied, he raised her until he could slide one arm beneath her thighs and scoop her up. He waited until Clive shoved the door wide and followed him inside.

Sally blinked rapidly to get her eyes accustomed to the absence of sunlight. The blinds and curtains were drawn inside the cabin. When the shadows started to take shape, she counted four more unfamiliar men, in addition to Yakim, scattered at intervals throughout the large open area that comprised the kitchen, family room and lobby for the Mathias family and their business. There were no guns in evidence, unless you counted the bulges under their jackets, and there was no denying who had control of the room. Luke's SEAL buddies lined a couch to Sally's right, all tense and angry—just like Luke.

Straight ahead, Daniel, Ellen and Bridgett sat at the kitchen table. Bridgett colored, seemingly oblivious to what was going on around her. Jen, sitting at the table with her back to the door, swung around at their entrance, her gaze narrowing in on the offending fragment that protruded grotesquely from Sally's leg.

"Mom? Are you okay?" Jen pushed away from her chair and sprinted toward her mother.

"Put me down, Luke. I don't want to scare Jen." She whispered the words in his ear.

Luke acquiesced instantly, keeping a firm hand on Sally's waist. She winced slightly when she tested her leg, but she caught Jen in a careful hug.

"Are you all right, sweetheart? They didn't hurt you, did they?" Sally stepped back and looked her daughter over.

"No. They were real nice—except they said we had to stay inside until you got here." Jen lowered her voice. "Travis was real mad about that." Jen glanced toward the three men on the couch.

Sally's lips pressed firmly together as resolve settled over her mind. "Well, now that I'm here, maybe they'll let you all leave." She met Luke's gaze as a warning glint darkened his expression.

"Don't even go there," he said. "I'm not leaving your side. Hold on to me. Let's get you on the couch."

His three friends scattered as Sally, Luke and Jen approached.

"MacGyver. Need you over here." Luke helped Sally lie back on the arm of the couch and stretch both legs on the cushions.

"What the hell happened?" Matt bent over her knee to assess the damage.

"I won the race." She offered the explanation with a slight shrug. From the corner of her eye, she observed her father as he moved to the table, where Daniel and Ellen sat with Bridgett. Sally tensed. She'd seen her father kill before and had long since given up on the idea he possessed an ounce of compassion. Were Jen, Luke and all her new friends going to die because of her? Clive could have shot her on sight. Why hadn't he? What did he mean when he spoke of making her comfortable as though it were a priority for him? Her breath stopped as he reached into his inside breast pocket...and started again when he drew out a thick envelope, which he laid on the table in front of Ellen. Words passed between the three of them before Clive nodded, turned and joined his men, speaking in hushed tones.

"How's it look?" Impatience edged Luke's question as he pressed Matt for a prognosis.

"Piece of cake. We can fix this. Might need a couple of stitches. Don't want to mar those gorgeous legs." Matt winked at her.

Luke slapped him hard in the gut. "Just keep your mind on your work, buddy."

Sally caught Luke's gaze. "Are you thinking what I'm thinking? Why fix me up so he can kill me later? That's why he's here, isn't it? We should be trying to make a deal to get everyone else out of here. I know you don't want to hear it, Luke, but someone has to take care of Jen. *You*. You have to take care of Jen for me."

Clive strode toward her as his men started to herd the others outside. Sally's heart rate kicked up as she watched Ellen and Bridgett walk out hand in hand. She pinned Clive with a heated glare. "What are you doing? Those people haven't done *anything* to you? Do whatever you want to me, but let them go."

Luke turned and stepped in front of her. "You'll have to go through me, Brennan."

Clive held up his hands in a gesture of surrender. "I wish to talk. That is all. Please...sit."

Luke stared at him for several seconds before stepping aside.

Her father's expression gave nothing away as his gaze slid to her. "It's good to see you, Annie. It's been a long time."

She barely recognized the name she'd answered to for more than half her life. How dare he use the name her mother gave her? Sally held his gaze, refusing to be the first to look away. A shake of his head and a subtle softening of his features surprised her. What was his game? She was never going to trust him again, and neither was Luke if his warning hand on her arm was any indication.

"I will not hurt your friends, Annie. Nor my granddaughter. This is between you and me. There are things we must discuss, and I prefer... privacy." Clive nodded toward the door. "But Jennifer, your young man and this medic will stay...for your comfort."

"Yeah, well, hold that thought for a minute, Pops." Matt gave her a confident grin. "This is going to sting so, Luke, why don't you distract her?" Sally barely caught Matt's words before Luke dropped down on one knee beside her.

"Hey, sunshine. I want to spend every minute of the rest of my life with you. I know you're tired of hearing me propose, but if you'll tell me you'll marry me...I'll stop."

With Luke's face in front of hers, Sally couldn't see Matt, and she didn't realize he'd jerked the wood free until he held the six-inch-long sliver up for her to see. Tears filled her eyes as she focused again on her Navy SEAL.

There were really only a few important things in her life. Luke and Jen were at the top of that list. She loved Luke, and she couldn't think of one reason why she shouldn't snatch up this little bit of happiness with both hands. She'd certainly lived enough of her life in fear of Clive Brennan. It was almost a relief now that he'd found her.

If the past was any indication, she couldn't believe a word her father said, meaning her happiness could very likely be short-lived. Still, committing to Luke was what she wanted to do...and no one, least of all her father, was going to stop her. "What do you think, Jen?"

The girl was smiling from ear to ear as she jumped up and down. "Yes! Finally!"

Sally laughed. "Looks like it's unanimous. Yes, I'll marry you."

Luke's eyebrows flew toward his hairline. He leaned toward her as he flung an arm around Jen and drew her into a group hug, along with Sally. Leaving a trail of kisses all over her face, he bent close. "You're mine. Thank you," he whispered.

Matt coughed, drawing their attention. "Sounds like congratulations are in order. I'm starting to feel like a fifth wheel around here. Sally, your knee's going to be sore for a while. No racing. I gotcha butterflied together for now. You can decide on stitches...later. Same with the rest of the slivers. We'll worry about them after you hear this man out." Matt nodded toward her father. "Jen, want to come with me and make sure Travis is behaving himself?"

She giggled. "Is it okay, Mom?"

A moment of trepidation sent her worried gaze toward Luke's friend. "Sure, baby. Stay with Matt, though, okay?" Sally dreaded her father's discussion. At the very least, it would be uncomfortable, and Jen should get to be anywhere but here. He'd said no one would be hurt—that it was between him and Sally. Even if he was lying, she'd put her money on Matt to keep her daughter safe.

Jen held her arms up, and he swung her onto his shoulders. She waved as he ducked down to go through the doorway.

Luke stood and pulled a chair close to Sally's head. Clive positioned a kitchen chair about five feet from the couch. For the first time, sweat glistened on his brow, and he looked nervous—but he couldn't be as nervous as Sally.

In all the nightmares in which she and Jen were killed mercilessly by the man now sitting down to have a chat with her, not once had he offered to talk things over. Either she was going crazy or the script had taken a 180-degree turn.

Clive sighed deeply. "You've thought you were hidden for a long time, Annie, but I have known where you were from the beginning, thanks to intelligence supplied by friends in the Russian GRU. You believe me a monster—a ruthless killer—a traitor to the country in which you were born. All true. I am not ashamed of what I am or what I've done. What I am *not* is a father who would harm his daughter...or anyone she holds dear. You did what you believed to be right—you testified against me. I would have preferred it differently, but I've paid my debt to your society. I am here to tell you to stop hiding and start living. You have nothing to fear from me."

Sally glanced toward Luke, half-afraid to believe what she was hearing.

"I didn't expect to meet my granddaughter. She's a good girl. You've done well with her." He held up his hand as though to keep her from interrupting. "You needn't worry. Neither you nor Jennifer will ever see me again after today. I will return to Russia to live out my life as a hero to my country. It is the best thing for both of us. And you have your young man to watch over you. This is good." His eyes shifted toward Luke. "Take care of them."

"I intend to," Luke said.

"Wait. If you meant no harm, why did you rig my house in Huntington to blow up?" Sally pushed herself up with the sudden urgency to hear his answer.

He narrowed his eyes. "That was not my doing. My friends and I arrived the next day, after you had left town. At first, I suspected your boss, Purnell, but after extensive questioning, he convinced me he did not possess the intellect to carry out such a plan."

"We saw the results of your questioning." Luke regarded him with a smirk pulling at his lips. No doubt he was thinking Emmett had gotten what he deserved.

"And I suppose you didn't ram your car into the back of Luke's truck that night and try to run us off the road?" Disbelief strained her voice.

Her father shook his head. "I swear to you on your mother's grave, it wasn't me, Annie."

Luke and Sally exchanged a glance. If this man wasn't responsible for the attempts on her life, who was?

Chapter Seventeen

Everything had happened so fast, Luke still couldn't get it straight in his head. As unbelievable as it was, Clive Brennan had tracked his daughter down to tell her she was free and clear as far as he was concerned. He'd left Daniel and Ellen an envelope stuffed with hundred-dollar bills to cover the rental of six cabins for a week with boats and tour guide included. He'd also apologized politely, asking that they not blame O'Sullivan, their regular client, who had made the reservations for them. Apparently, the poor guy truly believed they were going to stay and fish out the week.

Learning that Brennan meant no harm to Sally was a relief, but it left some rather significant unanswered questions behind.

Reclining on a grass-covered bank, Luke looked out over the lazy bend in the river where Jen and Sally fished. Five-year-old Bridgett sat not far from Jen and kept up a running stream of one-sided conversation. Jen's occasional comment seemed to be all Bridgett required to keep her talking. The innocence of the two made him smile...until he remembered the puzzle he'd been trying to figure out ever since Brennan and his entourage were picked up by two additional men in black SUVs. No one had been sorry to see them go.

"Maybe your house blowing up was accidental—a gas leak or something. And maybe those men who rammed us were drunk out of their heads and just looking for trouble. We should call the sheriff to see if he's found anything." He threw out the ideas, even though they were baseless. He wasn't ready to give voice to his hunch yet, mostly because Sally had made it clear the subject was off-limits.

He should have known she wouldn't buy it. Sally didn't even look at him. "The house was all electric—no gas leak. And those men? They shot at your truck after it went off the cliff, remember? You're right, though. We should call the sheriff." Sally whipped her line over her head expertly, casting and landing her fly on the water with a delicate touch.

Luke grinned. Where had she learned to cast like that? It was a thing of beauty. Jen was nearly as good. Perhaps he'd talk them into giving him some lessons before he embarrassed himself.

Sally swiveled to look at him without moving her feet. "You should call your brother too. He'll be worried."

True enough, but there was still something hinky about this whole setup. With the lack of anyone to blame, suspicion had been cast far and wide. "What about Lambert? He'll want to know what happened." Luke would be interested in how the man responded when he learned of Brennan's visit. Did he already know Sally's father wasn't a threat? The marshal's high-handed method of trying to force Sally to leave with him suddenly seemed blatantly fishy. *No pun intended.*

She reeled in her line and stepped from the ankle-deep water a foot from shore, exchanging words with Jen. The girl smiled and continued to fish from a gradually sloping bank a dozen feet upriver. Sally strode toward him, with only a slight limp. An easy smile contradicted the strain she'd undergone a few hours before. Luke's gaze swept over the gauze wrap covering the heel of both hands as well as her right knee. MacGyver and Luke had spent the better part of an hour removing dozens of small slivers from her scraped-up hands while Travis and Coop entertained her with a PG version of life with a SEAL unit. Luke couldn't tell if it was her interest in their stories or the wine they held so she could drink or Brennan's abrupt exit from her life that was responsible for her relaxed and mellow state.

His gaze followed her as she approached, and when she sat gingerly beside him, he hooked his arm around her waist. "Doing okay?"

Sally leaned over and dropped a kiss on his mouth. "Stop worrying. Other than making it hard to dress myself, this is nothing." She held up her two gauze-wrapped hands.

Luke chuckled. "I'd be happy to help you with that."

An unladylike snort issued from her throat. "Yeah, I just bet you'd be all kinds of help."

He increased the pressure of his arm around her, bringing her closer. "Are you sure about not getting those stitches?" This wasn't the first time he'd brought it up in the hopes she'd reconsider. She'd decided shortly after they'd finished digging slivers from her hands that she'd been poked and pinched enough for one day.

"I've made up my mind, so let it go, Luke. The cut isn't deep and Matt cleaned and disinfected it. I had a tetanus shot less than six months ago, so I'm good to go. Better than good—I'm free of my father's shadow for the first time in eleven years."

Concern jabbed him as it had a number of times since Clive Brennan gave his speech and walked out of her life, leaving them with more questions than they had answers. Was Sally's old man playing a vicious game of his own? Was he lying when he told her he had nothing to do with bombing her house or trying to run them off the road? The only thing wrong with that line of thinking was they'd all stumbled unwittingly into Brennan's trap this morning. He had them. What possible benefit would he derive from lying at that point?

"Free from your father, but the shadow's still with us."

Sally wrinkled her brow and studied him thoughtfully.

"Emmett Purnell was pissed as hell the night the fire started. Are you still convinced he wasn't involved?" The list of people who might have thought they had a score to settle with Sally was short and improbable. Still, Luke ran through the list once again, biding his time.

"Emmett isn't my favorite person, but I don't think he plotted to kill me. Don't forget, he came to warn us about Clive being on our trail. He's a woman-beater, which doesn't place him high on the list of morals, but no... he's not a murderer." Sally fingered the still-tender spot on her cheekbone where Emmett had belted her.

Luke gently brushed her cheek with one finger, gritting his teeth until his instant rage came under control. "I agree, but I should have kicked the shit out of him when I had the chance."

Sally lay her right hand on his chest, drawing his gaze to hers. A teasing smile lit her eyes. "Were you serious when you asked me to marry you?"

"Which time?"

Sally slapped him lightly on the stomach, then cradled her hand and gave him a pretty pout.

"I was serious each and every time. I have to admit, you took me by surprise when you said yes. There I was without a ring, in a room full of hostiles and MacGyver grinning like a monkey."

Sally laughed softly. "I figured we were all going to die. I wanted you to know that even if all we had left was a few minutes, I wanted to spend them with you."

Luke's hand slid slowly down the column of her throat. "Oh, I see. The only reason you agreed to marry me was because you thought you were going to die any minute?"

Sally tilted her head and regarded him. "I didn't say that...exactly."

"Since your life has been extended indefinitely, you're not going to change your mind on me, are you?"

She lay her head on his shoulder. "Just try to get rid of me, sailor."

A chuckle rumbled from his chest as he kissed the top of her head. That was the answer he wanted to hear, and his heart skipped lightly in response. "No way. I'm going to try like hell to keep you right here." He pulled her closer to his side.

"You might be up to the challenge." Mischief flashed in her eyes.

"Damn right." He tipped his head and landed a kiss on the tip of her nose, then moved to her lips as he placed his other arm around her and molded her to his chest. A few seconds later, he heard childish giggles, and little Bridgett groaned.

Sally pulled away, mirth reflected in the blue of her eyes. "No private moments when there are kids around."

Luke sighed. "Damn, I hope that's not true."

Sally just grinned as she sat next to him again.

A few feet away, Jen laid her line across the water in a perfect cast. Luke stole a glance at Sally. "Do you have any enemies we should check out? Anyone who might hold a grudge?"

Her forehead scrunched as though concentrating. "No one I can think of."

Luke took a deep breath. If he couldn't get her to volunteer the information, he'd have to pry. "What about Jen's father?"

Sally tensed instantly and tried to pull away, but Luke rolled to a sitting position and tightened his hold on her waist. "Wait. Tell me it's none of my business if that's the way you feel, but please don't run away from me."

Anger flashed in her eyes and, for a moment, it seemed as though she would repeat his words back to him, effectively shutting down his line of questioning. He quirked an eyebrow as she stared at him. Finally, she dropped her head away from his gaze and her face turned red, whether from anger or embarrassment remaining unclear.

Luke hooked one finger beneath her chin and repositioned her face so he could see her eyes. "Trust me, babe." Pulling her toward him, he crushed his lips over hers possessively.

What in the hell was he doing? He couldn't force her to reveal details about a man and a time in her life she'd just as soon forget. Except for the sake of determining whether the man held a grudge bad enough to do her harm, Luke wouldn't have brought it up. He didn't want to put her through the pain of remembering but, damn it, her safety was at stake.

She closed her eyes for a long heartbeat, and when she opened them, she nodded determinedly. "If you ever tell Jen any of this, I'll…well, I'll pretend I'm going to have sex with you in a public place and then take all your clothes and leave you there naked." The lack of a smile at the end of her statement spoke to how angry she would be.

Luke winced. "Yeah? I think I saw that in a television sitcom a few years ago. Not something I'd be looking forward to."

She raised her chin. "If we're in agreement, ask me what you want to know."

"Does the man live around Huntington?" Luke rubbed his hand up and down her back.

"He lives in Grizzly Gulch, near the lodge."

"He doesn't have any contact with you or Jen?"

"I'd see him now and then when I used to visit Rachel. He's a pig, so I didn't waste time being cordial. He never knew about Jen…until a few months ago. Came snooping around, asking questions. Wanted to know who Jen's father was. I lied and told him it was Jonathan, but he didn't believe me. He said Jen didn't look anything like Jonathan." Sally's gaze wandered to the girls on the riverbank.

"What was he after? Visitation? Did he want you back?" Luke nearly choked on the words.

She shook her head. "He holds a notable public position in the county and he's afraid if anyone else makes the connection between him and Jen, I might be able to cause trouble for him. He doesn't want anything to do with me or his child. He suggested strongly that I take Jen and leave Idaho."

"Did he threaten you?" Luke tamped down the rage building inside him.

"Not in so many words, but it was there in the way he sneered and the way he talked to me—like he couldn't use big words because I wouldn't understand them."

Luke was on the verge of seeing her face through a red haze. He had to throttle back his fury. There was a chance Jen's father was the one who'd blown up Sally's house and tried to run them off the road. On the other hand, would someone so concerned with his public image take that kind of risk? He seemed more at home using innuendos and threats than getting his hands dirty. What was he hiding that would make the risk worthwhile?

Luke moved closer, bringing Sally between his legs so she could lean back against his chest. He joined his hands around her and hugged her tightly. "What did you mean when you said you might be able to cause trouble for him? What do you have on the guy?"

Sally went quiet. Didn't move. Didn't speak. A hitch in her breathing was an obvious indication of her distress. Luke gave her what time she needed, counting the minutes as he watched the sun disappear behind the mountains to the west. Damned if she didn't start to tremble, and he wrapped himself around her to offer what warmth he could.

"If I'm going to tell you the rest, you have to promise you won't do anything that will make it worse for Jen."

Luke got the uncomfortable feeling he was being torn apart. Instinctively, he sensed something bad was coming—something he'd feel duty-bound to avenge—but she had him with her request to protect Jen. "I'd never hurt her, Sally."

Again, she let some time pass. "I met him at the Cougar Ridge Watering Hole one night when Rachel was working behind the bar. I'd had a couple of drinks without eating and they hit me pretty hard. Rachel cut me off and said I'd be staying the night with her at the lodge, but he offered to take me home. I'd have never accepted...but he was the sheriff. You should be able to trust a sheriff." Sally covered her face and burrowed against his arm.

"Sheriff Mike Connors?" It was everything Luke could do to remain sitting with his hands quietly laced around her. His brother had butted heads with Connors when Garrett first arrived—enough to know the sheriff wasn't above stretching the law. Apparently, he wasn't above breaking it either. Luke could guess what Sally was going to say next, and if she thought he was going to let that son of a bitch get away with hurting her, she wasn't thinking clearly. Reminding himself to breathe, he leaned his head toward her ear.

"It's okay, babe," he whispered.

"I had to get up early the next morning and I just wanted to go home and crawl in bed. By then I was really feeling the drinks. It was stupid—I knew better—no amount of rationalizing will ever excuse what I did. God, Luke, I let him take me home." Her voice broke and she swiped at tears falling freely down her face.

"I fell asleep in the car. I don't even remember arriving at the house. The next morning I woke up naked in my bed...and I knew. The bastard had drugged me...and raped me."

With a gargantuan effort, Luke kept his voice calm and nonreactive, because anything else would only make it harder for her. "Did you call the cops?"

Sally shook her head miserably, issuing a cynical laugh. "What part of sheriff didn't you understand? I don't know how it is where you're from, but here all the law enforcement officers belong to a good-old-boys club.

I was barely twenty, new to the area and trying not to undo what Marshal Lambert had done for me by having my face splashed all over the media. Who was going to believe me over a cop?" She lost it then, covering her face as she leaned into him, her torso shaking with her sobs.

Luke held her close, using his body as a shield from young, inquisitive girls who might otherwise see her and come running to find out what was wrong. "Go ahead and cry, babe. You've earned the right. I'm sorry I wasn't here then to take care of that piece-of-shit sheriff." Barely breathing the words, he doubted if she heard him…and it was just as well. He was here now, and he wasn't going to let an opportunity to kick the man's ass pass him by. Luke would gladly accept Sally's threatened retribution for the privilege of unleashing holy hell on the sheriff's good name.

Sally gradually settled, crossing her arms on top of his and glancing at him over her shoulder. "Morning sickness was so bad with Jen I knew before I ever took the pregnancy test. It was just a formality. I don't think I've ever been more alone or scared as I was then. So sick I couldn't make it to work half the time and barely making ends meet as it was. I didn't know Rachel very well back then, but she could tell something was wrong, and I finally told her I was pregnant." Sally stopped and leaned her head back on his shoulder.

Luke had never felt so helpless. He was used to being in the thick of battle, making shit happen, but there was nothing he could do but listen, and it was killing him.

"I wouldn't have made it through the next eight and a half months without Rachel, Peg and Jonathan. They literally saved my life. And then Jen was born, and I couldn't believe something so good, so perfect, had come from all that ugliness." Sally shifted in his arms, turning sideways, love shining in her eyes for her daughter, who was currently helping Bridgett examine some treasure she held.

"She's pretty incredible…and you're an amazing mother." Luke pressed his lips to her ear, wiping an errant tear from her cheek, happy to hear her chuckle at his compliment.

"I am, aren't I?"

He snorted. "And humble too. How many more would you like, sunshine?"

She shrugged one shoulder. "Babies? A couple should do it."

The idea of creating babies with this beautiful woman made him smile. Sally and Jen had been all the family he'd craved, and they'd seemed unattainable a few short days ago. Nine months ago, he'd been faced with the possibility of never walking again. Only a week before that, he'd accepted the fact he would likely die in a filthy shithole somewhere in

Afghanistan. Now, babies? Luke buried his face in the crook of her neck as his vision blurred and his eyes burned with unshed tears—the first he'd allowed since Ian's death.

Sally shifted again, her front meeting his as she slid her arms around his neck. "Thanks for not judging me, Luke."

He squeezed her tighter, not trusting his voice, and they stayed like that for a long time, listening to the chatter of the kids and their carefree laughter.

"Hey, Harding, ya wuss! Dinner's ready. Quit screwin' off and get your ass up here." Travis's gravelly drawl intruded into their peace.

Sally's head jerked up. "Travis, you promised to work on the language thing." She raised her voice to the same level his had been and glared at him where he stood about a hundred feet away. Tall grass, driven by a light wind, fanned around his legs. Behind him, all the lights were on in Daniel and Ellen's cabin and, for the first time, Luke noticed the aromas of good home cooking wafting on the breeze.

"Oh, sh…I mean shoot, Sally. I'm sorry. I forgot about the kids. I swear, it won't happen again." Travis shook his head, turned and stomped toward the cabin, still talking and waving his arms.

"Mom, are we going to eat?" Jen rose and started gathering her fishing gear. "I'm starving."

Sally's eyes shone with love for her daughter, and, again, Luke felt an inkling of possessiveness.

He caught her gaze and held it until her smile faded. "Thanks for letting me in, sunshine." He would call Sheriff Anderson in Huntington first thing tomorrow and get the lowdown on Connors. Then he'd ask Ben to check the whereabouts of Jen's father the night Sally's house burned. The man wouldn't be the sheriff for long if Luke had his way. He almost hoped Connors didn't have anything to do with the events at Sally's house or, later, on the road to Aunt Peg's. Luke would much rather Sheriff Connors remained free so he could take his time destroying the man's fucking life.

Chapter Eighteen

Sally glared at the digital clock beside the bed. *Midnight.* She reached out and slapped the top of the clock sharply. The darn thing must be broken. Time couldn't possibly crawl that slowly. From somewhere in the covers behind her, a soft whimper sounded, and Sally held her breath.

Jen had gone to sleep as soon as her head plopped on the pillow, even though the girl had had the same traumatic day as Sally. Maybe meeting the grandfather she hadn't known existed wasn't as scary for her. After all, she hadn't seen him with blood on his hands.

No, I'm not going to think about him. It's enough to know he's out of my life, and Jen's, for good.

She'd been looking over her shoulder for so long, her watchful gaze scanning the faces in every crowd, she couldn't stop her brain from replaying the unbelievable scene that had unfolded in Daniel and Ellen's cabin that morning. Analyzing. Second-guessing. Doubting. Finally allowing herself to hope it might actually be true. She was a mess. No friggin' wonder she couldn't sleep. Where was Luke when a girl needed him?

A groan escaped her lips. As though things weren't chaotic enough, she'd told Luke about Jen's father, something only one other person in the world knew about, leaving out none of the dreadful details. He'd been angry. She could tell by the heat of his body and the way his jaw tightened. But he'd listened, asked a few questions and hadn't tried to fix everything. That was a good sign. He always seemed to know the right things to say.

She slapped a hand over her eyes. *Oh. My. God!* She'd forgotten momentarily. *Please...someone tell me I didn't say* yes *to his marriage proposal this morning in the middle of a scene right out of* The Godfather.

Something sounding suspiciously like a hysterical giggle rose within her, and she moved her hands to cover her mouth so she wouldn't wake Jen. As though that was even a possibility. Her daughter had always been a sound sleeper, even as a baby. A herd of cows stampeding through the cabin would have trouble waking her.

On the other hand, I'm going to lay here wide awake for the rest of the night!

She listened for a moment but heard nothing from the front room, except the sound of the wind rattling the front door. Luke had insisted she and Jen take the bed and he'd sleep on the couch. His six-foot-three-inch frame wasn't going to fit well on the barely five-foot couch. Could he possibly be sleeping soundly? Maybe she'd just take a peek.

Carefully, Sally slid from the bed, waiting a few seconds to make sure Jen still slept, then tiptoed away. The cut above her knee stung as she took her first step, and the cool air slid over her skin. The tender flesh at the site of the rough-edged wound was sore and slightly swollen. Matt had said that was to be expected, but if it appeared red or infected by morning, they'd be making a fast trip to urgent care. Sally had waved away his warning, hoping a day of rest was all she needed.

Crossing the threshold into the front room, she padded softly to peer over the back of the couch. Luke lay stretched on his side, arms and legs dangling over the edge of the cushions. His mouth barely open, his breaths worked in and out with the slightest wheeze. Long strands of hair cascaded over his forehead and into his face. *Peaceful.* Sally didn't have the heart to disturb him.

A flash of light from beyond the window snagged her attention, and she walked silently across the floor until she could peer outside. A staggered shaft of lightning split the darkness and lit up the night sky to the southeast. She counted off—*one thousand one, one thousand two, one thousand three*—until she reached one thousand eighteen and a rumble of thunder cut her off. Sally smiled. According to the lesson her mother had taught her when she was a little girl—younger than Jen—the storm was still eighteen miles away. One count between lightning bolts and the resulting thunder marked each mile. She used to love thunderstorms…before her mother died.

Two minutes passed before another lightning bolt zigzagged to the ground. She flinched, only reaching one thousand five before thunder crashed nearby, fading to a rumble until it finally disappeared beneath the sound of the wind. She'd always loved the smell of the air right before a rainstorm, so she strode toward the door and pulled it open. The wind, whipping through the opening, nearly jerked the doorknob through her fingers.

She started when Luke caught the edge of the door with one hand as he stepped up silently behind her and slid his arm around her waist, pulling her back against him. The storm picked that moment to hurl another lightning bolt, closer this time, and she barely made it to one thousand two before the thunder boomed and sent them both back a step.

Luke braced one shoulder against the door and joined his arms around her, holding her tighter. "What are you doing up? Couldn't sleep?" He spoke close to her ear and still the wind tried to carry his words away.

"Not a wink." She leaned against his strong, hard chest and folded her arms over his. "I didn't mean to wake you, though."

"I'm a light sleeper these days." He planted a kiss below her ear, and his warm breath on her cheek sent a shiver racing through her.

The storm had cooled the day's heat, but now the wind across Sally's skin wrapped her in a chill not caused by the temperature of the air, and she trembled for a different reason as a pinprick of anxiety invaded her space.

"Are you all right?" Perceptive as usual, she felt him tense.

No. She wasn't all right, but how could she explain that to Luke when she didn't understand it herself? She sensed something…and the odd feeling in the pit of her stomach felt strangely like dread where only happiness had rested a moment ago.

The next instant, the sky opened and the rain poured down, soaking the earth and beating out a staccato rhythm on the roof. *Lightning flashed and the thunder rolled. There's a song with those lyrics, isn't there?* That damn hysterical giggle was back, but she refused to allow it to surface. Sally was glad for the darkness. If Luke couldn't see her face clearly, hopefully, he wouldn't read the apprehension that was surely visible there. She should tell him she was fine, but that would be a lie. Something in the air—the darkness—the wind and the rumble of thunder across the meadow—

A sudden shudder caught her off guard and stopped her in midthought. "Do you feel that?" She rubbed her arms, rough with goose bumps. Logic told her she was being ridiculous, yet the certainty that someone or something was watching them grew until no doubt remained.

"Feel what? Are you cold? Let's go inside." Luke tugged her toward the warmth of the cabin but, held captive by something just beyond the fringe of her senses, Sally's legs wouldn't cooperate.

She'd never been one to believe in premonitions or unseen evil, but the fear tap dancing along her spine wasn't normal. *It's only the storm. I'm having a panic attack over nothing. Just breathe.*

Luke took her by the shoulders and forced her inside, closing the door. With the storm locked out, she should be okay…but she wasn't. The presence was all around her. *I'm going crazy.* All the warmth seemed to have left her body. She pushed Luke away and hugged herself, rocking back and forth on her feet. As though awakening from a dream, she slowly became aware of Luke saying her name, worry and confusion evident in his voice.

"Sally? What's going on? You're freaking me out, babe."

It seemed as though a great deal of time had passed, yet it couldn't have. It was still dark. The wind still blew the rain into the side of the cabin in gusts and the thunder rumbled, though farther away now. She met Luke's gaze and held it as though it was a lifeline. "It's not over, Luke."

"Fuck!" Apparently, his patience was growing thin. He scooped her in his arms and marched to the couch, sitting with her on his lap. The light of the lamp dispelled the darkness as he flipped the switch. "Talk to me, sunshine. What's not over?"

A sob shook her, but she pulled herself up straight and looked him in the eye. "Whoever tried to kill us isn't finished yet. I know it sounds crazy, but I can *feel* him—I can sense his sick, twisted desire to kill us—even Jen, if he finds her here." She tried to jump from his lap, but Luke tightened his arms and wouldn't let her go. "Luke, we have to get Jen out of here." Hysteria was a breath away, but she had to hold it together or he wouldn't take her seriously.

The expression on Luke's face hadn't exactly screamed *we need a straitjacket over here*, but clearly he was biting his tongue to keep from saying something that would make the crazy lady go off. Sally didn't blame him.

"Babe, Jen's safe here with us. We'll make sure she stays that way." He stroked her bare arms as though she were a child scared of the boogeyman. *Well, one of those is true.*

She jerked away from him and gained her feet.

* * * *

Luke stared into the panic-filled blue eyes above him. His gaze took in her heaving chest, her determined stance and her hands fisted at her sides. What the hell had put her in fight mode? "Sally, let's talk about this—" He reached for her only to have her slap at his hand.

"Luke, I'm getting Jen as far away from me as I can. This madman, whoever he is, will kill her too if she's here with us." She stopped and shook her head, confusion etched on her face for a split second. "You can either help me or stay out of my way." She whirled and started for the bedroom.

He rose, ignoring the twinge in his back objecting to his quick movement, and reached her in two strides. Careful not to touch her, he placed his body in her path. As he towered over her, her hands plopped onto her hips and she stared at him with a did-you-have-something-to-say lift of her brow. She was so damn gorgeous when she got all riled up. Too bad he had no idea what had caused her strange mood.

"You know I'll help, sunshine. If you want Jen away from us, I'll call Garrett and ask him to come get her. We'll see if Ellen and Bridgett want to go with them."

"Yes, *yes*! That's a good idea. They'll be safe at the lodge with Garrett and Jonathan." She moved as though she would go around him.

He held his arm out to stop her. "Tomorrow," he said firmly.

She shook her head and opened her mouth, clearly to argue the point.

Luke put his fingers to her lips to stay her words. "Tomorrow will be soon enough, Sally." He turned her away from the bedroom. "Come and sit with me. Tell me why you can't sleep. Is your leg hurting?"

She was calmer now. Apparently, making the decision to send Jen away from them had been enough to forestall her hysteria. Where had it come from? Was it simply a feeling? Or something more? He'd come back to his many questions about her prediction later, when she wasn't so agitated. He'd learned over the past year not to discount his, or anyone else's, gut instinct.

"No, it's fine. You and Matt should stop worrying."

"Not going to happen. MacGyver's always concerned about infection because we saw so much of that overseas. A person can lose a limb in a couple of days if it's not taken care of properly. As for me? I'm going to worry about you—get used to it." He settled her beside him on the couch. "So...what *is* keeping you awake?"

She dropped her gaze, her cheeks flushing to a pretty pink. "Aside from strange premonitions? It's been quite a day. My mind won't shut off. Luke, how do you think my father found us?"

Luke had asked himself that question more than once and had never come up with a satisfactory answer. "A retired Russian spy probably still has a few resources at his disposal. There's always someone willing to take a bribe in exchange for information. Even someone inside the US Marshals Service."

Sally frowned. "He could have found out the marshal was coming for me and had him followed."

Luke issued a noncommittal grunt. Apparently, they'd never agree on the integrity of Marshal Lambert. At least she'd recovered from her panic attack enough to mention the incident, and although Luke was tempted to ply her with questions, he'd let it go for now. He shifted until his legs stretched lengthwise on the couch, his shoulders wedged between the arm and the back cushions. Then he pulled Sally on top of him, her breasts plumping against his chest and her hips resting between his legs. "I should have been paying more attention. I promised you he wouldn't sneak up on us." All the more reason Luke should take heed of her warning. His right hand splayed across one cheek of her ass, pulling her tighter against him, awakening desire once again. Hell, he couldn't get enough of her.

One index finger touched his mouth softly. "Shh…you were distracted." Her smile was reflected in her eyes until she stretched toward him and touched his lips with hers.

"True that," he whispered as she pulled back. Fisting his free hand in her long, wavy tresses, he held her head in place while he plundered those soft, sweet lips at his leisure.

Luke awoke to bright sunlight invading the room through open blinds, his body melded together with Sally's on the couch. He groaned at the stiffness of his back, although it wasn't nearly as stiff as a body part that resided below his waist. Sally opened her eyes, kissed his jaw with a smile and slowly unfolded her legs as she started to slide off the couch. At the last second, Luke tightened his arms around her and kept her from leaving.

"Um…hard-on alert. Why don't you grab me a pillow before Jen pops out here unexpectedly?" This kid-in-the-house thing was a killer—one he'd happily get used to.

She grinned but quickly wiped it away and stretched again. "Hmmm… sounds like a personal problem."

He cocked one eyebrow and moved his hips in a circular motion as he ground his thick and hard arousal against her. "It could be *our* problem easily enough." His lips teased her throat and the tops of her breasts while his hands dove beneath the waistband of her pajama bottoms to cup her butt cheeks and squeezed. A squeal escaped her for a fraction of a second before he covered her mouth with his. Her nipples pebbled against his chest through her silky top.

She broke the kiss, a flush highlighting her cheekbones. "Okay. I see your point."

Luke smiled, glad she appeared to be back to normal this morning, acknowledging for the first time how badly she'd scared him last night.

"What's it going to be? You could slide one of those long, sexy legs over and straddle the problem...and take care of this for me...or...you could grab the pillow we knocked on the floor."

Sally tapped her chin with her finger and narrowed her eyes. "Would it make me a horrible mother if I chose the first option?"

Damn it. Sally had accepted his dare and gone one further. If only Jen wasn't a mere thirty feet away, he'd show her which option he'd choose. The smug grin she fixed him with seemed to indicate she'd won...and damned if she hadn't—this time.

Luke laughed. "It's not nice to tease, babe. I might decide the risk is acceptable."

The grin disappeared. "No, you wouldn't." Suddenly, she didn't sound so sure of herself. She set her feet on the floor and grabbed the pillow, tossing it at him. It hit the tented front of his sweats and Luke grunted, clutching the pillow in front of him.

With her running interference, he retreated to the bathroom. His shower was quick and filled with speculations about how best to convince Daniel and the guys to send Ellen and the girls away because of Sally's premonition. *No, that'll never work.* He'd have to approach them as though the idea had been his and do whatever it took to sell them.

When Luke sauntered from the bathroom, dressed in jeans and a black T-shirt, Sally sat cross-legged on the bed beside Jen's sleeping form. Hair mussed and pajama top hanging off one shoulder, she took his breath away. His ego got a boost when her gaze traveled over his body appreciatively, and her smile made him feel like a million dollars. Striding to the bed, he leaned his arms one on each side of her and locked his lips with hers for a sweet, lingering kiss. When he pulled away, she kept her eyes closed for a beat or two, and he heard from his dick again.

With a low chuckle, Luke reached beyond her and shook Jen's leg. "Time to get up."

Jen yawned, then sat straight up in bed. "Why's it so early?"

"We're taking a little ride today. Your mother will explain while I arrange our transportation." His gaze swept back to Sally for a moment before she nodded solemnly. Dread stirred in his gut. Damned if her sense of foreboding didn't seem more plausible in the cold light of day.

Chapter Nineteen

Sally woke slowly from a deliciously naughty dream. One that she wished she could go back to sleep and finish. A disappointed sigh echoed around her until Luke filled her mind's eye. He would no doubt be more than willing to help her begin and end her dream...when he returned. She glanced at the bedside clock. *Ten forty-five? No way.* She'd only meant to close her tear-filled eyes for a few minutes' rest after saying an emotional good-bye to Jen and Luke. Not an hour and a half.

It'd been her idea to send Jen away. Yet when Luke had returned to tell her the plan had been set in motion and they'd be ready to leave within the hour, she hadn't been ready to let her daughter go. Through an abundance of caution, Daniel had agreed that Ellen and Bridgett would travel to the lodge too. Ellen would drive the girls in their Suburban while Travis and Coop followed closely in Travis's Chevy until their little caravan met up with Garrett and Jonathan. Then Travis and Coop would turn around and hightail it back.

The plan had broken down, however, when Luke discovered there was no cell service. At that point, the decision had been made that Luke would follow the others in the Jeep until he acquired a strong-enough signal to phone his brother and make the necessary arrangements. It'd been the last straw for Sally's frayed nerves to see them both drive away. She'd held it together until the three vehicles were out of sight, excused herself to Daniel and Matt, saying she'd been looking forward to a long soak in a bubble bath, and scurried back to the cabin before her tears betrayed her.

Enough of feeling sorry for myself. Jen will be safe even if the worst happens. Luke will probably be back by noon at the latest.

With a determined toss of her head, Sally slid her legs over the side of the bed. Forty-five minutes later, she'd showered, dressed in jeans and a pale blue tank top and tidied up the small cabin. With the aid of some plastic wrap she'd found in the cupboards beneath the sink, she'd been able to shower without getting her butterfly bandages wet. The wound looked good, just the right shade of pink, and the swelling had disappeared. Probably not ready for any races yet, though.

Sally's stomach grumbled loudly. Time to investigate the leftover situation in Ellen's refrigerator. Perhaps the boys would be interested in lunch too. She laughed at her choice of words to describe Matt and Daniel. No one would mistake those two for *boys*.

Savoring a deep breath of clean mountain air as she stepped from the cabin, Sally started up the foot-worn path. A slight wind tossed the tall grass around, and a host of lacy clouds dotted the sky with thunderheads building to the north. They might get some rain before the day was over. Hopefully, Ellen and the girls wouldn't get caught in a lightning storm.

Sounds of pounding drifted to her from the direction of the barn. Two bay horses and Bridgett's spotted pony grazed in a pasture nearby. Daniel, no doubt, working on something. Otherwise, the peaceful setting was undisturbed. She looked around for Matt but didn't see him. He was probably helping Daniel on some project in the barn.

The other cabins she passed all stood silent but clean, thanks to their frenzied activities the day before yesterday. Of all the things Clive Brennan had said and done, paying Ellen the full rent on the cabins for the length of his reservation was what had impressed Sally the most. Well...that and his informing her she didn't have to live in fear of him any longer. She still couldn't believe it.

As she walked by the last cabin before Daniel's, wood slapping on wood caught her attention. She stopped and searched the windows, porch and sides of the smaller cabin for signs of Matt. No one. She started to call out, but then the wind gusted again and a branch from a large willow scraped against the corner of the cabin.

Jumpy. That was apparently her lot in life now. It was true they still hadn't determined who blew up her house or tried to run them off the road, but they were a long way from Huntington. Besides, if she didn't count Jen's father, she didn't have any enemies. Try as hard as she could, Sheriff Connors simply didn't fit the role of killer.

As she stepped from the shadow of the cabin and continued along the path, suddenly an explosion rocked the ground. The tremendous roar deafened her. The air currents propelled by the blast, and a barrage of flying debris, slammed into her, knocking her flat on the ground and the air from her lungs. Ringing in her ears disoriented her as she tried to sit up. Heat from the inferno singed her skin. She pushed herself along the ground backward to escape the superheated air. A small particle of wood caught her above the eye as it flew by. Blood obscured her vision.

Daniel's cabin! What happened? Where are he and Matt? Please, God, don't let either of them be in that blaze.

The next instant, Sally was surrounded by blurry figures. The one straight in front of her smiled and said something. All she heard was the ringing in her ears. He reached out as though to help her up, and she let him have her hand. Gaining her feet at the expense of her equilibrium, she squeezed her eyes closed and refused to throw up.

"What happened? Who are you?" She addressed her questions to the nice-looking blond man who'd helped her up, but since she couldn't hear herself and all she got from the blond was a perplexed smile, it was quite possible she hadn't spoken out loud.

There were others as well. Were they ninjas? She sensed their blackness surrounding her...or was that her pending unconsciousness? That question was answered when someone behind her tugged a musty-smelling bag over her head. *What the hell?* She twisted away and brought her hands up to jerk off the offensive thing, but she was too slow. Someone yanked her arms behind her back. She heard a zip as they fastened her hands together cruelly, the bindings cutting into her skin the more she struggled. Everywhere she turned to get away, she ran into another body. Hands touching her, pushing her into the next person.

Finally, someone grabbed her arm and pulled her roughly against him, and she could feel his breath on her cheek through the bag. "Can you hear me?"

He must be yelling because she could. She nodded, biting her lip against the tremble that signaled her fear. She couldn't afford to be afraid.

"Good. It doesn't matter to me whether you live or die. You are insignificant. Only a distraction for me and my men while we wait." He trailed his finger across her throat and down to where the neckline of her tank top met her skin. A few of the other men laughed, speaking in a language she'd never heard before.

She shrank from him, but he apparently wasn't ready to let her go. His grip tightened around her arm. "There are some rules that will help your chances of staying alive. You will not speak unless spoken to. You will bow your head in our presence, and you will do exactly what we tell you to do. Do you understand?"

Not a chance in hell, buddy. Sally nodded again because she had no choice.

"That's good." He dropped her arm and ran his hand down her side until he reached her bottom, where he squeezed a handful.

Sally sidled away from him, bumping into the men on the other side of her. They all laughed crudely and then the apparent leader—probably the blond man—said something in their language. One man on each side, they dragged her along by the arms over rough ground, snickering each time she tripped. The good news was, the ringing in her ears was getting less noticeable and she could hear again. Or maybe that was the bad news.

They were getting closer to the river. Sally could hear the water lapping over rocks in the current. Were they taking her to the barn? She'd heard pounding there earlier. What if Daniel and Matt were there?

The silence was like a wall when they dragged her inside the structure. If there was anyone else here, they weren't letting it be known. The men jerked her to a stop while one of them shuffled another few steps. She heard a metallic click and the squeak of rusty hinges. Then the one beside her pushed her forward, bending her over with a blow to her stomach, and shoved her inside something metal. She sprawled on the rough flooring, unable to break her fall, her already painful knee taking the worst of the hit. Before she could move farther away from them, one of them grabbed her feet, holding them tightly together, while another bound her with a zip tie.

The rusty hinges squeaked again until the door she'd come through clicked shut and the men left her alone. When she could no longer hear their booted feet outside the barn, she struggled to sit up, drawing herself as far from the opening as possible.

This was *so* not good. Who were they? What did they want? And what had they done to Matt and Daniel? The roaring fire ripped through her memory and she shuddered. No. She wouldn't believe they were dead.

Minutes dragged by with only the sound of her breathing. She occupied herself by feeling the inside of her enclosure, pleased when she determined it was a cage of some sort. That was good. If she ever got the bag off her head, she would at least be able to see her enemy. A supreme effort had brought her heart rate down to a reasonable level. It was hard to be unafraid when she was absolutely, mind-numbingly terrified, but that was what it would take if she was to survive this ordeal. Not just survive. Somehow, she had to get away, find Daniel and Matt and warn Luke before he drove into the middle of whatever this was.

The worst was not knowing what these animals wanted. Blondie had said they were waiting. For what? He'd also said she was incidental. Meaning she was just in the way—they weren't out to kill her. Yeah; somehow, they didn't seem like the kind of men who would leave anyone alive. Were they the people who'd planted a bomb in her house? Their latest act of destruction seemed to support that. If they weren't after her, who were they trying to kill?

Luke!

But why? Luke had loyal friends. Did he also have enemies?

Sally jumped at the scuff of feet across the dirt floor of the barn. *Don't be afraid.* She clenched her jaw and looked straight ahead. Damned if she'd bow to them. What kind of a psychopath demanded that?

Blondie's tenor voice jolted her when he spoke from the vicinity of the door to her enclosure. "What's your name?"

She didn't answer.

"You may speak."

"Go to hell," she said.

Blondie's footsteps scuffed to Sally's right and then back, and she turned her head to follow his movements as though she could see through the bag.

"Would you like to know what happened to your friends?"

God yes, but she wouldn't give him the satisfaction.

"They're alive, and they'll stay that way as long as you don't cause me any trouble." His voice hardened, and she caught the barest hint of a New York accent. "What's your name?"

His message was clear. He would hold Daniel and Matt's lives over her head.

"Sally. What's yours?" She spat the words in distaste.

"Much better, Sally. Pretty name. Very American. Very Christian. My name is Ahmed."

Sally's soft intake of air was met with a laugh. *Ahmed.* The American traitor who tortured Luke—who killed Daniel's brother. Luke had told her he was dead.

"I see you've heard of me. Does the infidel tremble with fear when he speaks of me? He should. I'm here to finish the job I started. When your Navy SEAL is dead, I'll be a hero to my brothers, and justice will be furthered." Satisfaction rang in the creep's voice.

Terrorists? Dregs of the earth, monsters, killers of the innocent in the name of religion. She'd never hated anyone as much as this man who stood tormenting her. "Ahmed? Traitor? Murderer? Yes. Luke speaks of you…with pity." Hopefully, Luke would forgive the lie she'd blurted in her sudden, uncontrollable desire to punish this man for what he'd done. Judging by the slamming of his hand on the top of her cage, Sally had hit home.

Disgust deafened her to the warning bells in her head. "Do your terrorist buddies trust you, or do they see the American in you and despise you for it? The men you lead—do they beg to be assigned to another? Do you have any friends? Anyone left who's willing to watch your back? You're a loser. Luke beat you over there on your own turf. The truth is, you'll never stand a chance against men like Luke Harding. You have no heart."

Silence descended around her, and with it came the first inkling Sally might have gone too far.

When he spoke, the barely controlled rage came through loud and clear. "Are you finished? You are an infidel and, as such, you will die before the day is over—you and all your friends. Your Luke Harding will watch me plunge the knife into your heart as I spill my seed within your belly at my climax. You will die quickly, but I'll take my time with him. I will break him yet."

Sally bit her bottom lip to keep the tears poised behind her eyelids from falling. *Don't be afraid.* Right. Easy enough to say, but putting those words into practice would be tough. Somehow, she had to warn Luke not to come back here. To take Jen far, far away from here. And she couldn't do it trussed up like a calf at the rodeo.

"I have a few things to see to before our guest of honor arrives, but I haven't forgotten your creamy skin and your sweet little ass. I'll be back, and we'll see if you're still so arrogant when we're done." His nearly silent footfalls retraced his steps.

Sally followed his progress until she could no longer hear him. Then she exhaled the breath she'd been holding. She wrestled with the bindings on her wrists in despair but only caused them to cut deeper into her flesh. Her blood was warm as it ran down her fingers.

It seemed like a long time before she heard sounds again. She cocked her head as voices raised above the shuffling of feet. Matt, and from the sound of it, he was giving someone a thorough cussing. Her hasty prayer was answered as the commotion came through the open barn door.

"Sally? Thank God you're alive." If he was planning to say more, it was cut off hastily by an apparent punch to the abdomen. His breath expelled loudly.

She kept quiet so his captors wouldn't find additional reasons to serve up abuse. As soon as they were gone, though, and all she could hear was Matt breathing hard, she turned her head toward him. Seeing him was suddenly of paramount importance, but it wasn't happening with this damn bag over her head.

"Matt? Are you okay?"

"Yeah...just knocked the wind out of me. What about you? Did they hurt you?"

Sally pushed Ahmed's threat aside. "I'm fine. Where's Daniel?"

"I'm here too." A new voice joined the conversation.

"Daniel! I'm so glad..." She didn't finish the comment on her lips, but she was sure both of them could figure out what she'd been about to say.

"Sally, I'm sorry. I went by your cabin a half-dozen times this morning to check on you. The last time, those bastards came out of nowhere. Hit me with a chunk of wood, and I passed out. When I came to, Daniel and I were both hog-tied in the cabin next to his. I should have seen them or heard them. I let you down and I'm sorry. Luke is going to have my head." Regret was heavy in his tone.

From the little she'd come to know of Matt "MacGyver" Iverson, he took his duties very seriously. If he hadn't seen the enemy coming, it wasn't from lack of attentiveness. Of that she was sure. "It's not your fault. They're after Luke. That blond-haired guy is the one who interrogated him in the POW camp."

"Wait. Are you telling me that's the murdering snake who killed Ian?" All kinds of shuffling noises and grunts came from Daniel's position. Sally could only imagine he was frenziedly tugging on his bindings just as she'd done earlier.

"Take it easy, Daniel. We have to be smart about this," Matt said.

Daniel's activity lessened and then stopped. "Whatever happens, I want that son of a bitch. Promise me."

"We'll worry about that when the time comes." Matt understood—it was there in his voice. "Do you know what they're planning, Sally?"

"Aside from some of the gruesome killing stuff, no. He seems to be waiting for Luke to drive in." They couldn't let that happen. They had to warn him—but how? "Is there any way either of you can get loose?"

"We're tied to a post. Given enough time, I could probably work these ropes loose, but Luke could be here any minute." Matt groaned with the effort he was obviously expending on the knots. "Unless they cut one of us loose, we could be out of luck."

Don't sugarcoat it for me, Matt. Sally laughed softly for lack of anything better to add. "Ahmed may cut my bindings—at least my legs." She assumed they would make the connection and figure out what Ahmed wanted her for. In the ensuing silence, she was really glad she didn't have to make eye contact with the men she barely knew.

"Aw, fuck!" Matt's sentiment somehow made her feel better.

Chapter Twenty

It seemed like hours before Sally heard footsteps again. She picked up her head and strained to hear how many and how close.

"Remember what we told you, angel lady," Matt said in a stage whisper.

She smiled for a heartbeat, imagining the pained expressions on Daniel and Matt's faces while they'd passed along their knowledge of a man's greatest vulnerability and how to optimize the situation in her favor. Their conversation, while they waited for God knows what, was more than simply weighing their options, few as those were. They'd treated her like one of the team—like her opinions added value to the plan they'd devised—that very well might be their last. Of course, there'd only be one set of circumstances that would make escape possible, and without escape, there'd be no warning Luke about the trap he'd be walking into.

"Looking forward to it," she whispered back and heard them both snicker. If only she was as confident as she'd made herself sound. The truth was, she was scared shitless. If she couldn't make the pathetic plan they'd come up with work, they were all going to die. If the plan did work, Sally would no doubt die first. With that thought, her heart rate kicked up a notch, but she quickly got control of her fear. Luke would be here soon. She wouldn't fail him.

One set of footsteps entered the barn and scuffed across the dirt floor to stop in front of her prison. "Hello, Sally. I'm happy to say, we're ready for your friend Luke to return. I'm sorry I've neglected you, though." Ahmed clicked something on the door of her enclosure, and it squeaked. "Luckily, we can fix that. You may come out now."

Sally didn't move, except to jump when he raised his voice to repeat the invitation. With wrists and ankles bound, she had to lie down and crawl like an inchworm. Finally, he grabbed her arm and dragged her the rest of the way, then pulled her up on numb feet. She teetered precariously until he pushed her back against the cage, and it moved slightly with her weight.

Suddenly, he jerked the bag from her head, and she scrunched her eyes shut and turned her head to block out the afternoon sunlight. He took full advantage of her exposed neck, fastening his lips there and scraping his teeth against the pulse point in her throat. One of his hands palmed her breast roughly, then continued up until he grabbed her chin and yanked her head around to face him.

Sally meant to suggest he rot in hell, but before she could utter a word, his mouth closed over hers, sucking and licking, his tongue delving for the back of her throat. She gagged, and he drew back, delivering a ringing blow with his fist to the side of her jaw. Pain erupted in sparkly lights as bright as the Fourth of July. She sagged between him and the metal cage behind her. Watching him through lowered lids, she saw him unsheathe the knife at his side. Her breath caught as she tried to stand straight. She heard voices other than Ahmed's and realized Matt and Daniel were cursing. Tied to the same post not ten feet away, both men hurled insults.

Ahmed turned his face toward them. "I don't need either of you. You're only alive because of my generosity. That will end if you don't be quiet."

"Yeah, well, come over here and try to *end* me, you lily-livered Nancy boy. You think you're tough, beating on a woman. Come over here and see what you can do with a man." Matt's taunt roared in the open barn.

What was he doing? He couldn't defend himself, tied the way he was. Ahmed would kill him. "No, Matt, wait."

He glanced at her, regret and sorrow in his eyes, but then his gaze flicked back to Ahmed, and he opened his mouth, no doubt to mock their captor further.

Without warning, one of Ahmed's men appeared at the open door. Whatever he said to his boss in their strange dialect put a scary smile on both their faces before Ahmed issued an abrupt order that sent the other man scurrying back where he'd come from.

"Your friend is back. We'll have to postpone our playtime…but I think I'll let you come with me and watch." He fisted his hand on the neckline of her tank top and pulled her toward him until his breath warmed her ear. "I may have to change my mind and keep you alive for a while. You'd like that, wouldn't you, baby?" He slid his other arm around her hips and held her still as he ground his hard-on into her belly.

"I'd rather be eaten alive by lions than have you touch me." The words flew from her mouth before she could stop them.

She'd done it now. He was almost certainly going to kill her.

Instead, he shoved her away from him. The back of his hand landed across her face with such force it jarred every bone in her body. Her legs nearly gave out, and she actually looked forward to the blackness that encroached on the edges of her vision. The next blow, from his fist to her stomach, doubled her over and made her forget the pain that had burst through her jaw a moment before. Her insides burned and nausea washed over her. She dropped to her knees.

"You will learn your place...or you will die." Ahmed clutched her hair and hauled her back to her feet.

Sally pushed the pain from her thoughts and fought the urge to vomit. She couldn't ruin everything now, when Ahmed was about to cut her feet loose so she could walk with him to witness his triumph over Luke. *Not if I can help it...and there's a God in heaven.*

When she didn't struggle to get away, Ahmed smiled. "Hold still, baby, while I cut your ties." He held her gaze as he knelt in front of her, then glanced away for a split second to position the knife. An audible pop later and she could move her feet.

Too bad her legs were tingly from lack of blood circulation. They would only get worse when the flow of blood increased, so it was now or miss her opportunity. She glanced at Matt, and he nodded slightly.

Ahmed rose to his feet. "Ready?" He took a step back and swung his arm to indicate she should go first.

Sally kicked her leg with all the strength she possessed. The toe of her shoe landed firmly in his testicles, exactly where Daniel and Matt had instructed it should. Then she braced her foot on his sack and dug in, crushing any flesh that got in her way.

"Fuck!" Ahmed grabbed himself with one hand and went down on his knees, his eyes rolling back in his head. He clutched the knife in his other hand, holding it to the side of his body as though he were about to drop the weapon. Sally swung her leg again, flipping the knife from his hand and sending it flying toward the men. Matt and Daniel both slid their ropes down the post until they were sitting on the ground, but the knife was still two feet short.

Ahmed rolled into a fetal position as Sally started moving. He grabbed futilely for her ankle. Her hands still securely bound, she ran to where the knife had dropped and kicked it with her foot until Matt was able to grab hold.

"Good luck." She was already out of breath.

"Get out of here," Matt said.

Sally didn't look back. Sprinting through the open barn door, she picked up speed as she went. Luke's Jeep was stationary at the top of the last hill that overlooked the cabins and the river. Why had he stopped?

Of course. The remains of Daniel's cabin still smoldered. He would see the destruction and know something was wrong. If she could just get close enough to warn him before one of Ahmed's men shot her in the back, he might get away. Their plan had worked so far. *Please, God, let me do this one last thing.*

She ran, ignoring the pain in her knee, the sawing of the zip ties at her wrists and the blood still seeping from the wound over her eye. She strained to see Luke in front of the Jeep parked on the hill ahead. He appeared to be holding something big and black to his face. Suddenly, Travis's Chevy rumbled over the rise and skidded to a stop behind Luke's Jeep.

Staying purposefully away from the cabins and the road, Sally plowed through knee-high grass and jumped over rocks. Spotting two of Ahmed's men running to intercept her, she ran faster. Her breath labored in and out of her lungs and her heart hammered as though it knew this was her last run. Hopefully, Matt and Daniel had gotten away too.

She pressed on, running on sheer adrenaline now. Damn, if she could only wave her arms, it would be helpful. Just a little farther and maybe her voice would carry to Luke.

"Catch her, you idiots!" Ahmed's voice from behind her was steeped in pure rage. Obviously remembering himself, he repeated the command in the language of his men.

Sally took a chance and glanced over her shoulder. They were gaining on her. Apparently, they weren't going to shoot her. Guess Ahmed wanted her alive. That was sure to be a bad thing. Racing to the top of a small mound, her feet slid out from under her and she fell. Rolling to her back, she pushed to her feet. The men were so close—she was out of time.

"Luke!" She forced herself to run again, although she didn't have enough lung capacity for keeping her pace and screaming like a banshee. The men were gaining. "Luke, it's a trap! Don't come in! It's a trap, Luke!"

One of the men tackled her, and she was all out of fight. She'd done what she'd set out to do—warn Luke. Jen was safe, and he'd survive to take care of her precious little girl. Her lungs hurt. Hell, everything hurt. The men's faces, covered with black masks, blurred before her eyes as they stared at her. One of them said something, but he could have been asking for the next dance for all she knew. She didn't have the energy left to care. The smaller of the two drew a machete from inside his cloak and placed the tip on her chest, repeating his words.

"Go fuck yourselves." The second time in her twenty-nine years she'd dropped the f-bomb…and it felt pretty damn good. But what was the matter with her? She wasn't being very polite. She looked directly at the machete man and smiled. "*Please* go fuck yourselves."

The two men looked at each other and laughed. Sally chuckled along with them…until machete man raised his huge weapon, poised over his head for a few seconds, and slashed downward.

Sally wiggled onto her side and drew her legs up to her chest in a useless attempt to protect her vital parts. She closed her eyes. Why the hell did people have to use knives? Give her a nice quick bullet any day. Okay. Now she was rambling. Probably in shock. What would it be like to be dead? She'd miss her baby…and Luke.

The terrorist dropped to one knee against her back, and she heard the machete plunge home. A sharp pain…and then nothing. It didn't matter, though, because the darkness was already upon her…taking her somewhere safe…and quiet…

* * * *

He'd seen the plume of smoke from miles away, but when Luke topped the last rise that overlooked the resort cabins, he slammed on the brakes and stared at the devastation below. Daniel's cabin was gone. Still smoldering, a pile of charred rubble was all that was left, part of the blackened chimney standing sentinel over the rest.

"What the hell?" He tore open the glove box and rummaged until he latched onto a pair of binoculars. His brother was always prepared and evidently kept his Jeep ready to go as well. He glanced in the rearview mirror as he had repeatedly for the past half hour. This time, he spotted a cloud of dust racing along the rough and pothole-filled road three or four miles behind him. Luke grimaced. At the very least, he was going to owe Travis a new set of shocks.

Luck had been with them when he'd finally reached Garrett on his cell phone. He and Rachel were in Coeur d'Alene, picking up supplies for the lodge. They dropped everything and headed for Sandpoint. Luke had turned back about five miles out of town, leaving Travis and Coop to escort their charges to a prearranged rendezvous point north of Sandpoint. As Luke had expected, Travis must have hauled ass to catch up to him, probably urged even faster by the column of smoke.

Luke stepped from the Jeep and raised the field glasses. The place was like a ghost town. The old Ford pickup sat in its spot near the ruins of

Daniel's cabin. All the remaining cabins were closed tight, and there wasn't a soul to be seen. The horses and Bridgett's pony chomped the grass in their pasture, apparently unaffected by whatever had gone on. At the dock by the river, four small fishing boats bobbed with the current, securely fastened to the wooden structure. Had there been four boats? More? Less? He couldn't answer the question with certainty.

He had to get down there to assure himself Sally and his friends were safe, but his need warred with logic that said to wait for backup. Logic would have lost the battle if his buddies hadn't been a mere mile away.

Two minutes later, Travis's Chevy roared up behind the Jeep, skidding on the packed dirt as the engine went silent, and Travis and Coop piled out. Luke tossed the binoculars to Travis as the man shouldered up beside him.

His friend raised them and peered through. "Shit o' Friday. That must have been one hell of a blaze. Where is everybody?"

"Let's go find out." Luke started for the Jeep.

"Wait. What's this? Shit!" The urgency in Travis's tone immediately grabbed Luke's attention, and he whipped around just as Travis held out the binoculars.

Luke took the glasses, but he didn't need them. Sally, a small figure at this distance, ran headlong through tall grass and wildflowers, on a direct line toward him, but her gait was jerky and awkward. She raced over the ground, sliding, tripping, catching her balance, her hands held behind her back. What the hell was she doing?

"There!" Travis pointed toward the river.

Two black-robed, face-masked figures sprinted on a diagonal course that would soon cut her off.

Luke raised the glasses. He had to be wrong...but his gut told him he wasn't. *What the fuck are they doing here?* And where were Daniel and MacGyver? He groped for the weapon tucked against his back. *Shit! They were too far away.* In a blind rage, he tossed the binoculars to Travis and sprinted for the Jeep.

Another yell went up, and Luke swung around. The newcomer's height, shape, stance and coloring left no doubt in his mind. *Ahmed Kazi,* the snake who inhabited his nightmares, screamed at his men to catch her—to catch Sally—and finished his command with a volley of words in their native language. His blood turned to liquid fire in his veins. The son of a bitch had died the night Luke was rescued, or so he'd thought. He hadn't realized he'd spoken the name aloud until Travis grabbed his arm.

"Ahmed? You've gotta be kidding. Isn't that the SOB who killed Ian?"

Luke didn't answer, just started for the Jeep again, a singular purpose running through his mind…until he heard Sally's strained voice. He jerked around just as Travis grabbed a fistful of his shirt.

"Luke, it's a trap! Don't come in! It's a trap, Luke!" Her thin voice drifted to him on the wind, and he barely comprehended her meaning before she lost her footing on a small slope and fell.

Luke turned and tore the Jeep door open, but Travis's hand still held him. "I have to get to her, man. They'll kill her." He ground out the words, trying to shrug off his friend.

A glance down the hill confirmed his fears. The two fighters were on her. One of them raised a long knife, the type they favored for beheadings and such. *Fuck!* He swung on Travis, knocking him up against the Jeep, but suddenly Coop was there, pinning Luke's arms behind his back. He struggled as though Sally's life depended on it…because it did. Couldn't they see that?

He glanced toward where she'd fallen…and his world went still. The knife dropped in a long arc as the man wielding it fell to his knees to gain more force for the kill. *Just like Ian.* Luke had learned the hard way that the human head survived for a few seconds after being separated from the body. The horror consumed him all over again. His own blood, pounding in his head, deafened him. Coop released him and stepped away, watching warily…for the beating he expected, no doubt.

Luke's legs gave out and he dropped to his knees. He raked his hands through his hair helplessly. It wasn't supposed to end this way. Instead of keeping Sally safe, he'd brought the enemy right to her door. He'd been watching for someone who wanted to harm *her*, but it'd been him who was being hunted all along.

He'd thought he'd hit his lowest point in that prison in Afghanistan, but he hadn't even been close. Without Sally, there was no reason to go on.

Jen. Luke had told Sally he'd take care of her daughter—he couldn't let her down again. The game was still on. He had unfinished business and it was going to end here—today.

"How many are there?" Luke didn't miss the fact they'd both stepped back as he rose to his feet.

"I've counted six so far, including the blond-haired bastard." Travis offered him the field glasses, which Luke accepted and placed around his neck.

Six was doable. He'd taken out that many during training exercises. "Daniel? MacGyver?"

"No sign," Coop said.

Luke reached behind him for the handgun shoved in his waistband and pulled out the clip to check his load, an action born of habit and caution. Replacing the clip, he thrust the gun between his back and his jeans again, then met Travis's gaze. "I could have stopped them—distracted them long enough Sally might have gotten away. You don't know—we'll never know." His voice rising and close to breaking, he clamped his mouth shut. It'd been a mistake to start this now. Raw and bleeding, his emotions were too close to the surface. *Concentrate on what needs to be done.*

Travis strode toward him, and Luke tensed. "Your head's all fucked up, Luke. What's the first rule? Huh? Those dickheads are out for your skin. Why else would that traitorous scum be here? If you'd rushed in there, you'd be dead now."

Shaking with fury and despair, Luke closed the space between them until they were nose to nose. "Do you think I give a rat's ass? I'd gladly give my life if there was one fucking chance she could have walked out of this." He dropped back and turned to survey the cabins, now quiet and, for all appearances, deserted.

"That's why I stopped you. You weren't thinking straight. She would have died anyway, the minute they got their hands on you. They didn't need her for anything but drawing you into the trap. She said it herself. *She* made the choice to warn you. Don't you think she could guess what would happen when they caught up with her?" Travis pointed toward the meadow where Sally had fallen.

He was right about one thing. This whole damn clusterfuck was Luke's fault. "You and Coop head back to town."

Coop and Travis exchanged a glance.

"We're not going anywhere," Coop said, issuing a disbelieving laugh.

Travis folded his arms in front of his broad chest, making it clear he wasn't moving either.

"Yeah, you are. There's been enough collateral damage."

Coop's chest expanded and he took a step toward Luke. "Since when are your *brothers* considered collateral damage? Those dirty motherfuckers attack one of us, they attack us all. Or have you forgotten?"

Coop's words jarred Luke. Maybe he'd feel the same if he was in their place, but he wasn't, and all he cared about was finding MacGyver and Daniel, hopefully alive, then taking out as many of the murdering terrorists as he could…before they killed him.

"MacGyver is a SEAL. You know damn well he'll stay alive, and he'll make sure Daniel stays in one piece too, because he's Ian's brother and a damn good friend." Travis closed on Luke again, stopping in front of him.

"You made it out of that pigsty they called a prison. That's no small feat. Coop and I are stayin' to guarantee you make it out of this little shindig too."

Luke glanced away from Travis's determined face to see the same look on Coop's. Damn it. He was wasting time and he was dangerously close to losing it.

He dropped his gaze to the ground a few feet in front of him. "I made it out of that prison because of Sally. I—" Luke couldn't continue, grinding his teeth together in agony.

"She's not dead." Coop's voice was so low, Luke wasn't sure he'd really spoken.

Anger and pain surged through him. "Damn you. Don't lie to me." Luke took long strides toward Coop, who leaned one hip against the front of the Jeep. As Luke reached him, Travis pushed between them and shoved Luke back a step.

"You want to hurt somebody—hurt them." Travis's words were superquiet but laced with steel.

The man had earned Luke's respect a hundred times over in training, in firefights and on impossible missions. He'd also been a friend when Luke needed one most. Coop too. Shit. Luke was acting like an ass, but he was so messed up, he ranged between simply not caring and needing to physically pummel someone. Too bad his friends were the only ones around. He inhaled a long, deep breath and lifted his eyes to study Coop. "Why'd you say that?"

A slow smile materialized on Coop's rough features. "It's true, man. While you were down for the count, I watched them haul her to the barn."

Luke's breath stopped for a heartbeat. "They didn't…"

"Hell no. She's all in one piece. Through the binocs, I could see they cut her on the inside of her arm. They carried her with her arms and legs above her heart. She was bleeding pretty good—not bad enough that they got the artery—but it was running down her arm and soaking her shirt."

Luke had a hard time grasping Coop's meaning. He'd gotten stuck at *cut her on the inside of her arm.* Ahmed's men had cut her arm. The posturing they'd done with the blade must have been for Luke's benefit—making him believe they'd killed her in the most gruesome way—because Ahmed knew it would demoralize him. It had almost worked…but there was more in Coop's smug smile, now being shared by Travis.

Sally is bleeding. The dead didn't bleed—not uphill anyway. As soon as the heart stopped pumping, the blood stopped flowing unless the wound was at the lowest point in the body. She was alive, for the time being. His relief was so great, he grasped Coop's shoulder to keep from collapsing again.

He should've seen that. Instead of falling apart like a cheap pair of boots, he should've been paying attention to details. The theatrics with the long knife had obviously been orchestrated by Ahmed, and Luke had fallen for it like a wet-behind-the-ears sailor.

He glanced sheepishly between his friends, finding only understanding and determination in their eyes. "Guess I'm a little too close to the situation on this one."

Travis barked a laugh. "Ya think?" He slapped Luke on the shoulder while working his bruised jaw back and forth. "You've still got the best right hook in the unit...and you're still the man I'd want by my side if *my* woman was in a bad place."

"Damn straight," Coop said.

It was humbling, and a little awe-inspiring, to feel the strength of the bond between the three of them, but Luke didn't have time to fully appreciate it now. "What do you say we have a look around and make a plan? It'll be dark in a few hours. We need to be ready to move."

Sally was alive—he refused to believe MacGyver and Daniel weren't too. Any plan they devised needed to get him into that barn without being seen, take out Ahmed's men, who were no doubt digging in and lying in wait, and reach the target before the surprise wore off.

Easy.

Chapter Twenty-one

Sally moaned and attempted to sit up, but even that small movement sent shards of pain rocketing to her nerve endings. She went still and held her breath, hoping the worst would subside. It didn't, and eventually she had to breathe anyway.

Her arm throbbed. Turning her head to see what was wrong, she wished she hadn't. There was blood everywhere. She couldn't tell how big or deep the wound was…and it didn't matter anyway because her hands were still bound behind her back and she couldn't do anything about…anything.

Tossed in a corner of the barn beside two straw bales, Sally pushed herself up to lean against them. The action left her winded, and her harsh breathing was loud in the empty barn. Okay, so she'd apparently lost a fair amount of blood. Her new blue tank top was toast. At least the blond-haired freak wasn't there. Where was everybody anyway? How much time had passed while she was out of it? The last she remembered, the position of the sun made it about midafternoon. Now it was that period between dusk and nightfall, with a good bit of moonlight coming through the open doorway. Why had they left her alone?

Her gaze darted to the post where Matt and Daniel had been tied. It was empty. Her heart soared at the possibility they'd gotten away. If only she knew for sure that Luke and the others had escaped as well. It was a good bet she wouldn't still be alive if the terrorists had taken Luke. However, a nagging voice in her mind suggested he would never leave her…not in the hands of the enemy who'd killed Ian and tormented Luke. No, he was out there somewhere, in the fading light beyond the open barn door. Hadn't he said he'd stick with her?

A scuffing noise brought her attention back to the barn door. A man's figure slipped inside, hugging the wall as he peered out. Then, apparently satisfied with what he'd seen, he straightened and hurried toward her. His huge frame had given him away at first sight, but she'd never been so glad to see anyone's smiling face in her life.

Matt dropped to one knee beside her. "How ya doin', angel lady?" he whispered, already examining the cut on her arm.

"Not that great actually." She winced in pain as she leaned back against one of the bales. "Where's Daniel?"

"He took off toward the river after we cut ourselves loose. Said he kept a hunting rifle and a few knives in his boat." Matt shrugged. "Everything else he owned is gone."

Yeah. Sally had firsthand knowledge of how that felt, and her heart ached for Daniel and Ellen's loss.

Matt pulled a familiar-looking knife from his back pocket. "Lean forward."

Sally did as he said, and sweet relief poured into her limbs as he sliced through the zip tie binding her wrists. Her hands were numb—dead weight when she dragged them onto her lap. Dangerously close to dissolving into self-pity, she bit the inside of her lip in an effort to focus.

As Matt rubbed life back into her hands, she spotted a slash on his wrist that bled with his movements. He must have noticed her inspecting the cut and smiled ruefully. "Daniel's a civilian. He accidentally nicked me when he cut my ropes." Nodding toward the knife at his feet, he grinned. "Way to think on your feet. Getting that knife to us was genius."

For the first time, Sally's smile wasn't forced. "Glad I could help. I warned Luke too. At least I think he heard me."

Matt chuckled. "Everyone within a mile heard you."

"They got away, then?" She learned forward, intent on his answer.

"Last I checked, they'd moved the Jeep and Travis's car out of sight, but I wouldn't count on him bein' gone. That's not how SEALs operate. We don't give up and we don't leave fallen comrades behind. It's our way."

Sally sighed. "I know—but you can't blame a girl for hoping." She smiled slightly. At least Jen, Bridgett and Ellen would be safe. Luke had made sure of that. "Where's the blond guy and his horde?"

"One of them wasn't paying close attention out front when I came in. He's going to miss the end of the show. I hid his body the best I could on short notice. The others are having a discussion in the cabin next to where Daniel's was."

"What do we do now?"

Matt stood. "We're going to get you out the back." He strode toward the large front door and stopped to peer around the edge. Immediately, he whirled and jogged back. "I think they discovered my handiwork. Time to go."

He cradled her shoulders, and Sally leaned into his arm as he steadied her...just in time to double over and hurl the contents of her stomach at their feet. Her entire body went weak and sweaty. Her legs wouldn't hold her any longer. Saliva pooling in the back of her throat faster than she could swallow and her stomach roiling, Sally stumbled to the closest straw bale.

Matt dropped down beside her. "It's okay. You're doin' fine. This is common when regaining consciousness after a physical or emotional trauma. Does your noggin hurt?"

She shook her head, and the movement made her throw up again. Damn it. The voices of blondie's henchmen reached her ears. "Go. You have to go, Matt." Pushing on his massive chest was useless.

"No way am I leaving you, so you're coming with me." Matt stood and scooped her up.

"I'll only slow you down." She clenched her jaw tightly and focused on not throwing up on him.

"Naw. Stick with me, angel." He moved quicker and quieter than Sally thought possible toward the back of the barn, where a stall door had been left open about twelve inches. Matt put his shoulder against it, sliding it open enough for them both to fit through.

Across the paddock, Sally could see the doorway that led out into the night. There was some moonlight mixed with the shadows that stretched across the hard-packed ground. She glanced over Matt's shoulder. Why hadn't blondie and his crew entered the barn yet?

Suddenly, their escape route was blocked by several dark figures. The one who pushed to the front had blond hair and a smug smile. "There you are. I'm afraid I can't let you leave. I've got plans for sweet little Sally and they don't involve you." He stepped closer and leveled his gun at Matt's head. "Put her down."

For a moment, it seemed as though Matt would ignore the command, but finally he set her gently on her feet.

Blondie grabbed her wrist and jerked her toward the door. He barked some orders to his men as he pulled her between them and stepped outside.

"Wait." Sally's fear for Matt was so great, she didn't care what he would do to her for speaking when not spoken to.

Surprisingly, he halted, sporting an arrogant smirk as he nodded at one of his men, who raised a gun to Matt's temple. "Say good-bye to your friend, sweetheart."

"No!" Sally's cry was shrill in the eerie silence. She tried to break away, but Ahmed held her in a tight grip. What made it worse was, Matt refused to meet her gaze, staring, instead, at Ahmed.

Ahmed resumed walking again, dragging her along behind. "Come, Sally. I'm going to make you forget all about your friend…and Luke."

She had no control over the tears that trickled down her face. Nor did she care any longer. Maybe she wasn't so unlike her father after all. Given half a chance, she'd kill this piece of filth and not lose a moment's sleep.

They were almost to the cabin that stood next to the ruins of Daniel's home when a single gunshot broke the silence of the night.

* * * *

Luke, Coop and Travis disappeared beneath the water of the river filled with glacial runoff from nearby mountains. This would be a cold swim and a quick one if they hoped to avoid hypothermia. Luckily, under cover of darkness, they'd been able to sneak closer on foot than they'd originally planned. Now, they only had to swim three hundred yards or so, upstream, underwater, while holding their weapons above water, without a wet suit, and come out at the spot closest to the barn, all without being seen. *Piece of cake.*

Two and a half minutes later, they hauled themselves from the freezing-ass river and ducked into the tall grass along the bank. Luke wasn't fazed by the cold water or the soaking-wet clothes that'd resulted from his swim. His hatred for Ahmed fueled a fire within him that kept him plenty warm. Without a word passing between them, they moved out, performing the next segment of their plan. Travis and Coop angled toward the long side of the barn, where several horse paddocks offered access. Luke's job was to go in the front and find the hostages.

Hostages. That was the way he had to think of Sally. As though this were any other mission he'd ever been on. Otherwise he'd go stark raving mad.

As soon as he entered the barn, he heard voices and followed them to their place of origin. MacGyver towered a head taller than all four of Ahmed's cronies, who stood around him inside one of the stalls. They appeared to be taunting him and none too happy that MacGyver wasn't taking the bait. One of the men stepped up and slammed the butt of his handgun into MacGyver's head, knocking him down. *Oh hell. That is going to be one pissed-off Navy SEAL when he gets up.*

Nervous laughter went through the onlookers. The man who'd hit him pressed his gun to MacGyver's forehead.

"Fuck this," MacGyver growled.

Luke rushed forward and braced his handgun on the half wall of the stall. "Down on the ground!" His Arabic was limited, but at least he'd gotten their attention. "Drop your weapons!" Then again, maybe his grasp of the language was worse than he thought—no one moved. The four black-robed men simply stared

MacGyver let out a roar, bent his knee and brought it toward his chest, then slammed his foot into the leg of the man who'd knocked him down. A sickening crunch made Luke grimace as the poor guy let out a shriek and fell to the ground, clasping his shattered knee with both hands. MacGyver ripped his gun from slack fingers and quieted his screams with a punch to the jaw that nearly broke the guy's neck. *Yep—pissed-off SEAL.*

The other three raised their weapons and tried to back out into the paddock. They evidently didn't know their escape route was already blocked. Coop and Travis appeared, one from each side of the doorway, and their KA-BARs flashed briefly in the moonlight. The standard-issue knives wielded by his friends permanently silenced the two targets closest to the door. The third man started talking excitedly, his voice rising steadily. Finally, he lunged toward the door, and Travis jabbed with his knife. The man staggered back but drew his long knife as he righted himself and started forward again.

Luke pulled the trigger. A SEAL's every shot was a kill shot, and Luke watched him fall with no emotion whatsoever…because he had to. Because this time it was for Sally. He'd learned to compartmentalize death for the sake of the battle. No fucking wonder he had nightmares every time he closed his eyes. That shit had to come out somehow. But he'd use what the Navy had taught him one more time…until the woman he loved was safe and everyone who threatened her was dead. If that made him a monster, so be it.

"MacGyver, you okay?" Luke lowered his gun and pushed through the slider into the stall.

"Right as rain," MacGyver said. "Thanks for showing up when you did."

Luke glanced around at the four dead or wounded men. "There were five men and Ahmed. We're one short."

"No, we're not. The other one got in my way earlier. He won't be bothering us."

Luke extended a hand and helped the big man up. "Daniel?"

"He's around here someplace. Tell you the truth, I kinda lost track of him, but I bet he's not far from the blond-haired bastard who killed his brother."

"Sally?"

"He took her out of here minutes before you arrived."

"Is she okay?" Luke held his breath.

"She's got a few cuts and bruises. Nothing too serious. Your angel lady turned out to be one hell of a fighter." MacGyver shook his head. "This riffraff spent most of the day in one of the cabins with their boss. If I was a betting man, I'd say that's where he took her."

"Let's go." Luke pushed through the paddock door and his friends fell in behind him.

It wasn't hard figuring out which cabin Ahmed had taken over. Every light in the place was on. Almost like he was advertising his presence. Luke sidled up to Coop. "What do you think?"

Travis and MacGyver joined their impromptu meeting. "Well, he's not trying to hide. My instincts tell me he's probably set a few booby traps. Maybe even rigged the place to blow."

"Fuck." Luke received no satisfaction from the fact he'd come to the same conclusion. The image of Sally inside with Ahmed made his blood boil. The idea that their attempt to rescue her might be the catalyst to her death left him numb.

"Check the doors and windows for wires. We need a way in." As the others hurried away, Luke stopped Coop. "Once we're in, check the attic." That's where the fire started in Sally's house, so that might be Ahmed's go-to spot. Maybe he'll repeat himself.

A minute later, Travis returned. "The door and the windows on this side are clear. They open into a separate bedroom and bathroom. Lights are all on. Might be where he's holding Sally."

"Okay, I'm going in. Coop will back me up and look for bombs once we're inside. You two cover the front and back. If we get in trouble, you'll probably be able to tell right away. That's your cue to come in with everything you've got." Not that they had much. Three of them had handguns, and they'd lifted four more plus an AK-47 off the fallen men in the barn. It would have to be enough.

Luke and Coop approached the side of the house. Carefully, Luke peered through the bedroom window. The doors to the main part of the cabin and the bathroom were closed. Clothing was draped over the quilted comforter. Luke pushed the window open about eighteen inches, then pulled himself up to stick his head inside and double-check for hidden wires. Finding none, he shoved himself through the opening, rolling as he hit the floor. Five seconds later, Coop was beside him and closed the window behind them.

The next instant, the two heard the bathroom doorknob rattle and barely had time to flatten against the wall. Coop held a knife as they waited. Slowly, the knob turned and the door opened. Luke caught a glimpse of her in the mirror just inside the bathroom. His carefully controlled rage almost got away from him. Sally's face and arms were bruised, cut and swollen. Clearly, she'd tried to clean some of the blood off, but one whole side of her tank top was stained red, and an angry-looking wound on her arm still bled. He forced his gaze from her image and focused on what he had to do.

Luke waited until she was halfway through the opening before he slid his arm around her, pressed his hand to her mouth and pulled her back against him. She struggled in his arms with far more strength than he'd expected. "It's me, sunshine. Don't be afraid. It's me and Coop. We're going to get you out of here." As soon as he whispered the words next to her ear, she went still.

He released her, and she whirled, throwing her arms around him. Her head came to rest on his chest as a sob escaped. "Damn it. He was right. Matt said you wouldn't go. We're going to have a talk about that later, sailor." A sob that was half laugh bubbled from her throat.

Luke tugged her closer and kissed her neck, weak with relief. "We can talk about whatever you want, babe." He motioned for Coop to slide the window open. "You go first and catch her."

Coop nodded, opened the window and let himself down feet first.

Luke bent to scoop Sally into his arms and hand her out the window to Coop, when the bedroom door burst open. Ahmed filled the opening, an Uzi submachine gun pointed at them.

"Well, well. If it isn't Navy SEAL Luke Harding." Ahmed's emphasis on SEAL caught Luke's attention.

He set Sally on her feet and pushed her behind him. "Ahmed, you lousy maggot. I thought you were dead. I'm disappointed you're not. This is between you and me. Let's take it outside."

"You and I can settle our differences right here." Ahmed worked the lever on the top of the Uzi, chambering a round. He pulled the trigger, and a short burst of automatic gunfire strafed the wall beneath the window where Luke had seen Coop last.

Sally grasped Luke's shoulders and pressed closer to his back, her body trembling. He placed his hand on her hip directly behind him to reassure her.

"That should keep your friends away for a while." As Ahmed turned back toward Luke, he smiled. Eerie, detached, crazy—the light that shone from the man's eyes chilled every fiber of Luke's being. He had to keep Ahmed talking until Coop and the others could regroup. It was Sally's only chance.

"You had it in for us the whole time because Ian and I were Americans. Why? It was your choice to turn your back on your country. You let them fill you with hate for your own people."

As though he hadn't heard, Ahmed stared at Luke. "You and your Navy SEALs always thought you were stronger…faster…better than me, didn't you? Even after I proved your friend Ian was weak, you still didn't get it."

Again, the almost unnoticeable emphasis on the words *Navy SEALs* interested Luke. "Didn't get what?"

"I was like you—proudly American—until…" His words faded, and he glanced around as though he feared someone else might have heard his confession. When his gaze returned to Luke's, anger burned there again. "The American military—the SEALs you value so highly—discharged me after my brother and I had successfully completed most of our training."

The statement jolted Luke to his core. *What is he saying? He signed on to be a SEAL?*

Ahmed paced one way and then the other, always keeping the Uzi trained on Luke. "Do you know why? Not because I wasn't good enough or strong enough. Not because I wasn't the best sniper—I was. Even better than my own brother. No. They seized upon my only imperfection. Can you guess what it was?"

"Your humility?" Luke regretted his flip remark as soon as he'd said it, but it was too late.

Again, Ahmed seemed not to hear. "A fucking broken bone in my wrist when I was a boy. It healed and never bothered me again. But it wasn't *perfect*, and that break decreased my range of motion by three fucking percent…which made me not good enough for the almighty SEALs. That I could perform any exercise quicker and better than the rest didn't matter."

"So, you took a medical discharge rather than stay in the regular Navy? Hell, I'd have done the same thing. But that doesn't explain why you became a terrorist. That's a pretty big leap." Luke kept his gaze on the man's trigger finger. He and Sally would have only milliseconds to react when Ahmed tired of talking.

"Eight months later, my brother was killed in a training exercise. A Humvee he was driving, with four other trainees onboard, overturned. The others were thrown out, but my brother was trapped behind the steering wheel. The Humvee went over an embankment and burst into flames. If I'd been there, I could have saved him."

Luke shook his head, a vague memory of the incident on the news niggling at his brain. "What makes you think you could have done more than the men who were there?"

"Obviously, they didn't try hard enough. Every one of you is going to pay for that." Ahmed's voice held the rage that clearly seethed beneath the surface, and he tightened his grip on the gun.

"So, that's it, huh? That's why you became a traitor, became a terrorist and killed Ian? To make the SEALs—any SEAL—pay for the accidental death of your brother?" Didn't sound like the actions of a rational man. It was just a hunch, but he'd bet Ahmed had lost touch with reality when his brother died. Why else would the traitor come thousands of miles to hunt Luke down again? That made his first guess right—Ahmed was crazy. And Luke had learned to trust his hunches.

"You've oversimplified it, but yes. And now it's your turn. Then I'll take care of your friends outside. I knew Sally would bring you close enough to spring the trap. I had every intention of trading her for you…but now, I can't bear to part with her either—for totally different reasons, of course. But I'm not a monster. I'll give you a moment to say good-bye." Ahmed relaxed his grip on the Uzi and glanced toward the door behind him.

Yep. Crazy and overconfident. The latter will be his downfall.

Luke understood all too well that if Ahmed pulled that trigger, there'd be enough lead flying in this room to kill everything in sight. *Not acceptable.* He leaned toward Sally, who'd turned a ghostly shade of pale since Ahmed walked in. "Out the window, now."

He didn't wait to see if she followed his instruction. Clawing for traction, he burst into a full run. Getting to Ahmed before he fired was the only thing that would save them.

A malicious grin broke over Ahmed's face as he braced his feet and tracked Luke's progress with the barrel of the gun. Behind the madman, a shadow caught Luke's eye. A man with a rifle stood in the doorway.

Luke leaped sideways out of the way, rolling as he landed, and slid up against the wall, praying Sally had done what he said. A high-caliber rifle shot echoed in the room. Ahmed jerked as though a puppeteer controlled his movements. A burst of submachine gunfire riddled the ceiling with bullet holes. Ahmed couldn't hold on to the weapon any longer. He dropped it and crumpled to the floor, blood pooling under him from the rifle fire that entered his back and blew out through his chest. Ahmed was still breathing, gasping for air.

A glance toward the window told Luke what he desperately needed to know—Sally was out of harm's way.

Three more shadows materialized, flanking Daniel, weapons in hand. Daniel stepped all the way into the room and strode toward Ahmed until he looked in to his face. "My brother was a good man. The best. You and your scum killed him. Now, you die." He placed the barrel of the rifle against Ahmed's forehead and pulled the trigger.

Chapter Twenty-two

Sally jolted awake, the sound of gunfire ringing in her ears. Immediately, she leaned into the warm caress of the man curled around her on the bed. It'd been ten days since terrorists tried to kill them on American soil. She was the one having nightmares now, but Luke was always there to assure her it was only a dream. The doctor had said, along with her many cuts and scrapes, she had a mild case of PTSD, and he predicted it would fade as her memory of the incident did. The kicker was, Luke had been sleeping like a baby. She'd take that trade any day.

Luke stirred behind her, his arm over her torso drawing her closer. "You okay, babe?"

"I am now," she whispered.

The sun would be rising soon. They couldn't lie around in bed today.

"Luke?"

"Yeah."

"Why did Emmett Purnell fly me to the hospital in his helicopter?" She rolled back against him and looked at his sleepy face.

She'd apparently blocked out parts of her ordeal, but every now and then she'd remember something she'd forgotten, and she simply had to know how it fit in with the whole. Luke had been so patient, answering her questions, allaying her fears. What would she have ever done without him?

"What do you remember?" He almost always started with that.

"I remember the sound of the helicopter as he landed in the meadow and the wind he created. Then I woke up just before the orderlies rolled me away at the hospital in Sandpoint. Emmett was there, staring at me. I think he smiled...and it was kind of creepy." Sally laughed.

Luke dropped a kiss on her lips. "When he cornered you in Sandpoint and we learned he'd been mugged by Clive Brennan, the last thing he told me was to call if I needed help. I'm sure he meant help beating the shit out of your old man, but he came when I called him anyway. All that was left to do was get you to a hospital. He was glad to help."

She faced away from him again. "Thanks, Luke."

"For what?" He ran his tongue around the edge of her ear, and she shivered. His arousal pressed against her bare bottom.

Sally shimmied around within his arms until she faced him. She raised her lips to his and reveled in the hunger obvious in his kiss. With a slow hand, she stroked the length of him, offering her throat for the attentions of his searing lips. He groaned and rolled her onto her back.

"Hey, sunshine, are you using me for sex?" His teasing smile made her heart do a backflip.

She shrugged and batted her eyelashes. "What if I am?"

Luke laughed low in his throat. "I have absolutely no problem with that."

A knock sounded on the bedroom door. Luke and Sally barely had time to scoot to their own sides of the bed before Jen burst into the room. "Aren't you guys up yet? The others are starting to arrive. We're going to be the last ones."

Sally bit her lip and tamped down her amusement at her exasperated daughter standing at the foot of the bed, hands on her hips.

Luke cleared his throat, but she could still hear the laughter in his voice. "Your mom and I will throw on some clothes. It will only take five minutes. Okay? Tell you what. Why don't you start down there and we'll catch up?"

"That's a great idea, Jen. Don't forget your jacket. It's still chilly this morning. And take a bottle of water." Sally sat up and held out her arms. "Come here and give me a hug first." If nothing else, she'd learned not to take her loved ones for granted.

Jen climbed onto the bed and fell into her mother's arms. Sally squeezed her tightly and brushed her lips across her rosy cheek. Jen would never find out how close they'd come to never hugging again. As always, the melancholy thought brought with it the threat of tears.

Luke always seemed to know when she was about to lose it. "Hey, Jen, what did we decide about the bedroom door?" He captured the girl's attention, and she slid off Sally's lap to sit cross-legged in the center of the bed.

"I *knocked.*" Jen defended herself with a shrug and a flip of her arms in the air.

"I know, and that's good, but you also need to wait for an invitation before you open the door." Luke was always so good with her. No wonder Jen loved him unconditionally.

She dropped her hands on her knees. "Why?"

Sally snorted a laugh, but Luke wasn't intimidated. "Well, because I might be dressing. Believe me, you do *not* want to see this naked." One of his fingers pointed back at himself.

Jen and Luke busted out laughing. How did he always do that—get what he wanted from her by being totally honest and end up closer to her for the effort? After a minute, Jen slipped her skinny arms around Luke's neck and gave him a loud peck on the cheek. Luke caught her around the waist and whispered something in her ear. Instantly, she giggled and rolled off the bed.

"Okay, I'm going. *Hurry!*" Both doors slammed seconds apart in the wake of Jen's excitement, and then silence settled over the cabin once again.

Luke rolled toward her until he was half on top of her. "Now, where were we?"

Sally laughed and wrapped her arms around his neck. "I'd love to stay right here with you…but you're in charge of this cabin-raising. You probably should put in an appearance."

Luke groaned, dropping his forehead to hers. "Okay, but whose stupid idea was this anyway?"

Before long they were out the door, walking hand in hand up the path toward the concrete pad where Daniel's cabin had been. Overnight, a tent city had sprung up in the meadow among the tall grass and wildflowers. People were milling about, greeting newcomers who came in a steady stream of cars down the dirt road. Sally's excitement sizzled just beneath the surface.

"It was thoughtful of you to organize this cabin-raising for Daniel and Ellen." Sally was busting-at-the-seams proud of him. He'd worked his butt off the past several days, getting commitments from everyone he could think of to show up and work for as long as it took to replace Daniel's cabin. Between ordering materials, drawing plans and raising money to cover what Daniel's insurance wouldn't, he'd still taken the time to make certain she was comfortable and cared for while she healed. *Thoughtful* wasn't nearly a good-enough word to describe him.

"I have my moments." Luke smiled and squeezed her hand. "Don't forget about the dance tonight. I promised to take you dancing."

She glanced toward the crowd ahead and smiled. "I'm looking forward to our first real date—the first of many, I hope."

He brought her hand up and kissed her fingers. A mischievous grin appeared for a heartbeat before he looked away. When he met her gaze again, the same worried creases that had lined his face for days were firmly in place. "You know I'm here for you, sunshine, but let's try not to overdo it today. Okay?"

Sally refused to let her disappointment show. How many openings like that had she given him over the past week? He had yet to mention their future or his marriage proposal, changing the subject, as he'd done now, obviously uncomfortable with where the conversation was going. What was a girl to think?

Luke cared about her—desired her. There was no doubt about that. But it seemed everything had changed since he'd believed he'd lost her. It was as though he pulled back from her to keep from being hurt again. No one else was likely to notice the difference…but she noticed. *Paranoid much?*

On the other hand, who hadn't changed? There'd been a carefully orchestrated and carried out attack by a brutal terrorist group in a sparsely populated area of Idaho. The terrorists hadn't been content torturing and killing on the other side of the world. One man had conceived a plan to follow Luke from the pit of hell and finish what he'd started simply because he'd survived. The attack was nothing on the scale of 9-11, of course, but it served to remind many there was an enemy and he could strike anywhere. Whether a flesh-and-blood witness to the horror or seen through the eyes of news reporters, everyone's world had tilted a degree or two. Why would Luke be any different?

She squinted into the newly risen sun to look at him as another of her unending questions turned her attention from the ache in her heart. "Apparently, we suck at hiding, don't we? How did they find us?"

Luke's breath escaped on a sigh.

Immediately, Sally regretted bringing up the subject. "Forget I asked. I'm sorry. We don't have to talk about it."

Luke stopped, pulling her up short. "The truth is, I've been waiting for you to ask…and dreading the look in your eyes when you hear the answer." He cupped her cheek and teased her lips with a light brush from his thumb. "I've given that plenty of thought. Talked it over with my commander and Homeland Security. We'll never know for sure, but the most likely scenario is, they followed me to the hospital in Bethesda, and when I was released, I led them right to you and Jen." The tick in his jaw surfaced as he paused.

"Ahmed knew what you meant to me because of the picture. He knew I'd do anything to keep you and Jen safe. So he used you to get to me. The bomb in your house in Huntington was Ahmed's handiwork, and later on the road to the lodge—the cars that tried to run us off the road. It was me they were trying to kill, and you got stuck in the middle. I'm sorry, babe."

Her heart constricted at the misery and anguish in his eyes. Did he think she blamed him for any of that? "Luke, you have nothing to be sorry for. The responsible person, and I use that term loosely, is dead. He'll never hurt anyone again." Sally fisted her hands in Luke's camouflage jacket and pulled him against her. "I love you, Luke Harding, and I would do everything over again if it meant having you in my life." There. That was so in-his-face there was no way he couldn't respond—not say he loved her back.

A cute-as-sin grin settled on his mouth…and she waited expectantly.

"Hey, Harding, ya wuss. What's takin' you so long?" Travis's drawl drew their attention to the crowd of people watching them from a hundred feet away.

Luke's gaze swept back to her, and the moment was gone. "I guess we'd better join them. The crowd's getting ugly." He took her hand, an expression she couldn't read darkening his brown eyes. "Come on. Let's get this party started."

There were so many people, and they just kept coming. Travis, Coop and Matt had stayed, so they could be there to help Daniel and Ellen rebuild. She gave them each a huge hug, feeling as though they were lifelong friends, rather than the two-week relationship it had actually been. These men would always hold a special place in her heart.

The rest of Luke's SEAL team was there too, and Luke clasped hands with them all and introduced her to each of them. Name tags would have been a good idea. Too bad she hadn't thought of it sooner.

Luke's Aunt Peg, a petite figure beside all the brawny men, with shoulder-length silver hair and chocolate-brown eyes, squeezed through the crowd to greet Luke. Then she turned to Sally and dispensed a warm hug. "Thanks for making my nephew so happy, dear," she whispered.

Sally's eyebrow shot up as the friendly woman smiled and winked. What on earth? There was no time to contemplate the odd exchange as Luke's brother, Garrett, grabbed her around the waist and lifted her off her feet for a bear hug. Setting her down, he planted a platonic kiss on her cheek and reached for Luke's hand. "Damn, it's good to see you both in one piece."

It touched Sally deeply that Luke's family had made the drive from Cougar Ridge to help a family they didn't know for no other reason than that Luke asked them. Cowboy, Garrett's retired military dog, had come along for the ride too. The shepherd was currently being spoiled and treated like the hero he was by the large Navy contingent.

Sally scanned the grounds for Garrett's fiancée, Rachel, and spotted the pretty redhead talking to Jonathan. They were outside the crush of people waiting to be told what their jobs were as Daniel began organizing the workers.

Luke looped his hand around her neck and pulled her closer for a quick brush of his lips. "Daniel needs some help. You'll be okay?" Excitement shone in his eyes.

"I'll see you later," Sally said.

As he strode over to Daniel, her gaze slid back to Rachel.

Garrett moved alongside Sally. Cowboy loped up to him, checking in, no doubt, before racing off to join a group of young boys with a rubber ball. Garrett and Sally both chuckled when the dog stole the ball and joyously evaded the boys' attempts to get it back.

Jonathan stepped away from Rachel, joining the detail beginning to dig postholes at each corner of the concrete foundation. Alone, Rachel fidgeted, and Sally's heart went out to her.

"She's nervous," Garrett said, stating the obvious. "She was devastated when the truth came out about Luke's request not to see you in the hospital." He raked his fingers through his hair. "I love my brother, but…well, sometimes he can be a real ass. Rachel knew how much he hurt you, and she felt responsible, even though she wasn't. I know it's been uncomfortable for both of you when you've attended the same functions, but she's missed you—"

Sally lay her hand on his arm and smiled. "This past year has been one poor decision followed by misunderstandings and topped off with a lack of communication. We're starting fresh today."

The relief that slipped over his face spoke clearly of how much he loved Rachel and wanted her to be happy.

"Rachel." Sally called her name when she was a dozen feet away, and Rachel turned. Sally couldn't tell what was going through her mind, but it didn't matter. Striding straight to her, Sally threw her arms around Rachel's shoulders and hugged her tightly. Apparently surprised, it took her a few seconds to relax and return the embrace.

"I'm so glad you're here." Sally stepped back. "Did you change your hair color?"

Rachel laughed uncertainly. "Only about four times in the past nine months."

Sally brought her hands to her hips and studied Rachel's deep auburn tresses with caramel highlights. She shook her head. "Well…I love it!"

Rachel's eyes welled with tears, even as her lips curved in a tremulous smile. "I'm so sorry. I didn't know what to do to make things right."

Sally held up her hand. "We're not going there. You're here. Come on. There's someone I want you to meet." She dragged her by the hand to a row of tables that had been set up adjacent to the work area. "Ellen, this is my best friend, Rachel Maguire. Also engaged to Luke's brother. Rachel, I'd like you to meet Ellen Mathias. Ellen and Daniel own this place, and they've been incredibly kind to Jen and me."

Ellen shook hands with Rachel. "Thanks for coming. It's so nice to meet you."

"It's an honor to be here, actually. You and your husband are heroes," Rachel said. "So, I came to work. What can I do?"

"You're in luck. In the cabin next door, there's a bunch of women, and a couple of men, working their butts off to get lunch prepared for all these people. You'll have to introduce yourself because I don't know half of them. Seems there are people here from all over the western United States who came to do something nice for us just because we ended up in the news. The idea takes my breath away. I'll have to pay this forward for a long, long time." Ellen stopped talking and pressed her hand over her mouth, but a sob escaped anyway.

Sally put her arm around Ellen's shoulders. "It's okay. You're entitled to shed a few tears—we all are." She glanced to where the men worked and caught Luke watching her.

He gave her a thumb's-up and she nodded.

"Look, Ellen. They've started to notch the logs and stack them. You'll be back in your home in no time."

Ellen straightened and smoothed her hair away from her face. "You'll have to excuse me, girls. I wouldn't be so darn emotional if I wasn't pregnant."

"What?" Sally couldn't help but laugh. "Okay. You've been holding out on me. Rachel, I'll catch up with you later, okay? Right now, I'm going to find a nice, shady spot for this pregnant lady to sit."

"Say no more. Congratulations, Ellen." As Rachel strode by Sally, she grabbed her hand and squeezed. The happiness radiating from her gave Sally a rush of warmth.

Soon, the assembly of cooks and food preparers were filling some of the tables with every kind of salad, pasta, Jell-O fruit concoction, bread, sandwich meat and dessert. A round, loud-voiced man, with an apron Sally was sure used to be white, manned a huge outdoor grill on which cooked chicken, hamburgers and hotdogs. Stacks of paper plates and plastic utensils lined the end of each table. One person after another carried pitchers and jugs of iced tea and lemonade to spread around the empty tables where people would eat. Sally left Ellen sitting with her feet up, enjoying a quiet moment and a cold drink.

Jen and Bridgett were passing out ice-cold bottles of water to the sweating workers starting to break in anticipation of lunch. Sally's gaze drifted to Luke, who was working on flooring with Garrett, Jonathan and a half-dozen other men she hadn't met. The walls of logs were going up around them as they worked. Obviously engrossed in his project, Luke didn't look up.

"Well, sweet thing, you've become quite a celebrity. If you can leave your adoring fans for a minute, I'd like to have a word with you."

The voice sent cold chills up her back as she whipped around. *Sheriff Mike Connors. Jen's father.* Standing across the table from her—the very last person she wanted to see. What was he doing here? She wouldn't have pegged him as a Good Samaritan. With a narrowed gaze, she stared at him. "Really, Mike? It just so happens I have a word for you. *Leave.*"

"Is that right? Where's my daughter, Sally? If you won't hear what I have to say, maybe I'll go talk to the kid." He started to walk away.

"No," Sally screamed. The decibel level, coupled with the alarm in her voice shut down the rumble of the crowd as if she'd turned a spigot. She sensed dozens of eyes on her and a collective holding of breath.

Darting around the table, Sally placed herself directly in front of him. No way was he getting close to Jen. "Don't you dare go near her." Each word was punctuated by rage, the likes of which she'd never felt before.

"All right." He grabbed her arm roughly and jerked her close enough his breath blew on her face. "It's entirely up to you, sweetheart. Let's you and me find a nice quiet place to be alone." Still gripping her arm, he started to tug her farther from the line of tables.

Sally's stomach lurched at the thought of being alone with the man, and he seemed oblivious to the fact everyone within a thirty-foot radius was listening to his every word.

Luke was a blur of motion as he slid between them, forcing the sheriff to let go of her. Slamming his palms against Connors's chest repeatedly, Luke walked him backward until a dozen feet separated them from Sally. Luke's right hook caught the sheriff already off balance, and blood spurted from his nose. The powerful punch spun him around, and he sprawled face down in the dirt.

A spattering of applause went up. Sally glanced around and found Garrett standing on one side of her, Travis on the other. Ten feet behind them, Matt lifted Jen and set her on his shoulders.

So...this is what it feels like to be surrounded by friends. She'd tried to keep herself and Jen from being noticed by the wrong people for so long, their friends had been few. Sally almost didn't recognize the feeling of total safety that suddenly became a living force inside her.

Luke yanked the sheriff to his feet, and Connors swayed unsteadily.

"You broke my nose. You just made the biggest mistake of your life, you fucking squid."

Luke chuckled in a totally unamused way, and a chorus of boos and four-letter words rumbled from the crowd at Sally's back. Evidently, the term the sheriff had used was familiar, and not in a good way, to the sailors on the grounds. Even Cowboy stalked closer, growling low. Garrett called him off with a quiet command.

"Don't *ever* touch her again, Connors, or you'll have more than a busted nose. If it was up to me, I'd haul your ass through the court system for what you did to her, but I won't do that to Jen. She's *my* daughter now, and no one is going to hurt her. Are we clear on that?" He shoved the sheriff another step closer to the parking area and his vehicle.

"Fuck you," Connors sputtered through the blood that covered the lower half of his face.

Luke's fist flexed as though he was finding it difficult not to punch the guy again. "Enjoy your last few days on the job, Sheriff. I'm making it my personal mission to see you don't keep it for much longer."

Wait a minute. Did Luke just say Jen was *his* daughter? A quick glance at the girl confirmed an ear-to-ear grin. Was he planning on a future with them despite his reticence to speak the words? Shamelessly, she admitted to herself she'd take him any way he came.

Connors glared at Luke but pivoted and almost trotted to his car. As soon as he got it in gear, he hit the gas, throwing up a screen of dust as he flipped off Luke. Beside her, Travis swore under his breath, shaking his head as he headed for the chow line. The hum of conversation picked back up, along with the clink of serving spoons on pans and bowls of food, as though the confrontation had been an everyday occurrence for most of those present.

Luke turned slowly and regarded her. His sexy grin was a tad weak, as though he wasn't quite sure how she'd react. "Sorry, sunshine. I probably didn't handle that very well." He shrugged, brushing a stray lock of hair out of his eyes. "I went a little crazy when I saw his hands on you."

Sally felt his words to her core. She loved him so much at that moment, her chest ached. Striding to him, she slipped her arms around his waist and smiled up at him. "You did just fine, sailor."

Relief invaded his expression as he wrapped his arms around her, and the beating of his heart was balm to her soul. Yet one thing remained. "I have to talk to Jen. Connors said things. You said things. I don't know how much she heard." Under the circumstances, Jen was sure to be confused about who her father was.

"If you don't mind, I'd like to talk to her with you." Luke's earnest eyes pierced her heart.

"Are you two looking for someone?" Matt set Jen on the ground in front of them, and she immediately flew into Luke's arms.

He laughed as he picked her up and held her close. "Thanks, MacGyver." Luke exchanged a solemn nod with the big man before he turned and headed for the food lines.

"That was *so* cool, Luke. Are you okay? Did you hurt your hand? Did you mean it when you said I was your daughter now? Did you ask her?"

"Whoa. Slow down, Jen. Your mom wants to talk to you for a minute. Okay?" Luke set her down but didn't break eye contact immediately.

Sally's gaze swept between the two of them. Why did she feel as though they were communicating on some alien wavelength? She brushed her suspicions aside as she knelt in front of her daughter. "Honey, I'm sorry if anything you saw or heard upset you."

Jen looked about as far from upset as a person could, a perpetual smile glued to her lips.

"Sheriff Connors isn't a nice man. Years ago, he did something bad that resulted in something very, very good. You were born." Was Jen understanding any of this? Too bad there wasn't an instruction booklet for being a single parent.

"Remember when I told you that every child has a mother and a father, even if they don't all live together?"

"Yeah," Jen said.

"Well, Sheriff Connors is *your* father. But because I love you so much, I've never allowed him around you. When you're older, I'll explain the reasons, and when you're old enough, you can decide whether you want him in your life. I'm sorry you had to find out this way, sweetheart."

Jen shrugged. "I knew, Mom."

"What?" Sally nearly swallowed her tongue getting the word out.

Luke knelt beside them and smiled at Jen. "How did you know he was your father?"

"Last year, in school, some of the older kids teased me about it, saying I looked just like him…and saying bad stuff about Mom. She'd never talk about him…so I asked Jonathan."

"*Jonathan* told you the sheriff was your father?" Sally would kill him.

"No, but he didn't say he wasn't either. Later, I overheard him talking to Rachel. Don't be mad at them, Mom. They didn't know I was listening."

"Oh, no, sweetie. I'm not angry. I'm sorry you had to go to someone else to hear what you should have heard from me. Next time you have a question, please ask. I'll tell you everything I know." Sally gathered her into her arms and hugged her until the girl started to squirm.

Pulling away from her mother, Jen glanced toward Luke expectantly.

Sally heaved an exasperated sigh. "What's up with you two?" She rose to her feet at the same time Luke did. Was that a blush coloring his whisker-roughened features?

Jen giggled and skipped a few feet away before turning back.

"Well, I was going to do this after the dance tonight, when there weren't quite so many people around, but my support staff is getting restless." He crossed his eyes at Jen and elicited another giggle.

Reaching in his jeans pocket, he brought out a small, red-silk drawstring bag and dropped to one knee in front of her.

Shocked, Sally backed up a step...and might have kept right on going if he hadn't reached for her hand and held her in place.

Luke dumped something out of the silk bag onto his knee—something that winked and flashed at her as it moved. Laying the beautiful solitaire diamond ring on the red silk, he held it out, then grinned his sexiest grin. "You are literally my sunshine. Since the day I met you, you've never left my mind for a second. The more I come to know you, the more I need you. The truth is, I can't imagine my life without you and Jen. I love you, Sally Duncan...or Annie Brennan...or whatever name you choose to go by. Will you do me the honor of becoming my wife?"

When he stopped talking, Sally looked from his eyes, shining with love, to the ring and back again. She wanted to scream, *yes, I'll marry you*, from the highest mountain, but the words were caught in her throat at the moment. This was what she wanted—the man she loved loving her back...and excited about being a father to Jen. What was wrong with her?

As seconds ticked by, she lost track of time. Finally, Luke tugged on her hand, and she fell forward a step. "Um...Sally, marry me?" His brow was beginning to furrow.

"Yes," she said, bringing the grin back to his beautiful mouth. "Of course I'll marry you."

Luke rose and took her in his arms, lifting her off the ground. Applause and whistles filled the air. Sally started, having forgotten there was anyone else around. Then she laughed and threw her head back in pure joy. She met his gaze and shivered as he let her slide down his front, his brown eyes darkening with lust.

Jen ran to them, and they picked her up, putting her into the center of their celebration. She was so excited, she probably wouldn't sleep for a week.

Luke beckoned to someone, and soon Matt meandered over, scooped Jen up and deposited her back on his shoulders.

"Did you have that planned?" Sally plopped her hands on her hips.

"Yes, ma'am." Luke cocked an eyebrow and let his gaze drift to her lips. Not much doubt what was on his mind.

"What else do you have planned?" She glanced around. Many of the workers, including most of the Navy SEALs, were returning to their tasks. The women and a few of the men began to clean up. As soon as lunch was put away, they'd be starting on dinner. "There's so much to do. I have to help."

Luke caught her arm before she took two steps and pulled her around in a small arc until she bumped up against him. "Huh-uh." His lips fluttered over the sensitive skin beneath her earlobe. "Come away with me. Just for a while. Ellen had champagne delivered to our cabin for later, but we'll toast our engagement now. You, me, naked, bubbles." He captured her lips and demanded entrance. When she broke the seal for him, he plunged in, twisting, stroking and turning her on with only the movements of his tongue. God, she was weak…but she couldn't make herself care.

"Okay. For a while."

"Yes!" He bent and scooped her into his arms despite her protest. "Don't argue. I'm carrying you."

Sally curled one arm around his neck and placed the other hand on his heart. With the steady beat of her forever love beneath her palm, she lay her head against his shoulder, letting his gentle strength surround her.

After a minute, she raised her head and met his gaze. "Who *should* I be? Sally or Annie?"

Luke kissed her forehead, and the air around them seemed to pulse with expectancy. "Either. Both. Whatever beautiful, incredible name you choose, you'll always be my sunshine."

About the Author

Photo Credit: Stalnakers Photo Shop

Dixie Lee Brown lives and writes in Central Oregon, inspired by gorgeous scenery and three hundred sunny days a year. Having moved from South Dakota as a child to Washington, Montana and then to Oregon, she feels at home in the west. She resides with two dogs and a cat, who are currently all the responsibility she can handle. Dixie works fulltime as a bookkeeper. When she's not writing or working, she loves to read, enjoy movies, and if it were possible, she'd spend all of her time at the beach. She is also the author of the Trust No One romantic suspense series, published by Avon Impulse. Please visit her online at www.dixiebrown.com.

Printed in the United States
by Baker & Taylor Publisher Services